THE BRAW
AND THE BONNY

HARVEY HOWELLS

SIMON AND SCHUSTER · NEW YORK

First printing

SBN 671-20831-4
LIBRARY OF CONGRESS CATALOG CARD NUMBER: 71-139631
DESIGNED BY EVE METZ
MANUFACTURED IN THE UNITED STATES OF AMERICA
BY AMERICAN BOOK–STRATFORD PRESS, NEW YORK

PART ONE

AN END

Chapter One

ON A SATURDAY late in 1909, John Dougal's prize bull unaccountably turned on that gentleman farmer, hurled its three quarters of a ton forward on charging legs, and crushed the life from him against the rough-cut stone wall of the byre.

"In aw my born days I never heard tell of such," said James Grant, tenant farmer for the remains now blanket-covered on a gate. "Aberdeen Angus dinna kill. They havena the mind for mayhem. Nor the horns."

"Himself would be glad to hear that, poor soul," answered Pat Nolan on the other end of the improvised stretcher, summoned there from the gardens of the big house. "Is it the back door, Jamie?"

"No! John Dougal goes in his front entrance. Head first. Let his feet lead when he comes out again for the last time."

"But the little ones? They shouldn't see their da . . ."

"Look ahead of you, man. Aw the curtains are drawn. Mrs. Dougal has gathered her bairns around her at the other end of the house. Out of sight and sound."

But the oldest son, Lachlan, opened the big doors. White-faced, not looking at their burden, he led the two men up the shallow stairs to the bedroom where the children's nanny, the cook, and Grant's wife, dragooned by the family doctor, waited to perform their last service for the master.

"You shouldna be here, Lachie," whispered Cook. "A lad of eleven—"

"Mother sent me," said the boy. "I had to escort . . . Thank you, Mr. Grant—Mr. Nolan."

Funerals for ordinary Presbyterians started from the home, but John Dougal had been an elder, and four days after his demise he was honored by services in a kirk packed to capacity. Businessmen by the score arrived from Glasgow on a special train chartered by the deceased's brother Philip, head of the family firm of East India merchants. A power in the city for generations, Dougal & Company was a name to honor in death as in life. At least a hundred bearded gentlemen, caparisoned in black from cravat to silk handkerchief, debouched from first-class carriages at the Strathgryffe station to walk in mournful numbers along the village's one main street and up the brae of the Dambridge road to the ivy-clad stone church. From its steeple, every thirty seconds a passing bell tolled to the pull of the beadle below, throwing its death knell over a valley curtained tight in respect.

In the vestibule Philip Dougal greeted his peers. Accustomed to giving orders, he instructed them to pile their overcoats on the tables of carved black teak. "You'll need their warmth against the sorry business to come." The gentlemen obliged but retained their tall silk hats to slip upside down into the wire racks under their places on the hard wooden pews.

Inside the church a watery sun sent reds and blues flickering from stained-glass windows and made gold of the brass handles screwed to the coffin that lay on trestles between nave and choir. Behind the unpolished oak the Reverend Arthur Auchinleck faced out, stern, on guard, personification of the bell that tolled a hundred feet up. The deep-toned bong rushed away, then came surging back through the open door to stoon the ears of Harriet Boyd, oldest friend of the new-made widow. Mrs. Boyd shivered, slipped her gloved hand into that of her husband, and Robert Boyd squeezed back to strengthen his wife.

Sir George and Lady Biggart, parents of the widow, their only child, were sole occupants of the left-hand pew second from the front. Over the seat partition sat Mrs. Philip Dougal, joined now by her husband.

Just like a posh wedding, thought James Grant. Bride on the left, groom on the right. Why had his own wife insisted on coming? Because it was fashionable? Her stony face revealed nothing.

A sounding void told him that the bell had stopped. Through the door from the vestry came the choir, behind them the widow on the arm of her oldest son, the lad Lachlan, their heads on a level, for he was tall and she a slight wee thing. The all-enveloping black, the impenetrable veil to the shoulders, made her look no bigger nor a farthing, thought Grant. Lachie would soon top her, the length of his leg below the kilt sure sign of growth to come. Dorcas, the oldest daughter, was sonsy and big already, though you'd no ken it the way her head was bowed the now. If her brother Hugh, the second son, hadn't had her by the elbow she'd never have found her way to the front pew. The middle daughter, Elspeth, ended the procession, for John Dougal's last two bairns, Morag and the infant Sandy, were oweryoung for funerals. Below the half veil allowed a young girl, Grant saw Elspeth's lips tremble before mother and children turned to confront the minister across the chasm of the coffin. In time with his slow nod they sank to their seats.

> *God, our help in ages past,*
> *Our hope for years to come,*
> *Our shelter from the stormy blast*
> *And our eternal home!*

A childless man, James Grant felt outraged pity surge for the offspring. They should be allowed to sorrow in private, no beside a throned coffin before the whole kirk. Six bairns John Dougal had fathered on his wife Anna in fourteen years. Then he had to get himsel killed by an accident that a half-wit farm hand could have dodged. The prayers for "Thy dearly beloved servant" should be for those the damn fool had left behind.

If it were Robert lying there—thought Harriet Boyd, and released more tears for her friend.

Sir George Biggart found comfort in his daughter's good fortune in marrying a wealthy man. She'd never have to worry about the wherewithal.

Her mother, devoutly unimaginative, found a very present help in the words of the minister and the familiar psalms.

Pat Nolan set his mind forward to a pint of ale.

Philip Dougal reassured himself that the passing of John Dougal's shares to a trust for his issue would not upset the equilibrium of the family firm one iota . . .

"May the blessing of God which passeth all understanding be with you all."

The congregation stood still as the family, followed by Mrs. Philip Dougal and Mrs. Boyd, slipped away to the vestry. Ladies were spared the burying, and the gentlemen, busy with their overcoats in the vestibule, were careful not to stare at the curtained four-wheeler as it passed the front door of the kirk, bearing home the bereaved widow, daughters, and friends.

Into the all-glass hearse with Corinthian corner columns the coffin now went. Standing behind, two phaetons over-flowed with flowers and wreaths, the biggest a St. Andrew's cross from the Lanark and Renfrew Hunt, whose members had known John Dougal for a thrusting rider. Carriages stretched up and over the brae, in the shafts, matching blacks rounded up from the surrounding villages to pull the throng of mourners to the graveyard a mile away on the south slope of the glen's northern ramparts.

"Hugh and I will walk, Mr. Auchinleck," said Lachlan Dougal.

"As principal mourners, you should occupy the first carriage," said the minister.

"There aren't sufficient for all, sir. Father had so many friends . . ."

The great bell struck again; drivers and coachmen, black-cockaded like their charges, climbed to their stations, and the procession moved out, hearse first, then the floral tributes followed by two kilted boys marching in the waves of hothouse perfume that would always recall the moment; wheels turning slowly in front, kettledrum cadence of horses walking, creak of traces, spectators uncovering as John Dougal, Esquire, went his last mile.

"Eyes front, Hughie," said Lachlan. "Don't look at the people."

As they turned into the driveway between the gray stone pillars of the cemetery, the rain came to make velvet of the animals' coats and streak the silk hats of those not fortunate enough to find space to ride. It teemed on bald head and white hair, on grizzled and black, on old and young for the fifteen minutes it took the Reverend Arthur Auchinleck to beseech divine mercy for the deceased. It would cause two subsequent funerals among the mourners, elderly victims of pneumonia developed from the colds endemic to seeing a friend off with dignity in a Scottish winter. What good does it do John Dougal to bare these auld craniums? thought James Grant, whom the wet didn't bother. He was impervious to the elements in Strathgryffe, where for generations his family had farmed the land he had sold to the man now being lowered into the earth. Grant sent no bitterness down with the coffin. The Dougals had offered, he had accepted, and that was that; the only possessions he envied his landlord the bairns born one after the other at the house built new for the groom and his bride. Grant sighed. Bride no more, but a widow too soon. It was God's mercy Mrs. Dougal had her young for solace.

A tall man with a face like a sad Punch—that would be the brother—beckoned to the two sons, who moved away from the open grave. Grant watched the trio climb into a carriage that went slowly down the drive, then broke into a smart trot on the road as the diggers spaded back the wet soil to thud muffled and hollow on the oak below.

"Thirsty work, interments," said Pat Nolan at his elbow. "You'll be for a beer, Jamie?"

"Aye. But no till I've had a large whusky."

There was that aplenty at the big house, but not for such as Grant. As at a wedding, all were welcome at the ceremony, but the reception afterwards was for the favored few, the city gentlemen who needed the bulwark of spirits against the physical and mental chill of the grave.

"Mamá asks you to excuse her," said Dorcas Dougal in a choked voice from halfway up the stairs. "The strain of the past few days . . ."

"Quite. Quite." Philip Dougal took charge. "There is a cold collation laid out in the dining room, gentlemen."

Rare roast beef, saddle of mutton, pheasant, partridge, and duck, all carved and waiting; the Glasgow burghers made a good meal, funerals being hungry work as well as thirsty.

When the whisky brought the first restrained laugh, Philip Dougal frowned at the gaffe and crooked a finger at Robert Boyd, who worked for Dougal & Company.

"Time to call a halt to this, Boyd," he said. "As the host pro tem, it is hardly my place. Perhaps you would be good enough to tell the—uh—mourners that the special train will leave in thirty minutes . . ."

"Allow me."

Philip Dougal watched his employee circle among the others, dropping a word here and there. Reliable chap and not at all aggressive fortunately. While the gentlemen struggled into their overcoats for the carriages and the station, the merchant asked another favor.

"Mrs. Philip is returning on the special, Boyd. Perhaps you could arrange privacy for her. A carriage with just you and your wife. Sir George and I plan to catch a later train."

"Certainly, Mr. Dougal. It's been a harrowing day for all. I hope it won't be too prolonged for you."

"No, no. I have matters to discuss with m' sister-in-law. We can dispose of them quickly as soon as she's rested."

The quiet talk swirled past the widow, back and forth, back and forth.

"First thing the morn's morn the murdering beast goes to the slaughterhouse." That was her mother. "Killing her husband—orphaning the poor bairns—"

"Don't fret, Clara. It's all arranged." Her father.

"Have you any notion, Sir George, what John put out for his motorcar?" Her brother-in-law.

"Three hundred and forty pound, I was told."

"An Argyll, isn't it? And a year old. I might offer three hundred. Take it off her hands—"

"That's right good of you. It wouldn't fetch as fair a price lumped in with the estate. You know I've already put the property up for sale?"

"You told me, Sir George. Fast work, I must say."

"Aye. I was lucky to find a townhouse in Kirklee suitable for my daughter and the children. With a bit of ground too."

"It will be fine to have them near us," said their grandmother.

"Near good schools too, Lady Biggart. Dear establishments, of course, but my brother has left them amply provided for—"

"Stop havering, the lot of you!" Anna Dougal jumped up from the horsehair sofa and swept across the expanse of carpet to stand before the wide hearth, her slight figure dwarfed by the high mantel, her hands clasped across flat middle. But for the fair hair piled high and the angry glint in her eyes she might have been a child about to recite. "I ken you mean well, but you'll no go and set up my life course without so much as a by-your-leave."

"I begged you to take to your bed, Anna," said her mother weepily. "You're not fit—"

"—to watch out for mysel? I better be, starting the now, or yon two will cut me up like a piece of the estate."

"That's no way to speak of your father and Mr. Dougal," said her mother. "And that dreadful accent. I thought—"

"—that with John gone I'd revert to la-di-da West End? There's a put-on way of speaking for you. And it'd no bring me entry to the farms around here, as my country talk does. It stays, Mamá." She turned to her father. "And so do I, Papá. You had no right to put Glen Gryffe on the block, and you can damn well take it off."

"Anna!" Lady Biggart gasped.

"Is that wise?" Philip Dougal shrugged off the swear. "I'm sure my brother would want you to move back to town."

"Then why did he no stipulate that in his will? John didna agree with rights for women. If he'd been for selling Glen Gryffe he'd have said so, but he didna and I won't. I'd no stay in dirty old Glasgow again for aw the tea in Dougal and Company's plantations. So you can just unbuy that Glasgow house, Papá. I'll no live in it. Ever."

"You're overwrought, child," said her father.

"Child? I have six bairns of my own to prove I'm no one mysel any more. I'm thirty-five years of age with thirty-five more to come, if I'm lucky, and I'll no suffer them as a long-faced widow woman. I'm wee Anna Dougal, still with a thirst for life that I intend to slake. You and Mamá look at my bottle and see it half-empty. I see it half-full. I have three braw sons and three bonny lasses, plenty of money for their raising, and the grandest place in the world to do it. Why should I uproot them and plunk them down in strange schools just to be by their grandparents? As for the bull that killed John, Mamá, my husband paid a thousand pounds for yon Pride o' Fyvie. I'll no throw that away for revenge. He's a champion Aberdeen Angus, and he'll work off his purchase price and a lot more serving the best cows in the shire o' Renfrew."

"Anna, you shouldn't even be aware of these things—"

"I'm no as green as I'm cabbage-looking, Mamá. And that minds me, Philip. John's motorcar's no for sale."

"A lady cannot manage one of those dangerous machines—"

"Then mibbie I'm no lady, for I shall. And I'll also manage the farm. I'll show John's weans that their mother can do it as well as their papá. Aye. Mibbie better."

When her relatives left for the Strathgryffe station in the village four-wheeler, Anna stood in the cobbled courtyard listening to the trot of hooves dying away down the half-mile drive, leaving the frosty night to her and the pure white stars. Behind the high land on the far side of the glen and burn that gave her home its name, the torches of the Northern Lights flicked soundlessly on, stabbing up fingers of pale green, lemon yellow, silver white to blaze in a shimmering fan from earth to heaven. Folk said the aurora borealis warned of an untimely death. If so, it was too late for John. Or he was overearly. By twenty years he was early. You're on your lone now, Anna Dougal, she told herself as she entered the wide two-storied hall with the shallow winding stair, the credenza with the silver salver for calling cards, the elephant's foot for umbrellas, the mirror for the final primp, the stone hearth for the red-glowing coals. A fire burned bright, too, in the square, paneled morning room as the Skye maid she was training to the table followed her in with a bedtime snack for one.

"I'll no bother with tea the night, Mairi," she said.

Long lashes down in tragedy came up quickly. "Och, but Mistress Dougal, you have to eat, and you as thin as a plucked corbie."

"Havers, lass. I've aye been skinny. Take they things away and off to bed with you."

Picking up the silver tray, the maid shook her starched cap in disagreement and left the room. Her mistress went to the marble-topped sideboard, poured herself two fingers of malt whisky, and sat in front of the fire. Straight-backed, sipping slowly, she let the neat spirits soothe the nerve ends jagged from the past four days, and when the glass was dry, poured herself another. I'm no taking to the drink, she excused herself. It's med'cin the now, and by the Lord I need it. She locked the decanter back in the tantalus and looked up at the antique tapestry above it—an aged shepherd in a wooden rocking chair, at his side his loving wife, by his feet his collie dog and his cat, the end of the road patiently limned in wools of many colors, under all a verse of Rabbie Burns.

. . . ma jo, John, we climbed the hill thegether.
And monie a cantie day, John, we've had wi' one anither.
Now we maun totter down, John. But hand in hand we'll go.
And sleep thegether at the foot . . .

I'll have that lugubriosity taken down, she thought, for I canna thole it. Never could. It was John who liked the damn thing. Totter down, indeed! Not wee Anna Dougal.

The Edwardian sense of duty demanded that the loss of a father bring visible pain to his children, but the graces of possessions and money eased John Dougal's untimely passing for his young, his end making no material difference to their beginnings. Dorcas and Elspeth remained as day girls at St. Malcolm's, Strathgryffe's fashionable boarding school for young ladies. Lachlan and seven-year-old Hugh continued to wear the chocolate-and-gold tie of the venerable Glasgow High. Founded in the twelfth century, older than Eton, the school provided an unbeatable education and turned out men, a result not always achieved by the more expensive and, to the Scot, effete public schools of England. To attend "The High" meant an hour and a half travel by train and tramcar for boys from Strathgryffe, a grind in the dark mornings, but coming home a raucous delight to all but the rare swot who wasted his adult-free time in study.

The two remaining Dougals were not old enough for school. Morag, aged four, learned her alphabet at the knee of "Old Wattie," a spinster nanny who had been in Dougal service since the birth of Dorcas. It looked as if she would continue in that sinecure for several years more, the last-born, Sandy, being not quite a year old when his progenitor met his end.

The two hundred acres of Glen Gryffe were not to suffer materially either, as long as James Grant, the former owner, retained his life tenancy and worked the farm.

There was money in abundance to maintain the twenty-room manor house with its white exterior walls, dark wooden beams, and roof of red slate. Built in 1895, it stood high on a hill looking down on Grant's farmhouse, a three-hundred-year-old sprawl of whitewashed stone on the bank of the Gryffe, a shallow burn running fast and clear through borders of oak, ash, and fir.

Five months after the funeral, Anna Dougal stood at an upper window of her gracious Tudor-style residence, looking out on her valley. Snowdrop and crocus were past, gone with daffodil and narcissus that had bloomed by the thousand on the misty grass under the trees. The oak had leafed out faster than the ash, promise of fine weather to come. "The oak before the ash, we'll only hae a splash. The ash before the oak, we're bound to hae a soak." The old sayings were the true sayings, like "Cast ne'er a clout till the May be out." Now the hawthorn's pink-and-white petals shimmered everywhere, and Anna felt ready to burst forth frothy as the blossoms themselves. In a fit of exuberance that could not be contained, she packed away her widow's weeds and donned a green-and-brown houndstooth check with matching bonnet. Let them be scandalized. She would put on the long face no more. Five dreich months were enough. The prescribed year of it, and they'd be carrying her down the hill to join John.

She admired herself in the pier glass that she had avoided as long as it reflected the figure of mourning. This is a sight better, she thought. Mibbie it's only a half-hourglass figure with a wee face to match, but when it's aw you have, make the most of it. Now I'll awa and give mysel a driving lesson. I'll need some help, and I ken just where to look for it.

"Good day to you, Mr. Grant."

"Whoa, Nell." The tenant farmer pulled up the Clydesdale and looped the reins over the plow handle. "Good morning, Mrs. Dougal." He took off his cap of checked tweed and smiled down at her, looking not much older than the day she had met him, all of fourteen years ago.

"It's such a grand morn, Mr. Grant, I've a mind to take the Argyll for a wee airing, if you'll put the machine together again for me."

"You're giving me a grave responsibility, Mrs. Dougal. Should aught gang agley, the village would have my head."

"When did you care a ha'penny scone what the village thought?"

In the face of that truth, he could only acquiesce. Motorcars being fair-weather playthings which spent the winters on blocks, so he put back the wheels with the thick wooden spokes and pneumatic tires, hitched the plow horse to the rear axle, and pulled the tan car out onto the cobbles. Brass gleamed everywhere; acetylene lamps, door handles, radiator all had a polish to match the sheen of the leather on the high-backed seats.

"Someone's been at work with the Brasso and saddle soap," said James Grant.

"Only wee me, but you'll no let on, will you?" Nimbly she climbed in the near door and positioned herself on the off side under the wooden steering wheel. "You'll no have to worry with the petrol and magneto and such. I spied son Lachie with the bonnet raised yesterday, redding her up for the road."

"D' you ken how to work the gear box?"

"I've had practices between polishes." Seizing the long

outside lever, foot barely reaching the clutch pedal, she demonstrated for him.

"You're gey determined, Mrs. Dougal."

"I am that." She advanced hand throttle and spark on their ratchets. "Well, Mr. Grant, if you'll have a go at the starting crank? I wouldna presume to ask, but it needs a man's strength."

"Flattery now, is it?"

Reluctantly he freed the fixed handle from the leather socket, pushed in, dropped his right shoulder, and spun the shaft.

"Put some muscle to it, man," said Anna.

"Och, I'm praying it'll no catch."

But Lachlan Dougal had been a good mechanic. A few turns of the flywheel, and the engine of the monster fired and set its entire length shaking with the power of fourteen horses.

"Well done, Mr. Grant. Ho, for the open road!"

"You'll gang warily now."

"Canny as a wee mouse." Foot slipped off clutch, the Glasgow-built car jumped forward, jerked across the court-yard, and bang-banged down the drive, its operator pulling back on the wheel as if reining in a mettlesome team.

Yon's a game wee hen, thought James Grant as he stared after the machine till it vanished from sight, then followed it with his ears while he soothed the neck of the Clydesdale still white-eyed in fright. When the noise of internal combustion finally died away, he led the mare with the great hairy fetlocks back to the plow. I'm a regular softie for a bonny woman, he mused as he walked behind the coulter turning over the wave of brown friable soil. But what was a body to do? It was her motorcar. Aye, and hers the fruitful land he looked over now.

Never had the valley been more lush, its pastures the brightest emerald all the way to the gray-stone village. Above it, in terraces, rose the homes of the *nouveaux riches*, the in-comers whose slate roofs of red, gray, black, and yellow formed a patchwork pierced by the soaring spires of firs and the four kirks: Church of Scotland, United Free Church of Scotland, the Parish, the Baptist. The Episcopalians with their near-popish responses were too few to afford a church tower. Religious schisms had come with the Glasgow merchants, lawyers, stockbrokers, shipbuilders who could afford the best of two worlds—the thrust and parry of commerce among the city's teeming million, then a fast steam home first-class to sit at ease in oriel windows and stretch their eyes ten miles over the verdant Strath to the plateau of Misty Law, 1665-foot-high bulwark against the prevailing sou'westerlies sweeping in from the Clyde. Businessmen who had helped to make Glasgow the Second City of the British Empire had turned the sleepy market village into one of the wealthiest spots in all Scotland. Every tenth home, seventy in all, was reputed to house a millionaire.

But James Grant worked for wages, thanks to the cupidity of his wife. A wildflower from a Paisley tenement, Daisy Grant had seen no value in the soil unless it could be turned into cash. And he, a love-struck youth, let the termagant she had quickly become talk him into selling in the hope that pounds, shillings, and pence would change her back to the winsome lass he had courted. What a hope. She had sweetened only until she discovered how little five per cent meant on the capital he would not touch; he wasn't that soft.

So over the years he had plowed another's furrow as straight as if it were his own, for he was that kind of a man, and it wasn't the buyer's fault that the sale had not brought happiness to the seller. A bargain was a bargain. Would the Widow Dougal want to continue it now? He couldn't buy back the farm. Land values had doubled in the last fifteen years, but his capital hadn't.

The metal clang of a distant gate broke into his reverie. Below him he saw his wife walk away from the kitchen garden and head down the footpath to the village wearing city clothes—fitted knee-length coat, pleated skirt to the ground, beplumed hat, show-off umbrella. Wednesday. Country day in Glasgow, this husband's night out. He'd have a meat pie and a pint and good cheer the night in the pub at Dambridge. The sun turned brighter for the thought.

"Giddap, Nell." He flicked the reins on the Clydesdale's hurdies, and man and beast plowed on while behind them the pecky maws, the black-headed gulls, wheeled low for worms upturned.

A blue crocodile of schoolgirls crept up the narrow country road past the ninth and last hole of the public golf course. Elspeth Dougal, in the column's front rank, heard the uncommon noise first. "Motorcar ahead," she whispered, and the intelligence rippled back under forty identical velour hats with the ribbons of St. Malcolm's School until the message reached her older sister in the tail of the croc. In transmission it had become: "Laying tar ahead." Dorcas sniffed the air.

"No talking, girls," called Miss Cuthbert, the elite gym mistress, product of four years of rigorous Danish discipline in physical education. "Remember Napoleon's instructions to his foot soldiers. Keep the mouth closed and breathe deeply through the nose. That's it, Dougal Major."

The noise grew, and around the bend the Argyll came hurtling.

Elspeth leaped for the ditch. Like dominoes toppling, those behind her followed suit to fall among the wildflowers in a flurry of black wool stockings and similar under-bloomers. Eyes firmly on the road, Mrs. Dougal was none-theless able to bow gracefully from the neck as the Argyll swept by its indecently exposed flankers.

In the blue haze left by the smelly monster, their high spirits released by the communal tumble, the young ladies wrestled among the buttercups and purple foxgloves, each determined to be the last back on her feet. A hundred yards away on the ninth tee a golfer, his long-nosed driver arrested at the top of his half-swing, gaped at the peep show spread before him.

"You've torn my stocking and skinned my knee! It's all bloody!"

"Serves you right."

"You pushed me on a thistle! Ow!"

"Get off me! You weigh a ton."

"Stand up! Stand up!" shouted Dorcas, first to do so. "There's a gentleman over there."

"Back in formation, girls," said Miss Cuthbert, stifling laughter. "And straighten your uniforms. Be sure there's no grass sticking to your coats. I wouldn't like the headmistress to think I couldn't keep discipline. You wouldn't want me discharged, would you? All right, then. Forward, girls. Mouths closed. Breathe through the nose."

The crocodile moved on, the crushed weeds struggled to rise, the golfer swung and shanked his drive forty degrees off line into the heather.

Five minutes later at the top of the Port Glasgow Road, the Argyll ran out of petrol, its normal consumption of thirty miles to the gallon reduced to ten by the driver's exclusive use of first gear on her maiden run. Anna didn't mind. It had been a grand adventure. Making sure her immobilized vehicle left room for lorries to pass—they could if they took to the ditch—she set off to heel and toe the four miles home, choosing the moor and fields, then the steppingstones over the burn to avoid the main road through the village, whose spiering look would frown on her unwidowly mien. Fine fun to flout convention; no need to be brazen about it.

She was home in time to dress for dinner with Dorcas, Elspeth, and Lachlan. Sandy and Morag had already been fed in the nursery. Hugh was too old for that, but with a year to go before his etiquette would be up to the formal room, he ate betwixt and between in the kitchen, supervised by Cook, a motherly body longer on quantity than on manners.

Dinner for the others proved to be a mixture of spice and suet, the former supplied by Elspeth and Lachie, the latter by Dorcas, pudden-faced from the sheepshead broth through the lamb chops to the dessert, and it a jam omelet, her sweet-tooth favorite. The Lord loveth a cheerful eater, too, thought her mother as Mairi cleared away the dessert things and brought in biscuits and cheese board. Chitchat at table was as much a part of manners as which fork to use for what, but Dorcas had opened her mouth only to put food into it. Anna was quite put out with her oldest daughter.

"And you know, Lachie," said Elspeth, "Miss Cuthbert— she's a jolly good sport, really—took me aside when we were back at school and asked me to give her compliments to Mamá. Honestly, Lachie, you should have seen her. When she came charging . . ."

"Who's she?" Dorcas spoke for the first time.

"Oh, bother. I beg your pardon, Mamá. Anyway, when Mamá came charging over the hill at us, Mamá looked like Boadicea in her chariot putting the Romans to rout."

"More like Deirdre routing the Picts," said Mrs. Dougal happily. "I mind they painted themsels black and blue with woad. That's aw I could see out of the corner of my eye— black and blue."

"Mamá! Please!" Too old to ignore and too young to enjoy the ribald, Dorcas reddened.

Anna suppressed a sigh. "I think I'll have a wee oatcake, Lachie," she said, "just to clean my teeth. Now, lad, what are you up to for the shank of the evening?"

"That depends," he said warily.

"Och, you'll no object to running this wee errand for your mamá. I ken you've had many a sly go at the Argyll when you thought nobody looking. There's two hours of daylight left. Do you think you're up to bringing the motorcar back in that time?"

He was on his feet instantly.

"I'll help, Lachie." Elspeth jumped up, too.

"You'll not, but you can come with me."

"Get a tin of petrol from Speirs the Garridge," Anna called after them as they walked from the room as quickly as manners allowed.

"Last one to Mr. Speirs's is an Englishman," she heard Elspeth shout as they burst out the front door.

"Please may I be excused, too, Mamá?" asked Dorcas.

"No the now, young lady. I'm for a wee gab with you first." She rose and walked over to the north windows. Down the braeside by the edge of the ripening hayfield she saw them running, Elspeth's golden pigtails flying, Lachie behind, holding back. Anna knew that Elspeth was the sprinter in her class, but Lachie was a proper whippet. The Dougals should move to the city? Never. Never ever. Not when they could live in Strathgryffe's clear air, with no law of trespass to keep them off moors and fields, the whole countryside theirs to roam. Scotland belonged to all Scots, and this wee corner of it was the grandest place in the world for children to grow.

Then what was gnawing at her eldest that she had the sad face? For months now, she'd been like a Christmas card, aye greeting. Even before her father was killed.

"You wanted to talk to me, Mamá?"

Anna sat down again. "I have a wee feeling you were ashamed of your mother this afternoon, Dorcas. Why should I no go for a spin in your papá's motorcar?"

"How could you, Mamá? Such a lack of respect. You're supposed to be in mourning . . ."

"Would you have me commit suttee like a Hindu—throw mysel on his funeral pyre to make sure my life was over? Well, let me tell you, my life's no over, no by half. It doesna do the late John Dougal any good for his widow to owermourn. I only have one life—"

"Mamá, that's atheism!"

Worse and worse. "Dorcas"—gently again—"as the country folk say, we must aw dree our ain weird—make our own decisions as to the life we lead. You seem bent on joining the unco guid, who believe misery in this world guarantees joy in the next. I canna stop you, but I'll no collaborate with you. I sometimes think we make our own heaven right here and now. I ken some of us make the other place, too, for I've been holding mysel down in it for five long months. This morning I clambered out, and from now on I'll fight to stay out. Dinna try to run the wee world around you, Dorcas, lest it roll you flat as one of these oatcakes. Let your mother, sisters, and brothers dance to their own bagpipes. We'll aw be the happier for it."

"But happiness is not the goal, Mamá. Godliness is. I'm going to live a godly life and with His help lead other people into the paths of righteousness. Maybe I'll even be a missionary."

From worse to worst. A bairn of fourteen, and awready she sounds older than I hope I'll ever be. I canna reach her at aw. "A noble ambition for a young lass," said Anna, tired of the discussion. "Run along now and take a good walk to stretch your legs and lungs in the fresh air the Lord gave us to enjoy."

As Dorcas left, Mairi entered the dining room.

"Och, I thought you wass gone, Mistress Dougal."

"Carry on. I'll no be in your way."

The swish of silver crumber on starched linen was as soothing as Mairi herself, bonny in uniform of black cotton, white apron, starched cap. With her lilting voice, b's softened to p's, sibilants accented and gender added as she translated from her native Gaelic, she was a fair treat to the ears. In the morning when she wakened her mistress with "She's a peutiful day, Mistress Dougal. You'll pe wanting your tea," the refreshment was to sight and sound as well as taste.

It was hard to keep Catholic girls like Mairi in Strathgryffe when the nearest Mass was held miles away in Dambridge. Paisley, too, mounted an ever-present threat to the continued service of each domestic in the village. Paisley not only had Catholic churches but also J. & P. Coats, its thread mills eager to hire girls too unsophisticated to realize that a "screw" of fifteen shillings a week made a bad exchange for a home all found, good food, uniforms provided, and ten shillings every month to spend or send home. A still greater threat to tenure lurked even closer, on the moors where a walk in the spring gloaming on Wednesday night off could lead to a twosome in the heather and a by-blow nine months later.

"Are you happy, Mairi?" asked Anna, to enjoy the girl's voice.

"Happy?" she said, surprised. "Och yes, I'm happy, Mistress Dougal."

"Look at me straight, Mairi."

Gentian-blue eyes under black lashes, soft mouth, red lips smiling over teeth white as lamb's wool, blue-black hair, the whole a honeycomb to any village lad.

"She is a good situation I have, Mistress Dougal," said Mairi. "Why should I not be happy?"

"No homesickness?"

"That, yes, but there is nothing to be done about it."

"Why did you leave Portree?"

"She had no jobs for the likes of Mairi Maclean."

"And no lads?"

"But no jobs for them either. My brother Iain is in the Glasgow Police, a good job. He sends money home."

"But Scotland's never been better off. Why shouldn't Skye be the same?"

"My father says it is because they made too few big farms out of too many little ones. I don't know. I only know our croft cannot feed ten children. So my brother and I, the oldest, had to leave." The girl's eyes moistened. "Och, she iss beautiful, Skye. Rugged and beautiful. Not like Strathgryffe, which iss beautiful—but softer . . ."

"Now, now, girl. Don't talk yoursel into the dumps. Glen Gryffe's to be a happy home for everybody, although there's some folk have a proper knack for misery." What ailed Dorcas? "I'll no have it. And leave some of the starch on that cloth, Mairi. You're like to crumb it to death."

Her houseful of women and bairns suddenly stifling her, Anna escaped into the morning room, poured herself a masculine tot—the first in months—added two drops of water, and raised the glass to her reflection, alive and vital in the gold-framed mirror that had replaced the dying shepherd and his wife.

"Here's luck to the house"—defiantly she gave the traditional toast—"and de'il tak the one who'd pity hersel or anyone else in Glen Gryffe."

Anna Dougal was out of mourning less than twenty-four hours. As she was downing her dram, Edward VII, King of Great Britain and Ireland and of the British Dominions beyond the Seas, Emperor of India, lay dying of bronchitis. The lusty man who had survived typhoid, an operation for appendicitis, a crushed kneecap, an assassin's near bullet, and sundry previous bronchial attacks finally succumbed on the night of May 6, 1910, in his sixty-ninth year. His passing meant more to Anna and her countrymen than had the demise of his mother nine years before. Victoria was a woman, Scotland to her only a place for a holiday. Edward was a man and one who identified himself with his northernmost dominion, even using the incognito Baron Renfrew for his pre-accession peccadilloes. Although it didn't eradicate his German accent, he had received part of his schooling in Edinburgh, and after the appendectomy which made that surgery fashionable, it was to Scottish waters that he steered the royal yacht for his convalescence. As affection begets affection, his love for Scotland had brought him the natives' esteem.

"He'll be gey hard to replace, Mrs. Dougal," said James Grant, handing her the *Glasgow Herald* with its mourning type.

"That he will, Mr. Grant. Edward the Peacemaker. No many kings get their nicknames, and they still alive."

"Aye. It's farewell to Edwardian times. They've been good ones for Scotland."

"I could shed a wee tear for their passing. A Georgian era doesna have the same sterling ring. The Georges havena been overly kind to auld Scotia. No from the First."

" 'Wha hae we got for a king but a wee, wee German lairdie.' " He quoted the Jacobite sneer. "But that was lang syne. We havena had a Geordie in eighty year—no since the Fourth."

"A profligate and a libertine, Mr. Grant, I would remind you."

"This one'll be different. He's a family man, married awmost twenty year to bonny Mary o' Teck."

"Who was first engaged to his late brother. Yon was an arranged affair. There canna have been much love in it, no with Prince Albert Victor only eighteen months in his grave when they wed."

"Arranged or no, there are six bairns to show for it. And never a whiff of scandal."

"Would it reach our nostrils if there were?"

"You're no being fair, Mrs. Dougal," he chided her. "It's no like you to prejudge a man."

"Then I'll stop, for I wouldna like to lose your good opinion. I'll be needing it if we're to work thegether."

"Work thegether?"

"Aye," said Anna, enjoying his astonishment. "It didna seem proper to tell you sooner. It's me for the farming."

"But you—a lady—"

"From now on, put a hyphen and 'farmer' after that term, Mr. Grant. I'll need you to show me the ropes for a wee, whiles I catch on."

"But farming and cattling's the coarse life. It's no for the likes of you, Mrs. Dougal."

"Stuff and nonsense I'll no have. I'm a farmer's widow woman, and I intend to learn to do what my man did. I owe it to Glen Gryffe."

James Grant hid his relief. John Dougal's husbandry had consisted of poking his hawthorn walking stick into the haunch of the nearest cow, and his closest association with his animals, putting a mare over the drystane dykes with the Lanark and Renfrew Hunt. He had been good at the latter. If his widow interfered with the running of the farm no more than had her spouse . . . Her next words disabused him.

"I'll have a look at the books when you find time," she said.

"Books, Mrs. Dougal?"

"A farm's a business like any other. It must have books."

"I have a wee note pad," he said dubiously. "You'll no be meaning that? The rest's in my head. Perhaps Mr. Dougal left some ledgers?"

"I'll have a look for them then, and if I dinna turn anything up, I'll start some from blank pages. No books! How can you run a farm with no books?"

"I wouldna ken, for I havena run aught for near fifteen year. Mr. Dougal's bank paid me my wages and still does. If I needed supplies or equipment, I asked for them and they were aye there. Dinna forget, I was naught but your husband's tenant farmer."

She stood on the front steps, he on the cobbles, their heads level as he held her gaze for as long as it took her to hear a throstle warble to mark out its domain, a cow moo to have its full udder stripped, a rook caw for devilment. What was he thinking behind the gray eyes in that braw face? That city folk with their lawyers and their inherited gold had taken advantage of a country lad? There was no resentment in his steady look and no servility, but worse, an acceptance of his lot. She couldn't abide that.

"Tenant no more," she said abruptly, "but partner. From now on we go halvers. I'll tell the bank no to stop paying you, though, till the back end. By then we should ken if your share is more nor the wages."

Thrush sang, cow mooed, rook cawed.

"You'd no be joking?" he asked.

"Take hand of mine and we'll shake on it, Mr. Grant."

Eyes crinkled, brown leather split in a grin. "And here's a

hand o' mine!" he shouted, grabbing hers.

"Dagnabbit! You dinna need to crush my knuckles to seal the pact. The books'll have to wait now. I'll no be able to hold a pen for a fortnight." But I'm no angert. A good grip's the sign of a man, which you are, Jamie Grant. For you I'll keep my country talk. You'd give naught but the courtesy touch of your bonnet to the daughter of Sir George Biggart, yon affected-spoken lass.

She wore black for two more weeks, until May 20 when George V, his competitive cousin Kaiser Wilhelm of Germany, six lesser kings, ex-President Theodore Roosevelt of the United States, and potentates by the score followed the muffled drums, the reversed arms, the empty saddle of Edward the Peacemaker through the streets of London. In the procession, marching on foot and in the uniform of a naval cadet, came the heir to the throne. Thirty-four days later, on his sixteenth birthday, he would be named Prince of Wales, Earl of Chester, and Knight of the Garter.

With the interment of the bluff, hearty King in far-off Windsor, Anna Dougal packed away the widow's duds with a grand feeling of finality, then dressed soberly and took an early train to Glasgow.

"Yoohoo! It's only me, wee Anna Dougal," she called into the brass letter slot of the top-floor flat on University Avenue where Harriet Boyd lived. Behind the ornamentally frosted upper half of the door, Anna saw a dim shape scurry across the hall and knew the lady bound from kitchen to bedroom to redd herself up for her visitor. Harriet was not the one to relax propriety, although she and Anna had known one another since both wore bibs, and all the years between.

"Anna Biggart, you're really most inconsiderate," was Mrs. Boyd's greeting when she finally opened the door. "You know I don't receive until three. You nearly caught me in my bedroom slippers."

"Dinna blame me if you're *en déshabillé* and the sun full up and over."

Hazel eyes kissed and were kissed by the blue eyes of the unwitting hostess before she turned and led the way into a kitchen alive with the fragrance of baking.

"Shortbread." The caller sniffed appreciatively. "I dinna mind if I do."

"No such luck for you. It's for my at-home tomorrow. You'll have to put up with yesterday's German biscuits."

"You'd serve stale to wee Anna Dougal?" She swung her handbag up on the coal bunker, tossed her sealskin shoulder cape and kid gloves onto the built-in bed, rattled a poker through the bars of the grate. She did not remove her Robin Hood bonnet with the jaunty green feather. "Where's the kettle?"

"Oh, Anna!" Harriet burst out. "If you only knew what an effort it's been to keep away from you."

"None of that, now. Pull yoursel thegether. You were aye the emotional one. Will you put the kettle on? Here, I'll do it mysel." She stuck the cast-iron kettle under the tap, and pure Loch Katrine gushed forth in its final leap from the mountains of Perthshire. "I'll give that to Glasgow—its water. I'm that drouthy, I could drink it neat."

"Save your thirst for the tea," said Harriet. She cleared her husky throat. "Robert brought home a chest of his newest blend. It's superb, if I do say so."

"Your grand man is Dougal and Company's number one asset." Standing at the scullery sink, Anna looked out over the backgreen four stories below, across the slate roofs and jutting chimneys of the West End flats to the spire of the Botanic Gardens United Free Church piercing the skyline half a mile away. She and Harriet had been baptized there. "You were right to stay away, my auld china," she said, back to her friend. "You ken me that well you didna have to be told it was what I'd want. To be by my lone in the den with my cubs till the wound healed a mite."

"And it has so soon? I've thought and thought—if it had been Robert . . ."

"There's a daft way to torture yoursel."

"It wasn't that, Anna. I was thinking how long it would take me to face the world again. I never dreamed you would do it this quickly."

"Och, I was aye the fast healer." Anna brushed off the faint criticism. "I'm convalescent awready, with no complications. There's no a blemish on wee Anna Dougal. Now"—briskly she lifted a stove lid with the short poker and placed the kettle over the coals—"put the pot on the hob to warm, Mrs. Boyd."

"I gave the children sixpence apiece today for their lunch at Colquhoun's." Harriet pulled up the leaves of the oak table. "Almost I could believe in mental telepathy. We'll have the house to ourselves till half past three."

"I wouldna mind having our wee tête-à-tête interrupted by your husband."

"You know he never comes home for the midday meal. And just as well. You act like a school girl any time you're in the same room with him."

"Fair sickening, isn't it?"

"And a compliment to my good taste. Would you fancy a bite of cold veal and ham pie? With a tomato? Only hothouse, I'm afraid."

"Hoity-toity. You must have laid out more than a bawbee for *pomme d'amouri*es grown under glass. It is no awfu the way prices are going? My butcher had the nerve to charge me tuppence for a wee calf's liver. Just after me buying a ten-pound sirloin."

"But you raise your own beef . . ."

"For sale only. My partner and I have decided we canna afford to eat up the profits."

"Your partner? Anna Biggart, what have you been up to?"

"No a thing I canna let on, when I'm ready. Which'll be after the tea's infused."

"I can't wait five minutes." Harriet poured the bubbling water into the heated china pot. "You're into some kind of mischief."

"My, that's a grand cup," said Anna. "Your Robert can be

gey proud of his new blend. And I suppose now you'd like to hear my wee surprise."

"It's probably nothing at all," said Harriet, stirring vigorously in her excitement.

"Leave the bottom in the cup then. You'll mind Mr. Grant?"

"The man who helped John run the farm?"

"Aye. Although John did more riding than running. I canna find even a wee bit paper to tell how the farm's done aw these year. It's frustrating for fair."

"What about Mr. Grant?"

"I'm coming to him. It's no the thing to talk about money, Harriet, but I can tell you that John's heirs dinna have to worry about the lack of it . . ."

"Anna, you are exasperating."

"—only the excess. Whatna example is that for my bairns? I'll no have them thinking they can loaf through life just because their great-grandfather started Dougal and Company. With two hundred acre, a twenty-room house, four servants inside, Mr. Grant and two farm hands out, a motorcar, horses, cattle, aw without visible support from Dougal brain or muscle now John's gone—it'll no do, Harriet."

"Why on earth did you arouse my curiosity?"

"I canna wake up what hasna been asleep aw it's life. Anyway, I've convinced my three oldest that we canna afford to stay at Glen Gryffe unless the farm pays its own way. The tea's certainly flowing like treacle around here the day." She held out her cup. "So it's wee Anna Dougal, farmer now, my auld china."

"But Anna, you don't know hay from heather. That's the silliest idea. I hope Mr. Grant—" She stopped. "He's your partner."

"Took you a while, didn't it? You should have kenned that right off. See's the sugar."

"Mr. Grant's a fine figure of a man, Anna. How old is he? Pushing forty?"

"No any harder than mysel."

"What do you think of his wife?"

"She looks away while she talks at you, and gives hersel more airs than Misty Law. Bonny though and four year younger. I canna abide her."

"Can Mr. Grant?"

Anna cackled and put down her cup. "You're no being overcomplimentary to me, are you? Nor to Mr. Grant. Dinna fret, Harriet. Yon chap's too straight to squint at this wee bag o' bones."

"You could stand a little more weight," said Mrs. Boyd thoughtfully. "But you're young, attractive, a wealthy widow —I don't fancy the arrangement one bit. Just watch your step, Anna Biggart. How did the children take your news?" Harriet giggled. "What a fibber you are, pleading poverty."

"Lachie upped with his guernsey sleeves and looked for a pitchfork. It'll do the lad good to ken life is no aw cigarettes behind the barn and a peppermint to follow." Anna sighed. "I wouldn't mind if Dorcas took to smoking. It'd be better than steaming, which she does aw day. At her own mother. She doesna approve of me, Harriet."

"It's her age. Think back, and if you're honest you'll admit we didn't think our mamás were any great shakes."

"My Elspeth does." Mrs. Dougal preened. "She called me a jolly good sport. No to my face, mind. I overheard her telling Lachie—one time an eavesdropper learned good of hersel. Where's the nourishment you promised? I'm famished."

From the mesh-sided meat safe jutting outside the window, Harriet took a pewter-covered ashet. "Mix the Colman's, Anna."

"That I shall. Never eat veal and ham pie without mustard to clean the palate and make each bite taste like the first."

Harriet cut two-inch portions of the brown-crusted pink and white meat *en gelée,* placed them on Wedgwood plates, and flanked each with one of the precious tomatoes. Then she put her knife to a pan loaf.

"Dinna turn the bread on its side," said Anna, grabbing her wrist. "Are you for starting another massacre? That was the Campbells' signal to fall on their hosts at Glencoe. It's awfu bad luck."

"When did you become superstitious?"

"Any time I see a chance to show you I ken something you dinna." Anna cackled. "You can cut the loaf upside down for aw I care. John told me the grisly legend. He was a great one for hating the Campbells. So are aw the MacDougalls and Dougals."

Harriet spread butter on four thin slices, cut off the crusts, and added young watercress to make dainty sandwiches.

Anna eyed her plate. "You'd no have a wee spot of claret to go with this grand-looking repast?"

"Did you ever hear of a proper Glasgow house without it? Should we?"

"Why for no?"

Harriet poured. By the stem the ladies raised crystal to the light, admired the ruby red, lowered the glasses, sniffed the bouquet, raised the wine again in salute.

"Here's tae us," said Anna.

"Wha's like us?" responded Harriet.

"Damn few, and they're aw deid, thank God."

Chapter Two

ANNA DID KNOW hay from heather, but not much more. She was a city child of her class, offspring of a gentleman whose castle was one in a four-story terrace of stone built out to the pavement to make maximum use of valuable ground.

Then at twenty-one she married a man who plucked her out of civilization and set her down in the wilds of Strathgryffe surrounded by cows, where, as Mrs. John Dougal, everything hortensial was done for her, and the roses bloomed profusely from June to December without her aid. In boasting to her parents that she would manage the farm, she had accepted Kipling's challenge to "Plan for more than you can do, and do it." Wee Sandy knew as much about crops and cattle as she. Even the kitchen garden behind the courtyard was the domain of the cook, who divided it between table flowers and table edibles with a trellis. Sweet peas grew up one side, eating peas up the other, an intermingling of perfumed beauty and mouth-watering nourishment that made the gathering of either a heady joy to those permitted the task. Elspeth loved to be asked to pick the long green fingers multiknuckled by peas as big as her thumbnail. Raw, they were like nuts, crispy and crunchy. Cooked and steamed with a lump of butter, they remained firm, dry inside as a roasted chestnut.

"Off with you, Miss Elspeth, and fetch a bowl of peas," Cook would say. "And none o' your empty pods, mind. Whistle aw the time and leave the kitchen door agee so's I can hear you."

The fruits and vegetables were planted to Cook's specifications by Pat Nolan, whose Ulster thumb was as green as his native land. A modest man, he attributed his success with growing things to the virtues of liquid cow manure on everything, particularly rhubarb. His devotion to the natural fertilizer was almost the end of the adventurous Morag.

On a fine July day the child spied a ladder left upright against the mushroom shed, a roofed cave in the rock cliff that protected two sides of the kitchen garden. As precaution against her exploratory ways, ladders were always left flat after use, so this was a chance for Morag not to miss. Stretching and straining, she hauled herself up onto the shed's slates, then on hands and knees shuffled across to the far edge to look down on the strawberry beds. There was Hughie lying on his back, stuffing his mouth with the biggest reddest ones he could find. Cook would skin him alive. Turning stomach to slate, Morag wriggled backward until her feet touched the lid of the dung barrel, a hundred-gallon hogshead originally used for the transport of ale, Pat Nolan's preferred tipple. She stood up and turned around.

"I see you," she called quietly.

Hughie's head jerked up. "Down from there, daftie. You'll fall and break your neck."

"Will not. 'I'm the king of the castle, and you're the dirty wee rascal . . .' HUGH-IE!" Her impromptu jig split the lid and in she went, luckily catching the rim of the barrel as she passed on her way to the bottom.

"Hang on, Morag! I'm coming!" Hugh dragged the ladder around and clambered up, grabbed her wrists and clamped her fists to a rung.

"You won't tell?" she said, hanging there half in, half out.

"I won't have to. They'll smell you coming."

"You could hose me off."

"You'd catch your death."

"No I wouldn't. Pul-lease, Hughie. The dung's burning."

In a corner of the courtyard, below the windows and out of sight, he played a steady stream on her until she was standing in a wee pond of puddle.

"Hughie, I'm sticky. Can't I take my clothes off?"

"I don't mind."

When the icy spray had washed away the heat of the fertilizer, he dried the goose-pimpled little body with his handkerchief, then pulled his jersey over her head and down to her knees, knocking now from the chill.

"Slip up the back stairs," he whispered. "Don't make a sound, mind. Scoot, before Wattie catches you."

She scurried around one corner as Miss Watson came around the other.

"Have you seen Morag, Hugh?" she asked, then caught sight of the sodden garments. "I see you have. What mischief did she get into this time?" She sniffed suspiciously and looked at the telltale ladder. "Oh, no," she wailed. "Not the fertilizer container. What will her mother say?"

"Do you have to tell Mamá? It was an accident."

"Morag's mischief always is. Certainly I shall tell your mother."

"It'll make an awful stink if you do."

The nanny's smile came and went in a blink.

"The stink, as you so rudely call it, will not attach itself to you," she said. "Morag is my responsibility and mine the blame."

Miss Watson's mistress first clucked, then laughed. "Dinna fash yoursel, Wattie," she said. "I wouldna want your job for aw the crown jewels, no when it's trying to hold onto yon piece of quicksilver, Morag. And throw those clothes in the dustbin. I'll no have you wash them as a penance."

Dorcas was horrified. "She stripped to the altogether, Mamá! In front of Hugh!"

"With clothes as glaury as hers, I'd peel before the Strathgryffe footbaw team," said Anna. "Aye, and the village choir."

"Seeing you pulled Morag out, Hughie, I'll forgive you the stealing," said Cook. "But just this once, mind. You're worse nor the starlings."

Mr. Grant laughed. "Morag's a wee menace," he said. "You did a fine job, Hugh Dougal. Come with me."

He led the way down the pasture where the cud-chewing kye swung lethargic heads to follow their passing, and the purling of the Gryffe Water bubbled louder as they neared the farm. In a corner of the cavernous whitewashed stone barn, a black and white collie lay on her side in a straw-lined box while five fuzzy pups like woolly caterpillars struggled over her and themselves to reach her dugs.

"Bred for brain, Hughie. Gwen's the best bitch in Renfrewshire, and the sire is Rab o' the Moss. You can have your pick of the males."

For three weeks Hugh ran down to the barn at least twice a day to study growth, ran home each time filled with the misery of decision. They were all fine pups. At bedtime one evening he slipped through the gloaming to the dark barn, heard the mother growl deep in her throat. "It's only me, Gwen." He held his breath as a piece of fur detached itself, climbed over the wooden lip of the box, tumbled out, and headed for the open. None of them had shown so much spirit before. He followed the fluffball into the last of the daylight and gently turned it on its back while it nibbled at his fingers with needle-sharp teeth. A dog! Placing the morsel against his cheek, to his delight he felt the rasp of a tiny tongue on his ear. "I name thee Chieftain of Glen Gryffe," he whispered. "Chief for short."

"That was gey thoughtful of you, Mr. Grant," said Anna. "I'll no insult you by offering payment. Here's the Polled

Herdbook back. Thanks for the loan of it." She handed him the bible of the Aberdeen Angus breeder.

"Did it teach you much, Mrs. Dougal?"

"Aye. That I've a lot to learn."

"You'd gie awa your shirt, James Grant," cried his wife in a voice to turn the cream. "The Dougals own the world, and you hand them a dog you could sell for two pound."

How could a woman girn aw damn day every damn day about money? For seventeen damn year? James Grant took horn spoon and soup plate from the cupboard and filled his dish with porridge from the black pot that had been cooking on the back of the stove all night. Looking out the window, he ate standing up, a custom handed down from the bad times when no clansman dared leave his approaches unguarded even while he consumed his breakfast. A daft idea now, but still no countryman took his oats sitting down.

"I'm no surprised you dinna answer, for you canna," went on the voice. "You're a gowk, James Grant. Why I ever marrit you—me that could hae had the pick o' Paisley . . ."

But then your mouth was rosy and bonny, no twisted thin by mean words. He sighed for the memory of the lass who had knocked the feet from the starry-eyed lad he had been. But for her he would have finished at the Royal College of Veterinary Medicine, would have had a degree to his name. His porridge were finished, so he sat down for the knife-and-fork course. Tam McBride's Bess was in heat again, and he was bringing the cow over to be served once more. Every three weeks, like clockwork, the beastie was ready, but it wouldn't take. It couldn't be Pride o' Fyvie's fault. No with his record.

"How was I to ken you were aw pride an' poverty? You aye had siller to jingle in your pockets when you were walking me out . . ."

Bad as the porridge the scrambled eggs were. Overcooked, the milk separated and slopping around the ham slice. Did she do it deliberately? He took a soda scone to sop it up. When he had finished his third cup of strong tea—it was good; she liked tea—he rose from the table.

"You'll be for Glasgow the day?" he asked, pulling on his rough tweed jacket, not looking at her.

"Do you grudge me? The one pleasure I hae to mysel aw week . . ."

And so the Lord be thankit. He closed the door quietly behind him.

His wife crossed the flagstone floor at a run, wrenched open the door, and gave it a good slam. But Daisy was past the point where kitchen violence could ease her certainty that the world had ill-used her. She had married the last of the Grants of Strathgryffe in the belief that she would live happily ever after, at sixteen too young to realize that happiness to her would never be what she had but what she hadn't. She counted no blessings, only griefs with a misanthropy bred of adolescent determination to escape from a miserly father who had dominated his weak wife and daughters. *If only I had this or that, aw my troubles would be over* was so ingrained in her that the lad whom the valley thought a successful catch ceased to be one to her as soon as he was in the creel. With understandable perversity she blamed him for their domestic disharmony and spoke the truth when she said the weekly trips to Glasgow were her only pleasure. Then she could visit the Royal Polytechnic or any other fine shop, where, to keep their jobs, the saleswomen deferred to the customer. The love of money for itself being her only inheritance, she rarely bought anything, spent hours inspecting the wares before she did, and was known in the showrooms of Glasgow not as Mrs. James Grant of Strathgryffe, but as "Finger and Fault." *Drat it. Here comes Finger and Fault. Your turn this week. Me for the lavvy.*

Oblivious of the burgeoning beauty of the oats ripening in the August sun outside the window, she now left the breakfast dishes unwashed in the tin-lined sink, the rooms undusted, the beds unmade, to catch an early train for the city where they believed only millionaires lived in Strathgryffe.

Shite! That was a laugh. For a constant churchgoer, some of Daisy's unspoken thoughts were as unappetizing as her porridge.

Up the cart track by the burn came Tam McBride with Bess and herding collie at her heels.

"'Morning, Tam," said James Grant. "How are you the day?"

"Able to sit up and tak the top off an egg, Jamie. I hope that bull o' yours is in as fine fettle."

"Now, now, Tam. Dinna blame Pride o' Fyvie. He does his part. How's Bess?" He examined the animal. "Aye, she's hot aw right."

"Would I hae brung her unless?" McBride stroked the silky neck. "It better tak this time. I'm no about tae mak a proper whure out of a dumb animal."

"You couldna do that. Whures dinna pay. You pay them."

"Is that a fact now? I wouldna ken, Jamie. Och well, they're getting a fine day for it."

The gentle raillery, the high-up sun and puffball clouds, the water running clear over the stones; the big men, the couchant dog, the cow coal-black against green pasture formed a pastorale, bucolic, serene. It was broken by a roaring up the brae.

"Godsakes, Jamie, that'd no be Pride o' Fyvie getting wind o' Bess awready?"

"That would be Mrs. Dougal," said Grant.

"My, my. Bawls like a bull, doesn't she?"

"No her, you damn fool. Her motorcar. As if you didna ken."

Down the drive from the big house came the Argyll, Anna in veiled hat, clutching the wheel with elbow-length gauntlets, Lachlan at her side.

"It's grand tae see her taking that sair dunt sae well," said McBride. "I havena had a crack wi' her sin' the funeral."

"That's about to be remedied," said Grant as the car

reached the road, turned handily onto the cart track, and bounced toward them.

"Had we no better get out o' the way?" said McBride, putting Bess between him and the juggernaut.

"You dinna need to hide behind a female, Tam. Mrs. Dougal's a proper Jehu. She'll no knock you down."

The Argyll pulled up. "Good morning, Mr. McBride," yelled Anna over four popping cylinders.

"Good morning, Mrs. Dougal," he bellowed back. "I'm glad tae see you looking sae spry."

"Never spryer. What cow's yon you have there?"

"My Bess, Mrs. Dougal."

Anna pushed the spark lever all the way up, and the motor died. An elbow jab and Lachlan dismounted; his mother followed, walked over to Bess, and slapped her professionally on the rump.

"Nice-looking beastie," she said in tones of doubt. "You'd think she could drop a fair-to-middling calf, Mr. McBride. This'll be the fourth time she's come calling. Or is it the fifth?" She turned to her partner. "You'll have discussed our stand on stud fees, Mr. Grant?"

"We were engaged in the pleasantries first, Mrs. Dougal."

"My, gentlemen are proper sweetie-wives when it comes to gossip, aren't they, Lachie?"

"I wouldna say that," said McBride, overheartily. What for was she havering about stud fees? It wasna fitting for a lady. "We've no had a crack, Jamie and me, for a month o' Sundays. And you dinna hae to fash yoursel about the siller, Mrs. Dougal. Tam McBride pays in advance, and I did for Bess a time back."

"But for a try every three weeks? You're getting owermuch of a bargain, Mr. McBride."

Tam's face reddened. Fine sport to kid with a man, but this was proper embarrassing. He took off his cap and twisted it in his hands. "Well, you see, Mrs. Dougal, it hasna taken yet . . ."

"Watch what you're doing to your cap, man. You'll break the skip. I ken fine Bess hasna caught. Otherwise, why would you be back with her again?"

"Mrs. Dougal, I'd be obliged if you'd let me discuss the matter wi' Jamie."

"Now, Mr. McBride, I may no understand cattling yet, but I do understand profit and loss. We canna have a costly animal like Pride o' Fyvie serving a lot of barren cows for nothing."

"You've nae proof Bess is barren."

"I have more proof that she is than you have that she isna, Mr. McBride. You've paid for service aw right, but no perpetual. When there's a live calf standing on its feet as a result, you pay again. That's our new policy. Agreed, Mr. Grant?"

"But that's no legal!" shouted McBride. "It's no Christian . . ."

"Dinna bring religion into it. You're no that good a kirkgoer." She climbed back into the car. "It's right simple, Mr. McBride. If you want the strain of Pride o' Fyvie in your herd, you pay. On our terms. That's one law we aw can understand, the one about supply and demand. Now, Lachie, crank us up again, an we'll awa to town."

"Drive aw the way to Glasgow?" said Jamie Grant. "It's twenty mile . . ."

"On a grand road with my son for postilion. Hop in, Lachie. Ta-ta the now, Mr. McBride. Good luck this time, Bess."

She made a wide circle on the pasture—reversing was still tricky for her—swung back on the track, and vanished down the main road, her words lingering like the sound of the motor.

"That was bloody unfair, Jamie," said McBride. "I canna argy with a leddy."

"I didna invite Mrs. Dougal to join the proceedings, Tam, but that's by the by. She's right. Glen Gryffe doesna run a haphazard operation like some who throw bulls and cows out in the field thegether to breed catch-as-catch-can. It's aw hand-mating here, and if Bess does come fresh, you ken, I ken, and the Aberdeen Angus Association kens the proud name of the sire and puts it in the Polled Herdbook. You willing to pay for Pride o' Fyvie's services the new way, or am I wasting my time?"

"You were before. The village thought you were soft in the head."

"That was John Dougal's orders, no mine."

"An' no his widow's." Tam McBride shook his head in admiration. "My, she's a proper wee tartar, isn't she now? Where did she learn about the cattling? From you?"

"Me and some literature. She's a great one for the studying. Now give us your hand on the second fee, Tam, and we'll awa to the bridal chamber."

"Sho, Bess! Sho!"

Anna's decision to motor to Glasgow was a draft from her half-full bottle which, like the Biblical widow's cruse, was never to be allowed to empty. The motorcar was not only an adventure; it was emancipation. When Anna was at the wheel she did not doubt that some day soon Rights for Women would be a reality. And high bloody time.

"Don't you want me to drive through Paisley?" shouted Lachie, embarrassment rising as they neared crowded streets. Mothers should conform, forheavensake. "All that traffic . . ."

"Let me at it," replied Mrs. Dougal. "It'll be a fair treat jeuking around the lorries and tramcars. You'll have to wait your turn till you're older."

He put his school cap in his pocket and pulled the tartan rug up to hide his blazer and save the High's colors from disgrace.

"Cover your head before you catch the sniffles." She thumped the klaxon horn *ah-oo-ah* at a pedestrian and replied to his furious fist shake with a cheery nod.

Lachie slid down in the seat until he was almost sitting on his shoulder blades.

"Straighten up, Lachie. I canna stand a sloucher." Reaching the busy thoroughfare, she slowed to the speed of the horse-drawn lorries.

What a rude lot town people are, thought Lachie. Look at them. All stopping to stare. No damn manners. What a rotten place Paisley is. *What's the difference between Strathgryffe and Paisley? Strathgryffe is famous for its hills and moors, Paisley is famous for its mills and . . .*

"Drat it. What's wrong with this thing, Lachie? It'll no steer."

"You're caught in the tramway lines, Mother," he replied coldly.

"What do I do then? Gang to the depot to get turned around?"

Now he had to stand up in full view of everyone. Even with their four hands to the wheel, it took a hundred yards to break the tires loose from the sunken rails. Some clots on the pavement cheered.

"If you position the steering shaft over one tram line, Mother, the road wheels can't get caught."

"Where did you ever learn a good idea like that, sonny?"

Sonny! What a foul day this was turning out to be. They crawled over the bridge high above the river, the White Cart, slunk past the ancient abbey like the cat that crept into the crypt—that was a good joke—then finally the buildings began to thin out, bringing temporary relief. Five miles of open country, racing the speeding tramcars, and he would have to face the scorn of Glasgow. Maybe the Argyll would break down . . .

"How about taking a turn at the wheel, Lachie?"

Suddenly it was the grandest day!

As they changed places, Anna rubbed her right upper arm and complained, "My shoulder's fair aching with aw that gear changing." Better he should think her soft in the muscles than soft in the head. Spoil a bairn, but never let on. That didn't build character.

"No so fast! No so fast! You're like to blow me away!" she yelled five minutes later, holding her veil with both hands.

"All the new Scottish motorcars have windscreens," he shouted back, not slowing. "The Argylls, the Arrol-Johnsons, the Beardmores. We ought to sell this antique . . ."

"And be without a motorcar?"

"No bloody fear!" He glanced quickly to his left. "I beg your pardon, Mother. I didn't mean that."

"You did too, you wee rascal. It's no the first time. I've heard you letting go around the stable when you thought you were by your lone."

"I don't see why b-l-o-o-d-y is a bad word."

"It's blasphemy, Lachie, the Cavaliers' favorite when they were fighting that nyaff Cromwell. Only, then they said 'By Our Lady.'"

"How could that become blo—what it became?"

"The English have aye chewed their words."

"Look who's talking," he said, greatly daring.

"Never mind the cheek. English speech is an affectation. Mine is a dialect—the Doric—a canny blending of Norse, Gaelic, French, and broad Scots to give English a flavor it doesna have to begin with. Where was I? Och aye. 'By Our Lady' became 'B'Our Lady,' then 'B'r Lady,' then—what you just said. So dinna use it, or I'll throw a proper *butchoch* on you."

"What's a *butchoch*?"

"Gaelic for curse. One that'll shrivel up your tongue if you wrap it around that word again."

As Elspeth said, she was a jolly good sport. Imagine her talking to him about swearing. If only he didn't have to be seen with her. Did other fellows feel the same about their mothers? He'd never know, for he couldn't ask a pal such a disloyal question.

On Paisley Road they found a livery willing to risk frightening its horses and stable the topless Argyll under cover against the possibility of rain. The boy daren't and Anna herself was not ready—not yet—to contend with the fierce traffic of Glasgow, ten times the size of Paisley.

"Awa upstairs," said Anna as they boarded a tramcar.

"You don't mind?" he said.

"Och, you wouldna want to sit with the ladies. And you're no wearing your kilt."

He grinned and went clattering up the stairs to the open upper deck, man's domain, where he could view the sights and sniff the air fraught with the multi-odors of industry and ships. He couldn't see the vessels, not even when the tram crossed the Clyde. The railway bridge, the last crossing downriver, hid the great liners tied up at the Broomielaw: ships of the Clan Line, Donaldson's, Anchor, City. He heard one hoot farewell and wondered where she was bound. Montreal? Africa? New York? The Indian Ocean? He'd travel the world when he was a man. Right now he was only a halflin—half man, half boy—on his way to the final fitting of his new kilt. And with his mother, forheavensake.

They walked along Gordon Street, he half a head taller.

"Off you go, Lachie," said Anna. "You'll no be wanting your mother's advice on clothes any more. Just be sure John Ross hasna cut the Dougal tartan with your future growth in mind. I canna stand duck's disease."

"Duck's disease?"

"Its bottom's owernear the ground. Half an inch above the floor when you're kneeling, mind. No a hair less."

Happily he touched his cap and went swinging through the fashionable crowd, sturdy knees flashing between woolen socks and shorts of gray flannel. He shouldn't have donned them the day, she thought. Flannel was for Sunday best, brawer by far than the hard-wearing blue serge boys wore against the wooden benches of school. Och, t'hell. Toffs is careless. He'll be a big man. And a handsome. With money. A catch for some lass who'll no do him justice, drat it. Nowhere was Anna more feminine than in her conviction that her future daughters-in-law would be a feckless lot, just as her sons-in-law would be fine upstanding men. She turned into West Nile Street, bound for her lawyer's place of business, somber-quiet offices of dark oak paneling, copperplate from broad-nib pens in the hands of hushed clerks at high desks, legal phraseology; intimidation.

"Good morning, Mrs. Dougal," said Archibald, the latest Son of McFadden, Son & Laidlaw, Writers to the Signet and Attorneys at Law. He had started as the grandson of the founder, but the longevity of his forebears had kept him from the filial title until he was fifty-five, with still more years to wait out before moving into front-name position, his father being a hale seventy-nine. The firm had handled the legal affairs of Dougal & Company since the East India merchants' founding, also four generations before. By custom, the managing director of the tea firm was the senior McFadden's client; lesser lights were Son's, there having been no Laidlaw since the first had gone to his reward in 1795. On her husband's death Anna had inherited Archibald but had met him only once, at the reading of the will. No Glasgow man made a friend of his lawyer and vice versa lest sentiment cloud judgment. A wealthy widow, of course, was something else again, and Son, a bachelor, now turned on Mrs. Dougal—my, she was a bonny wee thing—what he hoped was the right mixture of sorrow and welcome.

"You'll be for a cup of tea after your journey, Mrs. Dougal," he said. "Our office boy infuses a grand pot. I taught him myself. That's one extra skill Dougal and Company's lawyers have to acquire—the brewing of tea. Or perhaps a glass of sherry?"

"Medium dry, please. And a wee nibble of cheddar, if you'd have it, to give me an appetite for lunch."

"I'd take it kindly if you'd be my guest." Now why had he said that? In thirty-five years he'd never squired a lady to the midday meal.

"I'm afraid no. I'm that busy I'll have to take it on the fly. I'll no keep you long, Mr. A. First, how much money do I have in the till?"

Stopper clinked in the decanter—Edinburgh crystal, circa 1720. What a question for a lady to put to her lawyer, to a trustee of her estate, to a guardian of her children.

"My dear Mrs. Dougal, has something come adrift? Has the last quarterly deposit not reached the Commercial Bank? I'm sure I transmitted it to Strathgryffe."

"Yon's no money. Yon's petty cash."

"I'm afraid I don't understand." Her country talk was a pleasing affectation. Too bad she wouldn't take lunch with him.

"My, this is good cheese," she said. "Just the bite to cut the sherry. Do you ken how big is Glen Gryffe?"

"Twenty rooms is my recollection."

"I'm no talking about my house. I'm talking about the productive part, although with six bairns you could say my home has no exactly been moribund."

The lawyer joined her in a wary chuckle. Infectious it was, levity where he had expected bereaving. "I would have to look up the papers to determine the acreage of . . ."

"Dinna fash yoursel. It's a mite over two hundred acre, half of them arable. The rest is taken up with house and grounds, trees, the Gryffe, driveways, a peppering of granite, and moor, where the grass is aw right to let out for sheep but too short for cattle. Now you canna keep growing the same thing on the same plot, or you'll take the nourishment out of the soil . . ."

"It's a wise farmer who conserves his land's virtue."

"He's daft if he doesna. At Glen Gryffe we follow the Norfolk four-course rotation that they worked out three-score year ago."

"The old ways often prove the best," said McFadden, reaching for bottom in this unexpected depth.

"Aye." Anna brushed aside the platitude. "So it's turnips one year—grand winter fodder for cattle—oats the next, then hay, then grass to pasture the cows whiles they fertilize the ground. And dinna look shocked. Manure is life to a farm. Now from my wee chronology, you can see that with a hundred usable acre on a four-year rotation, Glen Gryffe has around twenty-five acre per annum for cattle, its one source of cash money."

"But Glen Gryffe is your home. You have ample income to maintain it. Your husband never intended to put the burden of moneymaking on you."

"I took it on mysel. You'll no ken how many cows an acre of well cared-for land can support? One, and two followers, Mr. A."

"Followers?"

"A yearling and a new wee calf."

"Mrs. Dougal, you astound me. Where did you glean all this information about husbandry?"

"From books and a grand teacher. You'll mind him—the lad your papá talked into selling? Well, Mr. Grant's steeped in it aw. With encouragement he could have made the Glen Gryffe breed famous. But John wasna that interested."

"His passing was a sad blow—"

"Blows are to be countered. Anyhow, with about twenty-five acre, my herd is frozen at seventy-five head and yin stud bull. It'll no do, Mr. A. It's no economical."

"My dear lady, why fash yourself with considerations of finance? You have a solid income from the Trust."

"Immaterial and irrelevant. Also immoral, for Glen Gryffe is no a paying proposition, and that's the worst immorality of aw. I wouldna have slept for the past fifteen year if I'd kenned that. So, how much coin of the realm can I lay my wee hands on right the now?"

"May I freshen your glass?"

"Just a taet, Mr. A. I'm driving."

"You motored up?" That explained the duster and veil. "You're a game one, Mrs. Dougal."

"We'd aw be game if you gentlemen would let us. Out with it, man. How much?"

The lawyer set out to recapture control of this extraordinary consultation. "The entire estate is entailed. You have the usufruct . . ."

"Speak English, Mr. A."

"The life rent subject to the guidance of McFadden, Son and Laidlaw and the Commercial Bank of Scotland."

"Trust, they caw it. Mistrust is more like it."

Son glossed over the oft-heard complaint. "On your demise which, looking at you, won't be for half a century yet—"

"Spare a body the gallantry."

"It is spontaneous, I assure you. Anyway, when eventually that regrettable occurrence takes place, the estate is divided into nine parts; two each to the male offspring, one each to the female, a most generous disposition to your daughters, I must say. All shares, of course, are to be held in trust for the next generation. Capital must be kept inviolate."

"Which is a gey long-winded way of letting on I canna lay my hands on a bawbee."

"Yours was a thoughtful husband, his only wish to save you from worry."

"Aye." Anna's tone was medium dry, like the sherry, as she stared into the flickering fire and mulled the injustice of male control, even after death. "So wee Anna Dougal needna fash about a will of her own, for she'll have naught to leave. Ever. I dinna doubt my father will also be set to reach from the grave to preserve his capital."

"I do not know Sir George's affairs, but I should imagine yes. However, you still should let me draw up your wishes. To die intestate is always, forgive me, inconsiderate of those left behind. You did not come an undowered bride . . ."

"My tocher!" She slapped her knee. "Of aw the gomerils to forget that. The house was built with my dowry. Dinna tell me my husband forgot yon tasty morsel."

"I tried to convince him to put it into his estate, if only for the sake of tidiness, but he procrastinated overlong." Son frowned at the recollection. "Well, what is done is done, or rather not done. I strongly advise you to let me prepare a will for you disposing of the manor house and any personal effects, such as jewelry."

"So I'm no all beholden," she said to herself. "Wee Anna Dougal has something of her own." She sat up briskly. "What's it worth?"

"Goodness, Mrs. Dougal, you're not contemplating selling!"

"Devil a bit, but it's an asset, Mr. A., and I've heard tell you can borrow against an asset. So what's my house worth?"

Smiling avuncularly, the lawyer rose from his desk to take the command position; in front of the fire, hands on lapels of frock coat. "Suppose you tell me what the trouble is, Mrs. Dougal. Don't be blait about it. No need to be shy with your man of legal affairs. You can confide in me without fear."

Mibbie I have been a mite aggressive, thought Anna, and taking his cue, meekly dropped her eyes to the carpet—a Templeton, she noted. Lawyers did themselves right well. "You'll ken Lord Maclehose?" she said.

"The shipping magnate? By name only. I hear he is quite poorly."

"He couldn't be poorlier, the grand old gentleman." A sigh. "At ninety-one with the lying pneumonia, he's no long for this world. Alone in that ramshackle castle, his wife gone before him, his only child killed by the Boers, and him that fond of bairns. He's leaving aw he possesses to Strathgryffe's Home for Orphans."

"Is he now? That's a munificent gift indeed."

"I heard tell of it because I'm a patron of the orphanage. I canna do much, one wee woman . . ."

"I'm sure you are a great help."

"No as much as I'd like to be, but I try. I was talking to the Superintendent the other day, and he says they dinna ken what they'll do with aw the land. They canna handle it without employing more people."

"And the Maclehose policies march with yours?" said Son.

"There's not much misses you, is there?"

"It's my business to be informed, Mrs. Dougal. Don't tell me you would like to acquire some of the Maclehose ground?"

"My, you're quick. Glen Gryffe canna make a profit without more stock, and it canna raise that without a bit more pasture. No if the beasties are to be up to John's standards." Another sigh. "I wouldna let my husband's memory down for aw the money in the world."

"Your loyalty does you credit. If there were the slightest possibility . . . How much of Lord Maclehose's property did you have in mind?"

"The hundred and sixty acre running down to the burn." No supplication now. "It's aw arable and adjoins Glen Gryffe for twelve hundred feet. With canny planning it could support forty cows and eighty followers. A smart man like you probably could buy it for twenty-five pound an acre. Four thousand pound should bring it in nicely and be a proper godsend to the orphanage into the bargain. The wee shavers aye need cash."

"I wish I could help you." McFadden was surprised to find he meant it. Her enthusiasm was a blaze to warm the heart. "But we would have to liquidate capital, and that in law I cannot do. Your late husband's will expressly forbids it."

"Poor John was that careful of my welfare. I wonder—did he put the kybosh on a loan on the manor house?"

"Certainly not, for no bank would consider such, Mrs. Dougal. The encumbrances, the lack of freehold . . . Not a worthwhile risk for an outsider."

"Why no keep it in the family?"

The lawyer looked at her intently, then a slow smile enlivened his bland features. "You're a proper caution, Mrs. Dougal," he said. "Your Trust should lend you money on the security of your home so that you can increase the size of your farm. Fair Machiavellian." The smile vanished. "As your trustee and children's guardian, I could not approve.

Forgive me—you are too inexperienced to be a good risk as a farmer."

"Did I no tell you?" she said. "I have a partner. Mr. Grant. Ask throughout the length and breadth of Renfrewshire and they'll boast there's no a better cattle man in aw Scotland. Any bank would put money on him. Aye, mibbie even the Bank of England."

A knock at the door preceded the newest office boy complete with coal scuttle, sent by his superiors to learn the cause of the merriment; Son never laughed when he had a client. The halflin put on two quick lumps and bustled out to tell the clerks that 'struth, Mr. Archibald was drying his eyes.

"That'll be aw for the day then, Mr. A.," said Anna. "I'll keep you *au courant* with developments at the castle. And you'll draw up my last will and testament, leaving the house to Lachlan, the oldest son. Failing him, Hugh, then wee Alexander. It wouldna make sense to cut up the place six ways. I'll send you a note of the disposition of the jewelry. I'll no have the girls haggle over my leavings. My furs you can foist on the Salvation Army, if they'll take them."

Hand on her elbow, he walked her through the kirklike offices, the clerks and the apprentice lawyers stealing quick glances, and opened the door to the stone stairs down to West Nile Street.

"Good-by, Mrs. Dougal. Believe me, I hope you'll be back often to brighten my day."

"Och, we'll probably have lots to chew over." She paused on the threshold. "Put a wee codicil, if that's what you caw it, in my will. James Grant is to have the right to buy the Maclehose land at the price per acre John paid him for Glen Gryffe. I've aye felt you lawyers took advantage there. I'll no have that on my conscience. Ta-ta the now, Mr. A."

He bowed low over her hand, held it a telltale second overlong. And him a seasoned bachelor! A nice wee titbit, that, for Harriet.

On this uplifting note she left the law offices for those of Dougal & Company next door. Sixty years before, the East India merchants had allocated some of the profits of an expanding tea empire into property in their fast-growing native city. On this ground they had built a two-story building for themselves and four taller ones to let, all with the classic Grecian lines so beloved of Glasgow's principal architect, Alexander "Greek" Thomson.

With ease, Anna pushed open one of the expertly hung bronze doors and crossed the black and white marble floor to a poor bit laddie in a gray alpaca jacket.

"I'll have a word with Mr. Philip," she said.

"He's no Mr. Philip," the halflin replied with a touch of contempt. "No sin' his faither passed awa. He's Mr. Dougal."

"Very well." No country talk for this wee snob. "Mr. Dougal."

"You'll be having an app'intment?"

"I'm Mrs. Anna Dougal."

At the awesome name he swallowed and indicated a leather armchair vast as a dry-dock. "Tak a pew, Mrs. Dougal."

"If I sat in that, you'd not find me in a week. I'll stand."

She was at the foot-tapping stage by the time her brother-in-law came through a side door of heavy oak, top hat in hand, frock coat open over immaculate white vest and gray silk cravat. He could have attended a regal wedding without changing a thread.

"My dear Anna," he said, frowning. "This is an unusual pleasure. You should have rung me up first."

"And spent money unnecessarily?" No Doric for Philip either. He didn't appreciate it, and she was selling. "I was next door with my lawyer, right on the spot. I'm flattered. I didn't expect the Managing Director to come down from his eyrie to meet wee Anna Dougal. I thought I'd have to ascend for my audience."

"I was on my way out. A luncheon meeting of the Clyde Navigation Trust. You know they recently made me a member? Perhaps my son Colin could take care of whatever it is you have in mind."

"My business is with you, and it'll take only a minute. You were right about John's motorcar. Ladies shouldn't drive these dangerous machines. I've decided to accept your offer for it. Three hundred guineas is not much, but it'll have to do."

"That was months ago, Anna, and the figure was in pounds, as I recollect."

"You drive a hard bargain, but I'll not argue. Three hundred pounds it is, then. Send your man down for it any day after today."

The sun on West Nile Street was even brighter than before as she pulled her gold watch out on its spring chain pinned to her bosom. Ten to one. Time to walk up to Sauchiehall Street and meet Lachie in the Willow Room of Miss Kate Cranston's Tearooms. Wait till she told him they were going to shop for a new motorcar this afternoon instead of going to the picture show.

The village of Strathgryffe was as dry as a maiden aunt's peck on the cheek. Once there had been a cheerful pub sloshing ale from wooden barrels into pewter tankards to slake the thirst of those who had earned it by their labor. But no more. With the zeal of those who know what is best for the lower orders, the gentlemen of the new houses had eradicated this debilitating temptation for the working man. Having discussed the matter in train and club, the wealthy agreed to boycott the local and let it be known that those unfortunates who lacked the strength to keep away from the offensive establishment would receive no custom or employment in Strathgryffe. Prodded, the Presbyterian ministers preached the evils of drink, and the Episcopalians'—the "whiskypalians' "—references to Our Lord turning the water into wine served only to emphasize how effete was that form of religion. "Wha daur meddle wi' me" roared the stubborn who would rather drink than eat, but economics were against them and drove some to jobs in Greenock or Paisley. When the tavernkeeper was unable to pay his suppliers, the gentlemen gave him an excellent price for his building, tore it down, and built a library in its stead to slake the thirst of the mind, a vast improvement to the serenity of the village's main and only street.

Naturally, the private golf club retained its nineteenth hole for its members, and the vintners' lorries from Greenock and Paisley continued to arrive weekly at the well-posted tradesmen's entrances of the elegant homes with cases of claret from Bordeaux, great-year champagnes and vintage wines from other French cantons; oaken tuns of Devonshire cider and good Scots ale; whiskies malt, liqueur, and blended; sherries from Spain; port, white and tawny, from Portugal; *fin* cognac, Drambuie, Benedictine, crême de mènthe, the last known to gentlemen in cloakroom privacy as "whore's delight." Little gin, though. Gin was vulgar, English, cheap, reputed to take the lining off the stomach, and "Auntie's ruin and Mother's damnation" to the poor.

The lack of a village tavern was not at all discriminatory. Anyone could have a selection delivered to his door if he had the money to stock a cellar. If he hadn't, the gentlemen paraphrased "Let 'em eat cake" with "Let 'em walk to Dambridge," a mere three miles away and downhill at that. So the men of Strathgryffe gravitated perforce to the Dambridge Larder; not unwillingly because the required ale was served by an added attraction, namely the owner, fair plump Dolly, wife of the gardener, Pat Nolan.

"Jamie Grant, you're a shameful man," she said, giving the mahogany a wipe with her bar towel.

"For quoting Rabbie Burns, the greatest Scot of them aw?"

"And the wickedest. Fine I ken his dirty poems had tae be cleaned up before they were printed."

"No dirty, Dolly, but of the earth, earthy."

Both hands on the bar, Gwen the collie's head on one foot, the other on the wooden rail, James Grant had the drink taken. Not much too much, but the right amount to make him agree with Harry Lauder, currently warbling on the world's stages "For when I was single, my pockets did jingle, I wish I was single again."

Being a week night, the Larder was quiet. Pints in hand, two silent farmers from Bishopton stared into the smoke-blackened stone fireplace where the coals glowed against the autumn chill. A prosperous-looking commercial traveler sat in the corner steadily drinking whisky and making notes in his account book.

"'We twa hae run about the braes'"—Jamie continued with Burns—"'and pulled the gowans fine—'"

"Aye. Lang syne. You shouldna recall those days, you sentimental gowk."

"I like to see the blush mantle those bonny cheeks."

"And me an old married woman? It's the heat in here."

"Mind the time you turned your ankle up Misty Law, and I carried you home on my back?"

"And my faither wanted to take the whip to you for having your arms round my legs?"

"Light as a thistledown you were."

"I'd break your back now."

"It would be a fair treat, Dolly."

"Hey!" The commercial traveler's loud hail broke the mood.

"Hay is for donkeys," Dolly shouted back. "If it's a drink you're after, come where I can gie it to you."

Muttering something about savages, the stout man approached, glass in hand.

"You'll be from England," said Jamie.

"None of your damn business."

The farmers at the fire turned heads slowly to look.

"You proved it again, laddie," said Jamie. "Scottish savages never shout at ladies. No more do we curse in front of them unless to put 'bloody' before English, which is no a swear at aw but an accurate description and statement of fact."

"That was Bell's of Perth you were drinking, was it no?" said Dolly sweetly. "You'll be wanting a large one for the road. I'm hoping it'll be for what your Dr. Johnson miscawed the noblest prospect in Scotland—the highroad to England."

Gwen growled through closed muzzle, one farmer took a pull of his ale, the other whistled soundlessly, the stranger glowered then let out a bellow of laughter.

"I apologize, madam. Yes, a double Bell's, please. I've had a bad day and my figures won't come out right—but that's no excuse. For swearing, this round's on me."

"I'll hae a wee port and lemon," said Dolly.

"It's mine, then." Jamie turned to the farmers. "What'll you have, lads? The same? Three pints, Dolly."

"Here, here," said a deep voice from the door. "It's time you were close't."

"And it's time you were off duty, Angus," said Dolly. "Sneck the lock for me, man, and hae a wee dram."

"Dinna mind if I do." The policeman whipped off helmet and jacket.

" 'Oh, Mr. Constable, whatever shall I do?' " sang the Londoner. " 'I meant to get off at Birmingham, and here I am at Crewe!' "

"He'd no be daft?" asked the man in uniform.

"I'm going daft. Are you coming?" said Dolly, pouring herself another port and lemon.

"See's a whusky, and I'll awa, too," said Angus.

" 'My mither-in-law, she's awa, she's awa,' " sang one farmer unexpectedly. " 'She's gone where the bad folk aw go. Turn mither's face to the wa', love. Turn that sour face to the wa'.' Aw thegether now—"

" 'My mither-in-law, she's awa, she's awa. She's gone where the bad folk aw go—' "

The stentorian chorus wakened Pat Nolan, napping in the back room to ready himself for bed. On stockinged feet he came out behind the bar, mouth sunken without the teeth he had left in the tumbler beside the sofa. A little man, the gardener still found it hard to believe that Dolly had preferred him to the husky brutes who frequented the Larder as much for the server as for the ale. Dolly never did tell him that to her his lack of stature was an asset. Big men were bossy. Over the years, Pat had given her gratitude in full measure, his cup running over when her fearsome father died and left behind every Irishman's dream, a pub of his wife's own. Now he stood behind their bar, squeezing arm around Dolly's ample waist.

"I'm for the road," said James Grant abruptly and went out into the night, Gwen at his left heel.

In the white moonlight, man and dog were one shadow as they crossed to the bridge over the Gryffe high above the thundering waters of the dam. *You're jealous of the wee Ulsterman,* said the ale. Everything had been a lark to Dolly, and a romp in the heather had been the most of all, with laughter before and after, the walk home as gay as the walk out and never a word of blame for him or regret for herself. "Jolly Dolly's Folly" she'd called him once. *But it's no only Pat's wife you covet. It's his happiness, too. You get one in the wame every time you see him with Dolly and mind what you drew instead. You're a miserable bugger, Jamie Grant, to begrudge Pat Nolan what he had the good sense to grasp and you didn't, and that's a fact.*

"Come on, Gwen," Jamie said aloud. "We better awa hame, or Daisy'll play Katie-bar-the-door and lock me out to sleep with you in the bloody barn."

The bone-white moon climbed, foreshortening their shadows. A nighthawk swooped ahead of him, and he wished it good hunting. The sleeping orphanage brought as always the ache of a man without bairns for bairns without a father. He was near sober by the time he entered the last half mile, a lane between a high hedge of solid beech and the higher wall of the Maclehose policies, the stone baffling the purl of the burn on the other side, echoing back the clack of his steel-shod heels. He filled his lungs with the nippy air and felt shame for his envy of another's lot. He lived in health and strength and the beauty of nature, and the cry of his clan was "Stand Fast."

"Good evening, Mr. Grant."

"Godsakes, Mrs. Dougal! How the—how did you get up there?"

"No by a broomstick, for aw you might think." Sidesaddle on the six-foot wall, Anna waved down at him. "His lordship's stones need pointing, and the cracks make a wee ladder. Will you no join me?"

He pulled himself up beside her.

Beyond the Gryffe the silver sheen of grass spread out before them, rising gently to the castle half a mile away. The baronial building with the square crenellated towers was ablaze as if for a party, light shining from every window, but there was no sound of merriment, just cold silent brilliance.

"So it's happened then," said Jamie. "Maclehose no more."

"He had a grand run for his money, and I shouldna be sad. But I am."

The great doors opened slowly, and a kilted silhouette came through the shaft of light onto the terrace.

"That'll be Rory Tulloch," said Grant. "He'll give us a good blow. For ten year he's been practicing 'The Flowers o' the Forest' against this day."

They saw the drones go over the shoulder, watched three steps of slow march before the piper's ancient lament for Scotland's dead came downwind to uncover Grant's head and bow Anna's while the high strains pricked her eyes to wetness.

"Amen," said Jamie as the last skirl went through them and the door slowly closed on the distant light. "Can I help you down, Mrs. Dougal?"

"Wait a wee. That's no what I climbed to see. I didna expect it. I'm perched up here to look at waste, Mr. Grant. Flagrant immoral waste. Acre after acre of good land producing nothing, like a bonny lass that could bear fruit and willna. Does it no sicken you to see this grand soil aw run to seed?"

"I canna stand to think of it."

"Then you'd better start, Mr. Grant, for in a wee while those hundred and sixty acre will belong to Glen Gryffe. How many fine Aberdeen Angus will that lot graze? Close your mouth, man, before a bat mistakes it for a cave and flies in. And give us a lift from here. Posteriors with no meat on them dinna belong on rough stones."

Speechless, he jumped down, held up hands that all but encircled her waist as she put hers on his shoulders. For the second it took to pluck her off the wall, she felt like a girl again.

"I—I dinna ken what to say," he said.

"Let it wait till the morn's morn." Gently she removed his hands. "I'll continue my interrupted constitutional and see you then. Ta-ta the now." She walked on. Fancy wee Anna Dougal mentioning her backside to a man! Next thing she'd be calling it her arse. Och, t' hell. A night like this would make a witch out of Queen Victoria.

Dazed but thinking, Jamie Grant sat on the low bank of the burn opposite his house and waited for his wife to go to bed. With a hundred and sixty acres more, Glen Gryffe would blossom. After all these years he might yet become successful at the cattling. Would prosperity give him back a wife? Would he want Daisy back on those terms? Now, the Widow Dougal—there was a woman. Och, it's the booze and the moon and the loneliness. And a bonny face smiling down at you. Yon's a combination that would make a lecher out of St. Peter, let alone James Bloody Grant.

His wife's lamp went out. He waited another five minutes before crossing the steppingstones, Gwen behind him. " 'Sho," he whispered, flinging out an arm to the barn. The collie slunk off, and he entered his house in the black silence, creaking up the stairs to the other bedroom that was his now and had been for years.

PART TWO

A MIDDLE

Chapter Three

FORMAL ACQUISITION of the land nearly doubling Glen Gryffe's acreage came a year and a day after the death of John Dougal. On that anniversary, wearing a touch of black and carrying a small basket, Anna walked the three miles to the cemetery on the north slopes of the glen. To spare herself from eyes that would gladly give her the pity she despised, she avoided Strathgryffe and took the paths west of the outskirt houses on the edge of the village green with its sports pavilion, swings, and wide-flung playing fields. She climbed over the drystone dyke onto the Port Glasgow road, crossed it, and went up the winding drive under the trees. In the deserted cemetery, by the well-tended plot with the simple granite headstone, she looked over the valley he had coursed from end to end astride many a good mare. *You were braw on a horse, John. None brawer. But what were you thinking behind your great beard? Did you love me at all? You never told me, and now I'll never ken. When it was time for you to marry, the only child of a suitable father was handy. Papá gave his consent, and that was the thrilling courtship of wee Anna Biggart. No a patch on my auld china's. There was romance. When I see her smiling on her Robert, I could envy her . . .*

With a trowel borrowed from Pat Nolan, without mawkish reverence she dug a small shallow hole in the turf at the foot of the grave. From the basket she took a potato into which two months before she had inserted the stem end of a sprig of white heather. She laid the tuber in the hole, patted the turf around the flower's wiry stem, scattered away the handful of excess soil, and rose from her knees. *I'll tell your bairns what I've done here the day, John. They'll approve, for they ken you did love your moors and your fields. The heather's from one, the potato's from the other, and a grand wet nurse the spud has been. The bloom will stay awhile yet. Now I'm awa hame, as you used to say, and if you can see what I'm doing to build up Glen Gryffe, I hope you approve. But I dinna give a tinker's dam if you don't.*

That night over dinner she informed her three oldest of the morrow's momentous acquisition.

"You said we were poor," said Dorcas. "Where did you find the money?"

"I'm putting what they caw a mortgage on the house."

"Mamá! How could you! Supposing you can't pay it?"

"You'll be turned out in the snow," said Elspeth.

"In your bare feet and a shawl over your head," said Lachie with relish.

"Dinna fret about failure," said Anna. "I've made Mr. Grant our partner. He'll keep us solvent. And he'll make proper farmers out of the lot of us."

"I don't want to be a farmer," wailed Dorcas. "I'm going to be a missionary. In Africa."

"Oh, dry up," said Lachie.

"That'll be enough of that, Son," said Anna, although agreeing. She craved enthusiasm for her grand new scheme, not cold water. "I tell you, bairns, we'll make a name for oursels. It'll no be long till Glen Gryffe beef will be aw the go in the best grills in Glasgow—"

"And Edinburgh," put in Elspeth.

"And London," said Lachie.

"Aye, mibbie even in the sinfu' city," said Anna. "They ken down there that the best sirloin aw comes from Scotland. Up the Dougals! I havena been this excited since Granny kicked the cow. What's the vote on a blowout to celebrate?"

"Only a year after—ow! How dare you, Elspeth Dougal!" Dorcas leaned down to massage her assaulted shin.

"This house has been dull as dull owerlong." Anna closed her eyes to the byplay. "And it with a neat natty ba'room fair crying out for the jigging."

"May I invite Kitty Boyd?" said Elspeth.

"That you may. We'll ask the Boyd family *in toto.* You wouldna mind putting up with wee Willie, would you, Lachie?"

"He's not so bad. For a kid."

"Motion carried then. *Nem. con.,*" said Anna, ignoring Dorcas's dissent. "Aw we need now is a Saturday that's convenient for Cookie."

What with one thing and another—the avoidance of conflicting local festivities, the engraving of invitations, the month's notice to permit the frantic flurry of frockmaking—it was seven weeks before the party could be held. On a Friday in January, Kitty Boyd and her brother Willie caught the 4:15 train to Strathgryffe. Their parents would come down the following day after one o'clock, when Dougal & Company released the father for the week end. Let out early from Gilmorehill High, boy and girl dashed home and raced up the four flights of cement stairs, then down with the suitcases packed the night before.

"I'll take yours, Kitty," said Willie Boyd. "Girls aren't supposed to carry bags."

"Thanks awfully."

Politely, the ten year-old boy walked on the outside of the pavement down the Avenue to Byres Road and the yellow tramcar, swung the impedimenta up the two steps to the back platform, and, with the help of the conductor, stowed the luggage under the circular staircase to the top deck.

"I don't mind if you go up," said Kitty.

"No thanks. Mother said I was to look after you. We'll both sit downstairs." Later, as they sped along Dumbarton Road, he asked, "How fast do you think we're going, Kitty?"

"I haven't an earthly."

"I'll bet only twenty miles an hour. This is slow stuff. The Royal Scot averages over sixty miles an hour all the way to London, even with engine changes."

"Where did you learn that?"

"*Children's Newspaper*. If you skim through it, you can read lots of interesting things and miss all the stodgy school stuff."

A gaunt youth accosted them as they stepped off at Argyll Street, a-thrang with traffic.

"You'll be for St. Enoch's?" he said. "Carry your bags for two bawbees."

He swooped on the handles, but Willie hung on.

"My brother is quite capable," said Kitty haughtily.

"Mike Dowd, paws off they bags!" bellowed the traffic policeman from the center of the intersection. "Now! Afore I run you in." He made a move toward them. "I've tellt you before. Wait till you're asked."

As the keely vanished among the hurrying pedestrians, Willie put the bags down and waved his thanks to the policeman, who smartly saluted back.

"Want to ride in the head carriage?" asked Kitty, following him across the concourse to Platform 12. "It'll be empty."

" 'Course it will. It's there as a buffer against a head-on collision, just as the last one is against a rear-end. We'll ride in the middle."

A crowd of boys in chocolate-and-gold school caps swept past, among them Lachie and Hughie, carefully not seeing their guests. Willie knew that they had been recognized but philosophically shrugged it off. It was no snub. He was at a school of a different color and with his sister. He'd have done the same thing.

In the middle carriage they found a compartment with one lone occupant, collarless, a sweat rag around his scrawny neck. He helped Willie put the bags in the rack, then took a clay jaw-warmer out of his mouth. "The pipe'll no mak you sick, lassie?" he asked. "Tell me, an' I'll knock it oot. I'm doon tae the dottle anyway."

"That wouldn't be fair. You were here first, and it is a smoking compartment."

"Ta." He beamed his thanks. "It'll no be for long. I'm only gaun as far as Paisley."

Steam clanged under the seat, the heat rose smotheringly, the dirty old pipe smelled like an outhouse on fire. As soon as the man dropped off at Paisley with a cheery "Ta-ta the now," Willie flung down a window and stuck his head out into the rushing winter blast.

Kitty tugged his jacket. "Willie, come in before you catch your death."

"What a reek that was." He closed out the elements. "Worse than the fug in the dressing room after rugger practice."

"Willie, you are dreadful."

A crescendo of sound announced their entrance into the rock-sided cutting, then the brakes grabbed for the station where nine months a year a bank of multi-hued flowers spelled out STRATHGRYFFE. The village was perennial winner of the competition for the prettiest stop on the line. Now, in the dormant season, the name was written in smooth first-size stones, all whitewashed to catch illumination from the inverted cones of yellow gaslight. Before the train was fully stopped, doors thudded open and schoolboys leaped out running to vanish into the dark like a shoal of mackerel before a porpoise. Safe now from the scorn of his peers, Lachie touched his cap to Kitty.

"*Ceud mile failte!*" he said.

"Coo meel falsh?"

"That's Gaelic. A fellow in my class speaks it. He's from Mull. It means 'With a thousand welcomes.'"

"I like that."

"Aw, forget school," said Willie. "It's Friday. Like to carry Kitty's bag, Lachie?"

They climbed the wooden stairs to the viaduct over the double railway lines and marched off for Glen Gryffe, a bag shouldered by each of the older boys. The Dougal motorcar was up on its blocks for the winter, and while Anna could have sent the trap for them, it didn't occur to her. Children must not inconvenience grown-ups. Or ponies. The two-mile uphill trot would have soaked the piebald with sweat, and it was a bitter night. So the children stepped out, feeling no grievance and enjoyed the walking, the crackling stars, and the thought of hot cocoa waiting.

They drank it in the hall, all crowded into the big wooden inglenook while the fire, stoked high in welcome, warmed sturdy bodies, reddened icy cheeks.

"We have twenty-two new horses, Willie," said Lachlan.

"Twenty-two! I don't believe you. Your stables aren't that big. Where would you keep twenty-two horses?"

"Easy. They're all under one bonnet."

"Mother's new Argyll," explained Hugh. "It has a hood and a windscreen and everything."

"The morn's morn, I'll let you sit in the driver's seat, Willie," said Lachie. "If you don't kick me out of bed tonight the way you did the last time you slept with me. There I was, sound asleep. The next minute I was halfway across the room, flat on the floor."

"Gwan, you fell out," said Willie.

"Can I come into bed beside you and Elspeth in the morning, Kitty?" asked Morag.

"Like a wee mouse," said Kitty, "in case we're still asleep."

"But leave your own mouse behind," added Elspeth.

"I wouldn't let her in if I were you," said Hugh, holding his nose.

Three Dougals told the story, Hugh interrupting Lachie, Elspeth interrupting Hugh.

"Stop it!" shouted Willie. Ears reddening—he hadn't

meant to bellow—he mumbled, "You shouldn't pick on Morag. Three against one's no fair," and endeared the child to him for life.

"I don't mind, really," she said. "It was awful funny. Afterwards . . . Have a digestive biscuit, Willie?" She held out the plate like a votive offering.

In the nursery, Sandy was turning purple.

"He wants to go downstairs with the big children," Miss Watson told Anna. "And it's time for beddy-byes."

"Couldn't we give him a wee dispensation? It's no often Harriet Boyd's bairns are here, and he feels left out."

"You'll spoil the child, Mrs. Dougal."

"With you to keep order? No a chance." Anna's youngest let out his breath triumphantly, and she threw him a conspirator's wink.

Upstairs, Glen Gryffe was built like a hotel. The master bedroom, bath, and dressing room formed a suite opposite the head of the stairs so that the bay windows looked south over the rising moor to the jutting top of Misty Law a thousand feet above. A narrow hallway ran east, another west, each with a bathroom and five bedrooms with hot and cold running water. At the time of construction, the workmen had marveled at the overabundance of plumbing, and the topers at the Dambridge Larder wondered if Glen Gryffe was being built as a fancy brothel. "Wash basins in aw the bedrooms. Imagine!"

Anna walked along the west wing to her oldest daughter's quarters, knocked, and entered quietly. Curtains drawn over mullioned windows, gas low in the mantle, Dorcas lay on top of the bedcover, hands on her stomach, wet eyes to the ceiling.

"What's up, lass?" said Anna. "Is it that time again?"

"Every twenty-eight days you said, Mamá. If I have to suffer this every month—less than a month—for the next thirty years . . . Why did you tell me that? Thirteen times thirty equals three hundred and ninety."

"My, you're good at the mental arithmetic. It's no the best

arrangement, Dorcas, but ladies just have to suffer it."

"I hate being a lady!"

"How about a wee taet of med'cin? There's no a better way to ease the misery."

"You shouldn't give me whisky."

Anna suppressed a sigh. "Buck up, lass," she said, refusing pity. "Wash your bonny face and come on downstairs and join the frolic. Kitty and Willie have been here for an hour. They're aye ready for a laugh, and that's as good as med'cin. Well, awmost."

"It's all very well for you, Mamá. You can't know what pain means. Not and have had six babies—ow! Ow! Ow!" She rolled over and bit the pillow.

"Then I'll ask Mairi to bring you up a wee tray with some Bovril and biscuits and mibbie a scrambled egg. You get into your nightie now and have your bite in bed. You'll be aw better the morn's morn."

As Anna went to dress for the evening, she knew that dinner would be the cheerier for her oldest's absence and despised herself for the thought. Whatna way for a mother to think.

Willie Boyd wakened in the dark, lay quiet for a moment wondering where he was, then slipped gingerly out from under the two blankets and down comfort. Careful not to rouse the sleeping Lachie, on bare feet he scampered over to the window, closed it, and looked out. Promptly he lost consideration for his bedmate.

"Snow!" he screamed. "Beautiful snow! A million tons of it!" He shot across the room again, jumped onto the bed, and kicked Lachie's backside. "Get up! Get up! Snow! Snow!"

"You wee messan!" Lachie grabbed for Willie's feet and missed. Together they ran to the window to stare out on starlit white, dimly seen Misty Law an ice cream cornet with the filling running down the sides.

"How deep, Lachie?"

The older boy opened the window again and stuck his

fingers straight down into the accumulation on the broad sill.

"Six inches," breathed Willie.

"Five anyway. Mibbie it drifted."

"Naw. Close the window, Lachie. I'm fu-fu-freezing."

"Keep your voice down. If Mother hears, she'll make us eat a hot breakfast before she lets us out the house. Want to try my old riding breeches?"

Wearing two jerseys apiece, scarves, breeches, two pairs of stockings, and carrying their heavy boots, they crept out of the bedroom. Willie would have gone into the bathroom, but Lachie grabbed his arm.

"That cistern makes an awful bloody racket," he whispered. "Pee in the snow. It's soundproof." He slipped into the dining room and took two yellow-gold Oregon pippins from the bowl on the sideboard. They crept through the darkened hall, donned their boots in the vestibule, then opened the storm door reinforced with steel against nor'easters and stepped out onto a shadowless carpet of ermine under a diamond-studded ceiling of lambent blue velvet. Willie put two fingers to his lips, inhaled, and blew out, his breath congealing in the ten degrees of frost.

"Look, Lachie. I'm smoking."

"Come on."

There were five sledges in the tool shed. Made of stout oak by Mr. Grant, the oiled steel screwed to the wooden runners glistened dully in the light streaming from the kitchen window.

"Cookie's up," whispered Lachie. "She's as bad as Mother for the hot breakfast. Don't make a sound."

Once they had their two-seaters out, silence was no problem, the snow hushing every move as they crossed the courtyard past the stables and out onto the brae. Lachie turned his sledge upside down.

"Why are you doing that?" asked Willie.

"To pack down a run, you dope."

Dragging the heavy wooden platforms by their bridles, up

they climbed filled with soaring well-being from the rushing thrills to come and the stark grandeur all around; the black boulders dappled with white, the mountain looming, the squeaking crunch of their boots on the frost-crusted snow, their oneness in a world asleep. Lachlan shivered.

"What's the matter, Lachie? You cold?"

"A mite," he fibbed rather than admit to the stab of beauty. " 'Cold as charity, cold as glum, cold as the hair on a polar bear's bum. Cold as charity and that's pretty chilly, but it's no as cold as our wee Billy, for he's deid, thank God.' " He opened a gate in a wire fence. "No sheep up here, so I can leave it agee to give us a longer run. God bless the Lanark and Renfrew Hunt."

"Why?"

"If Father hadn't been a member, he wouldn't have put in all these gates."

"Why?"

"Hunters hate fences. The horse can't see the wire to jump it. If a fox leads the hounds to a fence, the whipper-in cuts it."

"I'd like to see him cut my fence."

"He bloody well would, but the Hunt would pay you to have it repaired. They have a wire fund."

"Then why did your father put in gates?"

"To save the Hunt money."

"Jolly decent of him. They must have cost a packet."

"He wanted to stay a member. He might have been dropped if he hadn't. Now save your breath to cool your porridge." They reached the top of the brae. "I'll go first. On my belly. You sit. You don't know the way, and I'd get hell if you split your fat head on a drystane dyke."

"Who's got a fat head?"

"Anyone that's daft enough to go to Gilmorehill High. Tally ho!" He hurled himself flat on his sledge and shot away, gathering speed through the elephant gray of morning coming, steering with body leverage and dragging toes, gateposts flashing past, over the sharp drop to the house where the level slowed him, then over the edge and chuting the sloping pasture. Faster than the new Argyll he was, the wind an icy pillow in his face as he swished down to the Gryffe. Ten yards from the burn he twisted his body, stuck out his left leg at right angles, forced the sledge to stop across the slope, and stood up.

"Gang way!" Head down, Willie came hurtling.

Lachie dived on top of him, grabbed his shoulders, and swept the pair of them off in one motion as the empty sledge slid across the farm track and flew through the air into the burn.

"You bloody wee menace!" yelled Lachie, cuffing his guest's fair head. "I told you to sit up and watch where you were going. If you've broken that sledge, I'll break your bloody neck."

"What for did you pull me off?" Willie howled back. "I was running fine . . ."

"Right into the drink, you daft wee bugger."

"Oh. I'm sorry, Lachie."

"That's all right. You've plenty of nerve for a kid."

They found the errant sledge grounded on a snow-covered rock jutting from dark chuckling water. Lying on the bank, Willie sitting on his legs, Lachie hooked the bridle with a stick and floated it back within reach. They made three more runs: fifteen minutes to climb up, a tenth of that to drop down the four hundred feet.

"I don't know about you, kid," said Lachie, "but my belly's rumbling something awful."

"Mine thinks I died."

As he said it, brass clanged from the manor house, where a dim figure stood on the front terrace vigorously waving a big bell.

"Good timing, Mother," said Lachie.

"Will she give us what-for?"

"Naw. She's a good sport. Come on. Let's see if there's anything to eat."

Pork sausages and calves liver, Wiltshire bacon tasty lean,

baked mushrooms, fried eggs, porridge—a great dish of it that had been gently bubbling and smoothing all night.

"Help yourself, Willie," said Elspeth. "Though why I should be polite to you, I don't know, sneaking off like that. Why didn't you waken us?"

"If you dinna see anything you fancy, Willie," said Anna, "Cookie has some grand Findon haddie. Would you like her to grill a piece with a nice lump of butter?"

"No thank you. I'll just have some sausages and bacon and eggs. And please may I have liver, too, Aunt Weeanna?"

"Aunt Weeanna!" said Dorcas.

"Willie Boyd! Apologize to Aunt Anna immediately," said Kitty, reddening for her brother.

"I didn't hear him say anything wrong," said Morag.

"I'm sorry, Aunt Anna," mumbled Willie. "I didn't mean to call you wee, only I've heard you do it yourself."

"It's a compliment, laddie," she replied. "It minds folk that valuables come in small packages. Like diamonds."

"Will you take me sledging, Willie?" asked Morag.

"You go with Lachie," said Dorcas. "Willie's not old enough."

"You're awful bossy," said Hugh.

"Don't talk to me like that."

"Oh, dry up," said the male head of the house.

She needs to learn to get along with folk, thought Anna. Mibbie boarding school's the thing for her. It wouldna have to be England. St. Thenew's at Helensburgh's no sae bad.

"I'll race you, Willie," said Hugh.

"You're on."

"Willie gets his choice of sledges then," said Lachie. "You challenged him."

Climbing sun from a cloudless sky to put golden lights in windows across the glen. White of snow to make red roofs redder, fir and pine greener. Five sledges, five Dougal bairns —Dorcas was still suffering—Kitty and Willie Boyd, a mother, a nanny.

"Put Sandy between Kitty and me, Miss Watson," said

Elspeth. "We'll keep our feet down and go slow."

"Slowly," came the automatic response, as the smiling Wattie placed the three-year-old between the two big girls. "Hang on tight, my little man."

"See me, Wattie!" cried Morag, flying past on Willie's back, arms tight around his neck, feet tucked under his legs.

Then on Willie's dare, sitting up behind him, Anna took a run.

"Fall off when I tell you," he yelled as they neared the bottom.

"You wee rascal! I didna ken . . ."

"Now!"

They rolled off and roly-poly'd on, Willie clinging to the bridle, snow under Anna's tweed skirt, down her neck, under her tweed tam. Spluttering, she grabbed a handful and slapped it over his open mouth, and James Grant, behind his window, laughed aloud and came outside carrying a spade.

"I'm thinking a wee snowbank would stop you with more decorum, Mrs. Dougal."

"Decorum and snow are poor partners, Mr. Grant, but go ahead."

Embankment finished, he wrapped sacking over a work-horse's big hooves, slipped on her collar and traces, and set the Clydesdale to hauling the train of laden sledges back up the brae, Willie on her broad back whooping like a cowboy. Then Lachie borrowed the spade and built a sharp edge on the down side of a hummock to make a jump. He hit it at thirty miles an hour, shoved down to lift his weight, and sledge and boy flew through the air for a good ten feet.

The senior Boyds arrived in the station four-wheeler at two-thirty, walking up the drive, its grade in the snow too much for the ancient horse.

"My, you both look grand," said Anna. "Robert, yon tall hat's a fair temptation for a snowball, but they wouldna dare, I hope. Lachie, take the bags. Do you ken what I was doing before you arrived? Sledging!"

"Anna"—Harriet giggled—"you weren't!"

"I was that. What's more, your son dumped me in the snow, as if I were fifteen again. You're no to scold him. It was fine fun. You're in the West Room. Och, it's grand to see you both. There'll be a cold bird and a bottle ready when you are, Robert."

Harriet's husband changed out of frock coat into worn Norfolk jacket and knickers and woolen stockings of a heather mixture pulled over his well-muscled calves, taking his time to give Anna and his wife theirs for the essential gossip. He stored his evening clothes in the wardrobe, his boiled shirt in the Sheraton chiffonier. It might be a children's party tonight, but there would be ladies present and the white tie mandatory.

"You don't mind, then, if we stay till early Monday morning?" said Harriet.

"Mind? I expected it. Fine I ken Robert wouldna travel on the Sabbath."

"He sets an awful good example, Anna."

"I dinna see how Harriet Hepburn's lived up to him for sixteen year."

"You wouldn't, Anna Biggart, because you couldn't."

"Sh-h, and haud your wheest. Here he comes now."

Although Anna had already eaten lunch, to keep her guests company she took a tender drumstick of the roast pheasant—*Choose the leg of a flyer, the wing of a walker*— and a glass of Bordeaux from the crystal carafe. Before they had finished, the early setting of the winter sun encarnadined the snow, and the children, shouting, clattered up the bare back stairs.

"Would you care to join me in a walk, Harriet?" asked Robert. "The light is going fast."

"No thank you, Robert. Anna and I haven't had a good crack in ages."

"Up to my room then, Harriet." Mrs. Dougal's eyes glinted with interest. "We'll no be disturbed there."

Robert Boyd, scarfed and gloved, went out into the red and blue-white gloaming where he found Mr. Grant plowing the drive behind the Clydesdale, whose nostrils snorted steam into the cold, caller air.

"Splendid evening," said the city man.

"Aye, for folk but no for cattle. They stay in the byre eating up hay by the ton, and it no as good for putting on beef as the grass they canna get at. Would you care to look at the herd?"

In the dark stone building it was easier to hear than to see the silky animals as they crunched their winter fodder. By the light of an oil lantern held high, the two men walked between the rows of twitching tails.

"The finest herd in Scotland," said James Grant. "No a swayback or a hump among them. All as straight as straight. And there's himself, the champion." Pride o' Fyvie swung his massive hornless head to the light, rattling the great neck chain worn since the day when he had crushed the life from his owner. "The past twelvemonth he's served twenty-nine cows, all in the Polled Herdbook. No doddies, no Angus cattle in the country, will have better bloodlines."

"Which must give you great satisfaction."

"The credit's Mrs. Dougal's. There were those who would have sliced Pride o' Fyvie for the table, but she wouldna let them. That took courage."

"Which she has in full measure."

"You'll have heard how she near doubled her acreage?"

"Your acreage too, now, I understand."

"To work, anyway. It's a grand thing for Glen Gryffe."

Upstairs, Anna and Harriet encompassed the latest gossip, reverted to reminiscence, returned to more current affairs. Anna sighed.

"What's that for?" said Harriet.

"Dorcas. You'll have noted her conspicuous absence. She's in her room feeling sorry for hersel. And dinna say she's at an awkward age, or I'll pour the tea over your carrot top. I hear that aw the time from Wattie. Drat it, we kept our sense of humor when we went through the growing up. I tell you, Harriet, it fair sickens a body the way she puts a damper on the whole house. Even wee Morag loses her sparkle when Dorcas moons around looking like Joan of Arc without her armor. I'll bet yon one didna ken how to laugh either."

"You can't expect a child to have your resilience."

"Dorcas's dumps started before John was kilt."

The casual reference to the tragedy brought a searching look from Harriet. If it had been Robert—she could never have been so—well, almost offhand. Anna's brittle acceptance of tragedy was more poignant than tears. "How does she get along with the others?"

"No worth a damn. Hugh says she's bossy, Lachie's aye telling her to dry up, and though Elspeth tries, Dorcas'll no let her near. She wants to be a missionary, of aw things. Wee Anna Dougal's daughter! If she were Catholic, I dinna doubt she'd get hersel to a nunnery."

"Is she running away from life?"

"Mibbie. She certainly wants me to. If she had her way, I'd be in the weeds of the widow for the rest of my natural. I wish to Pete I could pry out what's gnawing at her."

"And you'd like me to try. Well, if I see an opportunity . . ."

"If you don't, you'll mak one. You never yet lost a chance to spier."

"Same wee Anna. You even beg a favor with an insult."

"Same Harriet Hepburn. You were aye owersensitive. Let's awa down and let Cookie tell us what she has in mind for the party eats."

Cook had concentrated on the sweets. Boys ranging in age from eight—Hugh's friends—to thirteen—Lachie's—were not about to take up room with sandwiches when their palates were offered trifles, fruits, tipsy cake, coconut pudding, chocolate pudding, chocolate drink, chocolate ices, macaroons, meringues, jellies.

"Will you have a jelly or a meringue?" Elspeth asked Lachie.

"You're no wrang, I'll have a jelly."

"Lachie, you are a fool."

With the exception of the sultana cake, the girls pretended less interest in the sugary viands. But the cake contained their futures; a ring for first to marry, a threepenny bit for wealth, a thimble for old maid. Bella Cockburn, delicately pronounced Co'burn, youngest child of "Whisky" Cockburn, the distiller, nearly broke her tooth on the piece of silver money.

"Serves her right," said Hugh, who had hoped for it. "She doesn't need any more. Her father's dirty rich already."

To loud cheers and her blushes, popular Molly Smith of the shipbuilding Smiths, found the ring. Fortunately the cruel thimble went to Gladys Stevenson, Paisley Rope Works, who at eight did not worry too much about its significance.

Boys with the right to a family tartan wore the kilt and pitied the bifurcated few. Girls were bouffant in whites and pinks and ruffles and tucks and bows. Elspeth had warned the boarders at St. Malcolm's to bring back party frocks from the Christmas holidays, and the relief from school uniform was intoxicating.

"You wouldn't know they were the same brats, would you, Mrs. Dougal?" Miss Cuthbert's athletic shoulders rose handsomely from chic velvet of sophisticated black, the envy of her charges. There at St. Malcolm's insistence on a school chaperon, the gym instructress took care to stay in the background except when called upon to set up Musical Chairs, Kim the Memory Game, Spin the Plate. She did not arrange Postman's Knock. Bella and Elspeth did, right after the conjurer had performed his last magic.

"A letter for Lachlan Dougal," said Elspeth, intermediary for Bella, breathless in the dark outside the door.

"Not this chicken," muttered Lachie. Sliding behind a curtain, he opened the window and jumped out into the snow, to be copied a second later by Willie. Said Lachie, "Let's have a smoke till this blows over."

"Who has fags?"

"I hid a packet of five Wild Woodbine in the tack-room rafters. Heard any book titles lately? Or hasn't the latest reached Gilmorehill yet?"

"Gilmorehill can beat the High any day. How about *The Nail in the Banister* by R. Stornoway?"

"Kid stuff. *Lower Blouses* by Seymour Titts."

"*Thunder to Come* by Lotta Beans."

"I heard that in the Infants. *Hard to Be Good* by O. U. P. Rick. I don't see that one myself, but the guy that told me laughed like an idiot. He's ahead of me. In the third form. Can you make the smoke go up your nose? Watch."

"How can I in here?" said Willie. "I can hardly see my own puff."

In the Stygian tack room Lachie thought about this. "I wondered why these coffin nails had lost their taste. Eureka! The pleasure of a cigarette is in direct proportion to the amount of smoke seen. Q.E.D., I think I'll give it up."

"Me too, Lachie."

"Let's get a spot of claret cup. Wishy-washy stuff—six lemonade to one of Bordeaux—but it'll wash the taste out of our mouths."

The small ballroom easily held the fifty children, with room to spare for the five local musicians. Patriotic red, white, and blue streamers festooned the beamed ceiling, and the sprung floor swung under the Grand Old Duke of York, the Lancers, the Eightsome Reel. Three sets there were of the last and Rory Tulloch's bagpipes to stir the heart and feet of all, including those who watched.

"They make me feel like crying," said Harriet.

"I'd rather let go a hoo-oooch! and be out there mysel, birling with them. I havena done a *pas de bas* since I was wed."

"Mind your champagne ball for our engagements? Even now, if I close my eyes, I can see you waltzing."

"Yon was the night terpsichore died in wee Anna Biggart.

John was no much for the light fantastic. He no only couldna dance, he wouldna."

By ten o'clock the last favor and fortune had been exploded from the last cracker, the last prize awarded, the last balloon burst, the last of the ices left melting in its crystal bowl. About to sound a siren behind Gladys Stevenson's back, Hugh found that he couldn't close his mouth to blow for the tremendous yawn that cracked his jaws. Ties were slipping behind red ears; little ladies, manners already asleep, scratched themselves openly. The hostess nodded to the band.

" 'Should auld acquaintance be forgot . . .' " Children and grown-ups joined hands around the room. At " 'Now give us a hand, my trusty friend,' " the circle shrank as the singers crossed arms, then again took the fingers of those on either side. Faster and faster played the musicians, faster and faster pumped the handshakes until the last line of the last chorus, "We'll tak' a cup of kindness yet for the days of auld lang syne' " and a cheer to finish: "Hurrah! 'God save our gracious King, long live . . .' "

Sunday was a heartbreaker. Sunshine, no wind, crusty snow, every prospect pleasing for sledging except *Remember the Sabbath day to keep it Holy*. Who could forget it? The rules of conduct made that impossible; the careful dressing, the breakfast solemnity broken only by a robin redbreast that hopped through the open window onto the table. "He doesn't know it's Sunday," Morag defended the tiny bird as she made pellets of dough for him from the inside of her roll. "Here, Cheeky." Then the sedate walk to church, the two-hour service with forty minutes of sound theology preached to the adults and at the young, who mercifully lapsed into semiconsciousness or soared away on fancy's wing. Hugh and Morag were spared the sermon, marching out with other infants to their special service in the basement. As an assistant teacher Dorcas also escaped, but Lachie and Elspeth,

Kitty and Willie were chained in the Dougal pew to fight the fidgets while the pulpit tones droned on and the hands of the clock stood still. The penultimate act of worship, the final hymn, was sung fortissimo. From relief, Elspeth felt guiltily sure. Then the benediction, the blessed fresh air, and the visiting outside the great front door.

"Race you home, Hughie," said Willie.

"No running, now," said Robert Boyd. "Remember the day."

"Yes, Father."

"Wait for me," said Hugh.

"Good morning, Mrs. Dougal."

"Good morning, Mrs. Cockburn, Mrs. Stevenson."

"Let's go the back way, Kitty," said Elspeth. "Take my hand, Morag. Coming, Dorcas?"

The oldest sister smiled derisively and moved away from children to stand on the fringe of the befurred mothers chattering about last night's inane party.

"A huge success I hear, Mrs. Dougal."

"Wee Alec said he was fair stuffed."

"Aye, it was 'Put I to bed but don't bend I,' I'm sure."

"Mine had a good dose of Gregory's Mixture before they slipped under the covers."

"My Molly slept with the ring beneath her pillow." Molly's mother leaned forward to Harriet's ear. *Whisper, whisper, whisper,* and both ladies giggled.

Shut out, Dorcas stared up the Dambridge Road where silk-hatted fathers in galoshes were setting off on the customary half-hour walk to give them an appetite for the monstrous dinners looming. Then like boa constrictors they would all rest, to keep the Sabbath Day holy. Impatiently Dorcas moved from foot to foot.

Anna caught Harriet's eye and flicked her own at her oldest.

"Well, Dorcas," said Harriet. "What would you say to stepping it home with your old aunt?"

Two feet apart, they paced down the hill between the

dismounting blocks and the high stone walls that gave privacy to the mid-Victorian homes. Through wrought-iron gates Harriet glimpsed neat gardens, colorless now except for evergreens and the occasional startle of holly berries. At the village center, where four roads met, a Celtic cross carried the names of the Boer War dead and reminded the pedestrian that such gallant sacrifices were a thing of the past in this enlightened future. The shops of the main street were all shuttered; butcher, baker, grocer, greengrocer, fishmonger, ironmonger, chemist, shoemaker, plumber, the curtains of the three floors of flats above drawn in honor of the Father, Son, Holy Ghost. Harriet didn't break the silence until they had crossed the railway bridge and were headed toward open country.

"I hear you would be a missionary, Dorcas."

"I'd like to try, but I don't know if I'd be able to pass the exams."

"If you want anything badly enough, it will come to you."

"Do you really believe that, Aunt Harriet?"

"Certainly. Isn't the snow white? Won't you miss it when you're in the tropics? For that's where you'll be sent, to join the mosquitoes and snakes and crocodiles. Did you ever notice that the foreign missions never try to save souls in cold countries? I suppose it has something to do with trade. There isn't much wealth in the frozen North."

"I'm sure Dr. Livingstone wasn't thinking of that when he carried the Gospel to Africa."

"No, but others were, and have made millions, thanks to his explorations." Having denigrated climate and calling, Harriet now came about on the other tack. "It's a noble future you've set your mind on, Dorcas. Too noble for me. I doubt I could give up the fun of living in bonny Strathgryffe."

"I hate Strathgryffe."

It was a whisper, such a tiny whisper that Harriet wondered if she had been meant to hear it. She tried to see the face beside her, but it was turned away toward a roadside spring gushing into a high bowl, then into a trough, a "rest and be thankful" for human and horse. Gently she took Dorcas's arm and guided her to the stone seat, sun-cleared of snow.

"Sit down, lass, and tell your old Aunt Harriet what's eating you."

"I can't. There's nothing . . ."

"There must be something. Nobody hates the place where she was born. Not when it's as bonny as Strathgryffe."

"I wish I didn't hate it—I don't want to, but I can't help it."

"Then why do you? There must be a reason."

"There is—no, there isn't. I can't tell you. I can't tell anyone."

So there was something really bothersome, and when a girl admits that, the next thing you know she's pouring it out. Harriet was pleased with herself. A few more minutes alone with Dorcas and—drat it. Someone was coming up the brae, Bible in hand. Grant's wife. A fine figure of a woman, Harriet noted automatically; straight back, a waist that wouldn't go more than twenty inches, and a chocolate-box face above the fur tippet. No wonder Anna couldn't stand her. She didn't stop, merely bowed and swept by.

Harriet turned to Dorcas and caught a look of venom winging up the brae. Well, well. So it wasn't only Strath-gryffe that Dorcas hated. "A nice-looking woman, that," she said, and as she hoped, the innocuous phrase opened the sluice gate to the penned-up waters.

Dorcas jumped to her feet. "Nice!" she hissed. "Nice, you say! There's nothing nice about her. She's vile and evil and not fit to—to live." With shaking hand she pointed to the bend around which Daisy had vanished. "That woman was Papá's—*Papá's* concubine!"

The Biblical term in the young mouth made Harriet want to giggle before the import sank in, and the fountain at her back roared in her ears.

"What are you saying, child?" She laughed uneasily.

"Why, you don't even know what the word means."

"I do too! Besom! Courtesan! Prostitute! Whure!"

"Sh—h, Dorcas! In pity's name, wheest!" Harriet looked around wildly. "Here come your mamá and Uncle Robert. Quick. Let's walk on. Go to your room. I'll make your excuses—say you're ill—I'll be up as soon as I can."

The barley broth, the roast sirloin, the onions in bread sauce, the steamed pudding redolent of treacle—all of it tasteless—the half hour around the hall fire . . . *After dinner sit awhile, after supper walk a mile.*

"I think I'll slip up and see how Dorcas is feeling," Harriet said at last.

The girl was sitting on the window seat staring down at the farm, exhaustion in her shoulders. "I shouldn't have told you," she said dully. "I shouldn't have told anyone. All this time I haven't. I promised God I wouldn't if He'd help me."

"Maybe I'm that help." Harriet sat and took the girl's hand. "You must continue. You might be mistaken."

"If only I could be. My own father . . ."

A tear splashed on the back of Harriet's hand. "Tell me, lovey."

"I can't."

"You must. For your own sake."

"I'd like to—I will—I can't keep it any longer. I was out on the moor looking for him. I knew he would be hacking home soon. He used to let me walk beside him, holding onto an iron, and we'd talk a little. I saw his mare grazing by a big patch of bracken. Her saddle was empty—I couldn't believe he'd been thrown. Not my papá. I ran, anyway, in case there had been an accident, but when I reached his horse, there was no sign of him. Then I heard a woman laugh." She lowered her voice to a whisper. "He was—he was in the bracken—with her."

"You didn't actually *see* them?"

"The bracken was shoulder high . . ."

Thank God for that. "I'm sure there's some simple explanation."

"There can be only one, Aunt Harriet. I ran to the big crag and hid—like a sneak. When they came out, Papá remounted, then leaned over and gave her money. I heard it chink. She—she held onto his stirrup leather. They were arguing. He let out a big shout of laughter and gave her some more."

"And all this time you've told not a soul? You brave child."

"I didn't mean to tell you. It just came out. Aunt Harriet, what am I to do?"

"Probably the hardest thing of all. Nothing. We have to keep this to ourselves. Forever, Dorcas."

"I promise. Mamá mustn't find out that Papá didn't love her."

"Never that. I'm sure he did. Just as he loved all you bairns. It must be hard for you to understand. I don't myself. Perhaps it's best just to accept a fact of life." What could she say? "There are some gentlemen who—they say King Edward was one—they have abnormal appetites . . ." Truly not comprehending, her mind came to a stop.

"Including my father?"

Tell Anna's child that John Dougal must have been a faithless profligate? "No, of course not. You mustn't think that at all. Instead, set your mind on all the ways he showed his love for you."

"I would, if I could remember any. He didn't believe in spoiling us. Or Mamá."

Harriet held back her own tears until she reached the West Room and lay down on the bed to plan what not to tell her dearest friend. As the shadows deepened outside and in her mind, she heard a tap at the door.

"It's only me, wee Anna Dougal."

"Come in," she called, grateful for the gloaming, her back to the fading light.

"A fine one you are," said Anna. "Wheedling things out of my daughter, then going off for a nap and me downstairs full of what killed the cat."

"If I had found out anything, I would have told you right off." Harriet pretended a yawn. "You know I'm always sleepy after Sunday dinner."

"No if there is anything to hold your interest."

"There isn't. Dorcas's problem is not extraordinary."

"It's as extraordinary as you thinking you can hide whatever it is. Never in aw our lives have you done that. It has to be gey bad for you to do it the now." Anna walked to the window and looked out on the white fields and the dark trees waving. "It's easy to guess the straight of it. Dorcas kens her father was as randy as Pride o' Fyvie." She wheeled on Harriet. "That's it, is it no?"

"Oh, Anna!"

"That's why she would have kept me in perpetual mourning. To cover up for him. And now you, too, ken about John. I would never have set you onto her if I had dreamed—I didna work it out until I was alone with the knitting, waiting for you."

"I wondered—you didn't seem grief-stricken. Why didn't you let on? Maybe I could have helped. You should have left him."

"With five bairns and another on the way? I didna find out till I was carrying wee Sandy, though it had been going on since the beginning. John didna deny it. He didna see the need. How did Dorcas learn?"

"She saw him come out of the bracken with the Grant woman—saw him give her money."

"Her! The bloody fool! He promised no to foul his own nest. There were maids and servants aplenty on the other side of the burn. Aye, and fancy ladies in Glasgow. He was no to play *droit du seigneur* at Glen Gryffe. That was the agreement. That and to leave me alone."

"But, Anna, you were too young to be without . . ."

"Love?" said Anna. "I wouldna ken. I'll tell you this though. I was never too young to be without John Dougal. To him the palliardy was for the man's pleasure only, if pleasure it was at aw. Consideration for the one who shared his bed was left from his makeup. I doubt he kenned he was supposed to have it. For me it was a proper relief to find him out. It gave me reason to refuse him."

"But, Anna, it's—it should be love, a mutual—undertaking."

"To you. Everybody kens it's different with you and your husband. They only have to be in the same room with you five minutes." She smiled. "After sixteen year, it's fair sickening."

"How have you kept your sense of humor? Look at you now. Robert says you lift him like a glass of champagne. I could weep."

"Not I. No even for Dorcas, who comes out of this best of any. To keep her mouth shut aw this time . . .   This is what's back of the Darkest Africa nonsense."

"Maybe you should send her away for a little. She says she hates Strathgryffe, and I can understand why."

"Even before this—I've been cogitating, Harriet. Do you think boarding school might no be the ticket for Dorcas?"

"Well, it would get her away from . . ."

"The scene of the crime, eh? It'd no make me an unnatural mother, shunting her off on others?"

"It could do her good. She'd be one of a crowd, with no farmhouse at the bottom of the hill to remind her."

"I've made a wee investigation of St. Thenew's at Helensburgh. It's affiliated with St. Malcolm's, so she could transfer now, although the term has started."

"It would be best for everybody—you, the other children, the girl herself."

"Then by the Lord I'll do it." She paused at the door. "Do you no feel the need of a restorative, Harriet Hepburn?"

"A cup of tea would be nice."

"Tea after this stramash? On down to the morning room with you, and we'll have a wee nip before Robert gets back. Mibbie a big one."

Chapter Four

THE DAY AFTER Dorcas Dougal left for welcome exile at Helensburgh, James Grant took his single-barreled twelve-bore and went looking for the pup he had given to Hughie five months earlier. He spotted him in the drying green nipping at Mairi's heels as she clothes-pegged snowy sheets to the line, a bonny figure, lithe and shapely. She patted the collie's head, picked up the tin tub, and vanished through the kitchen door. Bereft of a human to bedevil, the pup made a fast barking circle of the green, chased and caught the corner of a flapping sheet, and served the Dougal bed linen like a rat, shaking it from side to side as if to break the rodent's neck.

First finger and thumb under his tongue, Jamie let out a shrill blast that broke the rookery in the elm into a hundred cawing birds. Instantly, Chief let go and dropped in a crouch. Another shriller, and he bounded over the turf, made a slow half circle to bring him within a yard, and then, belly to ground, crawled in and lay at the whistler's feet— sure proof that instinct was there before training.

They didn't walk far, maybe two miles for the man to the

coursing dog's four, until in a fold of the moor they came upon thirty blackface grazing, a curly-horned taup in charge. Breeding sent the dog after them, the sheep taking flight as the ram turned head down in protection. Grant locked and raised his gun in one motion and at sixty yards let Chief have the charge in the rump, sending him head over heels. Whining piteously, the collie pulled himself around in circles by his forepaws, hindquarters dragging as Grant broke his gun and walked over to the hurt animal. "'Twas only rock salt hit your arse, wee dug," he said. "It'll sting the morn's morn as well, minding you no to herd sheep unless you're told." In farm country a dog was allowed two bites at a human but only one at a sheep, and none at all during the fast-approaching lambing season. If a farmer saw a collie chase a carrying ewe, the offender was as good as dead, with none to blame the man who squeezed the trigger. Hughie's pet was now safe from that fate.

Jamie knocked on the kitchen door.

"You're early for afternoon tea," said Cook. "But I'll put the kettle on."

"No for me, thanks aw the same. If you have a knuckle-bone, you might give it to Hughie when he comes home. For his wee dug."

Wise in country ways, Cook looked at gun and dog. "I'll gie you the bone. Mak your ain peace wi' him."

"Not I. He doesna ken the skelp came from me, and Hughie's the only one to feed Chief. I wouldna wean a dug awa from his master."

"Jamie Grant, you're soft as crowdie cheese. Wait there and I'll bring you a glass of buttermilk. You've time for that."

The winds sweeping up the Clyde from the Gulf Stream had cleared the snow from the rolling hills of Renfrewshire. February's fickle sunshine was a benison on his hair and face, the tumbler of tart refreshment cold in his big hand. Feeling grand, he drained the glass like a pint of ale.

"You'll no have met Peggy," said Cook, pushing forward a younger version of Mairi. "She's down from Skye, too, to gie me a hand. Say 'how d' you do' to Mr. Grant."

"*Cia mar a tha sibh?*" In Gaelic, Peggy politely asked him how he was.

"Never mind that heathen tongue," said Cook, a Low-lander. "Part of your training's to learn the English."

"You'll be Mairi's sister," said Grant. "You're like as two pippins from the same apple tree."

Scarlet, she sidled around the kitchen coal bunker and out of sight.

The bonny young face, Cook's bonny old one, aye, and Mairi's bonny form walked with him as he went slowly down the brae, back to the icy reality of his wife and her slovenly cooking.

Better is a dinner of herbs where love is, than a stalled ox and hatred therewith. Proverbs 15:17. What about leftover cold mutton and boiled potatoes and her glower to chill them further? As he reached for butter and salt to make the dish edible, he noticed a letter propped against the cruet stand. Little mail came to the farm. Who could be writing to him?

"There's a letter for you," said Daisy.

He nodded.

"Open it."

The postmark read Glasgow. He didn't ken many folk in the city, visited there only twice a year for the Agricultural Show at Scotstoun and the Christmas Circus, to which he took half a dozen bairns from the orphanage.

"You're feart tae read it in front o' me." Slit-mouthed, she leaned on the table.

"Where would you get such a daft notion?"

"It's frae a woman. I can tell."

"Is that a fact, now?"

"If you'll no, I will." She swooped like a hawk on a mouse and clawed the envelope open with her thumb. Lips moving as she read, the color drained from her face. "Och, I'm sorry," she faltered. "It's nothing at aw, Jamie. Just a wee trick by some crazy . . ."

When had she last used his name? "Give it over."

She darted to the stove. Grant arrived there with her to close his hand over hers before she could drop the paper into the glowing coals. "Shite!" she screamed and sank her teeth into the fleshy part of his thumb. He pushed her onto the sofa, pried her fingers apart, and took the letter to the light.

> *Why did the late John Dougal, Esquire, give money to Daisy Grant?*
>
> *A Friend*

He read the badly printed words three times, not taking them in. Then he looked at his wife poised on the edge of the horsehair, her breath coming jerkily through open mouth, fists clenched, knuckles white. Guilty! By God, she's guilty!

"Well," he said. "Why did he?"

"I tellt you. It's just a wee joke."

"Is this, too, a wee joke?" He held out his hand, and blood dripped through the sun's rays to the stone floor.

"You were hurting me . . ."

"No when you ran to burn my letter."

"I didna want you upset. I couldna let anybody dae that tae ma husband."

"What the hell else has yoursel been doing aw these year?" He'd outrage the truth from her. "You're a liar, Daisy. You aye were. Now I find you're a part-time whure besides."

"You shouldna use such language tae your wife, Jamie. And it's no true. You canna believe a poison pen . . ."

"I can believe this." Again he held up the injured hand.

"Och, I'm sorry. I didna mean to."

"Liar, wife by name, and part-time whure by nature." He walked back to the table, sat down, picked up his knife and fork, and took a bite of mutton. He chewed a little, then spat it out. "One thing you're no is a cook. In fact, Daisy, you're fit for neither kitchen nor boudoir. It's hard to believe that John Dougal, *Esquire*, thought you worth a penny. Or did he give you tuppence?"

For certain no man would write such a letter. It must have been a woman, someone from around these parts, using her left hand probably, a woman who fancied herself a lady with her "Esquire" for John Dougal and "Mister" for him. What local female could have been in Glasgow yesterday? The answer came and sickened him. He had driven Dorcas Dougal and her mother to the train. Was this why the bairn had been hustled off to boarding school in mid-term, because she kenned about her father and James Grant's wife? If so, then the widow shared the knowledge. Anger and comprehension rose together. "You're a bitch, Daisy. A black lying bitch no fit for decent folk to spit on."

"I'm no a bad girl, Jamie . . ." A whisper, husky with fright. "John Dougal forced me. The wee bit o' money was tae shut ma mouth."

Now it was coming. "Where? In my own house?"

"Och, even he wouldna dae that. He caught me on the moor."

"And what were you doing up there? You're no such a lover of the outdoors that you'd be taking a walk. Did he carry you ower his shoulder or throw you across his saddle? It'll no wash, Daisy. No one damn word of it."

"It wasna ma fault—and it was once—just once, Jamie."

"That might be true. I canna see John Dougal wanting a second piece from Daisy Grant."

"You dirty rotten bugger!" she yelled. "He got whit you'll never get because he was willing tae pay. An' no tuppence either. Ten shilling the last time and worth every one o' them, he said. I gi'ed him value for his money aw right. An' I'll tell you something more that'll hurt. It was a pleasure. He was aw man an' he took whit he wantit. He wasna like you, a halflin begging me tae love him. You mak me want tae puke, James Grant. You aye hae an' you aye will." Fright gone before righteous rage, she carried the dishes to the sink, over her shoulder flung, "An' dinna think tae gie me the gate. Try that, and I'll tell them you kenned aboot John Dougal an' me frae the first—that you made me dae it an' took aw the money. They'll lock you up for a pimp." Angrily she pumped water to gush over greasy plates.

His hands went around her neck from the back. "I'll give you a choice," he heard himself say. "You can pack and get out, or you can stay and wonder when and how I'm going to kill you." Viciously she back-heeled him. He squeezed harder. "Dinna fret, Daisy. I'm no going to do it the now. I'll delay the pleasure so I can watch the fear grow in you. I might no do it for a year. On the other hand, the blind rage could come over me at any time. Mibbie when I come home from the Dambridge Larder the night. Or mibbie it'll be a cold rage and a pillow ower your face when you're sleeping." Again he tightened his grip. "You better no go down the stairs in front of me. A wee push and you could faw and knock yoursel unconscious. Then I'd lay you face down in the burn by the steppingstones. Would you like to be drowned, Daisy?" Despite his hands, her head twisted negative. "You better taste your food careful like, although they say ground glass has no flavor. Och, there's a dozen safe ways to rid mysel of you. I've been thinking them up for a long time. I could choke you the now, then hang you in the barn, and I'd no be blamed. The wee joke the postie brought would make a verdict of suicide certain." He took his hands from her, and she leaned over the sink, gulping air in horrid rasps. "I'm awa the now, Daisy. I'll no be back till the pub closes. Mibbie I'll go for the whisky the night, and you ken how spirits make me rambunctious. So you'd be smart to be gone when I get back. Leave your address, and I might send you a bawbee or two. I shouldna do it, but I married you for better or for worse, and you'll soon be owerold for the whuring."

He boarded a train for Greenock and the Tontine Hotel, where he had high tea that could have been a dinner of herbs or a stalled ox, for all he tasted. To think that a Grant should cause bonny wee Anna anguish. Along the wide Esplanade he walked and looked across the four miles of Clyde to the far shore and the winking lights of Helensburgh, the highest the windows of St. Thenew's. What a terrible burden for a young lass just growing into womanhood. Sma' wonder she sought to hurt the bitch-cause of it.

With the salt-laden breeze in his face, the mellow lights from the solid villas on his left, the moon's glow on the corrugated water to his right, he paced the Esplanade to its end at Gourock. On he went, the Renfrew hills above him, the river-sea beside him, while across the tidal water the lights of the villages clung to the skirts of the Argyll mountains rising black for fifteen hundred feet and more. As he returned along the Esplanade he gave a shout of laughter bitter as a warlock's. Not once had he felt jealousy or the blow to vanity that was the cuckold's portion. If Daisy left him, it would be a monumental relief, like sweet convalescence after a wicked fever. He caught the last local, and the coupled wheels picked up the refrain of his boots all the way to Strathgryffe.

"I wish I had kent you would be on the train frae Greenock, Jamie," said the stationmaster, looking up. "I wouldna hae been worrying about whit tae do wi' that cuddie o' yours. Your horse and cart's been out behind sin' Daisy took off for Paisley."

"Aye," said Grant, holding himself in. "She's awa to visit her sister." It was possible. Her sister Maggie still lived in the mill town.

"Will she be for a lang stay?" From under the flat cap, inquisitive eyes queried.

"Two, three days," he temporized, not yet ready to let the village in on his hopes.

"She took more luggage nor that. And never a tip. Here, whit's this? Half a crown's far owermuch. Are you drunk, man? I'll no tak advantage o' you."

"Keep it, Hamish. I'm no *fou*, no with whisky anyway." He climbed into the cart and like a tipsy reveler sang "Ma mother-in-law, she's awa, she's awa" the whole road home. What a daft gowk the woman was. He could no more have harmed her than pulled a hair from wee Morag's head.

Half an hour after the following Sunday's benediction it was all over the village. Daisy Grant had left her husband's bed and board, no concern of the rich but to the natives a grand puzzle to help while away the rest of winter's drabness.

"Sure'n we havena seen Jamie as carefree since he was wed," said Pat Nolan as he climbed into bed with his Dolly.

"You canna blame him. Yon lemon tart's been a sour taste in his mouth. Cuddle into my back, lovey. He should hae put her oot lang syne. It must hae been something awfu bad tae mak him do it now. She wouldna give up free room and board of her own accord. Pat"—a thought sat Daisy up—"do you suppose she's a shirt-lifter?"

"It's a high opinion you hae of Mrs. Grant." Pat yawned.

"Now dinna go tae sleep on me afore I puzzle this out. There's one thing for certain. Yon stingy besom wouldna gie hersel for love alone. She's that near, she maks an Aberdonian look like Father Christmas. So we hae to look for money, an' that means an incomer. If John Dougal was still alive . . ."

"Him? It couldna be."

"Why for no? He didna miss much that was available. Aye, an' some that wasna. A mean cow like Daisy Grant would be just the sort tae give in tae a man like him. If he made it worth her while."

Pat thought this out. He had respect for his wife's perception, but this time it couldn't be. "Mr. Dougal dead an' gone these many months. It couldna be himself unless Daisy did the dirty on Jamie wi' a ghost."

"Dinna be sae logical. It maks sense. Him with aw that money an' Daisy that handy . . ."

"But Jamie only finding out now?"

"It has tae be, Pat. I can feel it." She settled back onto her side. "You can go tae sleep while I work out how Jamie learned the truth."

In the village kitchens, opinions firmed along the same lines. Disliked Daisy Grant would never have given up her hearth voluntarily, and to make a long-suffering husband show her the door, her crime must have been the ultimate. But with whom?

Then the postie, emboldened but delayed on his rounds by door-to-door hospitality to honor his birthday, slipped when he essayed a tricky short cut above the six-foot salmon loup of the Moss Burn. A responsible civil servant, he clung to the mail bag as the abortive attempt to make up time sent him hurtling over rocks into the deep quiet pool among the fish. Although he saved the sodden letters, when he lost his foot he also lost his regulation cap, his whistle, his job, and, embittered at the fuss His Majesty's Government made over a wee dram, his loyalty to the sacrosanct Royal Mail. He told his wife about the letter addressed in an obviously disguised hand delivered to the Grant farm the day of Daisy's flight. "Yon's how Jamie found out," he said triumphantly. "Moreover, it cam' the day after Dorcas Dougal left the village in a hurry. Now, suppose the lass kenned her faither had been havin' a wee nibble at Daisy? That would be reason for the Widow Dougal tae send her awa tae forget. And Dorcas, cast oot, writes Jamie tae get her own back on the one who caused the damn mess." The pieces fell into place.

Cook asked for an audience with her mistress in the morning room, a portentous request.

"You'll no be here to give notice?" asked Anna.

"Och, no, I wouldna dream of it, Mrs. Dougal," said Cook nervously.

"That's a relief." A constant worry surfaced. "Mairi's pregnant."

"Mairi's a good girl . . ."

"I didna say she wasn't."

"You ken I keep a hawk's eye on ma girls, Mrs. Dougal. It's no that at aw."

"Then what is putting the red in your face?"

"Gossip."

"Ho, ho!" Unsuspecting, Anna leaned forward on the edge of her chair. "Where's the finger pointing the day?"

"At Glen Gryffe, ma'am."

"At me?" She was Glen Gryffe. "I'd be wearing a halo if they passed them out for dull rectitude. What am I credited with doing?"

"It's no really about you, ma'am. It's the—the master. I mean the late master." Cook squeezed moist hands together. "They're saying he's the—the reason Jamie Grant showed his wife the gate. Och, I didna want to tell—but then the bairns—I hae to warn you—put your guard up—in case they heard sic a dirty lie frae the village."

And you ken that I ken it's no lie, but the truth, you good and faithful servant. You're showing me my real husband again, just as you did when you sacked a girl for my sake. You said, "It's best for aw concerned that she's out o' Dougal service," and I didna quite catch on until that night—

Black brows, black beard jutting, the angry eyes, the spoiled red mouth. "Where's yon tablemaid, the Irish one?"

"Cook discharged her, John."

"Who gave her the right? Can you no control your ain staff?"

"Her going will no interfere with your comfort, John."

"She obliged me, Madam. Do you no consider that comfort?"

He had felt no guilt, shown no shame for the hurt to his wife.

"Thank you for telling me, Cook," she said. "Though I doubt a soul who kenned Mr. Dougal would believe such nonsense."

Cook smiled faintly. "It doesna mak sense, does it? But you ken what folk are. Gie them a suspicion, and they mak it Holy Writ."

"Then give them a flea in the lug from me for this latest phantasmagoria."

"Yes, ma'am." Satisfied, Cook returned to her kitchen, the deceit of John Dougal's rectitude still ostensibly intact between mistress and servant.

In black oilskin, sou'wester, and heavy brogues, Anna splashed through teeming rain to the farmhouse and pounded the knocker of the kitchen door.

"What are you doing out on a day like this, Mrs. Dougal?" said Jamie. "I would ask you in, but my wife's awa'."

Pushing past him, she entered his home for the first time. "When do you expect her back?"

"That's hard to say."

"Dinna lie to me, Mr. Grant. I canna stand a liar."

"Supposing I said I hoped she'd never step across my threshold again?"

"Then the village has the right of it. You put her out."

"She left on her own."

"I'm right sorry, Mr. Grant." Mealy-mouthed hypocrite.

"You're no to take it that way, Mrs. Dougal. Life with Daisy has been a sore trial."

"What made her decide to cut and run after aw these year?"

"Fear, Mrs. Dougal." His smile was benign. "She up and left for fear I'd put her down where she could hear the daisies grow."

"You? Dinna be daft. You're trying to save my feelings, Mr. Grant. There's no need. I ken aw about Mr. Dougal and her. What I'm after is how you found out?"

Frowning, he dipped into his pocket and let her see an envelope. "I'll no let you read it, Mrs. Dougal. Your hand shouldna touch such dirt. I'd burn the letter except it establishes who's at fault. With this I can keep Daisy awa from my hearth." He stuffed the letter back.

"Who wrote it?" It had to be Dorcas.

"I havena an idea. I wish I did. I'd like to shake the hand of the man . . ."

"Your tongue's twisted again and for the same reason. To save me. Fine you ken it was my oldest."

"And how would she find out, such a wee lass?"

"She saw the passing of the money. And no more."

"That's a ton off my back." His shoulders straightened in relief. "I havena slept proper, wondering how she got on to Daisy and—and . . ."

"Say it. My husband."

"No. Her father. She's naught but a bairn."

"With aw a woman's viciousness. We're no very nice, we females, Mr. Grant."

"I beg to differ. Dinna lump yoursel with the others. And the gossip will pass, Mrs. Dougal."

Warmed and comforted by a gentleman, she went back up the brae and by morning had decided how to silence the truthful tongues of the village with a most visible lie.

This took the form of a stained glass window depicting Mary Magdalen drying the feet of the Son of Man with her hair. In May it was presented to the United Free Church of Scotland, Strathgryffe.

IN LOVING MEMORY
JOHN DOUGAL 1859–1909
HIS WIFE ANNA
HIS SONS
LACHLAN, HUGH, ALEXANDER
HIS DAUGHTERS
DORCAS, ELSPETH, MORAG

The men of the village interpreted the lavish memorial as proof that the widow knew nothing of her late husband's activities on the wrong side of the marriage quilt. "Else why would she spend aw that money tae immortalize him in the kirk?" Less naïve, their wives concluded the reverse. "Else why should she spend aw that money tae whitewash him in the kirk?" All agreed that the subject matter was appropriate, the deceased having had ample experience of fallen women, including those he had tripped up himself.

"You're the only one kens why I did it, Mr. Grant," said Anna. "In the face of that bronze plaque of dedication, who'll speak ill of the dead to my bairns? By now, even Dorcas may doubt she caused your wife's exodus. At the Easter holidays I let on that Mrs. Grant had run away with a commercial. Right convincing I was. I put the home-wrecker in ladies' unmentionables and gave him a spiky waxed mustache. You dinna mind, Mr. Grant?"

"And you're the one who canna stand a liar."

"Unless it's wee me in a worthy cause."

"H.M.S. *Indomitable*, that's you, Mrs. Dougal."

"Where my bairns are concerned. 'Touch one, touch aw' is this Dougal's war cry. Well, that'll be enough of that. Now where do we get the Aberdeen Angus to stock our new acreage?"

"Pride o' Fyvie could manage it himsel if we had the cows. We have twenty-four in calf the now. We're like to get about twelve new cows out of the lot. But it's no good practice to introduce them to the bull until they're fifteen month old."

"To their own sire? I dinna hold with the inbreeding, Mr. Grant. Look at the Bourbons. How many cows find their way to the butcher shop?"

"You'd no be proud of a Glen Gryffe fillet from a cow, Mrs. Dougal. Cows we keep. It's stirks end up on the tines of a fork."

"Exactly what is a stirk, Mr. Grant?"

"The English caw him a steer," he said uncomfortably. "We take a sharp knife—well, let's say he's a bull calf when he's dropped, but no for long."

"Do you castrate aw the new wee bulls?"

Jamie Grant's head went down. "Stirks put on weight faster nor bulls," he mumbled.

Just like eunuchs. Right emancipating, this talk. "Man, I'm learning."

"Stirks, too, are easier to manage. They're no so rambunctious."

"That doesna surprise me," she said. "What does is the blush on my partner's cheek."

"I canna help it if my face is red."

"Will you forget I'm of the gentler sex? You're to look on me as a farmer."

He raised his head. "Now, would you really want me to do that?"

He smiled. She smiled. And heard a whisper in her ear loud as a bass drum. *Have a care, wee Anna Dougal.*

"I'll thank you to stick to business, Mr. Grant," she said. "How long till a calf turns into a working bull?"

"It's best to let them be eighteen month old."

"Fancy that. The girls grow up before the boys. Just like *homo sapiens.* How about letting some of the new calves keep their manhood? Or is it bullhood?" *Whatna way to talk, Anna Dougal.*

"You'd no be recommending some of Pride o' Fyvie's offspring give their sire a hand?"

"That would be inbreeding bad as the Pharaohs' and hurt the reputation of what's to become the best stock farm in Renfrewshire. Cattle buyers must ken our line is superior. The dining public should learn it, too. Would it no be a smart thought to raise a champion or two and have a belted earl present a cup to a Pride o' Glen Gryffe or a Prince o' Glen Gryffe or a—a Royal Son o' Glen Gryffe? With pictures in aw the papers of the noble beastie, and you at its head."

"Not I. You, Mrs. Dougal. You're a sight bonnier."

She ignored the flattery, although it was grand to hear. "What do you think of my wee idea?"

"It's no so wee. It would tie up capital. A show bull takes a sight longer to grow than a beef. He should be three year older—two, three hundredweight heavier to be a matinee idol. If we let three bulls grow to show-age and dimensions, there's three stirks we dinna sell. We're out that income till the bulls are marketable."

"But meantime they serve the cows we'll have to buy anyway."

"The byre would need to be expanded. I've a bit of money put by . . ."

"Son of McFadden has more."

"Beg pardon?"

"I said we'll have to see my lawyer man. The both of us. I'll simper while you smother him with the facts of life on the farm. It wouldna be proper for me to discuss them with a guardian of my bairns. He's a Victorian fuddyduddy in some ways."

He was not in matters of money. In Glasgow, prime starter of the Industrial Revolution, every business and professional man believed that the booming economy could only go up and looked for ways to give it a lift. With exports double imports, Glasgow was a self-contained empire, a conglomeration of manufacturing, the world a market for its wares which were carried in Clyde-built bottoms or hauled by Clyde-built railway engines. Increasing Glen Gryffe's beef herd appealed to the lawyer as an excellent gamble containing little risk beyond the possibility of disease. He recommended insurance against such.

"There's a ween of plagues." Jamie Grant cheerfully listed them. "Foot-and-mouth, Bang's, Johne's, tuberculosis, anthrax, black leg, and with four stomachs you aye have to watch out for the bloat."

"Did I no tell you, Mr. A.? My partner's the grandest cattle man in aw Scotland," said Anna.

"Mibbie no that, Mrs. Dougal," said Jamie, "but I do ken how to protect the beasts. And we'll no pay money to the insurance companies, Mr. McFadden. We'll carry our own. For every cow we buy, we'll put a wee bit aside in the bank and save the premiums."

"Sound thinking, Grant," said McFadden. "Indeed, the whole proposition is sound, for increasing the loan on Mrs. Dougal's home merely transfers funds from the house pocket to the farm pocket."

"And I have Son in my coat pocket," said Anna when they were out on West Nile Street. "He's an old sweetie-wife, but as long as he gives in to me, I can put up with him. Now, what do you say to a bite?"

"Would Miss Cranston's Tearoom suit, Mrs. Dougal?"

"I can lunch there by my lone, Mr. Grant. I fancy a lobster mayonnaise and a wee bottle of chablis at Ferguson and Forrester's, where I canna go unescorted."

Mr. Forrester recognized Mrs. Dougal as they entered, seated them himself in one of his private rooms, and ordered for them. To return the favor, Anna offered to deliver Glen Gryffe beef to the restaurant's chef at a very reasonable price.

"We couldna afford to sell so cheap were it no for the advertising," she said.

"Advertising, Mrs. Dougal?" asked the restaurateur.

"On F and F's fancy menus, Mr. Forrester. Promote Glen Gryffe beef there, and I'll see you're aye stocked. Although with the demands on us, it'll no be easy. My, that was a delicious mayonnaise. I couldna make better mysel. No wonder you're kent for setting the best table in the whole of Glasgow."

When Anna referred to Son as an old sweetie-wife, she knew whereof she spoke. Keeping the secrets of his profession made him a compulsive purveyor of those titbits not locked up by ethics. It was with pleasure, therefore, that he spotted Philip Dougal that evening in the smoking room of the Conservative Club.

"Lloyd George is a menace," said Son of McFadden, to establish rapport. "Labor Exchange and Insurance for the unemployed, indeed. Rank socialism."

"The seven shillings and sixpence a week for doing nothing was young Churchill's idea, I'm told."

"And to think he holds a Scottish seat in Parliament. It was a letter day for the Conservatives when he crossed the floor to the Liberal side."

"Yes. I'd rather know my enemy than harbor a traitor to

his class in our party's inner councils. Lloyd George is a natural Liberal."

"A man of no family. A Welsh troglodyte. Could I offer you a spot of brandy?"

"Certainly not." Impatiently Philip Dougal rattled his newspaper. "What's on your mind, McFadden?"

"Your sister-in-law was in to see me today."

"A tragic figure."

"Then I take it you haven't been with her lately, for she's more merry than tragic. You'll have met her partner?"

"Her what?"

"That's what she called him. He used to run the farm for your brother. A big fellow with the smell of the country about him."

McFadden meant no harm, but his little morsel sat sour on the tongue of Philip Dougal, lineal descendant of that commercial pirate king who had outwitted Napoleon and gone on to break the monopoly of the East India Company with ships sailing direct from the Clyde to Bombay and China. To the Managing Director of Dougal & Company (founded 1733) the family firm *was* the Empire, and it unthinkable that one of his illustrious surname should be running around Town boasting of a partnership with a common farm servant. He had not liked his late brother nor did he particularly care for the widow, but the Dougal name must be protected.

He rang up Sir George Biggart and made an appointment for luncheon the following week at the newly opened quarters of the Royal Scottish Automobile Club, to which he had recently been admitted; if one owned a motorcar, one lived up to it. Over the half-Coronas he broached his sister-in-law's habit of aping, and consorting with, the lower orders. The resultant letter from Sir George was the first Anna had ever received from her father. It took her to Glasgow again in a rage as hot as the radiator of her new Argyll. She drove all the way this time, crossing the Clyde on the Renfrew ferry to the admiration of the carters and the fright of their charges. She had done the eighteen miles in just over an hour when she pulled up at her former home and the Lord Provost's twin lampposts, the outward reward for her father's year of duty in the unpaid post. That and his knighthood.

Although the engine was stopped, the car quiet, she still shook as she looked at the city's coat of arms on the glass panels, *Let Glasgow Flourish* emblazoned under *The tree that never grew, the bird that never flew, the fish that never swam, the bell that never rang.* And the girl that never grew up as far as Papá is concerned, she thought as she stepped down onto the cement mounting block, swept up the stairs over the basement area, and rang the electric bell. To her further annoyance she had forgotten that today was Lady Biggart's weekly at-home and so had to sit on her emotions while silks and satins, sables and laces indulged themselves in tea, finger sandwiches, *petits fours*, biscuits, three different cakes, and sympathy for the young widow. Anna felt fair stifled. The initial surprise at her appearance soon gave way to commiseration, making her again want to shout "My bottle's no half empty! It's half full!" Philip's wife, the Honorable Margot, rawboned daughter of a baronet, seemed more quizzical than sorrowful. He's been opening his tight mouth to her about me, Anna decided. She ate little and said less until the last of the perfumed ladies had taken their leave and she was alone with her mother and two parlormaids, wraiths in black and white who made three journeys apiece to clear the silver and china from the high-ceilinged room before departing for belowstairs.

"And now, how are my grandchildren, Anna?" said Lady Biggart. "I don't like to ask about the bairns in front of our friends. So common. Is Dorcas happy at St. Thenew's? It was a proper shock to me when you sent her to boarding school. It seemed so—so callous of you."

"Mibbie. But I'm no that callous I canna be hurt mysel, Mamá, and that Papá has done. Clear to the quick. Will he be home at the usual time?"

"Lately he's been arriving earlier. He's at his three score and ten, and taking it a mite easier, dear."

"Then I'll hold my tongue till he shows up. The children are aw healthy, and Dorcas's wee letters dinna exhibit any misery from St. Thenew's. She's in her element. When did the Honorable Margot start gracing your bun fights?"

"She has never been before. When she rang up, I was quite surprised—almost as startled as I was to see you. I know that John—dear John—resisted the telephone, Anna, but you shouldn't. It makes common politeness so much easier."

"If I canna come to my mother's without first finding out if it suits her, then I'll no come at aw."

"You're always welcome, dear, but it makes it nicer for the servants. Are you staying to dinner?"

"I couldna swallow a bite, I'm that mad at Papá."

"I hear his feet now. Please don't be angry, Anna. It's not good for him."

A scowling George Biggart entered the drawing room. "Did you drive that infernal machine all the way from Strathgryffe?" was his greeting.

"It didna drive itself, Papá," said Anna.

"Don't be impudent, young lady. I'll not have you gallivanting the streets of Glasgow like a—a suffragette. Do you fancy yourself as one of the new women?"

"Aye, and I'll do as I damn please."

"Anna!"

"Keep out of this, Clara," said the father.

"You're right, Papá," said Anna. "The bone I have to pick is with you. What right have you to tell me to mend my ways?"

"When you visit your lawyer with a married man, a common farmer whose wife has left him . . ."

"How do you ken that?"

"Your brother-in-law made inquiries."

"How dare Philip spy on me!"

"He has your interests at heart."

"He doesna give a tinker's dam about my interests. I could walk the streets for aw he'd mind, if I wasna called Dougal. That's aw he cares about. The firm's precious name."

"I'll not have you miscalling one of the most respected men in the City."

"Respected, is it? He wouldna be if folk kent that he's never been near his only brother's children since the funeral. And the one time he's seen the widow was when I called on him unannounced in his office. He didna even have the grace to ask me into the sacred premises. He's a whited sepulcher, yon Philip Dougal, covering up dead bones."

"Don't defend yourself by attacking him. Have you obeyed my instructions to get that tenant off Dougal land? Have you given the fellow his marching orders?"

"No and never! What you call Dougal land was once aw his, until Dougal lawyers took advantage of the last of the Grants."

"More fool he if he didn't get a good price. And more fool you to take such a gowk for a partner."

"I couldna ask for a better than Jamie Grant. He may no be a match for city lawyers, but he kens cattle. Jamie stays till he dies or leaves of his own free will."

"So it's Jamie now, is it? Clara, please leave the room." He opened the door for his wife.

When she had gone, he pulled a handkerchief from the tail pocket of his frock coat and blew his nose, looking over the white linen at his only child. "Excuse me," he said, surprising her with gentleness. "I seem to have a touch of the sniffles. Sit down, lass, and let us see if we can't discuss the matter reasonably. Bear in mind that I'm talking to you for your own good." Anna suppressed a groan. "Your mother and I sheltered you as a girl, as was our duty. We brought you up in gentility with no mention of the coarser ways of the common folk. There was no need to warn you about them when you'd only encounter a few as servants. Now you are a widow going your own willful gait, which appears to include making a friend in the lower orders. It'll not do,

Anna. Common folk have common habits and worse, and we must keep them in their place. You'll not give this tenant of yours his Christian name to his face?"

"I wouldna presume . . ."

"The presumption would be his if he let you, but I wouldn't blame him. He has not had the upbringing of your husband."

"Are you implying that Jamie Grant is no the gentleman John Dougal was?"

"I don't have to tell you that. As a young man Grant was a menace to womanhood and probably still is. That kind of chap doesn't change. Even today your minister says he spends more time in the pub than in the kirk, though his wife never missed a service."

"Philip's spies were gey thorough."

"If you do a job, do it right." He brushed aside the interruption. "Grant isn't old, Anna. Quite a bit less than forty. That's young for an unprincipled man to be living alone, close to a pretty widow."

"You'll no give him credit for having learned self-control in seventeen year of marriage?"

"That class of people can't control themselves. Their morals are not ours."

"Good for them. The moneyed class—I'll no call it the upper class—doesna set a very good example. The goings-on at Edward's court were no aw confined to the King's bedchamber."

"Talk. Just talk. As Lord Provost I dealt with facts, and the most appalling of these was the amount of illegitimacy among the poor."

"That is Glasgow."

"What about Strathgryffe, where fifty per cent and more of the marriages are late for the child?"

"For good reason, Papá. A barren wife is no help to a farmer, as Jamie Grant found out."

"Why must you defend him?" He was turning angry again. "This conversation is sufficiently distasteful. I shall conclude it bluntly. John Dougal was a gentleman. Don't expect his code of honor in one who is for all purposes a servant."

It would have been gratifying to contradict, but the straight and narrow road he had traveled was coming to an end. To pull the blinders off now might hasten his feet down the brae. All she said was, "No, Papá."

"And you will see that this Grant fellow is discharged?"

"That's no possible. John gave him life tenancy. In writing."

Sir George sighed. "Then I must tell you our second plan."

"Our? Yours and Philip Dougal's?"

"Aye, but more Philip's. He's willing to buy Glen Gryffe—acreage, stock, house, buildings, the lot—to get you and the children to move back to the city."

"So that's why his horsey wife was here the day. Philip is after turning County on the cheap. I ken how yon one thinks. The poor bit widow with no financial acumen will sell to her kind brother-in-law at his figure. She wouldna have the brass to bargain with the head of the firm supporting her and her bairns. Glad I am that I canna oblige him, even if I wanted to." Make this a good one. "I've never told you John's parting words. I've never let on to a soul, for they were a proper curse. As he was slipping away, with his dying breath my husband said to me, 'Dinna let yon bastard Philip lay his hands on aught of mine.' "

"God bless my soul! I can't believe it!"

"Would I have sworn if those werena his very words? Did you never wonder why Philip was no named a trustee of his brother's estate?"

She left shortly afterwards. "Yon bastard Philip" is right, she thought as she aimed the bonnet of the Argyll at the West End. It was his fault that I had to lie to my poor old father. John would have named Philip if I hadna told him I'd bury him bare naked if he did and I survived him.

A successful down-change to climb University Avenue

revived her self-confidence, the tricky double declutching being accomplished without one clang of gears. I'm learning, she thought as she surmounted the summit and descended swiftly past the grounds of the University. At a corner lamppost, a gaggle of boys and girls played street cricket. She pulled over to the right, whistled through her teeth, and Willie Boyd came running.

"Is that gadabout mother of yours at home?" she asked.

"I suppose so. Can I get in, Aunt Weeanna?"

"No the now. Would she be alone?"

"Kitty's away to the piano teacher. When can I get in?"

"When I come back. I'll no be long. If you can keep these other ruffians from sliding down my mudguards with their tackety boots, mibbie I'll give you a run around the block."

"Get back there, Moira Clarkson. Who do you think you are?"

Visiting Harriet was an oasis of refreshment from the first "Yoohoo! It's only me, wee Anna Dougal" to the triumphant conclusion, "And there's not a damn thing Papá or that long-nebbed Philip can do about it. Aren't you proud of your auld china? She is getting to be a real artful dodger with age."

"I wish you were older," said Harriet.

"Here, what's this? I thought we agreed long ago never to grow old."

"As I've told you, you're too young to be left a widow."

"Harriet Hepburn, you'd no be siding with my Victorian papá?"

"Perhaps, but for a different reason. Jamie Grant may be the soul of honor. I'm not so certain of you."

Anna cackled. "Where would you suggest I put my silken love nest? Up a tree? For that's where I'd be. I better awa now before you find me wanton." She cackled again. "Me wanton. That's rich."

They passed out into the hall of the flat, where a straw hamper stood open, half-packed, harbinger of summer at the seaside.

"You'll be for Arran when?" asked Anna.

"Thirteen days. I can hardly wait. I know Kitty and Willie can't. They live all year for the first of July."

"They deserve it after putting up with Glasgow for ten months. Ta-ta the now."

She was still chuckling as she pushed her way through the children and climbed in behind the steering wheel. "All right," she called. "Hop aboard! Once around the bay for a tanner! Any more for the *Skylark?*"

Four times she circled the block, a mile ride for the five boys and three girls sardined on the floor and leather seats, Willie *ah-oo-ah*ing like the Klaxon.

"Put a paper over my beer, for I'll be back," she shouted above the engine's roar when the bairns were once more standing on the pavement.

"How soon?" asked Willie, ever one to nail an adult promise.

"No before you're off to Arran." She pulled clear of the curb.

Willie jumped on the running board. "You'll be down for your visit, won't you?"

"If your mother'll have me. Awa with you now before I get going fast enough to break your leg."

"Cheerio, Aunt Weeanna."

Traffic occupied her until she stopped her motorcar on the deck of the ferry.

"You're tae ge' off your seat, leddy," said the lone deckhand as he scotched her wheels with wooden wedges.

"I'm comfy here," said Anna.

"You'd no be if the bo-at went doon."

"Never has and never will."

"There's aye a first time. The rule is—naebody in a vehicle when under way. Ge' off."

"I'm no on a horse." However, she stepped down.

"That's be'er. Stop your engynes, leddy,"

"There's only one. And who'll give me a crank?"

"Och, I'll wind you up when we reach th' ither side."

"When will that be?"

"When yon packet's by." He nodded upriver to the towering bow of a ten thousand-tonner apparently motionless on the ribbon of black water between the ship-lined docks. "We hae the right o' way, but she has the size and the tide, so we'll no argy."

While the little ship waited, she pondered the fears of Harriet and her papá that wee Anna Dougal might come to no good with Jamie Grant. He who could have any lass in the shire if he had a mind for the hanky-panky. And she whose memories were not such as to make her yearn for more of the same. Is that what it would be, the same? As the tenement-high sides of steel slid past at three knots, for the first time in her life Anna let herself think what "it" would be like with one particular man, to wit Jamie Grant. To her surprise, she did not find the speculation revolting. Quite the reverse, in fact.

In the following weeks she broke her half promise to Willie to visit the Boyds on the Isle of Arran. To Harriet she wrote saying there was so much to do on what was becoming a proper farm that she could not be spared. Plain havers, that. Without her help Jamie could manage many more acres, much more stock than their growing herd, her principal contribution to the operation merely the encouragement she gave him. And you'd best stop thinking of him as Jamie, she chided herself. He's Mr. Grant and you're Mrs. Dougal. Dinna forget that.

"I've heard tell, Mr. Grant, that many cattle breeders find it easy to raise hogs alongside cattle."

The resultant sties were built close to the farm, downwind of the big house. "There are no dirty pigs, only dirty owners, Mrs. Dougal."

"If you say so, Mr. Grant."

A Tamworth boar and six sows formed the initial stock; heavy white animals of pure breed, capable of bearing litters of eight to ten that would dress out as well as did Aberdeen

Angus. Their long deep fleshy sides would produce quantities of lean bacon of the finest quality. A chicken run, too, was added, although Grant would have nothing to do with the fowl. That was woman's work which Mairi and Peggy took on in addition to their other labors, calling the birds to the mash in musical Gaelic.

"When do you expect the new cows, Mr. Grant?"

"Six doddies should be on the next cattle train, Mrs. Dougal. Lachie and Hugh have gone to herd them home. You'll no mind? Looking after the beasties and his brother is right good for Lachie."

If only he werena aye so considerate. If only he'd beat horses, get stotious drunk, give Mairi the eye . . . No. No that. She might take it. If only he'd be *in*considerate—och t'hell, Anna doused herself with cold comfort. The reality would probably no come up to the dream anyhow.

"It's a stranger you are, Jamie Grant," said Dolly Nolan, handing a pint over the empty bar. "I was feared you had signed the pledge."

"Devil a bit. But I'm no as drouthy as I used to be."

"You're enjoying your ain fireside, now you can stoke it yoursel?"

"Right for you. It's a fair treat to be able to throw on an extra lump without being called a wastrel."

"It's no decent. You shouldna be by your lone night after night. It's against nature."

"I'll no deny that," he said cheerfully. "But when you've been alone with a person for years, it's proper restful to be alone without a person. Every morn I wake up happy, for it's to an empty house."

"If it wasna for Pat, it'd no be empty long, I'm telling you. I'd lock the Larder and march you back up the brae this very minute. What about the twa Highland sisters at the big house? I hear tell they're bonny as the Island o' Skye itsel."

"And to me as far awa. You wouldna have me lead those lassies on, and me a married man?"

"Shed yoursel o' her then, you gowk. You hae the grounds.

There's twa whole villages that ken the laird got to Daisy
. . ."

He stopped her. "No one in Strathgryffe or Dambridge has proof of that. It's only gossip. And if it were true, would you have me drag wee Anna through my mire, bairns and aw?"

At closing time Dolly went to the back room and wakened her husband on the couch. "Time for bed, Pat." Under the cozy comfort, drifting into sleep she murmured, "You'll never guess what Jamie called the Widow Dougal. 'Wee Anna.' His face was that gentle when he said it. I wonder if there's aught going on there. Wouldn't that be the grandest tit for tat?" But the snore on her back told her Pat was already beyond caring.

Chapter Five

THE SUMMER OF 1911 was glorious, to Clydesiders a heavenly reward for past good behavior, a just dispensation to ensure the success of the Scottish Exhibition of History, Art, and Industry held that year in Kelvingrove Park. From Sauchiehall Street to University Avenue and beyond, the palaces of fine arts, history, aviation, industry stretched along the banks of the River Kelvin. Never was there a better time to visit "North Britain," as the condescending English liked to miscall Scotland, envisaged as home to savages stripped to the kilt, string of herring in one hand, claymore in the other. The indigenous culture was a surprise to daring Londoners who came exploring and stayed to marvel at the works of the natives. *Why Geoffrey, the people are civilized. Quite. What an unconscionable fibber you are.*

Anna visited the extravaganza only once; to enter the Argyll in the *Concours d'Elégance* where the latest vehicles from all over Europe were judged for style, equipment, and appearance. "If only we could at least win a bronze," said Lachie nervously as the judges neared them. He had come along to rid the machine of road dust and give it the final shine. When they were awarded a first-place silver medallion, he promptly appropriated it for his room.

"No fair," said Elspeth. "I did as much polishing as you."

"Me, too," said Hugh.

"Only at home," said Lachie. "It was the elbow grease I gave it at the exhibition that turned the trick."

"You'll no let the Argyll take credit?" asked Anna. "We'll attach the bauble to the dashboard, where it belongs."

Dorcas did not participate in this effort. She was spending the summer in medieval majesty on the treeless slopes of a deer forest high in the Grampians, guest of her first best friend, school chum Fiona Murray. A year younger and an only child, Fiona agreed with Dorcas that even between identical twins there never had been a more selfless mutual devotion. Like all Murrays, she was distantly related to the Duke of Atholl, hereditary Chief of Clan Murray. To Dorcas this touch of nobility offset the drafty passageways and damp stones of the castle, whose original walls dated from the sixteenth century.

"How lucky you are, Fiona, to have been raised with history."

"And chilblains, even in July. Brr-r. Button my jersey, Dorcas, before you catch cold."

"Good of you to let me borrow it. Let's take a canter. I love your hill ponies."

"But they're so tiny, after your hunters."

"Great rawboned beasts. Your horseflesh is much more companionable. And it's not nearly so far to the ground if you fall off."

"When have you ever? It would take a bucking bronco to throw you, Dorcas. I wish I had your seat."

She came home taller, slimmer, and prepared to make invidious comparisons between her summer and the humdrummery of Glen Gryffe.

"Quite weaned from Renfrewshire, aren't you, Dorcas?"

said Miss Watson, assisting the dressmaker with the fitting of new uniforms for school.

"Renfrewshire is adequate." Dorcas had heard Fiona's father apply the word to a bottle of Burgundy and now used it whenever possible. "What a bore, having to wear these ghastly uniforms again."

"My, it's a sophisticated wee hen, isn't it, Wattie?" said Anna. "You wouldna expect that kind of polish to be applied in the Highlands, would you now?"

"Mummy, Drumnadroit Castle is merely the Murray's summer place. Their Scottish town house is in Edinburgh, and their permanent domicile is in Berkeley Square, London."

"Mummy. Domicile. Are we no the West Endy ones?"

"Weaned from home for fair," said Anna later, when alone with Dorcas's old nanny.

"These are just growing pains, Mrs. Dougal."

"Growing-away pains, Wattie. And I dinna like the kind one damn bit. I'd rather have her a missionary to the Hottentots than a Scot who would be a Sassenach."

Unlike Shakespeare's boy, Dorcas did not return "creeping like a snail unwillingly to school." She went gladly, spirits rising with every turn of the wheels carrying her from the place where John Dougal's heel had splintered the rose-tinted glasses that show the future in the glowing colors of romance. Her father had become Everyman, and each stand of Strathgryffe bracken a reminder that he could be one with the beasts. At school it was different. School was the company of her peers, their talk of boys met in the past hols giving Dorcas hope. Without exception apparently, these darling young men believed that the playing of any game honorably was more important than the winning of it. *Vitai lampada!*

Winter arrived that year with a force-nine wind on the eve of the closing of the successful Exhibition. As if Providence still wanted to help, the gale razed some of the buildings and appropriately sent the roof of the Aviation Pavilion flying over the other palaces to make a landing high up on Park Terrace.

The day after the closing was *Please to remember the fifth of November, the gunpowder treason and plot;* Guy Fawkes Day to commemorate the failure of the knight who had been caught before he could send the House of Parliament skyward in 1605.

Anna saw the anniversary as a grand excuse for a blowout complete with the traditional fireworks and bonfire. For a month of week ends Lachie and Hugh had gathered burnables, including tarry railway sleepers pinched under the nose of Hamish, the station master. They did not know that Mr. Grant had asked the panjandrum to turn a blind eye to their pilfering in a worthy cause. The festival was to be held on the new Dougal property in front of the castle now filled with orphan children. For the benefit of the wee shavers who had little color in their lives there would be Roman candles, giant whirligigs, zigzags, Mt. Vesuviuses, and scores of varied rockets.

"It'll cost a packet, Mrs. Dougal."

"Do you ken a better way to bang a sixpence, Mr. Grant?"

The Strathgryffe Pipe Band caught wind of the affair and offered to play.

Elspeth, with an assist from Miss Cuthbert, received permission to organize a torchlight procession from St. Malcolm's. The Girl Guides, not to be outdone, proposed another.

The Ladies' Aid of the United Free talked the Paisley battalion of the Argyll and Sutherland Highlanders out of a bell tent to shelter the mutton pies, bouillon, and aerated waters the kirk would sell.

"For the benefit of the orphanage, no doubt," said Anna.

"Well, we thought for foreign missions . . ."

"No a hope. Charity begins where?"

"We could give the orphans a share."

"I'll settle for that," said Anna. "One hundred per cent, and no argle-bargle."

To rebut the United Free, the Parish Church promised to supply portable organ and organist for the singing.

The 14th Renfrew Troop of Boy Scouts requested a demonstration of bridge-building across the Gryffe.

"You'll no mind a wee favor in return?" said Anna. "We could do with a grandstand for folk whose feet give out. We'll seat them. For a price."

Using Morag's water paints, Wattie made a score of posters. "They'll have to go inside or the colors will run, Lachlan."

"Nae bother at aw," said Lachie. He covered Strathgryffe, then on his father's favorite mare rode over the moor to Dambridge to entice some foreign money to the affair.

"I'll be there masel with bells on," said Dolly when he gave her one of the bright advertisements for the pub's window.

Each minister of each kirk felt it his right to open the celebration, a religious superfluity which pleased Anna. She couldn't choose one without offending the others, so she would choose none; farm lads and servant lassies out for a frolic could do without the backward collar. Johnny Black-adder, the superintendent of the orphanage, was the man for the job. He had a voice like a bull, and he needed it to reach the rear of the vast throng that turned out for the burst. It was free, wasn't it? The pennies dropped into the collection cans of the girls of St. Malcolm's and into the wishing well didn't count. Nor did the penny surcharge on the tuppenny meat pies.

"There must be a thousand folk here, Mr. Grant."

"That and more, Mrs. Dougal."

Pipes skirled and lasses kicked off their shoes to dance, careless of hobnail boots on their bare toes. Girl Guides marched with torches held high; Boy Scouts built their bridge, suffering casualties—two in the burn—only when taking it down. Rockets sprayed golden rain from the dark heavens, rockets banged, rockets turned into colored stars. The Ladies' Aid ran out of food and drink when twelve pounds nine and six was in their till. Mairi Maclean never found out who caught and kissed her in the dark tunnel of the arching rhododendrons. At nine o'clock a solemn girl dressed in the Home's best had her hand held steady by the super as she put a flaming torch to the two-story-high bonfire, and scarlet lances soared twice that height with a roar to frighten the timid. After the cheers, the singing began.

Roamin' in the gloamin'
By the bonny banks o' Clyde
Roamin' in the gloamin'
Wi' your lassie by your side,
When the sun has gone to rest . . .

Head down, tweed cloak tight around her, Anna slipped away. Before it turns into a fertility rite, she told herself. Wi' you leading the parade if Jamie were to give you half an eye. The dark belongs to the young, so awa home and take your med'cin.

Now there's a cheery thought . . .

Guy Fawkes Day raised seventy-one pounds fifteen shillings and tuppence farthing, and led to nine March weddings and a proposal of another sort from Jamie Grant.

"It doesna pay to upset cattle with construction, Mrs. Dougal. I've been thinking why build onto the present byre? Would it no be wiser to have another one awthegether?"

"And hang the expense?"

"Never that. But if we could rework the old castle's stables? That would save a packet and wouldna upset the cows in calf."

"You'd no be thinking more of the entertainment of the bairns than the comfort of the beasties?"

"You're quick as usual. I've aye felt sorry for the weans, but since your Gunpowder Plot I canna get them out of my mind. No kith, no kin to give them a push. They're entitled to a hoist up the wall of life."

"It'd be gey inconvenient for you," she said, "with the byre a mile away from the farm."

"It's no that far, and it would be right handy for the bairns. They could help."

"No without pay. We couldna exploit them."

"No on your life. I've talked with the super, and he'd put their earnings into the Penny Savings Bank, where they'd make five per cent. That way, when the wee shavers went out into the world, they'd no be without a bawbee in their poke."

"And no without a trade either, Mr. Grant. You're for an agricultural school with wages for the students."

"You're on to me." His face split in a grin. "Pat Nolan's game for the flower and vegetable gardening. Harold Wilkie's agreed to do the building in his spare time. For free. Dolly Nolan'll supply beer for the workmen at the same price. Wilkie's a grand mason. And if he needs new stone, there's a ween of that begging to be cleared off Glen Gryffe land."

"Now you're making sense instead of sentiment. I can shake on that, partner, for it's gey practical."

"Awa with you, Mrs. Dougal. You're as sentimental as they go."

"Ditto wi' dots," said Anna.

Thus was born the Model Farm of the Strathgryffe Home for Orphan Children. It was formally opened in March by the Countess of Strathgryffe, chief patron of the Home, and the newspaper pictures of that titled lady flanked by Mrs. Dougal and Mr. Grant sent Harriet Boyd to her writing desk. ". . . *not only to have your picture in the paper, but with a gentleman who lives on your land and is separated from his wife. What's going on? Is this why you've been neglecting me? Never to Brodick last summer, and I've only*

*seen you once since. As I'm not appearing in public, you
come here and let me look you in the eye, Anna Biggart.*"

At thirty-eight, Harriet was expecting for the third time,
and no Glasgow lady six months gone would expose herself
to the rude stares and conjectures of the common people on
the street. Certainly not one of her age caught by a moment
of careless rapture in Arran's heather. Fancy Mr. and Mrs.
Robert Boyd throwing their hats over the moon like farm
hand and servant lass, a delicious secret Harriet had hugged
to herself until the prescient Anna diagnosed the resulting
condition on that last visit.

"You mean you didna ken?" she had said. "How could you
be a mother of two and no notice a third was on the way?"

"I'm nearly forty." Harriet drank whisky to counteract the
shock. "I thought it was my age." But a little later, the
masking spirits made her giggle. "Maybe I didn't know it
had happened, but I know full well when it did happen."

"Spare a body the romance."

Now, in the empty first-class compartment on the way to
see her friend again, Anna decided that envy had provoked
the wry reply, envy of the bliss that had given Mrs. John
Dougal the go-by. As the train charged between the culti-
vated fields, she half-closed her eyes to bring Jamie's face
swimming in to shorten a tedious journey. She hardly
noticed the stop at Paisley and was jolted back to reality
only by the clatter of points as the engine found its way
through the maze of rails high above the Clyde, then
plunged into the fetid glass warren of St. Enoch's. Hurriedly
she jumped up to repin her hat at the mirror. My God, she
thought, you look like you just popped out of bed and were
ready to pop back in again. Better unsmoke those eyes, wee
Anna Dougal, before Harriet Hepburn gets a keek at them,
or she'll be pulling at you like a throstle after a juicy worm
in the rain.

Harriet, however, didn't need new prodding to her curiosity. She plunged right in as she handed over a teacup, in
her agitation half empty.

"I'm worried sick, Anna."

"Tide's out." Anna passed back the china to be filled. "Put a head on that and dinna fret, Harriet. You'll have this bairn as easy as the other two. You have 'gee bee aitch,' as we say in the country. Good breeding hurdies. Are yon German biscuits fresh?"

"I baked them for you this morning, though why . . . What a thing to say about a lady! You make me feel like one of your cows."

Anna shrugged. "My, that's a frush biscuit. You'd get a *cordon bleu* in Paris for your baking. They almond fingers your own too?"

"Naturally. My worry has . . ."

"I hope they're as chewy as they look. I canna stand soft almond fingers. How are Kitty and the piano getting along?"

"Splendidly. She's up to Chopin now. My worry has nothing to do with the coming child. It's . . ."

". . . a boy. For a quid. You have the look of one to you. You dinna have to bet. I'll send you a pound note anyway to wet the new citizen's head with champagne. How's Willie?"

"Getting over an attack of *mal de cigare*. He stole one of Robert's."

"Did he now, the wee rascal? I'll have another cup just the same as the last."

"Anna Biggart, *what is going on between you and Mr. Grant?*"

"Wouldn't you like to ken?" said Anna. "Watercress sandwiches. My real taste. I'll have one to put the lid on the sweets."

"So there's nothing. You wouldn't whet my curiosity if there were. What a relief!"

"I'm no about to cock my tam o' shanter at a man at this late date."

"But you might. And when you set your heart on something you never rest till you get it. That's what scares me, Anna. You ought to go away for a while."

" 'Wha would be a coward knave?' I'll no run away from a

danger that doesna exist. Put that in your tea and stir it, Harriet Hepburn. You dinna ken Jamie Grant one wee bit. If I was so daft as to give him the eye, he'd say, 'I couldna love thee, dear, so much, loved I not honor more.' "

"Never mind Lovelace. When I think of you, I think of Montrose. 'He either fears his fate too much, or his deserts are small, that dares not put it to the touch, to win or lose it all.' You always were game for a gamble."

"I should have kenned better than to quote verse to an elocutionary. See's a digestive biscuit to clean my teeth and change the subject. I hear your bairns on the stairs." Saved by the school bell.

The newspaper story linking Mrs. Dougal, widow of the late John Dougal, and James Grant brought other repercussions. Sir George Biggart and Philip Dougal privily agreed that since the deplorable situation was now public, it must be given an air of respectability, whereupon Philip wrote to the editor of the *Glasgow Herald* announcing the creation of a fund for the Strathgryffe Home for Orphan Children, "my late brother's favorite eleemosynary activity." The letter also announced initial donations from Dougal & Company and from Biggart & Company, "owned by Mrs. Dougal's father, Sir George Biggart, formerly Lord Provost and generous benefactor of Clydeside."

"Two thousand bonny quid floating up the Gryffe," gloated his daughter. "And without me turning a hand."

"Shite!" said Daisy Grant, who now realized that in a weak moment she had been frightened from an expanded Glen Gryffe. She should have been standing there with the Countess right alongside Mrs. Toffy-nosed Dougal. It scunnered Daisy to have this sour ingredient thrown into her pot of self-satisfaction, up till then simmering with the certainty that she had bettered her lot since shedding her husband. She had a pound a week the gowk sent her plus her wages of fifteen shillings as an overseer of girls at J. & P. Coats. Tom Black, her brother-in-law and a master foreman at the mill, had found the job for her. He had also provided a place to live in one of the two tenements he had frugally acquired over the years. She paid no rent, an unusual generosity of which her sister Maggie was as ignorant as she was of the reason for it. Returning home from a trip to Glasgow shortly after Daisy moved in, Maggie had nearly caught her husband and sister in not-so-innocent play, a nice piece of timing on Daisy's part. Knowing exactly how long it took to walk from station to flat, she seated herself on Tom's lap when the train whistled its approach, jumped up and away the moment she heard Maggie's foot hit the stairhead. Illicitly preoccupied, the bemused Black heard neither signal and barely managed to cover blood-suffused face with a silk show handkerchief when Maggie rushed in, fortunately tea-filled and intent only on the w.c.

"That was owerclose," he muttered as the bathroom door slammed behind her. "I canna tak a chance like that again."

"You will, Tom," whispered Daisy. "You're aw man. You canna help yoursel. You'll hae to do something about it."

The something turned out to be a one room and kitchen flat on the ground floor of his other building, with a back door in the close concealed from nosy neighbors who spent half their time spying out of upper windows, bosoms and elbows comfortable on bolsters taken from kitchen beds.

"Are you sure you're aw right there by your lone, Daisy?" Maggie worried as they walked to the kirk behind her deacon husband. "Paisley's awfu rough, and the ground floor's awfu easy."

"Dinna fret, Maggie. There's no a thing in the place worth a burglar's trouble. No a farthing."

The latter was true. She was banking every possible shilling in a savings account which grew bit by irregular bit as others knocked on her hidden door, by invitation only and in the small hours when Tom was snoring-safe with Maggie; married men who daren't boast and spread the word.

Shite! And shite again. There she was, thinking she was on Easy Street, then the newspaper had to go and show her she had run away from an easier. She could go back. The dirty bugger didn't have the guts to strangle her. Hand flew to throat, and once more in rushed the sweat-panic of suffocation that never left her. He might. A girl never kent where she was with a man. You couldna trust a one of them. Go back? It wasna worth the worry, even a second's. The Widow Dougal could have him, her that couldna hang onto her own husband, let alone another's. What was she getting in return for helping James Grant? To Daisy there could be only one answer, and her sound commercial sense surfaced to plot how she could benefit by it.

Old Wattie was so loving proud of her employer that she sent a cutting of the story to Dorcas.

"Is it a good likeness of your mamá?" said Fiona.

"Adequate," said Dorcas.

Lachie acquired a black eye.

"Who belted you one?" Hughie asked.

"Nobody." Scruff O'Brien had sneered, "*I wouldn't let my mother kiss a countess's arse,*" and Lachie's fist had shot out instantly, following the advice of his gym instructor that "twice blest is he whose cause is just, but thrice the man who gets his blow in fust." Scruff had managed only one counter, but it had been a good solid straight left to the face.

"Aw, come on, Lachie."

"Don't fash your elders." Lachie was not about to let his kid brother know that some fellows were rotters, even at the High. "A goldfish did it. He didn't like me leaning over his bowl, so he louped up and slapped me with his tail."

"Aw, Lachie. You can tell me."

"Want to help me de-coke the Argyll when we get home?" said Lachie, to stop the inquisition. "We should have it ready to come off the blocks soon."

"You mean it? I'll race you the rest of the way."

"You're on, Hughie. How much start do you want?"

"Give me to the bridge, please."

"Fair enough. And I'll carry your books."

Lachie held back and did not catch the ten year-old until

they were halfway up their drive. Then he stopped.

"You shouldn't let me win," said Hugh, panting. "That's what cheats do to the Kaiser."

"Quiet, young 'un." Lachie pointed up the brae to a tall branchless tree that had sprouted in their absence. "Behold. Birnam Wood comes to Dunsinane."

"Lachie, you're daft . . ."

"Or, if you prefer it, the telephone has reached Glen Gryffe. Come on!"

Glasgow had installed its first instrument in 1877, but general acceptance of the convenience, including John Dougal's, was delayed by the number of exchanges that proliferated—the doctors', the lawyers', the stockbrokers', the steel trust known as "the Iron Ring," whose members were charged £15 per annum. There were also the Bell Telephone, named for its Scottish inventor, and the Edison Telephone. All these were subsequently amalgamated in one National Company, whereupon the Glasgow Corporation, quick to smell a profit, promptly set up a competing municipal system. Again business and professional men were forced to subscribe to more than one exchange until in 1910 the London Government voted itself a monopoly under control of the General Post Office.

The two boys burst in on their mother studying their latest acquisition, a black instrument standing on the monk's bench in the hall.

"There it is, lads," she said. "No only an invasion of privacy but ugly as other folks' sin."

"As long as it works, Mother," said Lachie. "Can I try it?"

"May I?" Elspeth joined them.

"No fair," said Hugh. "Lachie asked first."

"I was correcting his English, daftie," said Elspeth. "I've already had a go."

Lachie ran an eye over the meager list of subscribers.

"The Cockburns are on the list," said Elspeth.

"They're all girls," said Hugh, furiously protective. "And yon Bella's ancient. She's a year older than Lachie."

"One foot in the grave and the other twitching feebly." Anna nodded agreement.

The Argyll in his mind, Lachie finally settled on Mr. Speirs's garage.

"Johnny Speirs is away to Greenock, Lachie," said a male voice.

"Who's that speaking?"

"We're no allowed to give out our names lest the lasses fall in love with our voice." The operator laughed. "You'd be calling Speirs for petrol, I don't doubt?"

"Yes. I'll need four two-gallon tins."

"I'll tell him. No need for you to ring through again. Ta-ta, Lachie."

"Thanks, whoever you are."

Mairi and Peggy kept well away from the instrument.

"There's nothing to be afraid of," Elspeth told them.

"It's electric, is it no?" said Mairi fearfully.

"Yes, but . . ."

"I'll no touch it," said Peggy. "There wass a man in Oban—the shock went in one ear and out the other and burned up his brains."

"That's nonsense, Peggy. Look. I'll show you."

In tandem the girls sprinted back to the safety of the kitchen and built-in speaking tubes.

Few calls came over the newfangled machine, for few homes possessed one unless required by the head of the house for his profession or trade. Days would go by without a social ring to frighten the maids at Glen Gryffe. Then one weekday in May, two calls came within half an hour. The first was from Robert Boyd, who had been granted permission to use Dougal & Company equipment.

"My dear wife presented me with a bouncing boy at one-thirty this morning, Anna." He sounded embarrassed that he, at fifty-two, should be responsible.

"Good for you!" she shouted. "How's Harriet?"

"A little squeamish from the chloroform, but otherwise very happy. She wanted another lad."

"I could have told her she'd get one. In fact, I did. How's yoursel?"

"I survived the ordeal remarkably well."

"You're no sae bad for an old codger. What name will you give the bairn, or don't you ken?"

"Yes indeed. He shall be christened Duncan Hepburn Boyd."

"D. H. B. Damn Healthy Boy. There's my sweary wee wish for his future."

The connection broken, she jiggled the hook for the operator.

"Please, Mrs. Dougal," he pleaded. "You're clickety-clacking my ears off."

"Sorry, sonny. Can you put me through to Edwards' in Glasgow? They're on Buchanan Street."

"I ken that, but yon's a trunk call. It'll cost you."

"Toffs is careless," said Anna.

From the fashionable jewelers she ordered baby spoon, knife, fork, pusher, tankard, napkin ring, all in sterling and all to be engraved D. H. B. in nice curly script. It was her first telephone purchase, and that it should be for Harriet's wee afterthought made her feel warm all over. She was not ten feet from the bell when it clanged again.

"Is this Mrs. Anna Dougal?"

"Well, it's no Annie Laurie, for she'd deid. Who's that at your end?"

"Daisy Grant." Anna whipped the receiver away from her ear as if, like Peggy's myth, it had sent an electric shock to her brain. "Are you still there?" the instrument crackled, "or did you faw down in a fit at my name?"

"How dare you ring me up?"

"Dinna talk West Endy tae me, Anna Dougal. It's as fawse as the rest o' you . . ."

"I shall give you ten seconds to explain this intrusion, then I shall disconnect."

"You'll no cut me off when you hear whit I hae to say."

"You're wasting your time. You have five seconds left."

"Did you ever hear of a suit for"—Anna heard a rustle of paper before the next words came, slowly, obviously being read—"alienation of affection?"

Anna's laughter tinkled into the mouthpiece. "And all these years, Daisy, I thought you had no sense of humor."

"You'll no laugh when you're in court as a husband stealer, Anna Dougal, unless . . ."

"Unless what, Daisy?"

Anna heard a deep breath taken before the rush of words. "I get five pound a week for gieing you a free haun' wi' James Grant."

"Someone's been serving you bad advice, girl," said Anna, adding another tinkle of laughter to infuriate. "This has the odor of blackmail."

"No it's no! I hae a—a friend who's a lawyer, an' he says you canna dae a damn thing aboot it as long as I dinna put pen tae paper."

"It's a bad business having a friend for a lawyer. You'd be a lot better off if you paid"—a pause—"with money."

"You dirty-mindit bizzem!" yelled Daisy. "You think you can caw me names just because you hae money. If you want ma husband, you'll hae five pound a week less . . ."

"Goodby, Daisy, and thank you for the best laugh I've had in a month."

She waited half a minute, then lifted the receiver again and heard "Strathgryffe Exchange."

"That'll be Malcolm Loudon speaking," she said in her everyday voice.

"I'll no deny it," said the operator. "How did you guess?"

"Och, I've kent you since you were a halflin, Malcolm. I couldna mistake your voice just because it comes over a bit wire. How are Mary and the baby?"

"Both nicely, Mrs. Dougal. The wee lad never lets go the teddy bear you sent, and him almost five."

"Heaven's sakes, he'll be going to school next. Do you ken who you put through to me no five minutes ago?"

"Don't tell me you're being bothered by anonymous calls? It wasn't a local, Mrs. Dougal. It came from Paisley—J. and P. Coats—and I didn't hear the voice long enough to recognize it, if I could have."

"You mean you dinna listen in? You're missing a lot of juicy meat, Malcolm."

"I wouldn't doubt it. My Mary doesn't see how I do it, although I've told her what I don't overhear, I can't tell. It's worth my job if I pass on any titbits."

"You wouldna find a woman with that strength of character."

"Not in a million years." Malcolm laughed. "That's why we'll never have woman operators."

"Would you mind making a note of the day and time that you put somebody from J. & P. Coats through to Glen Gryffe?"

"Anything wrong, Mrs. Dougal?"

"Nothing I canna handle, Malcolm. Just sign the wee note and send it to me with the postie. Toodle-oo, and tell Mary I was asking for her."

She walked to the window and saw Sandy toddling down the driveway, his hand in Wattie's, both going to meet Morag, who went to school only in the morning. *Touch one, touch all.* Any dirt thrown at wee Anna Dougal would splatter her children. *Wasn't their mother mixed up in a scandal suit some time back? No truth in it, I'm sure, but they say he was quite a handsome fellow. Managed her farm, as I recall.* Anger swept in to make her hands tremble; she had to get away before the bairns returned. "Please give the Argyll a crank," she said, and Pat Nolan, noting her tone, obliged without his usual pleasantries.

She drove with the top half of the windscreen open, the rushing wind to cool the rage, the steering wheel to still the hands. Through the village and up the steep sharp-angled brae past the stone entrance pillars of the baronial hotel with its acres of lawn and blossoming bushes, of flower and vegetable gardens. Past the golf course where she had sent the girls of St. Malcolm's tumbling, hats over the seat of all trouble. Past hawthorn in bloom, apple trees too, pink and white against greenest grass. Over narrow roads between drystane dykes banked with thistle. "You can sit on the shamrock of Ireland, on the leek of Wales, on the rose of England, but you canna sit on the thistle of Scotland." And by God, you'll no sit on wee Anna Dougal, Daisy Grant, for I'll sting right through your drawers to your dishonest backside. The vulgarity pleased, the spring flowers soothed her. Soon thistle would bloom, foxglove too, and the bell heath, badge of Clan MacDougall—all as purple as the heather that came last to signify the end of summer.

She stopped with the bonnet pointing down a brae so that she could start the motor in gear, an emancipating trick learned from Lachie. Over a five-barred gate she climbed and up a steep hillside on the brown and greening heather to the high point of the moor walk they called "The Pad." Dutifully she replaced a fallen stone on the cairn marking the top, then turned to look north to Dunbartonshire and the beginning of the Highlands. Seven hundred feet below, two miles wide lay the Clyde, shallowed by the long bar which gave its name to the village Langbank, hidden by the swell of the slopes. She could see two dredges of the Clyde Trust—what would yon trustee Philip make of a husband-stealing suit?—their chain of buckets busy at the endless job of keeping the man-made channel open for the biggest ships in the world, Clyde-built the most and best of them. Opposite her on the far bank, castle-crowned Dumbarton Rock guarded the mouth of the River Leven, route of the spawning-bound salmon to Loch Lomond, eight miles off. She could see a blue corner of Britain's biggest body of inland water and in the distance the bulk of Ben Lomond dominating the lesser mountains. The solacing view arced one hundred and eighty degrees before her; from the smoke pall of Glasgow in the east to the Tail o' the Bank in the west, the mighty anchorage for oceangoing liners and tramps and paddle steamers churning between them from Greenock and Gourock to the holiday resorts—Sandbank, Kilmun, Blairmore, Cove, Kilcreggan, Roseneath, Rhu, Helensburgh. What devil had possessed Dorcas? "The de'il's no aye the ill child he's called." He'd put in a grand day's work when he used Dorcas to flatten Daisy. Now if Auld Clootie would guide wee Anna Dougal to the same fine result . . .

She let wind and sun, color, movement of ships, sparkle of sea, shimmer of mountain combine to free her subconscious, and when she rose from the turf half an hour later she knew what to do about Daisy. Not until morning, however, could she set events in train, for the children were home and the telephone exposed. I'll have the instrument moved to the morning room for privacy, she thought as she waited for Malcolm Loudon to put her through to McFadden, Son & Laidlaw.

"Good heavens," said Son, startled. "What possible need could you have for an investigator?"

"It's no for mysel, but one of my staff's in a wee bit of bother." Jamie was almost staff.

"Surely the police . . ."

"It's no a police matter, Mr. A. And I've aye been attracted to the private detecting ever since I came across yon book by Allan Pinkerton about his exploits in the States. My, his *Thirty Years a Detective* was exciting. You'll have heard of it, no doubt?"

"I'm afraid not, Mrs. Dougal. Our practice doesn't require such knowledge."

"I didna read his book for learning, just for fun. Did you ken he once saved President Lincoln from assassination? And captured a gang that stole seven hundred thousand dollar? When one Glasgow lad has such muckle success abroad, there's bound to be a body that copies him at home."

"In all my years at the bar, Mrs. D., I have never required the services of a private investigator."

"But you ken everything and everybody in Glasgow. I'll bet you could lay your hands on one this very minute."

Ex-Police Sergeant Ivor McNab arrived the following morning, a bluff hearty man with a heavy mustache of ginger red that belied his age. Anna thought he looked like a commercial traveler, one who enjoyed the good things of the table in the best restaurants and bars. His attaché case of Moroccan leather added to the impression.

"I hae to warn you, Mrs. Dougal," he said after an hour of answering her questions about his exploits. "I charge by my time plus expenses, and my biography's no that interesting."

"It is too, but mibbie you're right," said Anna. "To business then. I want to find out aw I can about a Mrs. James Grant—Daisy Grant, who works at J. & P. Coats in Paisley. At least she uses their telephone."

"When you say 'aw,' what do you mean? It could be a gey big job. Can you define it a wee?"

"Daisy was a bad girl no so long ago. I dinna doubt she still is, but I need proof."

"Is there a James Grant?"

"He's my partner in the farm."

"Is he now?" McNab stroked his mustache. "And I suppose he showed her the gate when he found out she wasna a good wife. Why isna he the one tae want my services? I'm hardly partial to a man that lets his lady dae his dirty work for him."

"Och, t' hell!" said Anna. "A wee minute wi' you, and you're as bad as the others. I'm no his lady. I'm his partner and friend. That's aw. A-double-L aw."

"Look you now, Mrs. Dougal, in my business I hae to act like a priest as far as the confessions are concerned."

"I've naught to confess."

She glared at him, but he met her gaze calmly. "Mibbie I shouldna hae used that particular word," he said, "but I must convince you that it's safe tae confide in me. I must ken everything before I accept a job. Daisy Grant's blackmailing you, I take it."

"No yet, but she's trying. You were quick to sense that."

"I can smell blackmail through the wall of a stone byre. Whit does she think she has on you?"

Why not tell him? "Och, here's the tale then. Although it makes yours truly look like a damn fool. Daisy Grant was obliging my late husband, and James Grant found out and gave her the go-by. He could divorce her but he won't, for it would mean giving me and my six bairns a black eye to share among us. He'd rather stay single though married. If ever nature made a gentleman, it's Jamie Grant. Now, being a bizzem hersel, Daisy thinks I'm playing tit for tat with her husband. She doesna mind—if I buy her off. Five quid a week, she says, or she'll sue me." Anna cackled with exasperation. "Me that's never called him aught but Mr. Grant in aw the years I've kent him."

"If she couldna win the suit, what gives her the idea you'd pay tae stop it?"

"She kens we'd have to bring up her hanky-panky with my husband to prove Jamie had no affection to alienate. What would that slap at their papá do to my bairns? So a mess in the courts isna the answer, Mr. McNab. But you get the goods on Daisy, and I'll make her wish she was behind bars where I couldna get at her."

"I'm glad I'm no Mrs. Grant."

"Then you're with me?"

"It'll be a pleasure."

"That calls for a wee nip, if you'd no mind being a solitary drinker. I never touch the stuff mysel. Except as med'cin."

Mournfully he shook his head. "I darena. I hae a hard head but a weak stomach. I havena enjoyed a meal in ten year. Bread and milk's my portion."

"My, that's awful. And here I was, thinking you looked a proper *bon vivant*."

"I would if I could, ma'am."

McNab walked slowly down the drive between lilac purple and laburnum yellow. He had an hour before the train, and it was a day to make a city man tolerate the country; mild and sun-filled with strange perfumes, sights, and sounds, none identifiable but all pleasurable. A bird—a lark, had he known it—soared up and up to hang in the air on a wing and a burst of song that he took as a special treat to flatter him. Bluebells—bobbing flowers—nodded from the dappled shade of tall trees. An insect—a bee or a wasp? —droned lazily around his head twice, then fell off on the wind before he had decided whether it was the stinging kind. At a bridge over a river he put one buttock on the stone wall and looked back up at the white and brown-timbered house he had just left. His new client had made a favorable impression on him. She was honest—that he would stake his pension on—but more impressive had been her—courage, you might say. Blackmail was the ugly crime, poisoning the victim's day from first uneasy waking to more uneasy sleeping. McNab had known strong men to lose weight and brain before its self-engorging terror. But Mrs. Dougal faced it foursquare with her jukes up, like a sturdy wee bantam ready to take on all comers. Because she was innocent? Perhaps. The detective had known the most honest to lie for love, but even if there was an affair between her and the man, it couldn't be alienation of affection. That much was clear.

The thud of wood on wood turned his head as a country man swung through a gate enclosed on three sides, a stile manageable by humans, unmanageable by animals.

"Grand day," said the man courteously, but taking in the stranger from head to toe and back again.

"It is that." McNab did not resent the scrutiny; the more observant the public, the more aid for the law. He nodded toward the manor house. "A grand home you hae."

"No mine." The country man smiled. "It was built by John Dougal. Now it belongs to his widow. I live in the farm down by."

So this was James Grant, nature's gentleman. Big as Mc-
Nab but heavier in the shoulder—the outdoor life would do
that for him. Strong jaw below a full mouth, strong nose, and
eyes as blue as yon flowers back there. High forehead and a
good head of hair without gray. Healthy. Probably with a
stomach that could eat nettles, thought McNab with envy.

"It's a gey big place," he said. "What kind of farming do
you do?"

"Mostly beef cattle."

"Are those your cows over there?"

"Mine and Mrs. Dougal's," said Grant. "But you'll no mind
me telling you they're no aw cows?"

"But they havena any horns—I thought that was how you
told a cow from a bull."

"No quite." The farmer smiled. "I'll confuse you further.
We breed Aberdeen Angus, called polled, meaning bald.
There's never a horn on either gender."

"Is that a fact now? I come out for a wee walk, and my
education is improved. I'm a fair dope when it comes to the
country."

"Do you aye take your tashy case wi' you on a walk?"

"You're on tae me," said McNab ruefully. "I'm a peddler,
forbye a high-class one." He opened his attaché case and
took out a large book bound in leather. "The *Encyclopædia
Britannica,* eleventh edition, new out last year. I've been up
at the big house trying to sell a set, but Mrs. Dougal already
has one." He'd telephone her from the station and ask her to
back him up. "Would you hae any interest? This wee sample
is volume number one. There are twenty-eight more, including the index." When the detective prepared a camouflage,
he did it thoroughly. "Seven year in preparation, edited in
London and New York wi' the help of Cambridge University. Note the thistle o' Scotland on the cover to mark its
Edinburgh origin in 1768."

"Stop, man. Stop. Dinna waste your selling on me. My
money aw goes into cattle. I havena any left over for a new

Britannica. My father's old one has to suffice."

"A proper shame," said McNab sadly, putting his wares away. Then he brightened. "But you'll aye be able tae use the big house's. Mrs. Dougal looks the kind of lady who'd share her treasures."

"I wouldna impose on her."

You could if you tried, thought McNab. She'd give you the damn books if you as much as hinted. Aye, and aught else you asked for. "My, she's young tae be a widow, and a bonny one at that. How far does her land go, or is it your land?"

"I just manage it. It was two hundred-odd acre when John Dougal was killed. When that happened, Mrs. Dougal didna give up, as expected. She squared her shoulders, grabbed a better hold on the place than ever her man had, bought another hundred and sixty acre, aw pasture, and took aim on doubling the herd."

"A driving lady."

"Aye, and a smart one. She's also plucky, she's generous, and as you say, she's bonny into the bargain."

"Well, I better awa for my train." McNab stood up. "And in case you're still worried about my loitering here, I'm no a Raffles making a plan of action. I was thirty year in the Glasgow Police Force before I retired."

"You'll no mind my suspicions?" said Jamie.

"As a law abider, I welcome them."

McNab walked on, pleased with the chance encounter and sure there was nothing illicit between his client and her partner. They had been too open to him for that to be on their consciences. Strong character, yon Grant. And considerate. His erring wife must be a damn fool.

He stepped off the train in Paisley for a visit to J. & P. Coats, where a longtime colleague, also retired, was now a guard. Over an ale, McNab obtained the subject's address. And more.

"She lives on the ground floor," said the guard, looking into his tankard.

"Does she now, Gregor? A woman alone usually goes for the safety of the top story."

"The flat belongs tae her brother-in-law, Tom Black."

"Mibbie it was aw he had to let."

"No Black. He put his savings into twa wee tenements. He and his wife are in one, your subject in the other."

"They'd no be wanting to be overclose, Gregor. I've seen many a fight when a body's in-laws lived under the same roof."

"Mibbie so, but I hae ma doubts aboot the Blacks. Tom's that fond of his wife's sister, he got her the job at the mill, too. And her wi' no experience." He belched and in apology added, "Better oot me than in me."

"What kind of person would you say the subject was, Gregor?"

"No very friendly tae the lassies. Whiles, though, she'll let slip a wee whisper out of the side of her mouth tae an older man. Around payday, I've noticed."

"You'll no mind if I sit in your wee cubbyhole for an hour or two the morn's morn, Gregor? I'd like a wee keek at her."

"I'll do better nor that, Ivor. I'll gie you a tour o' the works."

Clanking machinery transforming cotton from the States into thread to be wound on bobbins that would go all over the world. Steam, noise, dye vats, and the smell of commerce. Girls and women, heads bent to their work, and Daisy Grant to see that there was no loafing by those in her charge. Yon owerthin upper lip doesna shout generosity, thought McNab. Apart frae that, no sae bad-looking.

His guide squeezed his elbow and mouthed "Black" as they passed a dour face topped by the foreman's bowler hat. About forty-five, judged McNab, the ripe age for Mr. Hyde to win the best of three falls with Dr. Jekyll. No doubt a singer of psalms in the kirk and a snapper of fingers in the home. A tasty bite for shark-mouth Daisy.

"Well, Gregor, I've seen aw I need for the now. I'll be around on payday, which'll also be rent day."

"Aye, the landlord grabs his before it's aw boozed awa."

Forty-eight hours later, McNab descended on Daisy's neighborhood in the disguise of a water inspector; flat silver-braided cap and black double-breasted jacket with silvered buttons. All residents of Paisley paid the same unmetered water rate, consequently the Corporation frowned on leaking plumbing. McNab's wasn't a popular garb, but it was Authority and a reason for prowling about the area.

Tom Black's middle-class tenement housed three groups of flats, each with a separate close, a cemented entrance level with the pavement. McNab dutifully climbed the stairs and examined the plumbing in the first close, giving stern instructions to replace worn-out washers in three of the homes—"Next time a fine, d'you hear?"—served the second the same, then entered the third, Daisy's, and although he knew she was at work, pounded on her door while he examined its approaches. There was an entrance from a back lane where the middens were. Right convenient, that, for the surreptitious after dark; nobody carried out ashes then. Satisfied, he finished his self-imposed duty by putting the fear of Corporation punishment in one old biddy whose water closet was a constant Niagara. The Water Department would be gey proud of me if they kenned, he congratulated himself, crossing the street to a fish-and-chips shop opposite. The delicious aroma of the food frying in wire baskets suspended in caldrons of boiling fat made his stomach growl like a hungry lion. He carried a plateful over to a window table facing the mouth of Daisy's close. As he waited, the mill hooter signaled the end of the day shift with a blast that set salt and pepper shakers and vinegar cruet to jiggling on the bare wood. There was no cutlery to rattle, fish and chips tasting best from the fingers. With a pocket knife, mournfully he cut away the golden-brown crust of the filleted haddock and exposed the gleaming white flakes inside, all that his miserable maw would tolerate without retaliation.

Daisy now came down the street head up, eyes straight ahead, and vanished into her close as if she couldn't wait to slam the door on her neighbors. Thinks she's too good for them, thought McNab. Her kind aye does. He settled back to wait for the next performer in the wee drama.

Ten minutes later came Black, bowler square and forward on his head, in his right hand the black bag of the landlord. Moving ponderously he entered the farthest close. McNab checked his watch. In sixteen minutes the rent collector came out and started into the next entry, where he spent sixteen and a half minutes. When the broad back walked into the third close, the detective ordered another plate of fish and chips.

"You didna finish the first," scolded the motherly woman between kettle and counter.

"It's ma stomach. It canna abide lard."

"I'll fry you a spud whole, then, and you can eat the middle. That canna hurt you. Here! Take a kitchen fork and wait."

It was an hour all but five minutes before Tom Black came out of the third close. That doesna prove a thing, but it's damn coincidental, thought McNab. He paid his bill, with thanks for the potato which had been a fair treat, and at the railway station retrieved his suitcase from the left luggage, changing into his own clothes in the lavatory. Now all he had to do was wait for dark.

The time passed pleasantly for him watching play at the Paisley Cricket Club, although like all soccer fans McNab scoffed at the slower pace of the English sport. This evening match, however, went a mite more quickly; each side was limited to one inning of two hours with a half-hour tea interval for the twenty-two white-flanneled amateurs. Daft game, thought McNab. About as thrilling as watching a faucet drip. He enjoyed the fielding though, the leap in the air and the bare one-handed catch of the leather ball rifled off the sprung bat. At 10 P.M.—Greenock C. C. 87 all out, Paisley C. C. winning with 89 for 8—he walked back through the gloaming to his job, the lamplighters scurrying before him on their tackety boots, with long flare poles to turn on and ignite the gas in the asbestos mantles. It was full dark when he reached the back lane, where there were no lampposts to shine down on him. Heels up, he tiptoed over the flagstones of the lane, past the midden, through the wash green, and into Daisy's gaslit close, the glow not reaching the space under the stone stairs marked that morning as his observation post. He concluded it was a dandy one after two douce couples had passed him unseeing, leaving behind the perfume of fish and chips carried home in newspaper poke for a bedtime snack.

Daisy's caller arrived by the back way, the first intimation of his presence a single rap on her door, which opened instantly onto a dark room.

"Who's there?" A whisper.

"Arthur Cochran." Another low murmur.

The man left at twenty minutes to twelve. McNab swore softly. The law said a couple alone behind a locked door after midnight were presumed guilty, no further proof needed. He decided to wait. You never could tell about a baggage like Daisy. A drunk stumbled in from the street, sliding his shoulder along the wall for support and falling up the stairs. At his door on the second landing he was greeted by a blast of invective that made McNab shake his head in admiration. Twelve forty-five and there came a light footfall from the back. Again the single rap, again the low voice.

"Who is it?"

"Charlie Baird."

"I shouldna let you in."

"You said I could."

"For twelve-thirty. Now it's awmost one."

"I couldna help it. I was playing cards . . ."

"Keeping me waiting . . ."

"I was winning, Daisy. I couldna leave without giving them a chance to get their losses back."

"Did they?"

"Naw. I was too good for them."

A pause. "If I let you in, you'll no stay owerlong?"

"Aw right."

What a gowk, to let yon shark ken he'd won, thought McNab. Charlie's wee delay'll cost him.

He gave his report to Anna at Miss Cranston's, using a maximum of euphemisms to save himself from embarrassment. "So there's nae doubt about it, Mrs. Dougal. The subject is a *fille de joie*," pronounced "fill de joy."

"I canna comprehend her, and that's the truth," said Anna. "To want money that bad—do you think she's no right in the head?"

"Her kind is aw ower Glasgow, Mrs. Dougal. What'll you do now?"

"Cogitate, Mr. McNab. I'll push your information to the back of my head and let it simmer a wee."

Cogitate she did as she sat with Harriet that afternoon in the intimacy of nursing the baby, his pink foot in her brown hand, the feeding child an umbilical cord between them.

"You've something on your mind, Anna Biggart," said Harriet, shifting the baby from left to right.

"My, the wean enjoys his nourishment," said Anna. I shouldna have come straight from McNab. Have a care, wee Anna, or you'll coup the beans into the fire. "Dinna let an excess of curiosity sour wee Duncan's snack."

The letter slot in the hall rattled loudly, followed by a piping treble. "Yoohoo, it's only me, wee Willie Boyd."

"Hoho! So you let your lad imitate me." Anna jumped to her feet. "Wipe your mouth, Duncan. Pub's closed." She sped to the front door and opened it wide, herself behind it. As Willie stuck his fair head around to see who was hiding, she grabbed him by the nose. "A copycat you've turned into, Willie Boyd."

"I knew you were dere, Aunt Anna. Dat's why I did it. I saw de Argyll."

"And a tease as well. Say you're sorry."

"I'b sorry."

"Prove it."

"Can't, till you let go by dose."

She did, he kissed her cheek, and she whacked him affectionately on the seat.

"Say, Aunt Anna. What do you think of wee Duncan?" he asked. "Is he asleep?"

The baby was barely awake, eyes closing slowly as Willie stared down at him with a look that made Anna want to cry.

"He's big, isn't he?" whispered the brother. "I bet he'll be a grand rugger player."

"If he's as good as you, he'll do fine," said Anna. "How's your school work, Willie Boyd?"

"Not as good as his rugger," said Harriet.

"Then a day off couldna make it any worse. They're holding the sheep-dog trials for the West of Scotland at Glen Gryffe tomorrow and Saturday. How would you like to drive down with me and stay the week end? Lachie told me to ask you."

"Anna Biggart," said Harriet, "not content with spoiling your own children, you'd spoil mine into the bargain."

"I'm a nuisance for fair," said Anna.

"I don't know what his father will say."

"We could be gone before Father gets home," said Willie.

"Leaving me to weather the storm?"

"Robert storm?" Anna hooted. "That's a sheep-bites-shepherd story. Your husband would agree that every lad should see dog trials as part of his education. I'd ask Kitty, too, but I doubt you can spare her, with the wean to care for."

"Very well, Willie," said Harriet. Lessons weren't that important. "Pack your bag and don't forget your toothbrush."

"Yoicks!" He galloped from the room.

Lachie and Hugh stayed home from school, too, a dispensation not permitted the girls of St. Malcolm's.

"No fair," said Elspeth at breakfast.

"A fib's no a fib till it's found out," said Anna. "I'll no write a wee excuse, then have your teachers spot you and Morag careering over the braes right as rain."

Trains with contestants, handlers, and supporters from neighboring shires converged on Glasgow early in the morning, there to transfer to locals, the first arriving in Strathgryffe at eight o'clock. Out stepped the stolid tweed-capped shepherds and their collies, mostly black with white markings, mostly bitches, they being more biddable. With never a leash among them, each close behind its master's left heel, the pick of the snub-nosed working breed came walking up the brae to Glen Gryffe. Four barnlike tents had been set up to the west of the Grant farmhouse, two for judges and contestants against the chance of showers; one for a buffet of tea, lemonade, and mounds of mutton pies, sausage rolls, Forfar bridie, cakes; and, by special dispensation to the Dambridge Larder, one for ale and whisky. Food and drink would not be given much play until Friday evening when the char-a-bancs—horse and motor—would arrive.

The course was set on the wide expanse of moor; from the Gryffe up the brae a half mile and into the dip where Hughie's Chief had been salted in the tail. Spectators and contestants stood quiet by the start as the first shepherd waited for the signal to send his entry into action. On the timer's nod, out went his long staff, pointing uphill, and his collie was off on a wide and silent sweep, moving close to the ground.

"Why doesn't the dog go straight up the hill?" asked Willie.

"Bitch, you city nyaff," corrected Lachie. "She's circling to get behind the sheep."

The black speck disappeared over the browside, and the small crowd waited tensely, envisioning the contest of animal wits going on out of sight. The man whose entrant was working seemed unconcerned, his face calm, right hand high and steady on his staff, its butt on the turf.

Over the center of the knoll four Blackface sheep came trotting, no daylight between them. "Five and a quarter minute," said a farmer, watch in hand. "No sae bad for a young bitch." The small crowd could see her now, five feet behind her charges, swinging from flank to flank to keep the animals in formation. Halfway down the brae in a direct line to the shepherd stood an open-sided hay cart, a narrow ramp at either end. The sheep trotted directly to it, stopped, and the collie closed in, baring her teeth to snap at the air behind the lead animal's leg. Its companions wheeled to run, the collie circled and stopped them, then drove the leader up onto the wagon. One at a time the others followed.

"Are the sheep trained?" asked Willie in a whisper, and Lachie gave him a withering look.

The Blackfaces milled around, the clump of tiny hooves on wood coming clearly to the spectators. On lowered belly the bitch crept closer, closer, until they were squeezed onto the downhill ramp. *Meh-eh*ing, they trotted out again and scattered. Like a flash the collie was after them, and in seconds the quartet was proceeding as before.

Four narrow planks ten feet apart spanned the Gryffe. As sheep neared shepherd, he pointed his staff at the gangway specified in the rules—the one farthest away, and the collie drove them to it. One at a time they crossed the rushing water, the bitch at the rear. Now the contestant pointed to the plank two from him, and the collie reversed the crossing. The shepherd walked forward to a small fenced enclosure.

"That's the only time he's allowed to move," Lachie told Willie. "When they're to be penned."

With one hand the dour-faced countryman opened the gate and swung his other arm and staff wide to make a lane to the pen. Warily the collie moved his charges forward. The sheep stopped and started, tried to turn aside, stopped and started, trotted in, and the gate closed.

Willie opened arms to clap, but Lachie grabbed his hand. "Not yet, Willie. Watch."

The collie crawled into the reopened pen, worked her way around behind the sheep, and drove them out again. With a quick silent charge in the move called "shedding," she split them two and two, chased one brace away, penned the other, and lay down guarding the entrance until her master closed the gate with finality, doffed his cap to the plaudits of the crowd, and smiled for the first time.

"Twenty-nine minute, forty-three second," said the spectating farmer with the watch. "Yon's a game wee bitch. We'll hae tae keep an eye on her." He clapped the shepherd on the shoulder. "Brawly done, Jock. I'll stand you a pint, for yon's thirsty work."

"Come ahint my heel," said Hughie sadly and led his Chief away, a pet who could have been a champion if his master had been half up. Almost he wished himself at school, where old Clark would be *mensa mensam*ing him to death. "Let's go for a walk up Misty Law way where we can look down on those stupid bitches. I bet there's not one of them can walk on her hind legs. Mibbie we ought to join the circus."

The first collie's time was still holding up when Elspeth brought Bella Cockburn home after school. Bella came to see not dogs but Lachlan, for although a year younger, he was a male. The pickings would improve when the public school boys were home on holiday from Fettes, Loretto, Sedburgh, one even from Charterhouse. Until then, Lachie must serve to determine whether men could be smitten by blue-black hair, brown eyes, a retroussé—*not* a snub—nose, and a large mouth. Lachie had known her all her life. If he rolled over, others shouldn't prove as difficult when she "came out." At fourteen, however, Lachie was more concerned with muscles than misses.

"Rats," he said. "Here comes old Cockburn." He pronounced all the consonants, and Willie sniggered.

"You wouldn't call her that to her face," he said.

"Let's hide in the boozing tent. They can't go in there."

It was quiet and shady under the vault of canvas, the turf green, the duck boards pristine in front of the temporary bar. By closing time the reek of ale and whisky, pipe tobacco, dogs, men, tweed, leather would be overpowering, but now the saloon tent held only a companionable fragrance that the two boys sniffed appreciatively.

"If they ever let women into pubs, it'll wreck them," said Lachie.

"Right," said Willie. "Men are best."

"Out!" called Dolly Nolan.

"See what I mean?" whispered Lachie. "Bloody well wreck them."

"I'm sorry, Lachlan," said Dolly, "but your ma would scalp me for letting you in here. If you're after a cream sodie or a ginger beer, skedaddle ower to the buffie tent."

"We're not thirsty," said Willie. "We're hiding from somebody."

"Shut up." Lachlan punched him.

"Hiding, is it?" said Dolly, all interest now. "From a lass, I'll be bound. Who?"

"Bella Cockburn," said Willie.

"Boyd, if you don't shut up, I'll give you a black eye."

"So the oldest Cockburn lass is sweet on you," said Dolly. "She has good taste."

"She has not!" bellowed Lachie. "I mean—och, I don't know what I mean."

"That's aye the way the first time," said Dolly tenderly. "Dinna run awa from it, laddie."

"Who's running away? I'm not a coward . . ."

"Lachie! Willie!" Elspeth's call filled the tent from the canopied entrance that blocked her view of the inside. "Come on out. We know you're in there."

Lachie vaulted the bar, dashed past Dolly and out the back flap, Willie at his heels. Together they belted away from the trial course, and not till they were behind the big house did they stop and throw themselves on the ground.

"That was too bloody close," said Lachie.

"I've got a cramp in my leg," said Willie, panting.

"Boy, are you out of training. Keep your knee stiff." He bent the toes of the offending limb back with all his strength and straightened out the muscle knot in the calf. "I should have let you suffer. Telling Pat's wife we were hiding from Bella . . ."

"Is she really soft on you?"

"How the hell do I know? Now we can't go back to the trials. What do you want to do? And don't say tennis. The girls'd see us, and we'd end up playing pat-ball with them."

"Elspeth has as strong a serve as you."

"You're crazy. How about trying to ride a stirk? I'll bet you can't stay on one."

"What's wrong with the horses?"

"By the time we had boots and breeches on us and saddles on them, Mother would want us in for dinner. Besides, stirks are more fun. They don't like being ridden very much."

The evening meal was broth thick with barley, Dover sole, roast saddle of mutton with red currant jelly, new potatoes boiled in their tender pink skins, and the first of the new peas. As a party sweet, Cookie had prepared a trifle—layers of sponge fingers, raspberry jam, custard, and, on top, a blanket of whipped cream. The sponge should have been soaked in sherry, but Cook was not one to start bairns on the road to ruin. It was bad enough that Mrs. Dougal had insisted on serving claret cup. Cookie had demurred against chilling it with the ice on which the fishmonger had delivered the sole, but the mistress of the house insisted that nothing sticks to ice if you wash it, and the festive drink didn't taste of the sea at all.

Willie's Glasgow pallor had vanished in the day of wind and sun. With that fair hair and quick wee smile, he'll be a proper menace when he's twenty-one, thought Anna. Aye, or before. Lachie too, even if he's shy of Bella Cockburn as a partner the night. Every time he passes her something, he turns chill as the claret cup. It doesna fash her though. You'll bear watching, lass, if you're that womanly wise awready.

"Off with you now and take advantage of the long light." Anna rose, releasing the young. "Keep awa from the tents, mind," she called after them. "Grown-ups are entitled to freedom from bairns in the evening. Is that no right, Mairi?"

"Och yess, Mistress Dougal," said the Skye maid, who was not much older than Miss Cockburn.

"Then see you and Peggy behave like two. Ten-thirty taps, mind."

Jamie Grant saw the highland lassies surrounded by a group of young men and made for the pub tent.

"See's a pint, Dolly," he said, "to wash the sour taste of envy out of my mouth. I canna get it through my head that I'm no twenty any more."

"You'll aye be that tae me, Jamie." Pat was out of earshot at the other end of the bar, so busy serving ale that his own tankard kept falling flat before he could finish it.

"Here's to the lassies, Dolly. Every last mother's daughter of them."

"I canna drink tae masel, but here's tae the lads. Lachie Dougal was in here this afternoon."

"He was?" Mr. Grant put down his ale. "I'll put a stop to that. You didna serve him?"

"He wasna here for any of ma produce. He was hiding from a girl. Lachie'd no be backward, would he, Jamie?"

"At fourteen?"

"He's big for his age. When I think of aw the fun coming tae him . . ." Dolly sighed.

"You wouldna mind being twenty again yoursel, would you now?"

"I wouldna say that. Each year I hae is the best year o' ma life."

"And it shows in your bonny face."

"Dinna look at me like that, Jamie, or I'll forget ma wee man."

"No you, Dolly. You're owerdecent."

"You'll no mind if whiles I wish I werena."

"Come on, Willie," said Lachie. "Let's work on the Argyll. No girls, though. They get in the way."

"Thanks," said Bella.

"Let's go down to the Maclehose pasture," said Elspeth.

"Why?" said Lachlan.

"I saw a big trout in the pool there yesterday. You could try to guddle it."

"What's guddling?" Bella was County, not country.

"You tickle a fish with your fingers," said Willie. "Then when he's gasping with laughter, you stick your thumb in his gill and toss him on the bank. I've done it many a time in the Cloy Burn at Brodick."

"I don't believe you," said Bella. "He's lying, isn't he, Lachie? You couldn't do it, could you?"

"Of course I could."

"I dare you."

"You're on."

The girls walked in front, Elspeth throwing a wink to her friend. Boys were easy to manage if you played to their conceit.

"You'll look like a dope, Lachie," muttered Willie. "Even if there is a fish there. I've only poached one in a hundred guddlings."

"I'm better than you are," said Lachie. "I've been at it longer."

As they crossed over into the east pasture, still Maclehose by courtesy, Bella stopped. "What's wrong with that cow?" she said, pointing.

Lachie followed her gesture. "Face this way!" he commanded, spinning her around away from the animal. "Eyes front! You too, Elspeth!" His sister obeyed. "Now, up to the house . . ."

"I don't want to go to the house," said Bella.

". . . and don't look back."

"We'd better, Bella," said Elspeth. "When Lachie takes that tone . . ."

"Oh, all right." Huffily she tossed her head and marched back up the hill.

158

The cow mooed loud as the Cloch Light and arched her back. Below her tail hung a shiny black head and two legs.

"How did that get in there?" Willie cackled and dodged as Lachie threw a slap at him.

The cow mooed again and began to swing her hindquarters from side to side, the calf's head and legs a pendulum just above the turf.

"It's stuck," said Lachie. "We'll have to give her a hand. You game?"

Willie swallowed. "No, but I'll try."

"Take hold of one hoof and I'll take the other, and pull straight back gently. Imagine you're pulling a cork out of a bottle."

"Uch. It's sticky and slippery at the same time."

"Shut up and pull. That's it."

The calf oozed onto the grass, struggled up on shaky legs that carried it to the waiting udder, and was suckling not ten seconds after its arrival in the world, its hindquarters toward the tongue-rasp of the mother cleaning it off.

"A bloody miracle," whispered Willie.

"A bloody bull," said Lachie. "Wipe your hands on the grass."

Bella was overwhelmed by Lachie's consideration for her purity. "Positively *gallant*," she told Elspeth. "*Un parfait gentilhomme*."

"Don't get carried away, Bella. Lachie's careful of any girl."

"I don't care. I think he's marvelous. If only he weren't a year younger."

"If it will make you feel any better, you're one-fourteenth older than he is now, but in ten years you'll only be one-twenty-fourth."

"Who cares about ten years from now? I think your brother is grand."

Unfashionably, Anna watched the evening trials for an hour. Saturday afternoon was the prescribed time for the

Strathgryffe gentry. She slowed as she passed the pub tent, wondering if she was hoping to run into Jamie Grant. Lonely as Wordsworth's cloud, she wandered around the canvas bulging with the good cheer and camaraderie forbidden her sex.

Passing a suddenly silent Mairi and Peggy and five cap-touching halflins, she gave them a severe nod to let the lads know she was watching out for her girls, like the spoilsport she was, drat it.

When she went in the big front door, Sandy had been in bed for two hours, and Hugh and Morag were downstairs ready for theirs. Morag kissed her cheek, then darted across to Willie and pecked him too, making him misthrow the dice, the ivories landing on the parquet instead of the card table. His face flamed.

"You miss your turn, Willie Boyd," said Bella, bored with childish Snakes and Ladders.

"No, he doesn't." Defiantly Morag handed him the dice. "It was my fault."

"Bella's right," said Lachie.

"Why? Just because she's a guest? Willie's too a guest."

"Bella's a lady."

"Then so'm I."

"Shoo, bairn, shoo. You're disturbing your elders and betters."

Morag snorted.

"Haven't you a hankie?" said Elspeth.

"In my nightie? Good night, all." Tenderly: " 'Night, Willie."

The youngsters were upstairs by the time Mairi came in from the servants' quarters, hat and coat still on, rosy-cheeked, bright-eyed, breathless.

"We're home, Mistress Dougal," she said.

"Two minutes late." How red the lass's lips. From good use? "That's no sae bad. Off to bed with you, and dinna forget, down on your knees first."

Her brood now safe for the night, she poured two fingers

of whisky. "All day I've been doing for other folk. This is for wee Anna Dougal hersel." She pulled a chair into the bay window, looked down at the tents where orange and red flares made a false sunset, and wished herself there, off for a spree with the gentlemen rankers. "God, have mercy on such as we. Baa, baa, baa." This poor little lamb better have another wee nip to put her to sleep, or she'll loup on her broom and go flying in his window like the witch she is. The mixed metaphor brought a chuckle without humor.

At four o'clock in the morning an explosion of thunder directly overhead shook the sleeping house, sending Wattie speeding from room to room to check the children. Sandy hadn't wakened, Morag was easily pacified, Elspeth was laughing at Bella, who had her arms wrapped around her bedmate in fright. Hugh was at the window enjoying the lightning that flashed the moor into black and white relief. Willie Boyd and Lachie were also intent on the display and didn't hear Wattie open and as quietly shut the door.

Eyes closed tight, muttering, Cook adjusted her bosoms, disarranged in the convulsive leap brought on by the thunder. Mairi sat up, listened for a moment, then, hearing no sound from Cook's room or Peggy's cell at the end of the corridor, lay down and pulled the covers over her head.

The lad who had climbed in Peggy's secluded window at eleven climbed out again, grateful for the bang that had wakened him before full daylight.

The bombardment of the white-forked storm moved up the Clyde against the going tide. On slate roof and cobblestone the rain teemed a steady lullaby to soothe the manor house back to sleep.

"Dry by seven, wet by eleven," said Lachie at breakfast, looking out at the effervescence of fresh-washed greenery.

"That's backwards, and I'll no except the vicey-versy as true," said Anna. "Judging by the wee lochs in the courtyard, we must have had a gey good storm last night to clear the air."

"You didn't hear it?" squealed Bella. "I thought Halley's comet had struck."

"It'll not be by again for another seventy-three years," said Lachie.

"Is that a fact now?" said Anna. I must have been drugged. It couldna have been yon wee tipple I had. "Help yourself to porridge, Willie."

He did, generously, then dipped his spoon into the milk jug, cut a neat hole in the center of his smooth plateful, and, pouring from a height, made the fluid lift the oatmeal free to float. With the spoon he spun the porridge like a tiny merry-go-round, then felt eyes on him and knew himself guilty of Playing With One's Food.

"These are good, Aunt Anna," he defended himself. "Porridge never float unless they're the best."

"I'll give your compliments to the chef," said Anna. "Morag! Dinna try it. Least, no when I'm looking."

"You know the big oak beyond the tennis court?" said Hugh.

"What about it?" asked Bella.

"It isn't any more."

"Let's see!"

"No on an empty stomach," said Anna. "Finish your breakfasts."

Like a death in the family it was, as Dougals, guests, and kitchen staff stood and mourned the body of the centurial giant split asunder, one half pointing west, the other east.

"I kenned that first bolt was awfu close," said Cook.

Surreptitiously, Peggy crossed herself. Had God meant it for her? In Purgatory she might have been, stricken off this earth in the most sinful state. Then her belief in the Almighty's omniscience said that if her Creator had been after Peggy Maclean, He wouldn't have missed. It was a warning. She'd be a good girl from now on and lock her window. But even as she made the vow before the evidence of Heavenly wrath, she knew there were too many *tearlachs*, too many darlings, around for her to keep the promise.

Up the brae came a team of horses followed by James Grant, Pat Nolan, Gordon Morton the Joiner, his helper, and a wheelbarrow load of axes and saws.

"A sad sight, Mrs. Dougal," said Morton in the tones of the undertaker he was when occasion demanded.

"Aye," said Anna, "but you're a sadder, here to cut up the corpse awmost before it's stopped breathing."

"The tree's no a very guid one for ma purposes, Mrs. Dougal, it's that gnarled. I'll no get many solid six-foot-six planks oot o' that. But as you're a guid neighbor, I'll pay you five pound for what I can get."

"Grave robber. You'll make twenty coffin from that fine oak."

"And there'll be a wee charge o' five pound for hauling the timber awa. So it'll be a wash."

"Using my own horses. You're near enough to be an Aberdonian, Gordon Morton."

"No quite a wash, Gordie," said Jamie Grant. "There'll be a charge of a sovereign for the team."

"An' a bob an hour for ma labor," said Pat.

"Och, go ahead," said Anna, seeing Glen Gryffe come out ahead. "I canna argue the cost of an old friend's funeral. And Pat Nolan, you find me the finest tree you can plant where that beauty stood, for I canna abide a vacuum any more than nature can. Make it a rowan for luck."

The shepherds and collies eliminated the previous day had already departed Strathgryffe, and Saturday morning's defeated left on the one o'clock. The locals and those remaining in contention were now matched in number by the elegant in bespoke tailoring. Gentlemen in Norfolk jackets and knickers, their ladies wasp-waisted in twill and pin-striped serge from which peeped the shiny toes of high-button boots and, from one daring fashion-setter, a glimpse of ankle; feather-trimmed toques, wide-brimmed bonnets, each a garden in itself; kid gloves, parasols, shooting sticks; wicker baskets for the china, cutlery, roast chicken, and wine; comments about the dear wee doggies. "Fit to gar you scunner," said the countryfolk, and the Dougals agreed it was fit to make you sick.

At four o'clock Bess o' Duncrag, a black bitch with one white pad, took off up the brae, ears back like a stoat after a rabbit pack. Down the brae the sheep came running, up over the hay cart, across the Gryffe, then back again to be penned, shed, and repenned with never a falter.

"Ma Goad," said the farmer with the watch. "Twenty-four minute, thirteen second." He shook gunmetal, then held it to his ear in disbelief.

"Trained sheep," said a fashionable gentleman in a tweed suit of black-and-white houndstooth check with the new cuffed trousers, and Willie, copying Lachie, gave the dope's back a withering look.

Two more collies made their runs to no avail, and at five-thirty Bess o' Duncrag's owner accepted the silver mug from the Countess of Strathgryffe, the presentation of awards being her life work. Prizegiving was followed by a Member of Parliament, an English Liberal substituting for Great Britain's Prime Minister Herbert Asquith, M.P. for East Fife. Whether the Sassenach orated on the topics of the day—Home Rule for Ireland, the packing of the House of Lords, Votes for Women, or pensions for overage collies—no one ever found out, thanks to his accent—*Yon's no English, Gordie*—and the drowning roar coming from the Dambridge Larder tent, jam-packed with thirsty alers.

"Now is the time for aw good bairns to come to the aid of the party and gang awa hame," said Anna. She winked at Jamie Grant and led her brood away.

Now why in the name of the Earl o' Hell did I do that? she thought in the kirk next morning. My age, and winking at a man who couldna tell a come-on from a go-by, he's that honorable. That brought back the problem of his bizzem wife, and during the forty-five minute sermon, Anna decided her course of action.

Next morning at his mother's request, Lachie positioned the Argyll on the downgrade of the drive. No man should crank her up for this day's skulduggery. She left motorcar, duster, veil, and gauntlets on the outskirts of Paisley, donned white gloves, and boarded a tram for the city's center where, taking her cue from McNab's report, she went on watch in the fish-and-chips shop. To justify her vigil she had to sample the viands, but it was no hardship. Haddock and potatoes were to her real taste, better than Cook could prepare them, but then she didn't have such deep hot fat.

Mill hooter blew, the street came alive, Daisy turned into her close, fumbled with the lock, kicked open the door, and marched in.

"Good afternoon." Mrs. Dougal of Glen Gryffe followed, her accent big-house-on-the-hill. "You can close your mouth as well as the door. I'm not a ghost." Leisurely she toured the one room and kitchen flat, taking in the distempered walls, the fumed-oak furniture, the dark-painted wood, the sink colloquially known as "the jaw box" for the duet of chattering that accompanied dishwashing. With dainty finger she lined the dust on top of the coal bunker and shook her head. Having established herself, she then turned her attention to the woman, who had shut the door but was having trouble with her mouth. Daisy could sneer wholeheartedly at what she called "the upper crust" in its absence. She had also found it easy to snarl into an ear held to a faraway telephone. Face to face was another matter.

"Ah dinna hae time tae redd up the place in the morn," she faltered, the underling caught in neglect. "Ah dae it when ah come hame."

"You should rise a few minutes earlier. It cannot take more than that to run a duster over a couple of rooms."

"Whit dae ye want, Mrs. Dougal?"

"Just a little chat. Don't bother about tea. I'm glad you seem comfortably settled, Daisy. You're a fortunate woman to have a brother-in-law who can supply such pleasant quarters. Rent-free, too."

"That's a lie!" Servant vanished, and virago counterattacked with a vehemence that confirmed McNab's deductions.

"As I was saying, you are most fortunate." Anna ignored the denial. "You are also courageous. Myself, I would not want to be occupying this flat when Tom Black finds out about Arthur Cochran and Charlie Baird and the others. He will, you know. These things get around. Remember years ago when he was charged with assault and battery? Yes, I've learned about that, too. Let off with a warning, wasn't he, because it was proved that the man he thrashed had looked sideways at your sister Maggie? I fear Black has quite a temper where women are concerned, Daisy."

"Whit if he has? That has nothing to do wi' me."

"Ah, but it has, Daisy. Not last payday, but the one before, it was your brother-in-law in daylight followed after dark by Arthur and, last, Charlie. At least as far as my information goes."

"You've nae right tae come here uninvited and tell sic a pack o' lies tae ma face. It's you that's the bad woman . . ."

"No lies, Daisy. I have proof."

"You canna prove whit's no true . . ."

"Sergeant Ivor McNab of the Police has it all down in his wee book." No need to say *ex*-Sergeant.

"The Poliss!" Daisy's hand flew to her mouth.

"Yes, Sergeant McNab can prove that Charles Baird entered these premises at twelve forty-five A.M. and stayed with you behind locked doors till one-thirty. And you must know what an assignation after midnight means to the courts."

"The courts?" Despite her telephone threat, to Daisy the law existed for the protection of the rich. "You'd drag me through the courts?"

Nine—ten—out . . . Having worked up to the bout for months, to floor her opponent in the first round was a decided letdown. All that training for nothing. "Drat it, woman, blow your nose and stop sniveling."

"Ah'm only a poor wee country girl . . ." Had Anna been

a man, Daisy would have fought on, but with a lady she knew when she was beaten. "Whit are ye going tae do?"

"I, Daisy? Nothing. But you are going to write a letter to your husband."

"Ah—ah havena ony notepaper."

"Didn't I know you would say that? I brought you some of Mairi's. She's forever writing home. See, the envelope's even stamped. I've written out what you should say. Start it any way you like, though perhaps not 'Dear.' That wouldn't be quite honest, would it? Perhaps 'James' would be best."

"It's no a confession of what I havena done?"

"Look at it and find out."

Fear speeding comprehension, Daisy scanned the printing penciled on a sheet torn from one of Elspeth's jotters. Then, unable to believe her luck, she studied it word by word, looking for the trap.

"Why dae you want me to write this?" she asked suspiciously. "It doesna dae me any harm."

"It puts a stop to your nonsense about the alienation of an affection that does not exist."

"That's aw you're after? If I send this, you'll no go spreading lies about me?" Had positions been reversed, Daisy would have been pouring the policeman's report into Tom Black's ear. Fear of Black made her shiver involuntarily. Quickly she discarded the prospect of extra income from the Widow Dougal. Shite! No money was worth the risk. "If you promise no tae open your mouth . . ."

". . . to your brother-in-law? Rest assured, Daisy. He'll never hear about your other friends from me."

Toffs were soft aw right. Soft and easy. She wouldna be so easy. Daisy rummaged in her purse for a penny and threw it and the last word on the table.

"Here's whit you paid for the postage stamp. I'll no accept even a copper frae you, Anna Dougal."

Mairi ushered Jamie into the morning room the following evening, and without preamble he handed Anna the letter.

Had he spotted the ghost writer? It was gey hard to think and spell like a Daisy.

> *James*
> *I dont want you thinking Im sorry. January 11, 1911 when I left you was the hapiest day of my life. Your no a man James Grant. I dont love you and I never did. So put that in your dirty pipe and smoke it. I wouldna come back to you for all the money in the Bank of Scotland.*
>
> > *I am*
> > *Yours truely*
> > *Daisy Grant*

Predictably she had added a postscript of her own.

> *P.S. Your lucky getting off with a meesley quid a week.*

"That's one to the bread basket," said Anna.

"Fair sickening," he replied cheerfully. "I'm wondering why she wrote it, after aw these months?"

"You havena tried to get her back. That's the kind of contempt a wife canna stomach, no without retaliating sooner or later. I'm gey sorry that the postie should bring you such a low blow to your pride."

"Dinna fret, Mrs. Dougal. It's been hanging ower my head like a thundercloud that Daisy might come back."

"See's that nasty letter again." Anna studied the ill-formed writing once more. "It wouldna surprise me if she hasna overreached hersel," she said. "Spite's a bad counselor. It's no for me to advise you, Mr. Grant, but I'd show this to a lawyer."

"Well now. I might at that." He replaced the letter in his breast pocket. "Did you have a nice wee run in the motorcar yesterday?" Without waiting for an answer he walked over to the bookcase and examined the spines of the *Encyclopædia Britannica,* the new edition. "I was right sorry for that book salesman who called on you a wee while back on a fool's errand. He seemed a decent chap. Did you ken he had been a policeman for thirty year? We had a wee chat, and he told me, though there wasna any need. It stood out all ower him. I bet he misses the detecting. You'd think he'd keep his hand in, wouldn't you now?"

"Och, where are my manners?" Was he on to her? "You'll have a dram, Mr. Grant? Help yoursel to the decanter there. You'll find soda siphon and glass in the sideboard."

"Will you no join me?"

"I'll have a taet of sherry to keep you from drinking alone."

"Aye. I wonder why Daisy waited till yesterday to get rid of her spleen," he said, pouring, his back toward her. "She must have posted the letter a wee while after you went for your tootle up the Paisley Road. You canna have gone to Glasgow. You werena awa that long." He gave her a searching look, handed her a stemmed glass, and raised his own goblet high. "I'll gie you a toast, Anna Dougal. Here's tae you, H.M.S. *Indomitable* hersel."

He was on to her aw right. Did she care? No one damn bit. She raised her own glass to eye level and looked across the rim at him.

"And here's to Jamie Grant," she said. "My colleague and my friend."

Son of McFadden did not relish advising the partner of Mrs. Dougal on matters conjugal. However, a client was a client, the law the law, and he an expert trained to guide the ignorant layman.

"This letter might have been written to establish a case of desertion, Mr. Grant. Can you assure me that your wife left of her own free will? You didn't turn her out?"

"I wasna even in the village when she put her foot in my cart and went birling down the road."

"Have you made any attempt to get her back?"

"Would a rabbit ask a ferret into a burrow?"

"Hm. Still, to establish your good faith, you must now write—or better yet, I shall write as your lawyer, formally inviting Mrs. Grant to return to your bed and board."

"Think of the danger, man! She might accept."

"Then I will have done my job. The authorities look with favor on the preservation of the home."

"They've never lived with Daisy."

The lawyer suppressed a sigh for the misery he had avoided. So far. "If she doesn't accept, then on January twelfth, 1915, she will have been in desertion for four years and one day, statutory grounds to establish your freedom." From a well-stocked bookcase he pulled a tome and opened it. "The Divorce Act of 1573 spells it out quite clearly." Sonorously he read. " 'Divertis fra utheris companie without ane ressonible causand remains in their malicious obstinacie be the space of four years.' "

"Couldna be clearer," said Jamie.

"Unless—unless you were guilty of—uh—infidelity. Were you? Was that why she deserted you?"

"You're no to mention it to a living soul, but that cap fits her, no me."

"When did you discover this?"

"The day she up and went."

"The day? She didn't stay the night? Careful now, Mr. Grant."

"Awmost as soon as I found her out, I left the house. When I came back, she was ower the hills and far away."

"Can you prove what you say?"

"Aye. Hamish, the stationmaster, saw her leaving one way and me arriving the other. By train."

"Then Mrs. Grant could not claim you condoned her offense, even if she had a mind?"

"There'd best be no need to mention said offense, for I'll no do it, McFadden."

"Four years' desertion is sufficient grounds, Grant, without bringing up the reason for it."

The injured party reported Son of McFadden's legal opinion that evening, although it was not necessary. Before forcing and guiding Daisy's hand, Anna had found these legal niceties under the D's in the *Encyclopædia Britannica*.

Chapter Six

THE OBITUARY for Sir George Biggart ran a column and a half in the *Glasgow Herald*, so many were his accomplishments, honors, civic contributions, clubs. Gentlemen filled the Botanic Gardens Church to its twelve-hundred capacity for the service conducted by the Moderator of the General Assembly of the Church of Scotland, the Right Reverend Dr. Alfred Newton. The City could not be said to have come to a standstill, but its pace was definitely slowed while the business and municipal leaders attended the passing of one of their own. In the front pew, Anna and her oldest son sat on one side of Lady Biggart, Harriet and her husband on the other. The daughter and her oldest friend took the widow straight home from the kirk.

"You're to stay in bed, Mamá," said Anna, pulling up the sheet and quilt. "Lachlan and I will be there to accept the respects of the gentlemen."

Such as Philip Dougal, who stood over Anna, weak whisky-soda in his tapering fingers, and made noises of condolence as feeble as his drink before moving away.

Ahead of him, Lachlan saw an endless line of funerals

which, as head of the house, it would be his duty to attend when these old crocks died off. For once he envied Hugh and his sisters, their presence not required even for a grandfather's burying.

McFadden the younger appraised the evidence of wealth surrounding his client. Despite the slump in the cotton trade, Biggart would cut up not so bad, and there would be only three portions—the widow, the daughter, and charity. Anna Dougal was a young woman yet, a bonny one worth the wooing for herself alone. In his thirties, Archibald Mc-Fadden had suffered a scornful rejection by a brutal beauty, and the refusal had instilled lasting timidity. Now, however, the sober circumstances of the moment, which precluded any overture, lent courage to his mind's eye, and almost he saw himself proposing in the vague future when the mourning would be past.

Harriet had her first close-up of James Grant. His presence surprised her, as did his appearance. He looked nearer thirty than forty, in plain black suit a sturdy yeoman among the portly gentry all in the full fig of the formal Prince Albert prescribed for funerals.

"You were good to come," said Anna.

"How could I no?" Harriet heard him reply. " 'Touch one, touch aw.' "

"Glad I am you feel that close to the Dougals."

When the four-wheelers had clipclopped back to the heart of the city—no one was so unfeeling as to bring an odiferous motorcar to a funeral—Lachie went for a walk to free his brain, and Lady Biggart went to sleep on a teaspoon of laudanum. Without asking Harriet's wishes, Anna poured two glasses of the whisky they could not touch in front of gentlemen.

"Here's to absent friends," she said, "and absent papás."

"Absent papás," Mrs. Boyd responded, "though my own was not worth the toasting."

"He was a man, Harriet."

"So is your Mr. Grant."

"He's no mine, more's the pity."

"Then why did he say, 'Touch one, touch all?' "

"That's the farm's slogan. Are you no glad there's a braw man to look out for helpless wee me?"

Despite the occasion, that made Harriet giggle. "He's the one needs protection."

"Whiles. I gave him a mite the other day. From his wife."

"Anna, you didn't!"

"Did too. I'll tell you about it. Some other time."

"It *would* be disrespectful to unburden yourself now," said Harriet. Doubtfully.

"I suppose so. Though I've aye held that funerals are to comfort those left behind."

"In a way, at a time like this, it's not good for you to have other pressures on your mind."

"I never was much of a one for the sackcloth and ashes."

"I should hope not," said Harriet, firmly now. "Overgrieving is so unbecoming. It's boastful, that's what it is."

"Papá used to say that if I followed Harriet's advice, I'd no get in trouble."

"You know you can have my counsel any time, Anna."

"Like right the now?"

"If you feel up to it."

"You'd no think me disrespectful?"

"I'd as soon think that of myself, Anna."

"Then sit back in your chair, for here goes."

The telling and the whisky routed the day's gloom as Anna recounted her foray into a world unknown to ladies. She concluded, "Now aw Jamie Grant has to do is let time roll by."

"I'm shocked more than I can say, Anna. That dreadful woman."

"Och, t' hell with Daisy. I've turned her gas down to a peep. Are you no proud of your auld china? Sherlock himsel couldna have done better."

"You shouldn't have done it at all. Now James Grant is more than ever beholden to you. The way you looked at him today . . ."

"After greeting yon Philip, Son of McFadden, and the other professional mourners, you canna blame my wee face for lighting up at him. It did for your Robert, too."

"That's different. That's friendship, not—not—the other. Anna Biggart, do you imagine yourself in love with James Grant?"

"My, whisky takes hold of you fast. You'd no have found the courage to pop that question without it. You're out of luck. 'A *fou* man's a true man' doesna apply to me at aw. Nor *in vino veritas* either."

"Because if you are, you're laying up heartache for yourself. Even if he were free, you could never marry. What would your friends say?"

"Good for wee Anna Dougal, I hope. The real ones anyway."

"Of course I would. But people like your brother-in-law . . ."

"Yon gomeril? The fool wouldna approve unless I married the Prince of Wales. Now there's an idea, Harriet Hepburn. How do you fancy me in a coronet?"

Mrs. Boyd giggled again, then hid her mouth behind a lace handkerchief as a knock came at the door.

"See's your glass." Quickly Anna placed the telltale tumblers on the sideboard before the maid entered with tea. "Put the tray over here, Isobel. And take they whisky goblets awa. A couple of the gentlemen must have left them behind." She peered at the dainty sandwiches of tongue, cucumber, watercress, tomato. "Nae French cakes? What kind of a five o'clock's that?"

"They didna seem appropriate the day, Miss Anna."

"Och, but they are, Isobel. Papá was a great hand for the *petits fours.*"

James Grant was not much of a one for cakes of any land. Returning from the funeral, he dropped off the train at

Dambridge for a tuppenny pie and a pint with Dolly, who would not be busy at that hour and should be glad to hear the lawyer's heartening interpretation of Daisy's letter. But the owner of the Larder was more worried than pleased.

"That's a lang time tae behave yoursel, Jamie," she said. "Ower three year."

"What's three year to a man o' character?"

"It's no natural. The law shouldna expect you tae be a bloody monk."

"I'd crawl up Misty Law on bare knees every day of the while it takes to be legally rid of Daisy."

"Yon's no a penance at aw by comparison. Wi' aw the lasses around—I saw Mairi Maclean the other day. There she is, just up the brae." *And so is the Widow Dougal. She's the yin worries me.*

"Mairi might as well be back in Skye. You canna think I'd harm a bairn like her."

"Fine you ken the Auld Adam has nae conscience when he's roused, and if Daisy caught you . . ."

"She's no going to, for I'll do naught for her to catch."

One who did get caught was Peggy Maclean.

Anna was snipping dew-fresh roses on an August morning when the maid passed on her way from the vegetable garden with a bowl of French beans.

"Behaving yoursel, Peggy?" said Anna, meaning nothing in particular.

The bowl crashed, the beans went bounding, and the girl let out a wet wail disproportionate to the minor accident. Anna dropped the cut buds—only another kind of deflowering could have provoked such an outburst—and taking Peggy's hand led her away from kitchen eyes to coax the old story out of her. It came easily.

"Dinna greet so, lassie," said Anna. "It's grand to have bairns when you're young. I'll put up the wedding, if your church'll take money from a Protestant."

"There's to be no wedding," wailed Peggy. "He's bound for Canada . . ."

"No if I ken it. When does he plan to run off?"

"Last week."

"You let him slip awa?" Here was reason for tears. Who had emigrated lately? "Sandy Tulloch! The miserable wee—taking my five-pound note to help him get started in Manitoba. And him no more nor eighteen . . ."

"Seventeen!"

Anna studied a linnet busy at its nest low in the dog rose hedge. She didn't blame the lass, she didn't blame the lad, she blamed nature for giving the power too soon for the brain. And she blamed herself. Bars must go on that window, locking the stable door after Peggy was three months gone, but saving other Peggys from future fly-by-nights.

"You're no to think badly of Sandy, lass," she said. "He's awfu young to accept the fathering of a bairn. But if you love him, I'll send you out to Canada with a wee dowry, a tocher to help you over the worst of the money troubles."

"The only water I'll cross is over the sea to Skye!" cried Peggy, not at all sure that Sandy was the culprit. Peggy was overpopular, as only a lass can be who offers the warmth of bed and blanket as well. Sandy had been allowed through her window but once, and then purely because he was pleading so noisily that she feared he might waken Cookie and spoil the game for his betters. Of all the *tearlachs* who had thrown their legs over her sill, he was the last she'd choose for a husband.

A week later, to avoid village eyes and comment, Anna drove Peggy and her box by the back road to Dambridge, then on to Glasgow's Buchanan Street Station and the train to Fort William. There she would catch the West Highland Railway to Mallaig and the ferry to the south end of Skye, where palm trees grow above the 57th parallel, thanks to the Gulf Stream. Peggy's home lay in the harsher north on the shore of Loch Bracadale, and Anna worried what reception would be given the girl who left there one and came back two. Peggy, however, didn't let such a natural happenstance interfere with her childish pleasure in her first motorcar trip. She prattled all the way to the city. Like a simpleton, thought Anna, which was unkind but probably true. Inbreeding had been a matter of survival in the Hebrides, depopulated by the brutal evictions that followed the defeat of the clans in 1745. Despite sentimental song and story, there was little romance in the aftermath of Bonnie Prince Charlie and the '45. Nor in the emigrations a hundred years later when mid-Victorian landowners discovered that sheep required less human care than did cattle. At least Peggy was bringing back new bloodlines.

"I've telegraphed your father to meet you at the ferry. Here's a few bawbees to buy a bun on the journey. And here's your ticket." Anna banged the third-class compartment door shut on the girl. She couldn't have Peggy arrive home pregnant and with a pokeful of silver. She'd send a postal order later to help with the bairn; to the girl's father in the name of her employer, which might soften the byblow. "Be a good lass and keep in touch with me. There might be a wee present for you every now and then."

"Mistress Dougal, if she iss a girl, can I christen her Anna?"

"Get along with you. Anna's a cow's name," she answered, gratified nonetheless.

Having waved the train away, Anna went to the Royal Scottish Automobile Club, an establishment so enlightened that ladies were permitted membership in their own names. The building, new in 1909, boasted a fine wine cellar and set an excellent table with only one shortcoming in Mrs. Dougal's eyes. It did not purvey Glen Gryffe beef. After lunch—the strawberry water ice tasted as good as the smell of the fresh fruit—she paid a visit to the office of the secretary. That gentleman was so taken aback by the solecism of a member, a lady, peddling her wares that she drove home with a respectable trial order to put through the club's butcher. A stock farm has little beef to sell, and Glen

Gryffe's belonged only in the best restaurants if the name were to earn prestige.

To Dorcas and Elspeth, with charity and compassion Anna explained the reason for the departure of Peggy, the wayward.

"Oh, the poor wee thing!" cried Elspeth.

"Little idiot," said Dorcas. "Now, Mamá, you promised to give your answer before I return to St. Thenew's, though how I shall put in another ghastly year at that childish establishment is beyond me. But after that, may I go to Le Manoix to finish? Fiona Murray is, and lots of other girls."

"How many?"

"I told you. Lots."

"And your china, Fiona, is exaggerating the same way to her mother, I dinna doubt. We'll see. Swiss finishing schools are gey dear."

"But we must have plenty of money now, with Grandfather's estate . . ."

"Next you'll be telling me you want to be presented at Court."

"But of course, Mamá."

To Lachie, Anna categorized Peggy as a bad girl out to snare a lad in the old proven way. This might make him think twice when he started to look at the lassies with a man's intent. Hugh, Morag, and Kenneth learned only that Peggy had been overcome by homesickness. Lest they think her soft in the head, to no one did Anna confide that she would pay for the borning, outfitting, and a fair amount of support for mother and child thereafter.

Feelings at the Dambridge Larder ran against Sandy Tulloch, whose coincidental emigration was looked upon as dishonorable until Pat Nolan told Dolly he had seen never a weed grow outside Peggy's window. "Sure'n not a seed planted there would sprout."

"Gie ma back a wee rub," said Dolly, digesting this. "Och, that's nice. Ma shoulders too, Pat. Are you telling me moss doesna grow on a busy thoroughfare?"

"Either that or Sandy was a bloody centipede wi' aw kinds o' different-size feet."

"His mother'll be glad tae hear that. I'll not tell another soul though. I wouldna want tae hurt the lass's reputation."

With the purpling of the heather, the children went back to school, Lachlan and Hugh not unhappily as September was the start of the seven-month rugby season. Elspeth, too, found the return to discipline bearable because the new term brought her the captaincy of St. Malcolm's lacrosse team. She played first attack, her speed having won her the position and her colors two years earlier, the youngest in the school's history to play for the First. Dorcas returned to St. Thenew's able to face the prospect of her final year because it would be followed by the glamor of finishing school in Switzerland, to which her mother had agreed.

"It's up and awa from your family for good, Dorcas. If I say aye to Le Manoix, it'll be the last slice at the tie that binds."

Dorcas did not answer. She did feel more at home with the Duke of Atholl's kin and their like. Although the Dougals had pots of money, they never did anything stylish with it. They hadn't given a hunt breakfast since Papá's death. Nor a garden party, when they could invite people like the Countess of Strathgryffe and the Honorable Margot, her own aunt. Dorcas had long since discarded her mother's fib that they had to make the farm pay. She was Dorcas Dougal, tea and cotton heiress, but who would believe it when all their riches went into cows? The girl never admitted to herself that her constant distemper at Glen Gryffe stemmed from the sins of the father. When she was away, she could accept her mother's tarrididdle about Daisy Grant running off with a commercial traveler, but at home her mind strayed to the bracken and stayed there.

Sensing this, Anna knew her eldest better off elsewhere. Dorcas was onion grass in the pasture, tainting the sweet milk of home.

"You can go," she had said, and had gone outside to sit with her youngest on the velvet lawn and make a daisy chain to drop over Morag's fair hair.

"Sandy, too," demanded her last-born.

"Flowers on a lad? Never." She held a buttercup to reflect yellow under his chin. "There you are, Morag. Wee Sandy loves butter, as if we didna ken."

Seeing them from her window, Cook squeezed lemons and strained the juice into three tumblers, vigorously stirred in sugar, and sent Mairi out with a tray of salty digestive biscuits and a siphon of soda. Anna let Morag push the lever, and the fizzy water splashed her silk frock, a small price to pay for the mischievous look that accompanied the mishap. Then Wattie arrived to take Sandy for his nap, and Anna, restored, went off to look for James Grant.

She found him in the orphanage byre, a lesson in progress for a clutch of ten-year-old girls to the *hiss-hiss* of the milk, the blurry Glasgow voices, and the deeper tones of the country. Instruction ended, the children went off with the pails, two to each handle, and with a glance and a smile at his vanishing pupils, Jamie came toward her.

"Overdoing it, are you no, Mr. Grant? Asking beef cattle to sustain their calves and also an orphanage?"

"Isn't that strange now? I had it in mind this very day to suggest two, three milkers. We're doing that well, I've more nor sufficient put by."

"It's a spendthrift I have for a partner. The farm's to be self-supporting. How much does a milker cost?"

"An Ayrshire would go for about the same as an Aberdeen Angus, give or take a bob."

"And you were planning to acquire how many of the latter? Ten?"

"Aye. But we could go seven and fill in with three Ayrshires. It would mean a bit extra labor. Milch cows have to be milked twice a day. I'd give their care as well as their output to the orphanage. That way they'd no mean extra work for us."

"Listen to the man. Advocating child labor."

"Three milkers would feed a ween o' bairns."

"Then three Ayrshires it is. You're gey persuasive, Mr. Grant."

"You're no sae bad yoursel. Glen Gryffe beef featured in the four best restaurants in Glasgow . . ."

"Did I no tell you? Five. The Automobile Club joined up the other day. The peripatetics who slice Glen Gryffe sirloin in that dining room will soon be crying our virtues aw ower Scotland."

"What about the rest of your grand idea to put oursels on the map?"

"We canna hurry nature, Mr. Grant. The new bulls are no old enough for show yet."

"Pride o' Fyvie'll soon be owerold. Look. I'll be at the West Highland as a buyer. It'd cost only a bawbee or two to be a shower as well."

Honor the brute that caused six orphans? "I dinna ken about that . . ." It would drive her mother down the hill. And the bairns? Bairns have short memories—the youngest anyway—and anything she did had the approval of Elspeth and Lachie; Dorcas might find out. "Could yon beast take a blue riband?"

"I'm sorry I brought it up," he said, seeing her swithering. "I'd no have you hurt for aw the blues in Scotland."

"I asked could he win?" His solicitude made her gruff.

"I couldna guarantee it, but I'd bet on it."

"Then you show him, Mr. Grant. But change his name to Pride o' Glen Gryffe." That would put the blinders on Dorcas.

"I doubt we can do that. He's registered in the studbook."

"You could put *né* Fyvie in the sma' print. There's little profit to us in giving an Aberdeen village a leg up."

He took his cap off to her and stood there in the sun, braw as any clan chief. "You said 'You show him.' I was hoping you'd come along yoursel, for you'd be grand publicity. There's no another lady cattle breeder in aw Scotland."

"Get along with you. Who would mind the farm?"

But the idea grew on her. The farm could run itself under Johnny Blackadder's eye. Why should cattle shows be all-male affairs? She was as capable as most men—aye, better than many. Look at the way she could handle the Argyll. She could probably drive it clear to Oban. There was a thought. Damn. You shouldna have had it, Anna Dougal. Now you'll no be able to live with yoursel for a coward if you dinna. I wonder how far it is? It wouldna commit me to telephone and find out.

Her club advised her that Oban was one hundred and ten miles from Strathgryffe via Glasgow. Or she could take the ferry from Gourock across the Clyde to Kilcreggan and go by the shores of the Gareloch and Loch Long, but they didn't advocate the latter route. Boarding and leaving the steamer by two narrow unsided planks was a dodgy business, a job for an expert. A low blow, that. Better to go the longer way through the city. If she would stop at the club, they would supply road maps and conditions and a last-minute check of her machine. They didn't try to dissuade her, which made the acceptance of her own dare mandatory.

Her children received her offhand announcement with open mouths.

"Like a nestful of throstles waiting for worms from the mamá bird," she said.

"You just gave them to us," said Lachie, for once disapproving. "A bait bucket full. You can't go gallivanting off to the Highlands by motorcar. Not without a man to look after you. It's—it's just not done."

"Mr. Grant could accompany Mamá," said Elspeth.

"And the bull could ride in the tonneau," said Anna. "Dinna be daft. It's the cattle train for Mr. Grant."

"What if you burst a tire?" said Elspeth.

"Have faith in the Ayrshire lad who invented the pneumatic. Jimmie Dunlop's rubber will no let me down. And if it does, I'll have a patch outfit and an air pump with me."

"You can't repair a puncture," said Hugh.

"Then I'll teach a shepherd or a crofter how to do it for me."

Lachie rose early the next morning to enlist Mr. Grant's support.

"If Mrs. Dougal's mind is made up, it's made up," he said. "You have a holy terror for a mother, Lachie. Be proud of her."

"I am, though at times she'd scare the trews off a Hielander."

While still hoping that male logic would prevail, Lachie and Hugh worked on the Argyll for three nights, changing the oil in the transmission and sump, packing grease into the nipples with the grease gun, cleaning and setting the gaps in the plugs. They reamed the jets of the brass lamps, filled their water tanks and acetylene containers. A garage in the Highlands being as rare as a white stag, in the tonneau they put two two-gallon cans of petrol, water for the radiator, and lubricating oil.

"We're a couple of bloody fools," said Lachie. "Now she'll go, and we'll have to stay home and worry."

"'They also serve who only stand and wait,'" said Hugh, newly introduced to Milton.

"That's a job for women!" shouted Lachie.

To avoid final argument, Anna had Pat Nolan spin the crank for her before Lachie woke. She took off in the last of the small hours, hood up, clouds down, trees a-drip, the windscreen in constant need of the hand-operated wiper, her spirits as high as the ceiling was low. "'By Loch Tummel and Loch Rannoch and Lochaber I will go,'" she sang, although she would travel south of that poetic route. "'By heather tracks with heaven in their wiles. If you're thinking in your inner heart 'tis braggart's in my step, you've never smelt the tangle of the Isles . . .'"

The clouds were scudding, the sun throwing glitter on the wet pavement when she pulled up at the club to find an early morning bon voyage committee awaiting her. The R.S.A.C. was anxious to promote touring, and a solo journey to the West Highlands by the daughter of a former Lord Provost, a Dougal by marriage, was news. To the nice laddie with the pencil and notebook she gave the purpose of her trip: "To buy the finest beef on the hoof. Mind you, spell the name right. Two effs in Glen Gryffe."

By ten o'clock she was avoiding the clutch of the tramway lines on Dumbarton Road, bowling along the north bank of the Clyde where the ships of war were rising on the ways to give the back of Britannia's hand to a fat-headed Kaiser who thought it his turn to rule the waves. Few of their leaders and none of the populace took the threat of war seriously, but Winston Churchill, First Lord of the Admiralty, was not a man to sit into a game with a weak hand. "Two keels for one," he had warned the German ruler, the slogan a grand assist to employment in the West of Scotland. Faster keels, too, as he pushed through oil-fired engines to replace the coal burners. The force of rearmament hit at every gap in the tenements that lay between Anna and the river, the clang of riveting smacking her left ear in one solid blow. She saw no ships except at Clydebank, where the jutting red-leaded bows in John Brown's yard soared above the blocks of workers' flats to take her eyes off the road. Modernity vanished in the narrow winding streets of Dumbarton, "the Fort of the Britons," sixth-century reminder of the time when the Angles, the Picts, the Scots, and the Britons themselves fought for control of Scotland.

Her journey really began when the Argyll's bonnet pointed north to the far-off Highlands, ticking off the miles carved into the whitewashed stone markers sunk low in the roadside. At Balloch she stopped for morning tea and hot buttered scones on a veranda overlooking the Leven, where fresh-water Loch Lomond started down to salt-water Clyde. Houseboats, lifeboats converted into cabin cruisers, punts, dinghies, and plain rowboats crowded the short river in a bank-to-bank maze that seemed certain to defeat the spawning-bound salmon, but never would. Most of the craft were home-built, result of the Scots craftsman's love of water and of money.

As she paid her thruppence plus a penny tip, Anna realized that she had left the Argyll pointing up a small rise. Damn! Now where to find a cranker? After a moment's thought she raised the bonnet and took her time about tickling the carburetor, pushing the needle valve once every few seconds until the required crowd of inquisitive boys had collected at her back. To the one with the broadest shoulders she said, "How do you like my engine?"

"No sae bad."

"Blasé, aren't you? Do you ken what I'm doing?"

"Flooding the carburetor, if you dinna stop."

"Is that a fact now?"

"Aye. Ah'd no let you do that tae ma motor. Ah'm going tae be a charrybang driver."

"Awa wi' you. You're no big enough. I'll bet you couldna even start this wee engine."

"How much?"

"A penny."

"You're on, Missus. Whaur's your shover?"

"Right here." Anna hopped in and slid under the wheel.

"Christ Awmighty," muttered the cranker. "A leddy driver. Ah weel, here goes." The Argyll fired on the second spin of the flywheel, and he came running around to her. "Gie's ma copper!" he cried over his friends' cheers.

"Here's a thrup'ny bit. See and no spend it aw in one shop. So long, lads."

"Ta-ta, leddy."

All the twenty-four miles of Loch Lomond she put one Scot's invention to another's; Jimmie Dunlop's tire to the hard surface named for Johnny McAdam, a black strip winding around the bays between green-clad braes and blue water. At the start she caught glimpses of an archipelago of wooded islands, some a mile or more in length with here and there the remains of castle or kirk. There was man-made loveliness, too, at the clachan of Luss, village and seat of the Colquhouns, where a single row of whitewashed stone cottages slept under a blanket of climbing roses, and collies dozed in warm dust at open front doors. The loch narrowed to a mile or less now, the road became the shore, and for seven miles it seemed she was in a boat afloat, Ben Reach two thousand feet high on her left, Ben Lomond a crouching mass above the east shore. Walter Scott country, that, across the loch; Rob Roy Macgregor and Bailie Nicol Jarvie and the Lady of the Lake. A steamer lay at Tarbet pier, filling the road with late-season trippers, low-class ones who stared rudely. At the bridge over the Inveruglas Water she stopped the Argyll's wheels for a flock of blackface sheep, their ammoniac reek clearing her nostrils as the foolish animals flowed around the machine, pushing, *meh-eh*ing, climbing up each other's backs, two collies urging them on with snarls at the heels of the hindmost. "Good day," said the shepherd, touching his crook to his cap as if he saw lady drivers all the time. No rude stares from a countryman. She unfolded the inch-to-the-mile ordinance map furnished by the club, and across the water identified Inversnaid, the mouth of the Snaid falling like a gray mare's tail over the cliff beside the inn. North of that she could see Rob Roy's Cove; opposite it, on her side, a wee island barely sufficient to support the remains of an ancient keep, a broch. Nearer still stood Wallace's Isle; Sir William Wallace, murdered in London in 1305 by Edward I, the Hammer of the Scots.

The map said the loch was six hundred feet deep here. Hold your eyes and your off-wheel on the road, wee Anna Dougal. At Ardlui, Lomond narrowed to the waters rushing down from Glen Falloch, and up beside it her wheels climbed. Near thundering falls too high for salmon to loup, she found a dip in the road going her way and stopped at the top of it to cool the motor and investigate the picnic presented to her by the club. Spreading a rug of MacDougall tartan on the heather, she opened the wicker basket to find half a juicy roast chicken, butter sandwiches, salad sand-

wiches—the tomato moistening the good bread to her taste
—two kinds of cheese, two kinds of biscuits, pound cake,
strawberries, and a wee tub of Devonshire cream. Did they
no believe she was going it alone? She made herself comfortable in hip-soft heather and began to eat, the dreamy hum of
a bee working the blossoms coming to ears now adjusted to
the water's roar, her eyes, too, feasting on the colors spread
before her; blue of sky, dancing rainbows in the falls, green
of moor and bracken, multi-pastels of granite, and everywhere a purple mist from the full-blooming heather. The
map told her she was three hundred feet above Loch Lomond, six miles from the south end of the Grampian Range;
almost four thousand feet high; Ben Lui to the west, where
she was bound, three thousand seven hundred and eight;
Ben Cruachan, to whose southern flank she must cling, only
nineteen feet less than that. "Courage, brother, do not stumble," and keep the throttle open.

She was sinking her teeth into a three-bite strawberry
when the hair at the nape of her neck told her she was not
alone. Slowly she turned and saw two brown shapes side by
side at the road's verge, shoulderless as standing stones in
layer upon layer of clothing that draped them from head to
ground. Tinkers, and she with a bulging purse. More cheer-
ily than she felt, she waved to them and called in her
broadest Doric, "Come awa ben and hae a bite. There's a
muckle left."

Not until they were beside her did she recognize one as a
skirted woman, the other a trousered man, their rags hiding
the movements of their legs, sacking wrapped and wrapped
again around their feet until they looked like elephants', the
male's face so hairy that only his nose was visible in the cave
of his coverings. He stooped, picked up all the remaining
food, and dropped it through his outer layer into some
hidden pocket.

The woman sank to the heather and held out a claw. "Cross
my loof with siller, pretty lady, and I'll tell your future."

"Och, I'd rather it surprised me." Cross this beggar's palm

with silver, and she might cross the pretty lady's neck with steel if she glimpsed how much was in the purse.

"A sixpennyworth to learn if you'll wed again," said the crone.

Not much of a guess, that. Almost any lady driving alone and wearing a wedding ring could be a widow.

The man picked up the plates and cutlery.

"None o' that!" Anna lunged forward, but the woman put a hand on her shoulder and pushed her back on the rug. I'll give them my purse, she thought. That's what they want, the thieving rascals. Then she laughed. The graybeard wasn't out to steal the club's silver and china. He was washing the utensils in the Falloch, scouring them with a handful of gravel taken from a wee pool.

"He wouldn't do that for me, his woman," said the crone, "but you gave us food. Few *Gaje* do."

"What are *Gaje?*"

"All who are not *Rom,* or as you call us, gypsies."

"How old is he?" asked Anna.

"Ninety-two, and I am ninety-one."

And I was feart for my life. What a gowk. Reassured, Anna rummaged through her handbag and took a sixpence from her purse. "Here's a tanner. I will have a wee keek at the future." She settled back comfortably. "It must be a gey heavy burden for you to look at your friends and ken what's going to happen in their lives . . ."

"The *Rom* do not tell fortunes within their *kumpania.* We use our gift to earn money from the *Gaje.*"

As Anna put out her hand to be read, the male gypsy walked away down the hill.

"He will wait for me at the caravan," said the woman. "He does not wish to hear your secrets."

"Would he understand? He hasna said a word. I thought —mibbie he doesna ken English."

"He does, but he will not speak it. As head of the *kumpania* he tries to set an example for the young. Although we are British gypsies, we must preserve the *Rom* tongue that is spoken by our people all over the world."

"But it's no wrong for you to speak English?"

"The women are the contact with the outsiders. You would not pay me six pennies for a prophecy in *Romani*."

"Let's have a go at it then."

The nonagenarian peered into the palm she held. "You will have a long life. That is certain and what most *Gaje* wish. Though why, I do not know, when they spend so much time in this world praying for admittance to the next."

"I'm no in a hurry mysel. I dinna fancy sitting on a wet cloud, and my harping's no what you'd caw concert quality."

"You must not joke unless you wish the telling to be a joke also. The thoughts must pass between *Gajo* and *Rom*."

"*Gajo?*"

"*Gajo* is one. *Gaje* is many or all. There are two men . . ."

Bargain rates, thought Anna, still amused. Two for a tanner. The gypsy looked up from the hand and peered into Anna's face, brown eyes searching. "One of these men is young, like yourself. You would give that long life for him, although the husband you do not mourn gave you no reason to seek another."

Anna looked into her own hand. "You can see aw that in my paw? It's no canny. This chap I'm for—does he fancy me?"

"I read your palm, not his. The second man you treat lightly. You use him without thought to his feelings."

Sweetie-wife McFadden? "And what are they?"

"That, too, I cannot see, but if he obeys your bidding, you must know the answer to your own question."

"If it's the chap I think it is, I doubt he has feelings."

"Those who show the least, often have the most. You would do well to remember that. You can be ruthless. When you have a goal, you go after it in a straight line. I would not wish to be the one who stands in your way."

"I'm getting a lot for my tanner. A character reading as well as my future."

"The one is the other." Again the gypsy bent her head. "I

see many children, how many I cannot say. The number changes . . ."

"You'd no be counting on me to drop another bairn?" said Anna. "I'm no so young as aw that."

The wise eyes looked into hers. "I do not know, but you will not always have the same family. One is a trial to you now, but that will change." She closed the hand and gave it a gentle squeeze. "No matter what happens, you will fight to be happy. You need no *Rom* to tell you that." She rose as easily as a girl. "Now I will join the *kumpania*."

"I must have passed it on the way up. I didna see you."

"*Rom* do not hide, nor do they flaunt their presence. The camp is in the wood of Glenfalloch Lodge. The laird is a kind *Gajo*. Like you." She reached into voluminous folds and produced a trinket basket, intricately woven. "This is for the food you gave my man."

"I canna take that."

"He would not wish to be beholden." She held out the basket. "Smell."

Anna did, and the fragrance of sweet grass filled her head.

"Do that if you would recall this meeting," said the gypsy woman. "When, in time, the scent appears to fade, a night in the dew will restore it."

The gypsy woman glided away, taking her spell with her. By the time Anna had all evidence of her stop stowed in the car, she had found a rational explanation for each fact "found" in her palm. Many widows had no love for their deceased, and all would like to have a Jamie tucked away in their thoughts. As for the bairns, numbers could trip the best of spey wives, and this one had been canny about the size of the Dougal family.

She climbed behind the wheel and picked up the sweet-grass basket. Worth more nor a tanner, it was, even if the hand reading hadn't been. She'd banged a sixpence for less many a time. Fingers skilled by heredity had wound the natural and green-dyed stalks into a bonny pattern. It would look fine on her dressing table holding a thimble and a wee pincushion. She opened the lid and smelled again. Then she let in the clutch. The Argyll gave one convulsive leap and stopped dead, trapped in the dip.

"Damn and hell and bloody!" Her known swears went winging across the heather, and like grouse disturbed, one, two, three brown heads popped up on the left, one two three on the right. "Spying on me, is it?" she shouted. "Stand up and let's see the size of you!" On bare feet the gypsy children ran to the motorcar and stood staring, solemn, silent. "Welcome to wee Anna's folly," she said. "If you were bigger, you could dig me out of this hole I'm in, but I doubt all six of you could shove me back up the brae for another go at it."

The mites looked at one another, then four sprang to the bonnet, two grabbed the wooden spokes of the front wheels, and pushing and turning they inched the Argyll back up the incline.

"Easy, now! No over the knoll, or you'll have me skiting back down into Loch Lomond."

Forward again, the boys giving an added push from the rear, and the motor fired. Letting it warm up in neutral, she handed the biggest child a shilling.

"Tuppence each, and if your *kumpania* is ever down Renfrew way, tell your chief this *Gajo* says he can set up camp at Glen Gryffe and welcome any time. That's Glen Gryffe with two effs. Up the *Rom!*"

In second gear the Argyll climbed to six hundred feet, and the rushing burn left her for its source high on Beinn a' Chroinn. A mile more, and she trundled through the only street of Crianlarich, where the shootin'-huntin'-fishin' crowd outside the inn God-bless-my-soul-ed her as she drove by to Strathfillan, a valley running almost flat for a while. Beyond St. Fillan's Chapel, up it went again, corkscrewing like a tramcar's staircase. Cutting one righthand bend too fine, she stamped on the brake just before her rear wheel left the road. "Close," she muttered, looking straight down to the boulder-strewn river two hundred feet below. Gingerly she backed from the corner and had another go at it, swinging wide from the precipice. Too wide. She reversed again, and on the third attempt turned the corner. Well done! But she had to pull up once more to give her kneecaps a minute to stop their uncontrollable jumping. At the tiny clachan of Tyndrum cupped in a glen a thousand feet up, tarmacadam disappeared as she swung west for Dalmally along a cart track, two ruts dissolving in clouds right down on the moor. Miles and miles of damn-all, not another clachan or even a shepherd's wee house on the map. Dinna let me down, Jimmie Dunlop, for my heart's no in the Highlands at the moment. It's like to fall out of my mouth. The next five miles took thirty minutes, her vision limited to a fifty-foot arc, the River Lochy unseen and roaring in spate on her left, the Argyll eerily pushing the mist ahead of itself, the day ripe for the Wee People to be out looking for a hostage. Through the gray cover loomed not a tiny sprite but a big reality, short, red, and hairy, and with a six-foot horn-spread to bar her way. Whether Highland cow or bull she could not tell for the beast's shagginess. If it were the bull turned loose to serve the cows at will . . . Waving an arm from her door she shouted, "Gang way, you ugly menace!" and the animal lowered its head in threat. "Ignorant brute doesna have the English." She remembered Mairi's Gaelic when the cattle threatened the kitchen garden. "*Erichay! Macasho!*" she yelled, not knowing what either command meant, but the Highland bull did, for he tossed his head, spun around, and trotted down the brae, the Argyll not a wheel's turn behind. A quarter-mile of this bovine pace and her hand went to the klaxon. It's no unlike his mating call, she thought. The cows may come panting, but—here goes! *Ah-oo-ah-ah-oo-ah!* The bull took a galvanized leap across the narrow ditch and vanished into the mirk. "'Toreador, now guard thee . . .'" sang Mrs. Dougal happily.

Three miles and a sharp bend aimed her at the roaring Lochy. If she had to ford the burn, she was done. Hosanna! There was a stone bridge, wide enough and no more. The Argyll charged up its hump almost into the chest and forelegs of a horse that pawed the air in fright, bringing a barrage of oaths from his unseen master. Quickly Anna half covered her ears and bowed her head demurely.

"Motor-effing-cars should effing well be kept . . ." The profane one's voice died away as he came in sight. "A—a leddy," he groaned and swept off his hat to femininity affronted. Red-faced, he backed his quivering charge to a passing place, and Anna took advantage of his shame to have him top up her petrol tank.

"They cans are gey heavy, "she said.

On now, wheels in the ruts, the grass in the middle seeming to tickle her through the chassis, a daft but uncomfortable notion relieved by the return of tarmacadam for the drop out of the clouds to Dalmally, a douce whitewashed wee bit of a village. She swept through it and on to the shores of Loch Awe, where a promontory jabbed into the water like a green thumb to uphold the ruins of Kilchurn Castle. "Thy hour of rest has come and thou art silent in thy age," Wordsworth had sung of the ancient keep. It hadn't been quiet when it was the seat of the grasping Campbells, hereditary foes of the MacDougalls and most other Highlanders. John Dougal had deived her with "From the greed of the Campbells, O God deliver us," an anguished plea of his forebears slaughtered by the unholy clan in the Pass of Brander. The road now took her there, and a fearsome narrow strip it was, the rushing River Awe on one hand, the unclimbable three-thousand-foot cliff of Ben Cruachan on the other. A place of ghosts. Nowhere to run. no place to hide, no recourse but to fight and scream the MacDougall war cry, *"Buaidh no Bas!"*—"Victory or Death!" —and be dealt the latter to a man. From the carnage the Campbells took their battle slogan, *"Cruachan!"* and the first step toward the fame and fortune still possessed six centuries later by the clan chief, His Grace the Duke of Argyll. John cursed all Campbells to his dying day.

Once out of the spectral pass, she stopped at Connel Ferry to view the salt-water Falls of Lora. On a twelve-foot coming tide the Atlantic swept in from the Firth of Lorne, running uphill over the ridge of rock at the mouth of Loch Etive, reversing the falls in the twice-daily surge to fill that arm of the sea. She watched a while, then drove on for a look at Dunstaffnage Castle, built on the site of the royal palace of Dalriada. This was MacDougall country, and she had been filled with its history.

Three miles more, one more stey brae, then over the hill . . . Done it! Below her wheels lay Oban, Charing Cross of the Highlands, Gateway to the Hebrides, the Isles on the Edge of the Sea. Ten hours from Glasgow. Almost ten miles per hour. And if she hadn't dallied along the way, she could have cut her time to eight. What do you think of that, Lachlan Dougal? Three cheers for the Argyll! And Jimmie Dunlop! And Johnny McAdam! And a tiger for wee Anna Dougal!

Her stops had brought her to Oban at the jewel moment when the setting sun throws emeralds, rubies, sapphires, gold-engarnished, over sea and crescent bay, islands, and the night clouds rising. On her left, the soaring columns of an unfinished coliseum stood stark in white and black with long, blacker shadows. "McCaig's Folly" folk called it, although the good man had beggared himself to provide a living for out-of-work stonemasons caught in the local slump of the 'nineties. Three steamers with the black-and-red funnels of the MacBrayne Line churned across the rays as they smoked into the piers from the Sound of Kerrera. "The earth is the Lord's and all it contains—except the West Highlands. They belong to MacBrayne's," said the monopolized natives. The Isle of Kerrera, due west, looked only a hop, step, and a jump away. The Lord of Lorne had granted twenty-nine merklands there to Alan MacDougall in 1457.

The red ball was going faster now to make a triangular silhouette of the Isle of Mull's Ben More. Then the sun dropped from sight, leaving behind upward beams to touch silver and gold to the under side of the clouds. Get a wiggle on, wee Anna Dougal, before the gloaming goes. You couldna light they acetylene lamps if you tried.

On the Esplanade she picked the Grand Marine Hotel because she liked the sound of the name, requesting a bedroom and sitting room from the elderly frock-coated gentleman behind the desk.

"The dining room closes in half an hour, Mrs. Dougal," he said. "I'd give my hands a wee wash and nip in there while they'll still serve you."

"Point me at it then, laddie, for I'm fair famished."

She ordered native oysters and followed the tasty appetizer with a clear turtle soup. Then came a center cut of native salmon, poached and served with salad cream, boiled potato, and peas. For entree, lamb chops well-done and French beans with a dab of mashed potatoes. "I'll skip the sweet," she told the waiter. "A wee savory will do fine." The bacon-wrapped prunes on toast fair hit the spot.

Her sitting room overlooking the Sound was light, high-ceilinged, and airy. She poured two fingers of whisky from a silver mutchkin, added a drop of water from the carafe in the bedroom, and sat in the bay of open windows, feet inelegantly on the sill, pleased with herself beyond measure. From the Esplanade rose the voices of the evening strollers and the quiet *roosh-woosh* of the wavelets on the pebble beach. The mountains of Mull were black against the deep blue of the star-studded western sky, and Kerrera only a lighter shape fading into the bigger land mass behind it. *Why did you never bring me here to the land of your sainted ancestors? I'd have been able to thole your pride in them better, then. But you'd have called that sentiment, and you were aye afraid of that. You were a plain bloody fool, John, and I'm no going to think about you any damn more.*

Morning tea and biscuits in bed, looking out on the busy harbor where the laden fishing smacks returning low in the water put her in the mood for a brace of fresh herring rolled in oatmeal and fried in their own fat, with a hot chewy roll, plenty of butter, and lashings more tea. And another roll for the tart Dundee marmalade. It was fair sickening that what she consumed did nothing for the figure taunting her from a shamelessly large mirror in the capacious tiled bathroom. Hollow hips, flat abdomen, and a bosom like two halves of one tennis ball. If you were built like Harriet, you wouldna mind seeing. Harriet's an armful, but you're no even a handful. She climbed into the tub in the center of the room. A girl could learn to swim, it was that big. She put her feet against the square end, shoved, slid up the back of the tub—and there were those dratted apologies for a bosom winking at her again. Gratefully she donned her concealing robe of flannel and unlocked the door to the corridor to find a gentleman holding the outside handle, he also in dressing gown, towel around his neck, toilet bag in hand, obviously bound for the same tub. "Oh, wash me in the water that you wash your dirty daughter in, and I shall be whiter than the whitewash on the wall." The old music-hall ditty sprang into her head.

"A dozen hotels in Oban, and we pick the same one," said James Grant. "You'll no have had breakfast?"

"Och, I had a wee tray in bed, but mibbie I could manage a herring to keep you company."

"Then you'll give me half an hour?" Away from the home ground he had a courtly dominance that nearly set her kneecaps off again.

"Good morning, Mrs. Dougal," said the tail-coated steward in the vast dining room. "Congratulations on your run from Glasgow." He pushed in her chair and brought her the *Daily Record*, fresh off the night train. There she was at the wheel of the Argyll, eyes closed, mouth open, a cod on ice. Drat that magnesium flare.

"It doesna do you justice," said Jamie. "But then no camera could."

And away went the kneecaps for fair.

"She's the mother of my nieces and nephews!" Philip Dougal waved the *Record*. "She's my sons' aunt! She's a disgrace to the name . . ."

"Which she has by marriage only," said his wife. "Why do you take that rag? It upsets your breakfast every morning."

"The *Herald* gives only our view of the world. I have to be *au courant* with other thinking, wrong though it may be. That my brother's widow should seek such cheap publicity . . . ."

"If it sells her beef, it might sell your tea. Look at Thomas Lipton."

"Please do not couple that guttersnipe's name with mine."

"Philip, you're positively frothing."

"Nothing of the kind. But if I am, it is for good reason. 'To buy the best beef on the hoof for Glen Gryffe.' 'Indomitable woman cattle breeder.' The rag dares to call her 'woman.' "

"But an indomitable one, Philip. I would be happy to have that description applied to me, for I admire spunk over any other attribute, be it in man or woman."

"GOOD morning, Mrs. Dougal." He left for the office in a sullen huff, a sunny mood compared to that occasioned by additional newspaper photographs five days later. There was one in the *Glasgow Herald* of James Grant, Esquire—*Esquire!*—Mrs. Anna Dougal, and the kilted Marquis of Lorne, Chief of Clan MacDougall, all smiling at a black head with a riband above its eyes. *Renfrewshire Bull Wins West Highland* said the discreet headline. No mention of Dougal & Company. Sound paper. Apprehensively he turned to the *Record* and was greeted by a half-page side view of Pride o' Glen Gryffe that exposed the bull's *raisons d'être*. Disgusting. The three other principals stood behind the animal. There was even an insert photo in the upper left corner of Anna Dougal—no Mrs.—simpering like a farm wench. With mounting distaste he read the lengthy account; daughter of Sir George Biggart; widow of John Dougal, late of Dougal & Company, East India Merchants; mother of six; intrepid motorist. The reporter, a stanch believer in Rights for Women, placed Philip Dougal's in-law somewhere between Grace Darling and Mrs. Sylvia Pankhurst. His day ruined, the merchant prince left for the office before his wife came down, taking the *Record* with him. Such a display of animal *genitalia* was not for her eyes. Moreover, she might applaud their sister-in-law's success.

Everybody in Oban did, the Highlanders and Islanders who had brought their own best to the show showering Anna with shy sincere praise. It had been a grand holiday, although she had not seen enough of Jamie, whose working hours had been taken up with inspecting and buying for the farm, his off-time spent with old cronies seldom met. She went with him to the show the first day, but after an hour of it realized that her presence inhibited him and the other men to a point of near strangulation as they fought to keep their talk suitable for her ears.

So while he was about man's business, she took to the shops, each of them a treat in itself. They had their winter clothes in now, with winter prices, and grand bargains in what was left of the summer stock. She bought skein after skein of yarn, the muted heathery tones no softer than the handle of the lanolin-rich fibers. She ordered bolts of Harris tweed sent to John Ross, the Glasgow tailor. Men were so much better than dressmakers for suits and coats. Garnet and cairngorm brooches in silver filigree for her daughters, Wattie, Harriet and Kitty Boyd. For Lachlan, Hugh, and Willie Boyd, each a *sgian dhub,* the black dirk of the Highlander, razor sharp, with handle of deer horn; they'd have to give her a penny apiece lest blade cut friendship. Wee Sandy's souvenir of Oban was a tin box of Edinburgh rock, hard peppermint sticks that would keep him going for a month of treats, the container itself a fine safe for future treasures with its bright-colored picture of the ruins of Dunollie, another MacDougall castle, high on the north horn of Oban Bay. It was gey hard not to think about John when evidence of his line was all around her; impossible when she was presented the silver tassie by the Marquis of Lorne, the MacDougall of MacDougall himself. What if he kenned that the black head of the winner had dunted the life out of a clansman? A wee shiver ran up her back as she accepted his praise, delivered in the accent-free speech of the well-bred Highlander educated in England. Jamie noticed her involuntary shudder.

"I shouldna have talked you into it," he said, even as he smiled and touched his deerstalker to the crowd.

"Och, t' hell with the animal," she said. "I'm for kicking up my heels the night."

"You're on. I'll be waiting for you in the lobby at seven-thirty."

Back to the shops for a floor-length kilt of Dress Stewart, the royal tartan favored by Queen Victoria. Any Scot could wear the regal sett, and not tonight would she appear as a Dougal. To top it she selected a white silk blouse with long sleeves and a flouncy front of lace, and for the sea breeze, a cloak of red velvet, the whole a compromise to go with whatever Jamie wore. She doubted full fig.

When she came down the wide shallow stairs, to her delight she found him in Highland evening dress—kilt and hose of the Grant tartan, velvet doublet, white jabot and foamy cuffs, silver buckle to the broad leather belt, sealskin sporran, dirk down his right stocking.

"You should aye put on the kilt, Mr. Grant."

"I do when the occasion caws for it. This is the first time in years that I've felt it right to wear what was my grandfather's. We're for the Great Western, Mrs. Dougal. We canna have you falling into the rut of the Grand Marine every night. I'll hail a brougham."

"Can we no walk? It canna be far."

Orange-and-lemon sunset over Mull under a mackerel sky, a soft breeze fragrant of the sea on her cheek, a muscled forearm under her hand, tide quiet against the shore, and the gulls *ky-iy*ing. Too soon they were in the wicker chairs of the Great Western's lounge, dry sherry in hand.

Afterwards she was not to remember much of the seven-course dinner. There was turbot and a Liebfraumilch, a Cabernet with the smoked tongue, and Mumm's '02 with the *coupe marron glacé—*

"To Glen Gryffe." He raised the celebration wine.

"To you, Mr. Grant."

"To you, Mrs. Dougal."

Coffee was served in the lounge where a gentleman could smoke if he wished; expensive cigars only, chosen by hallowed ritual. The picking of the brand from the boxes held out by the waiter, the sniffing, the rolling between fingers close to the ear to detect and reject dryness of leaf, the final selection; the removal of the band and the piercing of the end by the serious servant, the wooden match held the proper distance from the weed as Jamie drew gently to light it.

"A fine Corona." He nodded approval.

A lady liked her host to smoke a cigar, mark of a gentleman if done with grace. Jamie held his between his fingers, not in his teeth as John Dougal had, cabbaging the end in no time—drat it, I swore no to think of John again.

"Good evening, Mr. Grant. I hope I'm not late."

Jamie stood. "Good evening to you. Mrs. Dougal, may I present Mr. Sutliff, from the States."

"Kaintucky, ma'am. Lexington, to be exact. Bluegrass country."

"Blue grass?" She managed to smile and ask the interloper to sit.

"That's right, ma'am. Blue. Although disbelievers say you have to drink a quart of bourbon, then fall down and squint at the setting sun through the blades of grass before you see their true blue. Horse-raising country, ma'am. And cattle."

"Mr. Sutliff has what he caws a proposition," said Jamie.

"Re-ally? Would you care for coffee, Mr. Sutliff?" said Mrs. Dougal.

"Never touch the stuff. In the U.K., that is. Never touch tea in the U.S., so we're even, a loser apiece."

"A whisky perhaps?" asked Jamie.

"Don't tell me there's bourbon in Obán." He accented the second syllable. "Oh, of course you mean Scotch. Reckon I'll have a snifter of brandy instead. Now, ma'am. Has Mr. Grant told you my proposition?" Sutliff leaned forward. "I'm willing to give you a fat price for Pride o' Glen Gryffe. I've got the beginnings of a herd of Aberdeen Angus back home. Your beast would put the seal of champions on it. Six years old, isn't he? Good for another five, maybe six, at stud."

"You don't look like a farmer to me," said Anna.

"No, ma'am. I'm a whisky distiller. 'Old Sutliff.' Biggest seller in America. My thousand acres of bluegrass are just a toy. Building me a racing stable, too. So, wanting nothing but the best, I came to Scotland for cattle and England for horses. You know, I never realized that the Scotch were different from the English. I thought you were all British—"

"All *Scots* are British, but not all British are Scots."

"More's the pity. Say, did you know there's a monument in Edinburgh—on Prince's Street—to the Scotch who fell on our side in the American Revolution?"

"Your war of independence came only thirty years after the English cut us up at Culloden," said Anna. "Your ranks were full of Scots out for another bash at England, the Auld Enemy."

"I should have known that, Mrs. Dougal. I had a Scotch grandpappy. Name of Campbell."

From the greed of the Campbells—"What is a fat price, Mr. Sutliff?"

"You mentioned it to me," said Jamie. "You wouldna be swithering, would you?"

"I never vacillate," said the American. "But I thought—with a lady present—you people didn't discuss money."

"When it's business," she said, "you can ignore my garb."

"Not easy, ma'am, when you're attired in such handsome kilts."

"I'm wearing only one."

"I stand corrected." He turned to Jamie. "How are they—is it to wear in winter?"

" 'He who'd be cold with the kilt would be kilt with the

cold,' " said Jamie. "There's eight yards of sound Scots wool around my waist. And what was the wee figure you had in mind?"

"Twenty thousand dollars. At the present rate of exchange, that's four thousand quid, as you say. Why do you call a pound a quid? In America a quid is a chew of tobacco . . ."

Four times what John had paid for the bull. But from a thieving Campbell? "He's not for sale," she said.

"Mr. Sutliff," said Jamie. "Would you mind giving me a wee minute alone with my partner?"

"Course not. I'll go to the door and have a breathe of sea air. Wish we had that in Kaintuck. I could make a fortune if I could only get it over there."

"If he could suck as hard as he can blow, he'd have no bother," said Anna when he had moved away.

Jamie covered her hand with his, a touch to melt her. "I'll no have you shiver again because of yon murdering brute. As soon as the American approached me after the prizewinning, I bought not one but two registered bulls to take Pride's place, for he's a goner. If you'll no sell, I'll gang back to the showgrounds this very night, take him out behind his stall, and shoot him."

There spoke no partner. Eyes down, she said, "When you talk like that, I canna argy-bargy."

"I'll bring the American back, then."

"Yes, sir," said Sutliff. "If I could bottle that air, I'd clean up in the States. Well, ma'am, now you've had a chance to chew on my offer, what do you say? Four thousand quid."

"Guineas," said Anna, adding five per cent for his tainted bloodlines.

"Great!" said Sutliff. "A heap more impressive for the newspapers. They'll really play that up. Four thousand guineas. Tony. Just like the horse sales at Tattersall's." He pulled a small pad from his pocket. "I'll give you a note confirming . . ."

"No need," said Jamie. "We have a gentlemen's agreement."

"There's no such thing, Scotty." Sutliff began to write. "I learned that from my granddaddy." He handed over the note, made his farewell, then he was gone at last.

"It's Campbells we are," said Anna. "Four thousand guineas!"

"I wouldna let that fash me. He told me to check his credit with the Bank of Scotland. Their agent says he's a multimillionaire."

"But four thousand—his wife'll have his head on a platter."

The night clouds had rolled in by the time they walked down the steps of the hotel. A steamer—it could only be a MacBrayne—came around the north end of Kerrera, bow wave ablaze in the beams of her portholes. Close to, a ketch rode at anchor, her stem almost on shore, the soft glow of her saloon a world apart for a man and woman to open their hearts, with only the gulls for witness. Slack water, the healthy iodine of seaweed, a cool hand of breeze on her cheek, color muted to violet, they strolled along the Esplanade to the wooden acre of pier where the gaslight dropped gold on dew-wet deck and into the moats between the fishing smacks. Hushed by the night, another MacBrayne steamer embarked passengers for the Outer Hebrides.

"Lewis and Harris"—he read the destination board—"North Uist, Benbecula, South Uist, Barra. Nothing west of them but St. Kilda and Tir-nan-Og, Isle of the Ever Young. Where the sun shines aw day, rain faws only at night, and seas are aye sma. On Tir-nan-Og flowers bloom aw year, barley and oats grow themsels, fish swim ashore—" He laughed. "And James Grant would die of boredom. She'll sail past the Inner Hebrides first—Islay and Jura, Colonsay, Oronsay, Tiree, Coll, Mull. And Skye."

Where Peggy bided her time. Anna saw the window opening quiet in the night . . .

"Come," he said. "I'll take you home now."

The Grand Marine lobby still as still, the wide quiet stairs to the first floor and the long corridor dimlit to her door, and it opening silent as dust falling. She turned to him, he bent forward. And kissed her hand. Her hand! Here she was, ready to loup over the moon, and he kissed her hand . . .

Around the empty sitting room she stalked in a mood black as the Earl o' Hell's waistcoat. "I could not love thee, dear, so much, Lov'd I not honor more." Och, t' hell. And damn. Honor was a tepid water bottle for the feet. She flung off the royal tartan, hauled her night things out of the wardrobe, and marched down to the bathroom to mortify the flesh. As the cold tap gushed, the half-a-sixpence figure jumped back at her. Some *femme fatale*. She was that scrawny, she didna belong in the gender at aw.

After the icy plunge—hold the breath, count to five, then quick out, like a seal—she gave herself a brisk toweling. I need a wee taet, even if it shouldna go on top of champagne. My self-esteem's had a sore dunt the night. Aw the wrong folk see me enticing. My poor auld papá, nasty-minded Philip, Daisy the Bizzem, Harriet—aw sure I'll be wronged. I'd no be wronged, I'd be righted. I dinna doubt half the village believes that the Widow Dougal and Jamie Grant are at the hugmagandy . . .

The corridor was straight. Her feet sped along it, past her door to his, to crack it on a room pitch-dark. With her fingernail she scratched the wood. "Yoohoo," she whispered. "It's only me. Wee Anna Biggart."

Chapter Seven

ANNA DID NOT BECOME Mrs. Dougal again until Loch Lomond was by and sight of the Clyde reminded her that once across it she was the sole parent of six. And a better, now that she understood what her bairns must find out or have only half a life—a quarter—no life at all. Now she knew the secret of Harriet's smile to Robert, why his in return was a benediction. No need to envy her auld china any more. Wee Anna's bottle was full and running over. All the way across the mountains unseen pipers had blown a Highland fling for her who at last had discovered what the fuss was about. "Horo, my nut-brown maiden" they played for a maiden no more, but a woman fulfilled by a man in whom she had lost herself for her own sake first and then, in the gentling dark, for his.

There had been no sadness. None at all. Instead, laughter suppressed—giggles from her and deep chuckles from him. "H.M.S. *Indomitable* is right," and she whispering back in his ear, "Welcome on board." To that and other brazen memories she slapped the klaxon, and *ah-oo-ah!* roared over the heather to send the grouse a-whirr.

And no shame. Just gratitude to be passed back and forth until it melded into one thankfulness.

"I still canna believe, Anna. It couldna be the champagne?"

"It helped. Scrawny wee me . . ."

"None of that, now. You're no to miscall the bonny armful you are."

"Dinna fib, Jamie. Och, yes. Do."

"No lie. You're as young in body as you are in spirit."

"And you love me as I love you? You couldna."

"How can you doubt it?"

"It's five minutes since you kissed me."

The muted clatter of the tea trolleys in the hall roused her from a doze.

"My God," she muttered, scurrying. "I'll be caught *in flagrante delicto*." She cracked the door, keeked out on the momentarily empty corridor, and sped across into her own bed just in time.

"Six o'clock," said the maid, putting the tray in her lap. "You wantit up early the day. You'll pe leaving, Mrs. Dougal?"

"Aye, worse luck. Do you happen to ken if Mr. Grant left a call?"

"Och, yess. For eight o'clock. Gentlemen is sleepyheads."

She was packed and gone by seven-thirty on the long journey that seemed half as far going home. There wee Anna Biggart left the Argyll in the barn, and Mrs. Anna Dougal crossed the courtyard without a glance at his farm. "Yoohoo," she called. "It's only me, your wee mamá," and the bairns, waving, ran past her to hoist the Union Jack, telling Strathgryffe that she was once more in residence.

Chapter Eight

"H IT HIM with aw you have, Hughie," said Mr. Grant. "Right in the bread basket. Again. Put some beef in it, laddie. Where's your muscle?" Hugh bent his elbow, clenched his fist, and offered his biceps to the touch.

"I've seen a bigger knot on a flea's leg," said Lachlan.

"It's no sae bad. But you're not using it, Hughie," said the instructor. "On your toes now, left foot toward Lachie, left arm out and your chin into your left shoulder, right hand a wee forward of your solar plexus to protect it. Now a straight left."

"Straight, kid," said Lachie, easily blocking the punch.

"Now a right cross, Hughie. Put your shoulder behind it. That's better. And dinna stand still, Hughie. Move your feet. Keep jeuking."

The boxing lessons were Anna's idea. "I'll have men for sons," she had told her partner. "There's owermuch feminine guidance around here."

"I've noticed its effects on mysel, Mrs. Dougal."

"Do you have to call me that the now?"

"Och, it's such a tasty part of a grand secret."

"Which'll no be one long if you dinna take your tongue out of your cheek." Later: "The girls, too, could do with a wee dose of male discipline."

"Is it a stepfather you'd make me into the bargain, Mrs. Dougal?"

"Sh-sh, man." Then: "Och, t' hell with my bairns."

"You have progeny, Anna Biggart? It's no possible, and you that young."

He anticipated no difficulty with the boys and found none when he offered the rudiments of self-defense in return for keeping one byre clean to his strict standards.

"Fair's fair," said Lachie. "Boxing lessons in return for pitching in with the work."

"Pitching out, you mean," said Hughie. "Bet I can pile dung higher'n you can, Lachie."

The girls were different. Morag was young enough to accept discipline, but Elspeth was at an age when she might resent the authority of one who had no right to it, so Jamie decided to caw canny until given an opening.

It came one day when Elspeth and Bella Cockburn galloped home after hacking over the moors. Turning for the stables, although they knew better, they inconsiderately let the mares have their heads. Whooping "Tally ho!" and pigtails streaming, they hammered across the dry ground and pulled up in the courtyard with the horses foam-slathered and blowing.

"Think shame of yoursels!" said Mr. Grant. "Misusing beasts like that!" It wasn't only the animals. Either girl could have taken a toss; the moor near the stable was one big rabbit warren. "Dismount and offsaddle. Then dry and walk the mares in the paddock till I cry halt. Under blankets, mind."

"Ow, my feet," moaned Bella after twenty minutes of marching in skin-tight leather.

"Mine, too," said Elspeth. "Serves us right."

"My socks feel wet. D' you suppose it's blood?" She straightened up. "Here comes Lachie."

"Enough, no more, says Mr. Grant." He leaned over the fence.

"Will you help me off with my boots?" said Bella.

"When you've curried your mount. You're to do that every time you ride. You, too, Elspeth. There's more to nags than sticking on their backs at full gallop. Women!"

In the inglenook before the fire lit against the creeping chill of foggy November, he straddled Bella's right leg, back toward her, then took hold of the boot heel and pulled while she applied leverage against his buttocks with her other foot.

"I'm for handmade boots," he grunted, "but this is fair ridiculous. How did you ever get them on?"

"I—used—powdered chalk. Ow, thank goodness!" Bella wiggled her freed toes and looked in vain for blood. "Do one of Elspeth's next, Lachie. I'm puffed out."

The joy of fatigue after exercise, lamb's-wool slippers soothing feet held toward the fire, and Mairi arriving with the tea tray . . .

"The milk she is for Miss Morag and Master Hugh."

"I'm fair sick of the stuff," said Hugh. "I'll not drink it."

"Then you'll not be wanting the gingerbread either, and it fresh."

"Och, come on, Mairi. Can't I have content?"

"May I give him a drop?" said Elspeth.

"I brought an extra cup." Mairi left smiling, the onus taken from her.

Elspeth poured the milk, added a splash of the adult tea, two spoons of sugar, and handed the pale concoction to her brother. "Now are you content?"

"I want content, too," said Morag.

"You're too young."

Down the stairs, holding onto the rails, came Sandy, crowing, "Keecook-eecook-eecook. I want an eecook."

"Isn't he over that baby talk yet?" said Bella. "It's cookie, daftie. Where's Miss Watson?"

"Wattie's playing a game." The four-year-old eyed the

tray. "She lies on the floor. I wake her up. I want a German biscuit."

"Say 'please.' That sounds like a funny game."

"Please. I don't like it. I pushed and pushed, but she wouldn't move."

In the silence a lump of coal fell loud against the bars of the grate.

"I think I'll run up and see what's keeping her," said Lachie in a strained voice.

"I'll go," said Elspeth.

"Stay where you are."

Up the steps three at a time and down the hall to knock at the nursery. Wattie would shoot him if he didn't. No reply. Slowly he pushed the door and saw her on the floor, knees up as if she had been at prayer and fallen sideways. Lifting her—she weighed nothing—he carried her to the chaise longue where she liked to sit and read to Sandy. Then he left her, and went slowly along the hall and down the stairs to his brothers and sisters and Bella, all standing, all looking up at him.

"Hugh," he said, "find Mr. Grant. Morag, please take Sandy to the kitchen and stay there. Bella, I think you'd better go home. Elspeth, ring up Dr. Curle and say we need him right away."

"I'm going up," said Elspeth.

She tried to run past him, but he grabbed her arm, and her face crumpled toward tears.

"Stop that. Remember the kids," he whispered, then raised his voice. "All right, Morag and Sandy. Kitchen. And please ask Cookie to come here a minute. Hugh, cut after Mr. Grant."

Head down to hide her face, Elspeth went to the telephone, Hugh shot out the front door, Morag led Sandy away.

"Do I have to go, Lachie?" Bella laid a hand like a bird's wing on his arm. "I was staying the night anyway."

"It won't be any fun, Bella."

"Wattie's dead, isn't she?"

"Yes."

"There's Sandy and Morag to look after. I could help Elspeth with them."

"All right. But you're not to go near the—nursery, mind. Your mother wouldn't like it."

"I promise. What time is yours coming home?"

"She's staying in town overnight. At the Central."

"Shouldn't you try to reach her?"

"No. She's going to the theater. The last train will be gone when the show's over." Wattie wouldn't want him to spoil his mother's treat. She was always urging her to go out more.

"Heart," said Dr. Curle when he came back down. "I've been treating her for years. On the q.t. She didn't want a soul to know, though how she hid it . . . A brave woman, Lachie."

As the doctor left, Morton the Joiner arrived with his helper and a plain wooden casket. "I'll tak it back tae ma shop," said Morton. "It's no fitting tae leave a corpus in a housefu' o' bairns."

"We're the only family Miss Watson has," said Lachlan. "She stays here."

"Lachie, why no let her lie at the farmhouse?" said Mr. Grant. "That's a part of Glen Gryffe, too, and I'll be there. You'd no be turning her out."

He watched the boy struggle with the nicety of honor.

"I suppose that would be correct, Mr. Grant. In a way you're as much a part of the family as she—as Miss Watson was."

"They'll bring her down right away—" Meaningly, Jamie jerked his head away from the stairs. "Do you no think . . . ?"

Lachie nodded and ushered them all into the dining room. Despite the heavy oak of the closed doors, he heard a hollow bump, saw Elspeth start and at the shake of his head give him a faint wet smile in return. The clipclop of slow hooves died away down the drive.

Now that the coping was past, boy needed man. "I know it's awful late for dinner, Mr. Grant," said Lachie, "but will you stay?"

"Please," said Elspeth. "Mamá would want you to."

Would she? He had no way of knowing, but could not refuse the appeal from her bairns.

"I'd be honored," said Jamie, and pulled out a chair for Elspeth.

It wasn't easy to break news of death to a mother full of the antics of Charley's Aunt *from Brazil, where the nuts come from.* "And what a nut, Lachie, wearing folderol that got the go-by when the steam engine came in, yanking up skirts to get at a trouser pocket, lighting a cigar . . . No matter how often I see yon farce—and I ken aw the lines—I still hold my sides." With a sigh for the fun, she remembered the Sabbath. "I trust you didna take advantage of my absence and dog the kirk the day?"

"All of us went, Mother."

"All of you? No wee Sandy?"

"Wee Sandy, too."

"Och, Lachie, he's no old enough. Did he disturb the congregation? I'm surprised at Wattie."

He told her.

"Pull up, son," said his mother, voice faint as a chicken's cheep. "I'll foot it the rest of the way."

The trap jolted off up the brae, and the desolation dropped over her at the loss of a friend who had spent seventeen years looking out for Dougals. Six times seventeen equals a hundred and two years of soothing the growing pains of bairns who weren't her own; soothing the mother's as well, for she too had grown up in that time. A shipload of tea drunk together, and many a wee game of cards slipped over on John, who didn't believe in consorting with employees. But Wattie wasn't an employee. She was a chum, an intimate. And now she was gone. Gone to God, Who might at least have left her time to enjoy the pension Anna had planned for her. Mibbie He kenned she wouldn't have been happy away from Glen Gryffe. That first Christmas . . . *Wouldn't you like to join your family for the holidays, Miss Watson?* And she replying, *This is my family, if you'll have me, Mrs. Dougal.* She had made that true, to become the beloved spinster "aunt" of the Dougals.

And now no more. No more advice and flattery to give, no more laughs and confidences to share. Poor old Wattie, never given her first name, Mary. It was fitting she should lie by the burn she had loved so well. *My Mary's asleep by thy murmuring stream* . . .

Without knocking, Anna entered the farmhouse straight into sheltering arms.

"I kenned you'd come here," said Jamie into her hair.

"I had to. I hope she can see us, Jamie. She was aye harping on my happiness."

"Like a proper friend, Anna."

"Did she ken she was that to me?"

"Nobody could live so long by your side and no feel your affection."

"I feel the guilt of hell now, that I didna put it in words."

"Would you like to see her?"

"No. Lying in state is for popes and barbarians. Leave the coffin lid tight as tight."

"It's from your own oak tree."

"It's like you to think of that." She drew from him, crossed to the simple box lying on trestles, and laid one hand on the wood. "I'm awa hame to the bairns, Wattie. Thank you for aw the good care you gave them. I'll try to keep it up, for I'll stand *in loco guardensis* as sure as you did *parentis.*"

"You've both done a fine job. Lachie's the proof, Anna. You're to tell him you're proud of him. A grand head of the house awready, and he not fifteen."

"Hello? Hello? Is that you, Anna?" Harriet Boyd's tone over the wires made it clear that she still didn't believe the instrument worked.

"It's no Queen Mary."

"Who? Who?"

"You sound like a howlet. Wee Alec Bell from Edinburgh will be glad to hear you've finally caught on to his invention."

The other party wasn't listening. ". . . and so I wish to see you, Anna Biggart. And I don't want any excuses. With the baby to look after, I can't go gallivanting to town and certainly not to Strathgryffe. Can you hear me? I'm shouting as loudly as I can. Anyway, come to tea tomorrow. And don't say you're engaged or too busy. You've been neglecting me shamefully again. Why don't you speak? You're not usually this quiet. That's tomorrow at four o'clock. I'll hang up now before my pennies run out."

"Hold on, drat it," but the lady was gone. Anna jiggled the hook.

"Yes, Mrs. Dougal," said the operator.

"You broke the connection, Malcolm."

"I did no such thing. Your caller did."

"Can you stick it together again?"

"Aye, but it'll cost you."

"Never mind that."

"I wouldn't advise it, Mrs. Dougal. You were rung up from a pay box in Glasgow."

"Damn!"

"Mrs. Dougal, cursing is no permitted on the telephone."

She went in search of Morag. "Would you like to go to Glasgow with Sandy and me tomorrow?" Harriet couldn't spier in front of bairns. "It's awmost Christmas, and the shops'll be a fair treat."

"We're going to see Father Christmas!" Although she had lost belief in the merry gentleman, for her mother's sake Morag jumped up and down, clapping her hands. "We're going to see Father Christmas!"

They saw dozens of him. The Mass of Christ was not a legal holiday in Scotland—*Wha daur preach popery at ma lug?*—but the merchants saw fit to bring joy to the children, and in so doing filled their tills with legitimate serendipity.

Anna saved R. Wylie Hill's to the last. The elegant shop on Buchanan Street, its four floors filled with household furnishings, devoted its acre of basement to the little ones. Here toy trains ran, model boats six feet long fluttered sails taller than a man; ocean liners, battleships, and motorboats sailed white-capped blue canvas seas. Dolls said "Mama" and closed their eyes. Their houses, elegantly furnished, were big enough for a child to enter on hands and knees. Sets of doll china; sets of Meccano; rocking horses of real leather with real manes; gleaming scooters, pedal cars, bicycles, tricycles; Daisy rifles, bows and arrows, targets. Miniature forts with lead soldiers of famous cavalry and infantry regiments, brave in the kilt. Tennis racquets, hockey sticks, cricket bats, footballs, rugger balls; mechanical toys for girls and boys—*so simple even a child can work them;* cowboy suits, Indian war bonnets, policemen's helmets, firemen's helmets, pith helmets; dominoes, Ludo, Snakes and Ladders. In the booming city they would all be sold. For cash. Proper Glaswegians never carried debts over into the new year, and of all the proper, R. Wylie Hill's patrons were the most.

Sandy on one hand, Morag on the other, Mrs. Dougal stood in front of Father Christmas. "Here he is," she said. "Would you like to shake hands with him?"

"No a hope," said Father C., who looked and smelled like a beer barrel. "They fingers wipe sticky mouths, I shake hands, then stroke my beard, and what do I hae? A rat's nest I canna get ma comb through till Ne'er Day."

"Are they your own whiskers?" asked Morag.

"Lassie, would R. Wylie Hill hae anything but the real mackay frae the North Pole?"

"You sound Glasgow. My storybooks say . . ."

"I hope you had a nice trip down," interrupted Anna. "How did you leave your mother?"

"Wi' a runny nose. She will gang oot in the snow in her bare feet. I've tellt her a thousand times tae put on her rubber boots. The reindeer can wait for their oats."

"Horses eat oats," said Morag. "Reindeer eat lichen."

"No mine. They're Scottish reindeer. Merry Christmas!"

"Wasn't he grand?" said Anna, making a mental note to tell R. Wylie next time she saw him that his 1912 Father Christmas wasn't up to par.

They left by the Argyll Arcade, where a mass of mothers and children moved slow as treacle past shop windows bright with lights and extravagances to give in the name of the Child. "I'm no for a tramcar the day," said Anna. "We'd have to stand. We'll find a four-wheeler and hang the expense."

"Toffs is careless," said Sandy, and his mother squeezed his hand.

"You brought the children." Harriet greeted them each with a hug. "I knew fine you would"—a meaningful laugh—"so I asked Kitty to come straight home from school and look after them in the kitchen. I lit a fire in the front room for us."

Damn. Defenses breached before the first sally. "You aye were considerate, Harriet."

"Have you found a new nanny yet?" asked the inquisitor when they were behind the closed door.

"I'm no looking. I havena the heart to replace Wattie. I'll take on the job mysel for a wee."

"That should keep you out of mischief, I don't think. Anyhow, I didn't invite you up here to talk about bairns. There's a different look to you, Anna. So what happened in Oban?"

"Oban was grand. Winning the blue riband was only part of it."

"Yes?" Harriet sat forward eagerly.

"Right after the prizegiving a daft American showed up at the hotel. You should have heard him spout. I learned more about the States. One, anyway, that he called Kaintuck. Where he swore the grass was blue. Fancy that. You ken what they caw whisky over there? Scotch. As if there was any other kind. And the place he's from must be"—she held her nose to approximate his nasal twang—"the original one and only land of milk and honey, yes, ma'am."

"Anna Biggart, stop being silly and come to the point. What—happened—in—Oban?"

"I'm telling you, amn't I? He bought my bull for four thousand guineas. And him a Campbell from way back. He didna have their crooked mouth, though. Then I bought two new bulls, five heifers, four doddies in calf, and three milkers ditto, and still came home with two hundred pound more than I had to start. How's that for a success, my girl?"

"Well, if you're not going to tell me what happened, I'll just have to guess . . ."

Anna slapped her knee. "That minds me. Somebody else was guessing at your auld china. A gypsy woman by the Falls of Falloch. Gowk that I am, I havena told you a word of my adventures en route. Wait till you hear. Well, Harriet, I left at six A.M. Pat Nolan—he's my gardener, you ken—spun the crank for me so I wouldna have Lachie looking worry-faced over the bonnet at his daring wee mamá. It was raining hard when I drove through Dambridge. Did y' ever notice how still a village is when every soul's asleep in the morning light? Far quieter than in the dark . . ."

"Anna Biggart, what—happened—in—Oban?"

"Haud your patience. I'm coming to that." Not on your life. "The photographer at the club was a nice wee laddie . . . ought to find a way to take a body's picture without blinding her . . . a picnic basket with grub to feed Lachie and Hughie for a week. And Willie Boyd, too. Where is the lad? Practicing rugby, I wouldna be surprised. Clydeside must be building aw the ships in the world . . . Dumbarton Rock looks gey big when you're under it . . . so this wee chappie started the motor for me . . . are you game for an excursion on the loch? Take the steamer across to Inversnaid . . . Rob Roy country . . . Inveruglas . . ."

She was still only on Lomondside when Kitty knocked and stuck in her head. "Excuse me, Aunt Anna, but Sandy's ears are all red, and he's yawning something awful. Shall I give him a wee lie down?"

"Look at the time!" Anna sprang to her feet. "*Tempus* shouldna *fugit* like that. And here I promised Cookie we'd be on the six o'clock. Fling Sandy's coat on him, Kitty, and I'll help Morag. Och, Harriet, I'm right sorry I never even reached the gypsy part. I dinna ken when I've gabbed so much."

"Nor said so little."

As they were going out the front door Harriet pulled her friend toward her, laid cheek against cheek, and whispered, "Have a care, wee Anna Biggart. Have a care."

"Near as near she was, Jamie, to coming right out and asking me."

"Would you have minded?"

"Aye, for I'll no share thought of us with anyone. No even Harriet. You're aw that's ever been mine alone."

"I've a wish to shout it from the top of Misty Law."

"Go right ahead. The sheep'll no tell."

They made no plans for the future. Happiness was the here and now, decisions far off. Time to make them when the court intruded on Gryffe's Eden. Forget that, and hurrah for the hugmagandy.

"Your mamá is the youngest person, Dorcas," said Bella Cockburn. "Everything is so much fun to her."

"She makes me feel old." Nothing at home was joyous to Dorcas, over whose head dropped a black hood as soon as she passed Mr. Grant's farmhouse on the way up the brae. Try as she would, Anna couldn't induce happiness in her oldest child during those holidays, not until she had granted her leave to celebrate Hogmanay with the Murrays.

"I shouldna give in, Dorcas." Fine you ken you havena the heart to keep her home in the shadow of her father. "Bairns should bring in the New Year by their own fireside. But aw right."

"I'm not a child any more," said Dorcas, merry as Christmas, now that she had her own way. She had never seen Fiona's Edinburgh home, opened annually for Scotland's biggest celebration. Edinburgh was the "Naples of the North," according to its inhabitants, who considered themselves a social cut above the industrial West of Scotland. "The wise men come from the East," said the Edinburgher loftily, to which the Glaswegian replied, "Aye. And the wiser they are, the quicker they come."

"I'm no much of a one for Edinburgh," said Anna when she put her daughter on the train. "All east windy and west endy. Give Arthur's Seat a spank from me."

"Mamá. How—Glasgow."

Out of sight, out of mind, thought Anna as the train pulled away in a cloud of pungent steam. I worry less about my own daughter than I do about Peggy Maclean. There had been no correspondence between mistress and former maid. The check sent monthly to Peggy required no action on Anna's part, it being handled as a transfer from one branch of the Commercial Bank to another, and Peggy didn't write. Even to her sister. Indeed, recently Mairi had received so little from the postie that she had stopped watching for him. So the arrival of an envelope with the Skye postmark and addressed in a girlish hand to "Miss Maclean" sent Anna—solecism or no—knocking on the kitchen door.

"May I come in, Cookie? Here's a letter for Mairi. I dinna doubt it's from Peggy. The baby must have arrived early. Open it, lass. It'll no explode. Hurry up. I want to ken—a boy or another wee Anna."

Mairi read, then raised doleful eyes. "It's not either, Mistress Dougal. She's wed. To a Maclean of Mull. A second cousin."

Cook banged a girdle on the stove. "And her eight months along. The lad must be a sumph."

"He's not a lad. He's a bairnless old widower, and his croft she iss worn out. It's free labor of mother and child he's after marrying. And to live in Mull . . . "

"Is that such a bad fate?" asked Anna.

"To someone from Skye, yess indeed."

"Dry your eyes, Mairi," said Cook. "Here comes Mr. Grant for his buttermilk."

Like a rosebud hit by a shaft of sun, Mairi's face lost its darkness. She whipped into the cool-room and returned with a white jug, pupils sparkling in the momentary moisture left by sisterly sorrow.

"I'll awa," said Anna. "I ken my place."

"Och, you're welcome in the kitchen any time," said Cook distantly as she smoothed apron on oversize bosom and made for the outside door, hand outstretched for the knob, a hostess welcoming.

At her age, thought Anna, and left on an inward snort of disgust. You could expect Mairi to act foolish. She was young. Aye, and bonny. And at the kitchen door when Jamie came chapping for buttermilk. Jamie wouldna give a servant lass a tumble—unless . . . Many a girl has tripped many a man by giving him a pretty foot to fall over. Mairi wouldna dare—Mairi might . . .

Mrs. Dougal pushed the bell to summon from kitchen to morning room.

"Yess, Mistress Dougal?"

"Come in, Mairi. I havena had a chat with you since I dinna ken when. Can Cookie spare you for a wee?"

The girl smiled. Perfect teeth she had, drat it. "Och, ma'am, when Mr. Grant stops work, so does Cook. She'll not notiss I'm gone except with pleasure."

Daft auld coot. "Mairi, tell me. Do you plan to spend aw your life in the kitchen?"

"Not unless she iss my own, ma'am."

"Smart lass. Any particular lad caught your fancy?"

"None that I would run after. Or that I'd want to chase me."

"The young are shy and green, Mairi. We have to let them ripen before they find the nerve to propose. You havena come across any older men to cock your bonnet at?"

"I leave them to the likes of Peggy." The girl tossed her head.

Now what was ahint that flash of fire? "Then that cuts down the field and calls for the waiting game."

"The best game. Look at Mr. Grant, wedding young and paying for it still."

"Aye, yon's a sad case, but he carries it well."

"He's a fine man. Mistress Dougal. Strong and upright like my father, although he doesn't laugh like Mr. Grant."

"A sense of humor is the grace that saves us aw, Mairi."

"Och, yess. I learned that from you."

"It's a courtier you are," said Anna. "Well, that's aw the now for your problems. Let's take a wee look at mine. It's gey lonely upstairs with Miss Watson gone. Do you think you'd be up to handling Sandy for me?"

"And leave the kitchen? What would Cook do?"

"Mibbie you could help me find two Highland sisters to take the place of the Macleans."

"Och, Mistress Dougal, there are twin Macleods at Sligachan who would walk across the Sound of Sleat to work for you."

"They'll no have to be that miraculous. See's their address, and I'll send a wee note off to them right away."

"And it's a nanny I'll be?" Mairi's eyes grew at the prospect.

"Aye. With a touch of the governess. Morag's almost beyond one, but Sandy has to be able to read before he enters the Infants in September. Do you think you could handle that?"

"Indeed, yess! Mistress Dougal—could I alter Miss Watson's uniforms—"

"No a chance. We'll get the dressmaker ower to cut new ones to your own shape. How do you fancy navy blue?"

Mairi left elated. Anna cackled. Sma' wonder Son of McFadden called her "positively Machiavellian." Mairi was happy. Cookie would be pleased with two helpers again. Sandy would more easily perfect his ABC's at the hands of someone other than his mother. And she had removed an attractive nuisance from the kitchen door. Soon there would be no daily propinquity; Mairi, kicked upstairs, would look askance at downstairs gossip and clash-ma-claver.

The twelve o'clock chimes brought "And all's well" from Mrs. Dougal as she surveyed the rest of her domain. Dorcas was content at St. Thenew's, now that Switzerland was in the offing. Happiness for Lachie was the trip home on the last day of term exams; for Elspeth, a win at lacrosse or a tennis ball zipping down the sidelines past Miss Cuthbert. Morag and moping were strangers, Hughie likewise, as long as he could course the moors, which he did in all weathers. As for Sandy, his mother could praise the Lord for his sunny disposition.

Outside, too, things were bein. Above the kitchen door of the farmhouse a new sign swung in the wind. Cut in the shape of an Aberdeen Angus, white letters on black spelled out *Glen Gryffe Farm. Office*, an honest statement, the back room now a place of records, accounts, and a telephone, a legitimate private meeting ground for two partners in a business steadily growing. The Aberdeen Angus bulls were increasing the herd satisfactorily—hand-mating only, sire and dam unquestioned—the get automatically listed in the Polled Herdbook.

"Drat it, Mr. Grant, they restaurants would take ten times the beef we can supply."

"It's a grand wee promotion, Mrs. Dougal, our name on their menus. Glen Gryffe's future is tied to the selling of stock, no steak."

"If it works for cattle, should it no work for hogs? I'll make a call on wee Tommy Lipton. It wouldna hurt us if he pushed Glen Gryffe bacon in a shop or two."

The orphanage garden was producing Brussels sprouts the size of cabbages and cabbages as big as houses, thanks to the abundance of Pat Nolan's elixir. Superintendent Johnny Blackadder swore you could see the rhubarb grow. And he pointed proudly to the milkmaids' cheeks, where fresh roses bloomed from the butter-rich output of the Ayrshires.

Things improved, if that were possible, with the advent of the Macleod twins, Sheila and Nora, arriving posthaste from Skye. They brought the training received in kitchen and dining room of the Sligachan Inn, a hostelry for well-bred mountaineers who practiced on the Cuillin Hills for later assaults on the Alps. The girls' deportment left nothing to be desired.

All in all, 1913 was the year of the full bottle for Anna, not even her fortieth birthday lowering its level.

"I dinna feel it one bit, Jamie. When I was seventeen, I thought I was twenty. When I was twenty-five, I felt fifty. Now, thanks to you, I'm twenty again. It's only other folks' ages that mind me of my own. The First Lord of the Admiralty has no damn right to be a year younger nor I."

"Dinna fret about that, Anna. Winston Churchill's a child phenomenon."

"Aye, with the gift of the gab."

As well as forensic skill, Churchill also possessed the hardest head in the House of Commons, twin virtues to the chief of the Liberal Party. Because a glass of wine was not wasted on Herbert Henry Asquith, Liberal M.P. for the Scottish district of East Fife and Prime Minister of Great Britain, after-dinner speaking on Government policy increasingly devolved on Winston Churchill, who expounded everywhere on every subject, the most volatile of which was Home Rule for Ireland, a plank inserted in the Liberal Party platform by Gladstone in 1886.

Prime Minister Asquith had evaded the Irish question until the 1910 General Election left him an unworkable majority of two, forcing him to sue for the support of the eighty-three Irish Nationalist M.P.'s. There was but one way to gain their favor. Home Rule. Urged from on top, Churchill plunged into the Donnybrook raging since before the Battle of the Boyne in 1690, working the Liberal side into every speech he made, even to audiences assembled to hear him expound on his own Cabinet responsibility, His Majesty's Royal Navy.

"A disgrace to his father, who played the Orange card," said Philip Dougal, the Conservative. "When Lord Randolph said, 'Ulster will fight and Ulster will be right,' he finished Gladstone. Mark my words. Ulster will never accept separation from the motherland."

"What else can Winnie do?" said the Honorable Margot. "When he crossed the floor to the Liberal side, he had to accept all their tenets."

"I repeat, a disgrace to a great name. It comes from his mother. An American. A frivolous spendthrift . . ."

"With a loyal son to pay her debts."

"And well he should. She gave him his start when she was one of the Marlborough House set, courting King Edward's favor after Lord Randolph died. She showed her true nature when she married for the second time—a man twenty years her junior."

"And the handsomest in England," murmured his wife. "Cornwallis-West could have had any lady he wished."

"As he has proven by divorcing her to wed another *demimondaine*, Mrs. Patrick Campbell." The merchant prince rattled his newspaper triumphantly. "No, madam. You cannot deny that Lord Randolph weakened his great line when he married the American Jenny Jerome. Tainted blood, madam. Tainted blood."

"He tainted his own. Had I known, I would have pitied Lady Churchill, touring India with the great statesman, Lord Randolph, and he becoming increasingly unbalanced from a social disease."

"Madam! Repeating such gossip ill becomes you. When you hear such unfounded rumors, consider their source and discard them. Who could have foisted such a canard on you?"

"A certain young gentleman newly returned from his family's tea plantations."

"I, madam? I told you such an improper story? Impossible."

"You were not always so proper, Philip."

In her mother's natal month, Dorcas turned her back on the full-blooming heather and left on the long journey to the finishing school for young ladies at Le Manoix. She, Fiona Murray, and four other maidens departed Glasgow Central on the *Night Scot,* their excitement concealed under a blasé boredom as false as the daisies and forget-me-nots on their bonnets, their chaperone masking her trepidation with a mien stern as the gaoler she was.

At the same time, Elspeth, almost seventeen and ahead of herself, enrolled at Glasgow's College of Domestic Science, "The Dough School," to be taught the culinary arts of Scotland, the Land o' Cakes, and France, the land of soups and sauces.

"How demeaning!" Dorcas had said. "And unnecessary. If you mix in the right circles, it's easier to find a rich man than a poor one. Your husband should be able to afford a cook."

"Maybe not," said Elspeth. "Perhaps he'll be a plowman poet. Like Rabbie." Elspeth, the athlete, was also the romantic, daydreaming her way to the city on the same train as Lachlan and Hugh, but first class to their third.

"Dinna complain, lads," said Anna. "Ladies are entitled to airs."

Sandy, hands in Morag's and Mairi's, entered the great world of the Infants at St. Malcolm's, where boys were permitted up to age seven. Mairi would not accompany him to or from school after that first journey, any bairn of five being capable of the two-mile walk without a grown-up. After the first week he took to dodging his sister's care and scampered home over the fields in search of solitary adventure.

In the shank of September, Anna and her partner returned to the scene of last year's triumphs. She did not motor this time—she had proved she could, hadn't she?—taking the train a day later than Jamie lest the village try to put one and one together.

At Oban's spacious fern-decked station open to sea breeze and salt air, he met her with a spanking carriage and pair of matching grays.

"My," said Anna, "this rig'll make more of a splash than the Argyll at the Grand Marine."

"That's no where you're headed." He flicked the reins on the muscled rumps, and they clipclopped along the Esplanade. "You didna think I'd rent all this for such a wee drive?"

"Is it abducting me you are, then?"

"Aye. In broad daylight."

"Ho ho! Young Lochinvar rides again. Would it be all right to ask where to?"

"And spoil the surprise? I'll give you a hint though. You'll be crossing the Atlantic."

"Water-walking horses. Or do we take a wee bo-at?"

"Wait and see."

"As Mr. Gladstone said in 'eighty-three. Am I no going to look at cows and bulls?"

"I finished all the buying and selling yesterday. You'll no mind?"

"Mind? When I'm being abducted? I'm no as green as I'm cabbage-looking." When she had last proclaimed that, she had been greener than grass. "Gee 'em up, Lochinvar, for this fair Ellen is fair bursting with curiosity."

The grays took them south at a high-stepping trot to the head of Loch Feochan and along its two miles to Kilninver. Here they turned off on a dusty track between a hedge of dog roses and a low bracken-clad ben hiding the sea, their route twisting and climbing by a burn where lupines showed blue against the shingle. Then the Atlantic and the lower islands of the Hebrides stretched before them. Down they dropped, brake on, horses walking to Clachan, a line of stone cottages whose walls gleamed like bridal silk shot with palest blue.

"Whitewash aye looks fresh, Jamie, but never in my life have I seen a body putting it on."

"You've never seen a donkey lying dead either. Nature's phenomena. Whoa!" With the whip he pointed at a stone bridge below, narrow, steep up, steep down. "There. The only bridge that spans the Atlantic. Over that and we're in the Hebrides. Well, mibbie no quite. But near as dammit."

"And nary a witch can cross water." That for Daisy. "Were you thinking of Tam o' Shanter's escape from the hellion in her cutty sark?"

"I was not, but it's no a bad omen."

"If I kilted my skirts, I could loup across, it's so wee," she said.

"I dinna doubt that. But then you're a holy terror, no an unholy."

The horses pulled them over the ancient bridge to the Isle of Seil, and he stopped again to show her the tide flowing from firth to firth under the vaulting stones. On the glassy water, green from firs above, brown from seaweed below, a brace of mute swans floated majestically, at their sterns two puffy gray cygnets, like dinghies under tow. With the advent of humans, the female raised her wings languidly, the young ones struggled up the white slopes, and the wings came down to shelter and hide them.

"Welcome on board," said Anna, and at his laughter the waterfowl turned heads to stare at them down their flat red bills. Then his face became solemn as a deacon passing the plate in the kirk, and her heart, knowing what was coming, sang the offertory.

"Anna," he said, "around the bend is an inn. It's wee—six rooms at most, but licensed, so the food should be aw right. At this time of year I doubt we'll find a soul in residence. I'd like to go there with you as if we were wooed and wed and married and aw."

"What name would you give us? Mr. and Mrs. L. Invar?"

"To hell with the name. And to hell with you aye leaving me. For a year now I've reached out my hand for you every morning and found naught but an empty pillow. Tomorrow I shall waken to you lying beside me like a proper wife."

The thrill of the illicit entered her, crawled up, filled her bosom, stroked her shoulders, ran down her arms to set her whole body tingling as marriage never had, with its blessings and signings and wills and trusts and servants and houses to run and obedience to give.

"Och, Jamie, for mysel I dinna mind the risk, but what about you? If we were found out—you'd be guiltless no more. Son of McFadden told you . . ."

"I'll no wait on the courts!" he shouted, and the swans, feathers ruffled, glided to the far grassy bank of the miniature sound. "It'll be fifteen months and more before I'm free in the eyes of the law. If then, for well you ken plans can gang agley. If the Lord has his eye on me, he kins I'm free as ever I'll be, and so are you. The remembrance of you scurrying back to your own house aw these months is fair degrading."

"We canna have that, Jamie." She gave in as she had planned, ever since leaving Glen Gryffe. "If you'd asked me on the mainland, I'd have said no for your sake. But that wee body of water looks awfu big from here."

She never did find out how he signed the inn's register, the staff giving them only "sir" and "madam." They stayed three nights and three days, walking everywhere while the grays ate their heads off in the stable. Anna, too, found a monstrous appetite. "It's aw the sea air," she defended herself. She could put away a dozen local oysters before a brace of grouse. Her muscles had never felt so toned, her legs so limber as they scrambled around the island four miles long and less than half as wide. With more slate per acre than anywhere else in Scotland, the innkeeper told them, colorful slate, too, pitted with iron pyrites and yellow crystals.

In horizontal rain, wearing borrowed oilskins and sou'westers, they took the two-man four-oar ferry across the channel to Luing, then footed it to Ardlarach, heads down to the wet driving wind, until the cloud cover broke into outriders charging away to the mainland, and the sudden clearing exposed a handful of islands sprinkled like colored glass on the blue at their feet. Further out stretched the Isles of the Sea, battleships steaming line astern into the Firth of Lorne. North lay the Ross of Mull; south, Colonsay; in between only the wide sea route to Newfoundland and Nova Scotia, where the dispossessed driven from Scots soil gave their country's name to their place of exile.

"She's a better view from Scarba. Fourteen hundred feet high, yess," said a lobsterman from the cockpit of his boat fast to the pier.

"How do we get there?" asked Jamie.

"I could take you now, for it is slack water and the race will not be running in the narrows. If you go, you must wait six hours till the tide she is right to take you off and bring you back again."

"Are you game?" Jamie looked at her.

"She is an easy climb up Cruach Scarba," coaxed the local. "And at the south end you will see the *Cailleach,* the Old Woman, tramping her wash, for her Tub lies between Scarba and Jura, the whirlpool some call Corrievreckan."

"Can we no go aw the way in your boat?" said Jamie.

"Not in mine." The lobsterman smiled slowly. "If she was twice the size and ten times as engined, not even then. The very seals stay away from Corrievreckan when the wind is against the tide, as it will be today."

"I'm game," said Anna.

Great black-backed gulls, their wings spanning six feet, soared astern in the odor of paraffin and ripe lobster bait blown away from Anna by the wind of the fishing boat's passage. Gold flashed high across their bow as a line of plovers whistled overhead. Red head straight down, black-tipped wings and white tail stiff in a W, a gannet hurtled soundlessly into the sea for food. The lobster fisherman steered for a tiny bay on the northeast, nosing in between two yellow rocks where seals lay sunning. He put his stem gently on the sandy shore and held it there, his screw barely turning.

"I will set my pots now. You must be back here no later than four o'clock."

"I am a farmer," said Jamie. "I dinna carry a watch. Where will the sun be?"

"Halfway between the Isle of Colonsay and the Ross of Mull. If you are not here at that time, you will be here all night, for the tide will run a few minutes after four, and I cannot make way against her in this old boat."

Scarba was nothing but a mountaintop. Seven Highland cattle grazed its sparse and precipitous pasture, and the soaring antlers and head of a stag pierced the skyline while ten hinds browsed around him, safe in the care of their monarch.

"They must have boated the red deer here, too," said Jamie. "I doubt they could swim from the mainland. No in these waters."

As they climbed, out of their sight the Atlantic pushed silently up the broad Sound of Jura and squeezed into the narrow Gulf of Corrievreckan. At nine knots the mile-wide wall of water soundlessly climbed the rock cliffs and scoured the bottom a hundred fathoms down until it met a sunken pyramid a bare fifteen fathoms below the surface. Then the immovable rock forced the irresistible ocean up into a racing overfall twenty feet high that fell with the roar of a thousand bulls of Bashan bellowing in agony. The sudden barrage hitting Anna's head like a pole ax would have driven her to her knees had she not already been there, using her hands to scramble the last few feet to the top of Cruach Scarba. Limitless sea, islands, mainland; blues, greens, yellows, purples, and the lobster-olive of uncovered rocks all shuddered before eyes set jiggling by the cannonade of the sea in torment. She opened her mouth to speak, but the westerly ballooned her cheeks and rammed her words back in her throat. She pointed a challenge, he nodded, and together they slithered down to a cliff above the roaring pit. With the wind against the tide, the race of foaming breakers as big as two-story houses charged into the fury of overfall. Six hundred feet out, two hundred down from where they clung to one another the maelstrom spun and howled, ready to toss any MacBrayne's liner about like a toy while white waterspouts shot up thirty feet from the whirling, sucking cone. The salt-laden din of hell filled ears, the eyes, nose, mouth. Anna pulled Jamie's sleeve and ran from sight of the Old Woman's Tub.

By deer path they made their way back to the sandy rendezvous hours early, to eat the inn's picnic, to wade ankle deep, to sit hand in hand on the heather, to find agreement in the other's eyes and fall into hugmagandy as easy as kiss-your-hand, then to look at the mainland and wonder how it would be to live in the battlemented castle over there. They did not speak much. Corrievreckan, three miles away, made it impractical. At a quarter to four the Old Woman abruptly finished her wash, and the sudden quiet was a benison to hold to the cheek. Anna massaged her ears tenderly. "Gey big feet the *Cailleach* has," she said. "And here comes our gondolier, right on the sun dot."

"Do any ships try the passage of Corrievreckan?" Jamie asked the fisherman as they chuffed up and down waves gentle now.

"Only at slack water. This summer two daft lads in a sloop thought to go through with the tide, and they were sucked in. They battened themselves in their cabin and prayed. A stout ship she was with stout prayers for crew. After spinning them around and over for a week of an hour, the Old Woman spewed them out, the only ones I've heard to survive."

He would accept no money. "She was a pleasure to take the chentleman and his daughter."

"He didna say it for the tip," crowed Anna as they walked back. "Are you no proud of yoursel, Jamie Grant, for having such a young lover?"

Later, in the dark . . . "Listen." Through the open window came a steady unmistakable groan.

"Aye, Anna, yon's Corrievreckan. The tide'll be coming again."

"How far away?"

"Twelve, thirteen mile."

"No far enough. Och, I shouldna complain. It's no many folk can lie in heaven and listen to hell."

He went home without her.

"I canna go straight back, Jamie. I couldna wipe you out of my eyes for Glen Gryffe after half a week of being aw yours. No without a change of scenery. I'll clear my vision with a wee visit to Mull and Peggy Maclean. I worry about the lass."

She boarded MacBrayne's *Queen Alexandra,* named for Edward's neglected spouse, and to her delight the purser saluted and gave her her name in broad Glasgow.

"You're a well-kent face in Oban, Mrs. Dougal. I saw you win best-in-show last year. You'll be alone?"

No sooner had they cast off than he was back. "Captain's compliments, Mrs. Dougal, an' wud you join him on the bridge?"

As they sailed the twenty-five miles up the Sound of Mull, the skipper gave her the guided tour, a proper treat. Better than Thomas Cook himsel. "Castle Duart, seat of the Maclean of Maclean—" He indicated a stone tower of antiquity four-square above them on a black cliff. "Sir Fitzroy Maclean bought it back for the clan and restored it last year. He'll be in residence the now, for his standard is up."

It appeared the sailor would be a farmer. "You ken, Mrs. Dougal, I canna afford to start with a big herd. How long does it take for one tae double itsel? That's Grass Point. We used to embark cattle there that had been driven across Mull from the west. Scrawny beasts from the Outer Hebrides. No like your magnificent Pride o' Glen Gryffe. An' you sold him to an American? Well, well. Yon ruin on the mainland is Ardtornish Castle. You'll excuse me whiles we dock at Loch Aline. That's where they get the silica sand. For the spectacles, you ken."

It was warm behind the canvas dodger shielding her from the breeze of the steamer's twenty knots. Sun shone. Sea sparkled. One lone cloud perched on top of Ben More as white as the frosting on the cake the steward brought them along with clay mugs of strong sweet tea. Her visit to Peggy Maclean née Maclean and her daughter named Anna was proving another example of the good deed that brings its own reward.

"Castle Aros," said her braw guide. "Empty for three centuries—ever since the Lord of Ochiltree ravaged it. The Sound's two sea miles wide here. Way over the bow, that's Ardnamurchan, westernmost point of all Great Britain. And you find the Tamworth breed of pig dresses out best? I'll mind that when I find my wee bit o' land."

He stopped talking as they came abreast of Calve Island, the plug that made Tobermory Bay the quietest anchorage in the Inner Hebrides. Slowly now, he conned the steamer in toward the crowded pier, where the name MacBrayne was blazoned red as blood on the sheds. Half the population of a thousand seemed to have turned out to "meet the boat." Stone houses painted white and black and pink and cream lifted in terraces above the still, black water, the slate turrets of the Western Isles Hotel soaring highest of all. The clang of the engine telegraph reverberated from wooded cliffs as he maneuvered the vessel to take a perfect pier, not a scrape, not a dunt, not a foot between wood and steel. He rang "finished with engines" and turned to Anna with a self-satisfied beam.

"No sae bad," he said, taking her arm and walking her over to port, away from the landing. He pointed down into the water near the rocky shore. "There's a fortune in gold there. His Spanish Majesty's *Almirante de Florencia,* sunk after the Armada with three hundred thousand pound sterling in pieces of eight in her coffers. The Campbells located her last year. Under thirty feet of clay, a sad frustration for that hungry lot." He laughed. "If they could get her up, whatna bloody battle there'd be. The Macleans would claim the booty, for it was their chief who blew her magazine in 1588 when her commander wouldna pay for sanctuary." He carried her portmanteau ashore and gave it to a porter with Western Isles Hotel in gold on his cap. "Are you for a long stay, Mrs. Dougal?"

"Just the night, Skipper."

"I'd be right pleased if you'd share my bridge again on the return voyage. Perhaps you'd have dinner with me in Oban?"

"A wife in every port, is it?"

"None in any, Mrs. Dougal."

A conquest, she thought happily as she sat over lunch in a bay window of the hotel, looking across the Sound of Mull to the green mountains of Morvern. Or is it my farm he has his eye on? I'll no think that. The other is better for the morale. Wee Anna Biggart has come into her own, and high bloody time.

She hired a pony, trap, and driver for the ten-mile journey to the west coast and the clachan of Calgary. She'd heard that there was a city in Canada, now, named for the tiny village, as if the forced immigrants needed a reminder of the land they had wept to leave. It was a silent drive. The old man at her side apparently had only the Gaelic. The cart track wound and twisted over the high land of rough moor, whose wirelike grass was an autumnal bronze pocked by the curse of Mull, inedible bracken tall as a cow's shoulder. The wind whipped across a narrow empty loch, no sheep grazed, no birds sang, hooded crows croaked across the high desolation. She was ready to accept Mairi's opinion of Mull when the road dropped into Dervaig and changed her mind. Two-score houses, some thatched, a white school, an ancient kirk grew among roses, and trees sheltered by heathery hills at the head of a quiet arm of the sea. Beauty stayed with her the rest of the way and burst into grandeur as they came on Calgary Bay, a sweeping crescent of shell sand with not a rock or stone or footprint to mar the sugar-white surface edged by the green machair.

"Skye couldna be bonnier nor this," she said. "How could the poor emigrants have borne to leave?"

"They would eat," said the driver, her enthusiasm unlocking his English.

Peggy's home stood alone, surrounded by fields well-tilled for turnips and potatoes. A barn of stone dwarfed the thatched one-story cottage, putting the emphasis where it should be. On work. Peggy was on her knees in the kitchen garden behind the drystone wall. At the sneck of the gate latch she turned her head, and crimson flowed up the graceful neck into the bonny face. Then she was in Anna's arms, crying and laughing in a display that caused the driver to cluck his tongue and stare at the sky in disgust before leading the pony around to the watering trough.

Peggy recovered quickly from the role of grateful servant and became her new self, the mistress of a farm.

"Thiss iss Anna Maclean, Mistress Dougal," she said, presenting her as proudly as if the bairn had been born ten months after the wedding.

Anna studied her namesake but could see no likeness to Sandy Tulloch. "She looks just like you, Peggy."

"Like my husband, too," crooned Peggy into the infant's neck. And that puts the wean in the miracle class, thought Anna.

Over buttermilk—no tea—and hot scones—no costly bread—in the stone-floored kitchen where the peat smoored in the fireplace, Anna decided to send the luxury of a chest of Dougal & Company's best to the crofter forced to live off his land.

"Are you happy, lass?" she asked.

"Och yess, Mistress Dougal. Mr. Maclean is a fine man and a good farmer. Glad I am that he married me and not Mairi."

Hoho! "Was that ever on the docket?"

"Perhaps. He used to write her, until my father told him that the tocher came with the younger sister."

The pregnant one, thought Anna, dowry coupled with proof of fertility, making Peggy no gamble at aw. No a rollicking romance, but sane and sensible.

"I see you've kept up your English, Peggy."

"I use the Gaelic outside, but never in the house. Mr. Maclean insists. For Anna's sake. Already he is saying that if she goes to Glasgow, it will be to the University, not into a kitchen. My tocher and the money you send he is saving for that."

"Mibbie when the time comes there will be a wee bit banked, too, for the bairn you're carrying now."

Peggy dropped her head shyly, her manner ladylike compared to the angry confession announcing her first pregnancy. There's naught like legality to bring out the sanctimony, thought Anna, and rose to go.

"Mr. Maclean will be sorry he was not home to meet you," said Peggy.

"Tell him luck to the house from me, Peggy. And many more bairns to keep my namesake company." She had one more query. "How old is Mr. Maclean?"

"He'll have his thirty-eighth at Christmas."

Younger than hersel. Drat Mairi with her doleful reading of Peggy's fate. Plain bloody jealousy that had been, and it had sent Anna Dougal over the miles to do battle with an ancient widower for taking advantage of an unfortunate lass. Instead she found Peggy the proud queen of her own douce wee castle. Mairi not wanting an older man was stale ale. She hadna been asked, and kicking her upstairs away from Jamie was as smart a ploy as wee Anna Biggart had ever made. Och, t' hell. Mairi was a woman and not to be blamed for thinking of hersel. And the trip hadna been a waste. The deluded traveler had seen the Sound of Mull, Tobermory, Dervaig, and the crescent moon on earth that was Calgary Bay. And met the skipper. She'd meet him again on the morrow if this tipsy driver didn't coup them both on the road back to Tobermory. As she climbed into the trap, the aura of barley brew was fit to draw the bumblebees from the heather and melody from his throat.

" 'The Isle of Mull is of Isles the fai-rest—' " he sang as they left Peggy at her yett, bairn on one arm, the other waving her apron. " '—of o-cean's gems the first and ra-rest . . .' I should give it the Gaelic, but you'd not have the language, would you, lady? 'Green grassy is the land of the sparkling fountain, Of waving woods and high tow'ring mountain . . .' Dugald Macphail wrote the fine song properly, and a Macfarlane translated her into the Sassenach tongue. She's no the same in English, but she'll have to do the now. 'Tho far from hame I am now a ranger, In grim Newcastle a doleful stranger . . .' " He stopped the trap and after some difficulty steadied a wavy arm on a cairn rising from a knowe a mile off. "Yon's a monument of thanks to Dugald, the exile. 'The thought of thee stirs my heart's emotion, And deeper fixes its fond devotion . . .' She has six more verses, 'Ant-Eileen Muileach, The Isle of Mull.' You'll be wanting to hear them?"

"Sing on, troubadour."

The slurry lullaby, the sun on her eyelids, the gentle motion opened the sluice to sleep resisted. Immersed in green-and-gold waves, she floated back to the hotel, up to her room, and wakened at noon the next day with no recollection of undressing. I missed my damn dinner, she thought. And my breakfast. Godsakes. If hunger hadna nudged me, I could have starved to death. Och well, sleep is meat, but I better have a gey big lunch, or I'll eat the skipper out of a month's wages the night.

She boarded the steamer in a hissing downpour, the circular bay spotted like a pot simmering to the boil for the eggs. The cloudburst drove her to the saloon, where the purser found her putting a lid on the hotel lunch with tea and French cakes.

"Captain's apologies for the Scots mist, Mrs. Dougal. You're welcome on the bridge, but if you're feart you might get wet, he'll attend you the night wherever and whenever you say."

He took her to the Royal Oban Yacht Club— "Honorary membership goes with my rank, Mrs. Dougal"—where she was the only lady present. He talked of the sailor's dream—

the farm where disease never strikes, cattle multiply and never die, oat and barley ears grow fat while bracken withers, and drought stops outside your drystane dyke. "It's no so long off now, Mrs. Dougal. I swallow the anchor in two years." He could not know that his retirement was to take the form of a German torpedo in the bowels of the *Queen Alexandra*, she going down with all hands and five hundred Tommies in the English Channel on a moonlight night, a U-boat night, in September '15.

He was a grand companion, full of stories. "The bonniest girls in the world? After judicious study—purely sociological, you ken—I'd have to give the palm to Sydney, Australia, and Belfast, Ireland, and New York." Smiling, he appraised the face opposite him. "And, for tonight only, Oban, Argyllshire."

"You have a heavy hand with the trowel, Captain."

She bade him good night in the lobby of the Grand Marine. "Soon as you leave the sea, you're to visit Glen Gryffe, mind."

"I'll do that very thing, Mrs. Dougal. And no just to inspect the farm."

"Whatna man it is for the flattery."

Wrapped in flannel night and dressing gowns, she flung up the window to look over to Kerrera and Mull, darking in the moonlight, storm gone with the change of tide. As she debated a taet to that *femme fatale*, wee Anna Biggart, her head fell back on the overstuffed chair and stayed there until not hunger but the cold wakened her at two o'clock in the morning. Some folk would sleep their brains into train oil, she thought, but it's no like me. It must be aw the sea air. She cackled, climbed into bed, and slept without changing position for ten more hours.

PART THREE

A BEGINNING

Chapter Nine

F. E. SMITH, Privy Councillor and brilliant legal mind, was a member of the Conservative "shadow" Cabinet, his primary responsibility liaison with Sir Edward Carson, militant leader of the Ulster-will-fight faction. Half a million Ulstermen had signed a "Solemn Covenant to defeat Home Rule," which caused Winston Churchill to denounce Sir Edward and, by implication, the entire Conservative Party for engaging in "a treasonable activity."

Although politically opposed, F. E. Smith was a close friend of Churchill's, and to him the lawyer suggested separating the troubled country by a georeligious line drawn from Londonderry south, then east to Dundalk on the Irish Sea; green below, free of London, Orange above, free to be loyal to England. To the pragmatic Churchill it seemed a way to avoid bloodshed. On October 18, 1913, speaking to his constituents in Dundee he said, "The claim for Ulster cannot be ignored."

This first hint that Northern Ireland might be allowed a say in her own fate brought howls of rage from the Irish Nationalists; Churchill, false colleague, had betrayed them.

"We are irreconcilable to any break-up of the country," said "Tay Pay" O'Connor.

Prime Minister Asquith informed the King that the Ulster Volunteers planned to seize the police, military barracks, and arms depots, and His Majesty ordered the heads of the near-warring factions to Buckingham Palace; the Ulstermen, the Nationalists, the Conservatives, and the Liberals. The meeting lasted four days without any retreat from the brink because "The Irish couldn't agree and the British couldn't decide." On July 25, 1914, the Cabinet backed from the Royal presence and returned to Downing Street, still seeking a way to pluck the centuries-old thorn from the British Lion's paw. As the heads of government sat in dispirited session, an official message was delivered to the Foreign Minister, Sir Edward Grey. He excused himself to peruse it, then in dispassionate tones read aloud Austria's ultimatum demanding, among other insults, that she be allowed to search Serbia for the plotters of the recent assassination of Austria-Hungary's Archduke Franz Ferdinand. As the insolent words penetrated, the Cabinet knew that while the gauntlet came from the hand of Austria, the voice was that of her ally, Germany, bent on conquest.

Bound by previous commitments, the opposing sides shaped up automatically.

Belgium, Britain, France, Russia, Serbia, the Allies for the defense.

For the attack, Germany with her cohorts, Austria-Hungary and Bulgaria.

Before the specter of a general European war, the Cabinet perforce tabled the vision of an Irish Free State.

Next day First Sea Lord Prince Louis of Battenberg, a name soon to be anglicized to Mountbatten, instructed the Third Fleet, standing by in the English Channel, not to disband from the test mobilization ordered by the watchful and prescient Churchill. With twenty-nine capital ships at sea and thirteen on the ways to the Kaiser's eighteen and nine,

Britain's navy was at strength, not quite Churchill's two-for-one, but armed, manned, and steam up.

A frenzied week of arguing in the national chancelleries of Europe proved pointless before the ambition of the Kaiser and his generals. On July 28 satellite Austria declared war on Serbia. Four days later Germany declared war on Russia and next day sent a handful of troops into France, at the same time demanding passage for more through Belgium. On August 3 she declared war on France and twenty-four hours later marched into Belgium.

Immediately John Redmond, leader of the Irish Nationalists, stated in Commons, "Catholics in the South would be only too glad to join arms with the armed Protestant Ulstermen in the North."

At midnight of the same day, August 4, 1914, Great Britain declared war on Germany, and the street lights were turned off in St. James's Park. "The lamps are going out all over Europe," said Foreign Minister Grey, watching from his office window. "We shall not see them lit again in our lifetime."

Thanks to Winston Churchill, the Royal Navy was ready. So were the ordinary citizens of Scotland, England, Ireland, Wales, and the Empire, who clamored by the hundreds of thousands for the right to bear arms against the aggressor. Among them was James Grant.

"They'll no take you, Jamie," said Johnny Blackadder of the orphanage. "What's your age?"

"Thirty-five?" said Jamie tentatively.

The sixty-year-old superintendent eyed him. "Aye," he said. "You could pass for that."

"If I can get by you, I'll get by the recruiters. I'll feel easy about Glen Gryffe if your bairns will work it and you supervise. The big lads are coming along grand. I never thought when I set up the agricultural school that I was doing it for my own good."

"What does Mrs. Dougal say to your leaving her in the lurch?"

"I havena told her yet. I wanted your word first that you'd help."

"Here's my hand on it."

"I kenned you'd go," said Anna. "If it wasna for the damn biologic difficulty, I'd enlist mysel. I'll miss you like the breath I'll be holding, but I canna keep you back."

"I'll no be gone long," he said as if he were just off to the village for an ounce of tobacco.

Next day, with Elspeth, Morag, Sandy, and Mairi in the tonneau, Cookie beside her, and Lachlan and Hugh on the running boards, Anna drove into the village to see the men route-march off to Paisley to enlist. Dorcas was still in neutral Switzerland. It seemed rather inane, she wrote, to risk the new inconveniences of travel across Europe when the unpleasantness would be over in a matter of months.

Piper Rory Tulloch led the untrained column of sixty-eight men past the Boer War memorial. Girls waved miniature Union Jacks, servant lasses threw kisses, and lads off for a lark dashed out of line to claim the real thing. "Loose your lips, Mac," yelled a marching wag. "You'll be late for the war." Jamie Grant waved his cap, and Anna Dougal bowed in acknowledgment as the rows went up the brae by the kirk where the minister stood, his wrong-way collar and benign face a benediction for all, sinner and churchgoer alike. Then an oak-lined bend in the road engulfed Strathgryffe's finest, and the skirl of Rory's bagpipes faded to a whisper and silence.

"If only I were a man," said Elspeth.

"If only I were older," said Lachlan.

"Who's for a slider?" said Anna Dougal and democratically led her entire clutch into the shop nicknamed "the Tally's" for the immigrant Italians who had monopolized the making of ice cream in the West of Scotland.

In the bulging Dambridge Larder things were so chock-a-block that a man having a pint passed back over the heads of his fellows had a hard time getting the tankard down to his lips. The high notes of the pipes cut through the din.

"Out!" Dolly thumped the bar with a bung mallet. "Out! Here come the Strathgryffe lot. Faw in afore you faw down."

With nearby hamlets to draw on, the Dambridge contingent outnumbered the arrivals by thirty. To maintain position as first in line, red-faced Rory didn't stop blowing and squeezing, nor did the men from Strathgryffe stop their march.

"We were here first!" shouted Dambridge, blocking the way.

"Awa tae hell," Strathgryffe yelled back. "We started first."

"Save your strength to fight the Hun," roared James Grant, a sergeant born, and Dambridge opened up.

Dolly passed out five tankards, then ran to the head of the marching column with the sixth. "Here, Jamie. *Slainte mhor.*" She wished him health and walking sideways planted a kiss on his cheek. "Leave the pots by the road. Pat'll pick them up when he's ower sulking in the back room because he's too auld tae march with you. Good luck, Jamie Grant. Gie the Jerries unshirted hell frae Dolly Nolan!"

The lack of discipline would have brought tears to the eyes of regular Army men, but they were already on the Continent, a hundred thousand of them, to keep the British promise to Belgium. Rory Tulloch's piping pulled one hundred and sixty-six volunteers across the Gryffe, sixty-three— including Rory—on a one-way trip. When they reached Paisley they found the Argyll and Sutherland Highlanders unable to absorb the thousands of men swarming around the hastily set-up recruiting office. There were no barracks, no food, and the volunteers would not go home lest they lose their place in the queue and first bash at the Hun. The Lord Provost threw open the town hall to shelter them, and the good women of the city began a round-the-clock service of sandwich, stew, soup, and tea making. In disgust at the delay, James Grant went on to Glasgow to check the possibilities there.

In addition to the sixty-eight who jointly marched away

from Strathgryffe, twenty of her sons received commissions in the infantry, artillery, cavalry, and the Royal Naval Volunteer Reserve, known as the "Wavy Navy" for the gold sleeve-bar that curved to distinguish it from the straight-line R.N. Then there were six other lads, lucky ones who did not require to enlist; they had joined the Territorials, the Citizens' Home Defense Force, called up immediately for the overseas service they had unanimously voted to accept.

"A good thing it'll be over by Christmas," said Bella Cockburn. "Think how ghastly the parties would be if the boys left behind were all Lachie's age."

When Lachlan Dougal returned to the High in September, he found the Sixth Form virtually nonexistent. Its masters, however, had ample work in the lower classes, the teaching staff also having been heavily depleted. "Business as usual," the war's slogan, did not apply to the fit and ready in schools and universities, in offices and factories, on farms, at sea, each lad convinced that he was a secret weapon; the conscript German Army didn't stand a chance against the British volunteer fighting of his own accord for a principle.

In Glasgow, Lord Provost Sir Thomas Dunlop and his predecessor, Sir Archibald Innes-Shaw, did a magnificent job of recruiting excelled only by white-bearded Jimmy Dalrymple, manager of the Glasgow Tramways. That corporation department at the corner of Bath and Renfield Streets draped its fifth floor with dozens of flags, the Union Jack alternating with the blue-fielded white cross of St. Andrew, Scotland's patron saint. Between the lower floors, giant banners told how and where to enlist NOW! Illuminated tramcars ran with the same positive message. Concerts, parades, cinemas featured it, for Dalrymple used all the resources at his command, and some that weren't, ultimately to raise the incredible total of five companies of engineers, two infantry battalions, and a brigade of artillery.

This meritorious record had not been achieved, however, as Anna Dougal sat with Harriet Boyd at an upper window of Miss Cranston's Tearoom, looking out at a dreich November drizzle. The news in the morning's *Herald* was as dismal as the day. The British regulars in Belgium were still holding the German hordes at Ypres, but at the final cost. The remnants of the 1st Scots Guards, the 2nd Cameron Highlanders, the 1st Black Watch, reduced to eight hundred men by twenty-three days in constant action, had been wiped out by six fresh battalions of Germany's 1st and 3rd Foot Guards. That the Huns had later been annihilated by Sir Douglas Haig's artillery, the 1st King's, and the rifle fire of engineers, cooks, and grooms did little to lighten the heart.

"Robert is still sure it will be over by Christmas," said Harriet, trying. "Or soon after. We won't have to worry about anyone we love being in it."

That's aw you ken about the price of tea, thought Anna. He didna have to go. No at forty-one.

"More tea, leddies?" One of Miss Cranston's waitresses stood, two silver pots poised.

"Never mind the hot water," said Anna. "I need a cup that has body to it."

A drumming sound entered the cozy room and swelled into the cadence of marching boots. As they looked down on Sauchiehall Street, the buildings opposite them emptied, upstairs windows flew open, and from side streets poured a cloth-capped crowd filling the pavements six deep from gutter to shop as the 9th Highland Light Infantry passed through the rain on the way to France. Column of four in puttees and breeches, straight-backed, arms shouldered, Glengarry ribbons hanging limp, the H.L.I. marched at attention, eyes front, mouths firm for the newsmen who photographed their passing, not knowing the long record they would set. They, the Scottish Rifles, and the London Scottish were the only volunteer battalions considered fit to join the British Expeditionary Force in 1914.

The watchers honored them with complete silence. There could be no cheers now for Jock going off to war. Not while Ypres was in agony.

"The Glasgow Highlanders. My sister has a bairn in that lot." The waitress whispered as if she were in the kirk.

When the first battle for the Flanders town ended indecisively nine days later, the British Expeditionary Force had held against double its numbers, thanks to its training and superior marksmanship. But the five weeks of fighting at Ypres, at Armentières, and at La Bassée left alive few of the professional officers and soldiers of the B.E.F. For the immediate future, the British Empire would depend upon Territorials, Dominion troops, and three divisions from overseas as both sides dug themselves in for the new-style siege warfare of the trenches.

Jamie Grant was in southern England at Aldershot, a lance corporal in the 5th Cameron Highlanders known as "Lochiel's" for the chief of the clan. He considered himself lucky to be accepted into the regiment sponsored by the Glasgow Stock Exchange; Jimmy Dalrymple had recruited heavily for it, and the response had been sufficient to fill its ranks ten times over.

Anna wrote in January 1915:

Dear Mr. Grant,

The arrangements you made with Supt. Blackadder for the care of Glen Gryffe are working out well. Thanks to you, the young lads are surprisingly knowledgeable. I have put Mairi Maclean in charge of the girls, as Sandy is now almost seven and in no further need of a nanny. Elspeth, who has given up domestic science for the duration, is a great help to her. The Government is taking a canny view of the immediate future and is asking all farmers to accelerate production. When you return, you will find little of Glen Gryffe left fallow or in flowers. Your partner is also increasing the cattle per acre beyond what we consider ideal, again at Government request. I have donated all saddle horses to the Queen's Own Royal Glasgow Yeomanry and have retained the Clydesdales.

Our demand note is callable on the eleventh of the month.

*I hope in the midst of all your duties you can send a letter
to McFadden, Son & Laidlaw to make sure they start things
moving.*
  Everyone here sends good wishes, including
              Yours truly,
          Anna Dougal (Mrs.)

Some bloody love letter, she thought as she sealed it.
Damn the censors. Och well, the "our" before her canny
reference to his approaching freedom was a declaration of
love. He'd come home free in the eyes of the law as well as
the Lord's. And soon. Despite Ypres, optimism still prevailed
to the point where the 17th H.L.I. had petitioned for ac-
celerated training lest the war be won before they were
ready.

Like the Irish, the suffragettes tabled their private fight
and joined in the common cause. A prominent one, a friend
of Harriet Boyd's, rang up Anna. With a first husband killed
by the Boers, a second who had just exchanged ministerial
gray for the padre's khaki, and an officer son in Belgium,
Meg Dawson felt that her place was as close to the front
lines as she could get.

"What about your wee daughter?" asked Anna. "She's how
old? The same as my Sandy?"

"I'll find somebody to look after her."

"January's no a month for learning to drive a motorcar. A
body could catch pneumonia."

"It's not a month for the men to be in the trenches either."

"You have me there."

So the Argyll came off the blocks for the tuition of would-
be ambulance drivers, and Anna gave lessons during the
short winter days. On Saturdays Lachie taught basic me-
chanics to Mrs. Dawson and four other ladies who boarded
at Glen Gryffe, "built like a hotel." When Anna pronounced
them ready to take their official tests, Meg Dawson gave
Lachie an English £5 note, the first he had ever seen. Each
Scottish bank issued its own, colorful currency that looked

more genuine to him than the black-and-white Sassenach promise to pay in gold.

"I couldn't take money for helping you, Mrs. Dawson. I'm not going to profit from the war."

"I'm not paying you for your help, Lachie. This is for your birthday. I gave my son a fiver on his sixteenth, too. You remind me of him when he was your age."

"How old is he now, Mrs. Dawson?"

"He'll be nineteen next week."

"And he's been in Flanders for months," Lachie told Hugh later, angrily whacking the body of the Argyll. "A lieutenant in the Royal Field Artillery."

"It must be rotten for you, Lachie."

On April 22, Albrecht, Duke of Wurtemberg, Commander of the German IVth Army, commenced the Second Battle of Ypres, using poison gas for the first time. As the mysterious yellow clouds of chlorine drifted down on the French forces, they fled their ground, leaving their guns behind.

Son of McFadden wrote Corporal James Grant that his suit for divorce on the grounds of desertion would have to be delayed until his return to civilian life. *"Obviously the putative defendant cannot return to your bed and board when you are no longer here to share either with her. Legally, therefore, she has been in desertion only to August 9, 1914, the date of your enlistment. Thus I recommend you do not bring suit until you have been demobilized five months."*

Two days after receiving this intelligence, Jamie Grant sailed with Lochiel's Camerons to join the 15th Scottish Division in France.

Second Lieutenant Bruce Bairnsfather created the cartoon character "Old Bill," a walrus-mustached indomitable private who symbolized the gallant working man in the trenches. The nation hurrahed the drawing of the middle-aged Tommy in a rain-filled shell crater as he squelched a complaining youngster with "Well, if you knows a better 'ole, go to it."

Banners on the Glasgow Transport Building now shouted

Glasgow Territorials have covered themselves with glory at the Dardanelles and *Thousands of Glasgow Territorials still wanted to take Constantinople.*

Meg Dawson left the city for the south of England as a potential ambulance driver, first depositing her daughter, Shona, with the Boyds for the duration.

Harriet's daughter, Kitty, went to work as a secretary-typist for a firm making shell casings. "I'll go to the University when the war is over," she told her mother.

"What do you hear from Dorcas?" Harriet asked Anna.

"Damn little," said Anna, ashamed of her eldest shirking in a land flowing with Swiss milk and chocolate. Dorcas's infrequent letters bemoaned the war only because it had caused cancellation of the traditional presentation of debutantes at Buckingham Palace, or "Buck House," as she disrespectfully labeled the Royal residence. She could find her way home, thought Anna. Others had, through Italy and the Straits of Gibraltar, the U-boats a minor risk to take in order to report for duty. Women were pitching in everywhere, in munitions factories, public service, on farms, even as tram conductresses trim in tartan jackets and ties and short skirts three inches off the ground. Proper Army they looked; when Anna saw them, she had half a mind to tell McFadden to cut off Dorcas's funds.

"It's a selfish age, nineteen," said Harriet sympathetically.

"Och, t' hell." Anna jumped up and went to the bay window. "Is yon no Goat Fell?'

Harriet came to look. Between the nurses' quarters and the chimney stack of the Western Infirmary, forty miles away a blue cone of mountain beckoned. "Oh, lovely, lovely," she said. "It's months since we've seen Arran from here." Moving quickly for a stout matron, she sped from the best room and returned with her three-year-old, yawning from his disturbed nap. "There, wee Duncan, can you see?" She held cool cheek to child's warm one. "There's old Goat Fell standing guard over Brodick Beach, where you'll soon be playing in the sand with your spade and pail. Remember

Johnny Morey's Island? 'I'll tell you a story of wee Johnny Morey. And that's my story begun.' "

" 'I'll tell you another of John and his brother,' " Anna went on with the centuries-old rhyme to fob off children begging for a story. " 'And that's my story endit. The dog broke the sugar bowl, and I can't mend it.' "

"Anna Biggart, stop making fun of Johnny Morey in front of Duncan. Just because you don't believe in faeries . . ."

Anna cackled. "Och, but I do. Renfrew Ferry. Govan Ferry . . ." The baby belched to rattle the windows. "Here, here, laddie, my joke's no that bad."

Harriet giggled. "He thinks it is."

"Well, it's me for the five-fifteen." She patted Duncan's cheek.

"What about Mr. Grant?" said Harriet at the door.

"What about him?"

"Have you heard from him?"

"No in the last three weeks."

"That could mean . . ."

Anna looked in the hall mirror and adjusted her toque. "Aye. He could be on his way."

Having found that gas attacks did not terrify the British and Canadians at Ypres, the Germans unleashed an unparalleled barrage with their superior artillery, and on May 26, considering that they had achieved a reasonable advance, concluded the second battle for the strategic town. The allies retained Ypres but lost Hill 60; British casualties 2150 officers, 57,125 other ranks; killed, 10,519. German losses, 860 officers, 34,073 other ranks.

In the same month the traditional concept of war ceased to be. No longer was it an extension of politics. With the formation of a British government composed of all parties, the conflict became a war of the people. Winston Churchill, who had ensured Britain's readiness at sea, was not named to the new Cabinet ostensibly because of the failure of the Dardanelles invasion, which he had conceived but had not been permitted to execute. He was appointed instead to the paltry job of Chancellor of the duchy of Lancaster, where-upon he abandoned politics for active duty in France as commander of the VIth Royal Scots Fusiliers. He was then forty-one.

With the House of Commons finally geared for all-out war, "Business as usual" began its gradual retreat into the Edwardian mists. For Anna, the euphemism vanished completely with the sinking of the ex-MacBrayne liner *Queen Alexandra* and the loss of the skipper who would have been a farmer.

"Aye, I kenned him, Lachie," she said. "A braw man who should have been coming here to learn aw about raising Aberdeen Angus from Sergeant Grant."

"Where are Lochiel's Camerons now?"

"Loos," she said and went for a walk.

The battle of Loos was carried out by nine raw divisions, two of them Scottish. They were ill-equipped and not up to strength, but the French General Foch insisted on an immediate drive by the Allies, so the British acquiesced and moved into action on September 25. They gained a little ground, only to see some of it recaptured when the Germans recovered from their surprise. The French, starting six hours late, had no success and on September 30 ordered a temporary cease-fire to gain time for reinforcements, as the British had originally wished.

"Patriotism is not enough," said Nurse Edith Cavell on October 11, 1915. Next day she was placed against a wall in Belgium and shot by the Germans for aiding wounded Allied troops to escape. She was fifty years of age.

Bad weather and enemy interference delayed the restart of the Loos offensive until early November. The new push brought no strategic results, became desultory, and settled into the monotony of trench warfare for the winter. In the battle of Loos, three British divisional commanders, 2,407 officers, and 57,895 other ranks were killed, wounded, or posted missing. German losses were estimated to have been one third as great.

The noise of the white-hot rivets being hammered home on the banks of the Clyde now made the prewar clamor but the chattering of squirrels as the river built and repaired vessels and warships to beat the German blockade begun in February 1915. *Untersea boaten* even penetrated the mouth of the firth itself. Indeed, it was rumored that when one was captured there, her daring commander had in his possession canceled stubs for a recent concert at St. Andrew's Hall in Glasgow. The safety of the country depended on the speed with which Clydeside could turn out ships of war and bottoms for the mercantile marine. Meanwhile, in the city and its environs, steel, heavy engineering, locomotives, aeroplane engines were produced around the clock for the volunteers who joined, trained, and shipped across.

With January 1916 came conscription, and service to King and Country ceased to be the privilege of the patriot and became the duty of every man. Rationing and meatless days remained voluntary, although Anna Dougal did her best to ensure that Glen Gryffe beef went only to the boys in the trenches.

Despite the 200,000 Irish volunteers fighting in France, there were others who looked on the war as an opportunity to win Irish independence. One of these was Sir Roger Casement, a former British consular officer. Knighted in 1911, he had domiciled himself in Berlin, where he worked actively to defeat his former employer. Learning that the Irish Republican Brotherhood planned an uprising for Easter, he set sail from Germany in a U-boat, landed in County Kerry, and was captured immediately, thus missing the Easter Monday fracas that paralyzed Dublin for a week. Casement was tried, convicted of treason, and sentenced to hang on August 3, 1916. The Spanish-Irish-American Eamon de Valera, prominent among the captured rebels, was jailed but not executed because he had been born in New York and was considered a citizen of the United States.

"Silly buggers, both," said Pat Nolan from County Down, one of the Orange six of Ulster. "Poor bleeding Ireland. The

Catholics can't get along with themselves, let alone with the Protestants."

Leaning against the sunny side of the byre, he was enjoying a pipeful of cut plug, Lachie pretending to, Willie Boyd manfully trying to light a third. It was the first summer of his fifteen that Willie was not spending on the Island of Arran, but when invited to help the war effort at Glen Gryffe, he knew where his duty lay; Aunt Anna was willing to pay, and Willie liked money. He was also finding himself in agreement with the Burnsian philosophy, "What signifies the life of man, And 'twerena for the lasses O." There were those aplenty at the farm; not untouchables like Elspeth and the friends of the family at Brodick, but land girls from the orphanage, fair game for a rough and tumble in the gloaming. He found giving up his summer holidays no hardship, devoted as he was to his courtesy aunt. She was a great one for a laugh, although last Sabbath she'd been somber as the day itself.

"Who stole your scone, Aunt Anna?" he asked.

"No a soul, laddie, though I wish somebody had pinched the Yorkshire pudding before I had that greedy wee second piece."

Blaming Cookie's fare excused the heartburn caused by the memorial service held that morning in Glasgow Cathedral for the city's sons who "went west" in the first three days of the Battle of the Somme. Twenty officers and 534 other ranks from the 16th H.L.I. alone, the battalion recruited from the Boys' Brigade. And Lochiel's Camerons were in the line there, too. She retired to the morning room and poured herself a glass of courage. "Inspiring bold John Barleycorn, what dangers thou canst make us scorn!" But no another's jeopardy. Jamie, I wish to God you were down the brae, safe in your own but-and-ben. She raised the glass with her left hand, the one nearest the heart. "Absent friends," she muttered, then went for a walk over the Pad to look down on the Clyde and find strength in Britain's might lying at anchor off the Tail-of-the-Bank.

255

At 3 A.M. of a summer morning, Lady Clara Biggart died of "fatty degeneration of the heart." All fatalities being ultimately failure of that organ, the doctor would have been more explicit had he attributed the passing to the typical overeating and underexercising of her class and gender. In sixty-three years she had accomplished nothing but the birth of one child.

"She was a good woman," said Harriet.

"If that's aw you can say about me when I'm gone, I'll have wasted my life," said Anna. "Seems to me we're put on this world to do more than wait for the next. Och well. R.I.P."

The usufruct of the trust established by Sir George now passed to his daughter, giving her one of the bigger annual incomes in the West of Scotland, where wealth was not uncommon.

"I can't stand this funk hole one more bloody minute," said Lachlan Dougal, prone on the turf, staring at the clouds. "It's nothing but a ruddy nunnery."

"Some nuns," said Willie and sniggered.

"You and your gropes. I'm not talking about randy bints. I'm talking about ladies. God, Willie, I live with them all bloody year except for school, and even there the real men are all gone. It's Saturday, isn't it? Any minute now, nice-girl Bella Cockburn'll come traipsing up the drive with her bloody racquet to add one more skirt. God, if I ever have to play another pat-ball game of mixed doubles . . . The place wasn't so bad when Mr. Grant was around. At least in front of him you could call shite shite and not fertilizer. Honestly, Willie, have you any idea what it's like not to be able to let go a rousing fart in your own fields for fear there's a girl over the hedge?" He rolled on his stomach. "Do you have any money?"

Willie emptied his trouser pocket of a once-white handkerchief, a horseshoe nail, a paper-wrapped toffee, and four copper coins. "Thruppence ha'penny. Do you want it?"

"Hell, no. What do you do with your wages?"

"Your mother doesn't give them to me. She says she puts them in escrow, whatever the hell that is."

"If I lend you a couple of bob, you could give it back to me when she does pay you."

"Where could I get rid of two shillings in Strathgryffe? I'd cat all over the moor if I spent that much at the Tally's."

"They would just about cover a trip to Glasgow for the three P's."

"What the hell are they, Lachie?"

"A pie, a pint, and a picture show. You ever had a beer?"

"Dozens of times."

"Liar. I'll bet you couldn't get one down."

"How much? The two bob you're going to lend me?"

"Smart wee bugger, aren't you? You're on. It'll be worth a florin to get out of this fartless fortress for an afternoon."

"Shouldn't we tell your mother we're going?"

"There's Hughie. We'll leave word with him." He whistled through his fingers, and his brother came running, collie at heel.

"We're off to town, Hughie."

"Can't I come, too?"

"You're two years younger than Willie. Bad enough if I lead him down the road to ruin."

" 'She was roo-ined as roo-ined could be,' " sang Willie.

"Come on," said Lachie. "We'll go by the steppingstones. Then we won't meet bouncing Bella on the road."

"The wretches," said Elspeth when she heard of the defection. "Lachie knew Bella was coming for tennis. Now we'll have to play singles unless—Hughie, how about you?"

"Do I have to?"

"I'll play, too," said Morag sadly, facing a Willieless afternoon.

The young men did not return in time for dinner, which, with their appetites, wasn't like them.

"They must be making picture shows as long as a service at the Wee Free Kirk," said Anna.

After dinner she, Elspeth, Bella, and Hugh sat down to a rubber of auction. The hostess, a good player, revoked twice. When Bella left for home at nine-thirty, Anna pulled a deck chair onto the terrace to watch for the return of her son and her friend's son. The sun was still up, newfangled daylight saving time now helping conserve fuel for ships at sea and factories. It was a calm evening, soft and windless. A cow lowed. In the valley a cuckoo, seldom seen but often heard, sounded its plaintive double note. From the vegetable garden came the *teacher, teacher* of a tit. Lachie aye contended that the call was the wee bird sharpening its bill. When the telephone shrilled to drown the sounds of nature, Anna forced herself to walk slowly to the morning room. Elspeth was already there.

"I'll take it, Mamá. Hello? Hello? . . . No, this is Elspeth. Go ahead."

Anna watched her daughter's face blanch then redden before she turned and wordlessly handed the instrument to her mother.

"Mary Loudon here, Mrs. Dougal," said the wife of Malcolm, who was now in the Royal Signal Corps. "Lachie asked me to give you a message. I wantit to put him through to you, but he cut me off." Her voice broke. "He's joined up, Mrs. Dougal. The Queen's Own Royal Glasgow Yeomanry."

Heads up.

"Thank you, Mary. I've been expecting it. Did he say when Willie Boyd would be home?"

"Mrs. Dougal, they took wee Willie, too. And him naught but a halflin."

Anna replaced the receiver gently.

"I'm proud, proud, proud of my brother," said Elspeth.

"Then come with me and drink to him." For if you don't, I'll break down altogether. "It's time you learned the brave taste of whisky. We'll toast Willie, too, the wee beggar. Harriet Hepburn and I wanted men for sons, and by the Lord we have them." But och, I could weep for the wish come true.

As an aching tooth takes the mind off the greater pain of a broken leg, so Willie's enlistment overshadowed Lachie's. The younger boy had been in her care, had run away from her home with the instigator, her son, and now she must carry the news to the mother, her oldest and dearest friend. But first there was Sunday to get through. Anna saw the Reverend Arthur Auchinleck's brows rise at the two vacant spaces in the Dougal pew. As the sole parent, I'm in for a pious talking-to. I couldna stand a pi-jaw the day, so I'll no go back to the vestry after the benediction to satisfy his curiosity. If he told me the lads were in God's hands, I'd assault the cloth.

For the first time in her life she did not stand and chat outside the front door, but paced away with a curt nod before the ladies had time to change their minds from God to gossip. The quick uphill walk home brought second wind to lungs and brain. It took time to train recruits, she re-assured herself—almost a year—and Lachie was the rawest, for all he could ride. In a year the war would be over, and he could come home a proven man without being exposed to the frightfulness of the Hun. Aye, that was the way to think. At noon dinner she fought to keep her bottle half full. "You're the head of the family pro tem, Hughie. Say grace and make it short. I'm fair famished."

She rose at six on Monday and made a good breakfast of a Loch Fyne kipper, then Glen Gryffe ham, thin and nicely frizzled around the edges, with two Glen Gryffe eggs fried in the same pan. A sleepy Hugh put up the hood for her, cranked the Argyll into firing, and alone she took the route south over the moors to Lochwinnoch, not as rugged as the drive to Oban in another life, but a challenge just the same, the road rising almost six hundred feet, and Misty Law on her off side a thousand feet above that. By Kilbirnie Loch she went, then through Dalry's ancient narrow streets, through Kilwinning, Stevenston, and down to Ardrossan Pier for a vessel bound across the Clyde. Arran lay thirteen miles out, unseen in a soaking easterly that whipped smoke at right angles from clay chimney pots and pushed with giant hand at her back. Behind the breakwater no Clyde steamers lay waiting her custom. They, too, were gone to war, transporting troops at twenty knots across the Channel, and some to further places. In the gay pleasure boats' stead, a pinnace of forty feet overall pulled at her hawsers with no grip of the water, her shallow draft her only protection should a submarine lurking in wait for a ten-thousand tonner be foolish enough to waste a torpedo on such poor prey.

Except for four woebegone sheep, Anna was the only passenger. Scorning the cabin, she wedged herself in the forward corner of the open-sided shelter deck, looking aft at the red ensign blown straight inboard and the following sea that grew as the little ship moved out of land's lee. The waves climbed above the stern, the stern rose, the waves slid below, the vessel yawed to broach, came back on course, the next wave climbed. It's a gey good thing I had the gumption to eat a decent breakfast, she thought. An empty stomach couldna stand this.

A mariner ancient as Coleridge's strung a lifeline fore and aft, its thick strands nearly against her chest.

"Who's that for?" she yelled. "I dinna need it."

"You bloody well might," he shouted back from toothless mouth.

Ten minutes later he used it himself as he clawed his way back to her along the streaming canting deck. He grabbed her hand, slapped it on the hemp, and pointed north to a white double wave, a giant gull's wings charging at them. Then the gray cutwater of a battleship rent the curtain of rain. Rolling her turrets forty-five degrees in the beam sea, oil smoke pouring from two funnels, at thirty knots the warship crossed their bow.

"Hang on!" yelled the deckhand, slipping under the line to jam himself in beside her.

Under her feet she felt the engine revolutions slow. Over her shoulder she saw the man-made waves collide with the easterly's in giant teeth of white that leaped toward them.

The following sea lifted their stern and drove the bow under the first comber. It crashed aboard green, grabbed at Anna's knees, swept the helpless sheep into the corner of the solid gunwale. The little vessel shook herself free, her head went up, up, and solid water poured over the stern to poop her. Almost. Forward motion nearly stopped, her stern struggled up, the propellor raced in the air, and an unseen hand cut its revolutions to the minimum. She rolled her port scuppers under, then her starboard as wave after wave crashed aboard and the corkscrew motion set her timbers to groaning above the din.

"Damn the Old Woman," shouted Anna. "Could she no have stayed at Corrievreckan?"

Then the wash was curling away astern.

"That would be H.M.S. *Barham*," said the seaman. "Frae John Brown's yard. I heard tell she'd be running her trials the day. Look at they bloody sheep. I hope they're no mutton." He scurried away to the mass of wool, examined each one carefully for broken legs, and turned back to Anna with a cheery thumbs-up.

There was little to be seen of Brodick's crescent beach as the cabin cruiser came broadside, then into the wind to take the pier after a ninety-minute passage, twice as long as the peacetime voyage. Clouds sat on top of the multicolored bathing huts, filled the three glens, hid the Duke's red sandstone castle, the Sleeping Warrior, Goat Fell. It was low tide, the sand bars up, and the bay itself a fury of white breakers, the deck of the pier a long way above the pinnace's, even when the waves sent her surging up. Like an elevator she rose and fell, rose and fell while Anna clung to a stanchion and wondered how they would maneuver her feet onto terra firma. The skipper, a red-faced septuagenarian in streaming oilskins, solved the problem by calling for a sling from the disembodied face looking down at them over the pier's edge.

"What do you think I am?" said Anna. "One of they bloody sheep?"

"You're dafter than that," said the skipper. "They didna

make the trip of their own free will. You did." But he was smiling as he said it, a braw man for all his age. The spinning ride up at the end of the rope made her feel like a bairn again, and so did the venerability of the pier hand who hauled her in with the aid of a boat hook. She squelched her way over the boards, head sideways to the gale, the excitement of the journey having clean driven the reason for it from her mind. At the pierhead it was brought back forcibly.

"Defense o' the Realm Act," said the police sergeant when she asked what authority he had for questioning her visit.

"What's that sneaking old maid D.O.R.A. doing here?"

"The Isle o' Arran is strategic. I have tae file a report on every passenger that lands. Even if it's bonny Prince David o' Wales himsel."

The toll booth was closed.

"The wee collector joined the Bantams, the 18th H.L.I.," said the sergeant.

"Was he at the Somme?"

"Aye. He'll no be back." He looked over her head and out to sea. "What a pasting the wee fellows took."

She let wind and rain hurry her across the bridge over the Hotel Burn. The hedge of dog roses and the thick rhododendron gave her some protection as she climbed the path to the red sandstone cottage that Harriet and Robert had rented every summer since their marriage. And Harriet's parents and their parents before that in the douce life folk lived till this bloody war broke families apart.

"Yoohoo! It's only me, wee Anna Dougal," she called, waiting inside the back door, her clothes puddling the flagstones. To her relief, Kitty came running. It was lucky she was on a few days' holiday; three was better company at a time like this.

Bewildered by the totally unexpected, Harriet clung to what she understood.

"Willie had no right," she said. "Now he'll never pass his Highers. How can a boy go back to high school after he has worn his country's khaki?"

Unlike Elspeth, Kitty was more afraid for her brother than proud of him. It was she who suggested that her father could get the underage boys out of their enlistment. Unfortunately, Robert Boyd was in camp with the Citizens' Volunteers for Home Defense. "Playing soldier himself," said Harriet, anger rising.

"We should send Father a telegram, Mamá," said Kitty. "He'll know what to do. I'll run down to the post office with it."

"Take Shona and Duncan with you then. They haven't had any fresh air all day."

When the door slammed behind the children, shutting out the sooching wind and rain, Anna produced a silver flask, well knowing she would have to provide the vital spirit. Harriet's late father had inherited a fortune, made two more, and lost all three through taking to drink. Consequently his daughter's home rarely boasted whisky.

"To Lachlan Dougal," said Mrs. Boyd.

"To Willie Boyd," said Mrs. Dougal.

"Drat this weather." Harriet dabbed her nostrils. "It gives me the sniffles. Come ben the house while I put the scones on the girdle."

She would not permit Anna to return to the mainland while the easterly blew its ordained three days. Anna did not object. Glen Gryffe could manage without her; not for many years had she been able to spend so much time with her old friend. Meg Dawson's daughter Shona was a winsome wee thing who enjoyed mothering Duncan, Harriet's sunny-tempered afterthought. The eight-year-old lass was proud of her family—father, brother, mother all in the war.

"Now you can be proud of Willie, too," she told Duncan.

"Willie's the bravest soldier in the whole world," said wee Duncan, and politely Shona did not contradict him.

"I think I'll walk over to Lamlash by the Faery Glen," said

"Kitty's that moony, she could be in love," said Anna when tea."

"Watch out for the Hotel Burn," said her mother. "It'll be in spate."

"I know a way across it. There's a branch of a big oak . . ."

"Kitty's that moony, she could be in love," said Anna when the girl had gone into the storm. "Anyone I ken?"

"Meg Dawson's son writes her all the time. He's been in the thick of it since the beginning. She tells me he has his third pip." Brass sounded on brass at the back door. "There's Coley the Bakers. Anything special you'd like with your tea?"

"I canna tell till I look at the goods."

The two ladies threw oilskins over their heads and shoulders and stood under the canvas canopy of the cart drawn by a mare so wet that she looked like a seal fresh from the sea.

"See anything you fancy, leddies?" said the lad in charge.

"I could go one of they strawberry tarts," said Anna.

"So could I," said Harriet. "Let me have a shilling's worth, Sandy, please."

"Sorry, Mrs. Boyd. Half a dozen tae a house. Ma father says we hae to conserve sugar voluntarily or they'll make it compulsory. Nae mair butter for the morning baps, either. It's marjarine now. So Willie's joined up. Good for him. They turned me down, and me six months older. I mustna be as good a leear."

"Don't be cheeky, Sandy Coley, or I'll tell your father."

"Och, I'm joking, Mrs. Boyd. We're aw proud of our Willie. And you'll be Mrs. Dougal. We heard about your Lachie, too. Up the Queen's Own! Ta-ta the now, leddies. See you the morn's morn."

"Dougal, L. will be of age in a matter of months," said the titled staff officer when approached by Robert Boyd, whom he remembered from rowing days on the Isis. "By the time they had him processed out, he would be due back in. Now, your lad's a different vintage. Tell you what, Boyd"—Red Tabs beamed with pleasure at the chance to do something for a quondam fellow athlete—"I will see that he is retained on the Home Front till he's eighteen. No, no. Don't argue. I know you feel that's unfair to the other chaps, but—I insist. In two years he should be able to win a stripe or two. I'll keep an eye on him . . . We'll advance him as fast as we can. By jove, he's the right stuff. But what would one expect? He's your son."

Anna's prayers for the war to end now developed a new intensity. Before, they had been general; she had felt it not fitting to ask God for the preservation of her lover. Now she dropped his name entirely from her nightly litany lest it diffuse her plea for an end to hostilities before Lachlan was ready for duty overseas. The omission of Jamie was daft, a superstition, but like not walking under a ladder, it couldn't do harm and might, just might do some good with the Almighty.

The greater strength of her demand for Lachie's safety taught her that love took many forms. For Jamie it was a selfish heartache; for her son, a yearning for his health and happiness with no thought of her own, which she would sacrifice totally if it would benefit him. It was easy to pray for Lachie.

1916 ended without profit for the Allies, the small strategic gains not commensurate with the loss of lives. The British surprise weapon, the tank, introduced in the Somme before sufficient were ready for action, was mishandled because of inexperience. The juggernauts bogged down in the mud, dashing the hope that a way had been found to penetrate and cross the enemy trenches.

The French Army was at a nadir, high in numbers, low in equipment, lower yet in morale after the blood bath of Verdun.

Despite their capture of 200,000 prisoners from the Austrian IVth and VIIth Armies, the Russian forces were torn by dissension and ripe for mutiny.

Joining the Allies too late, Rumania fell, giving the enemy all her oil and wheat.

Britain still controlled the seas, but the Battle of Jutland waged by Admirals Beatty and Jellicoe had been a tactical triumph for German Admiral Scheer, who sank two of Beatty's six battleships before escaping. An expanded underseas campaign threatened when Deutschland's large submarine cruisers sank several neutral vessels off the coast of America.

The profit side of the ledger could show only the capture of Baghdad and the minor Italian success at Gorizia. These were not enough for the British Home Front. On December 11, 1916, Asquith lost to his fellow Liberal, Lloyd George, who became Prime Minister on the promise of "a more vigorous and more efficient prosecution of the war." The voters overlooked his angry espousal of arms reduction in the spring of 1914.

On December 12 the Germans, smelling victory, proposed the initiation of peace discussions. The Frenchman Joffre, however, misinterpreted the peace feeler as a sign of weakness. The Allies had never been more powerful; now was the time to smash *le salle Boche,* although Joffre did warn that after one more major battle his country would no longer have the reserves to replace the inevitable dead.

President Wilson of the United States asked the belligerents to define their war aims as a preliminary to peace talks. All replies were considered evasive at best, and the possibility of negotiation was shelved. The American, who had labored long for peace, did not comprehend the nature of the global conflict—that for the first time in history this was a war of the people and capitulation by either side unthinkable as long as the home fronts retained the will.

Lloyd George recalled Winston Churchill from command of the VI Royal Scots Fusiliers and appointed him to the Cabinet as Minister of Munitions.

Early in 1917, the all-out blockade of the British Isles

justified the fears of Coley, the Brodick baker: sugar, meat, bacon, and fats were rationed.

The limitless losses under Joffre caused his replacement by General Robert Georges Nivelle, whose *"ils ne passeront pas"* at Verdun in '14 had cost 350,000 Frenchmen but had stopped the Germans.

March brought the Russian Revolution. Under a headless provisional government, her armies began the collapse that was soon to be total.

With the sinking of unarmed U.S. ships and Germany's efforts to persuade Mexico to attack her northern neighbor, on April 6, 1917, the United States entered the war. Acquiring this new ally to replace the fading Russians gave a boost to morale but no immediate support to ground fighting. America must first enlist her manpower, train and equip it before she would be ready for battle.

Pour la gloire, Nivelle sacrificed his countrymen against the barbed wire and machine-gun emplacements of Champagne. Mutinies broke out in sixteen French army corps, and Nivelle was replaced by General Philippe Pétain, who proceeded to bind the wounds of his troops by leaving the fighting to others. With America not yet in, Russia making no contribution, France moribund, the sixty-four British Empire divisions under Haig were alone.

After due deliberation, the authorities decided that cavalry was outmoded. Along with other regiments, the Queen's Own Royal Glasgow Yeomanry was dehorsed and ordered to replace the empty ranks of the 18th H.L.I., the Bantams, whose annihilation begun in '15 had been virtually completed in the mud of Passchendaele. Among those sent to train for the Poor Bloody Infantry were Dougal, L., and Boyd., W. H.

A week after news of the transfer reached Glen Gryffe, Mairi Maclean came running from the orphanage, in her hand the *Glasgow Bulletin,* a lively picture paper founded two years before by the oracular *Herald.*

"Where did you get the rag?" asked Anna.

"From Johnny Blackadder. Oof! Wait, please, till I find my wind." At twenty-three Mairi was far removed from the shy doe who wouldn't answer the telephone. Responsibility upstairs and on the farm had bolstered the assurance that she found in her mirror. The demure Highland lass had grown to be the beauty of Strathgryffe, a tantalus to the lads of the village, had there been any left there to thirst. Her voice retained its heart-catching lilt and sibilant emphasis, but her words no longer reflected translation from the Gaelic except deliberately and for fun.

She's owergood for Glen Gryffe, thought Anna. Mibbie I could wangle her a position at the Dough School. Or send her to the Ayrshire School of Agriculture. Before Jamie comes home.

"Look, Mistress Dougal . . ." The farmerette held out the paper, and Anna recognized a picture of the building where she had put "finis" to Daisy Grant. *Entrance to Scene of Crime* she read below the photograph and alongside it *Sergeant's Wife Slain, Man Detained.* Daisy had been found in bed, death apparently due to strangulation. An unidentified citizen had been detained. *The authorities have asked for the return of the deceased's husband, Sgt. James Grant, 5th Cameron Highlanders . . .*

He's coming home!

"How soon will they have him out of the trenches, Mistress Dougal?" asked Mairi, eyes enormous.

"They can be gey quick when they have a mind." Anna cleared her throat. "Drat it. I aye get a wee hoast this time of year. But I wouldna look for the sergeant before week's end." How long a Blighty would he get? No matter how short, better a few days than a boot on the backside. "The twins should redd up his house."

"Och, it will be grand to see his chimney smoke once more."

"Aye." And you wouldna mind warming yoursel at yon fireplace. "Run along now and alert the kitchen." Dinna blame the girl; you're as bad as she, concerned only with yoursel and no a thought for the murdered woman. Whatna terrible end. Never mind how rotten Daisy was, Jamie loved her once, and no woman deserved such a fate. Anna saw again the petulant mouth, the shifty *stupid* eyes . . .

The telephone rang.

"Mr. McFadden here." For the first time in their association, Mr. A., still Son, asked if he might pay a social call on Mrs. Dougal.

"He was that portentous," she told Elspeth that night, "you'd think he was after an audience with the Queen." And that's wee me, if yon gypsy's warning held water. He's read what happened to Daisy, and he's out to get his oar in before Jamie comes home free."

"I wonder what he wants," said Elspeth.

"We'll find out soon enough. I invited him to take the top off an egg with us tomorrow night."

"There's a bobby coming up the drive," Sandy called down the stairs.

"You're supposed to be asleep, you rascal," said Elspeth.

"Och, it's too light. This old summer time . . ."

Sheila, the Macleod twin on door duty, ushered in the uniformed police sergeant.

"Well, well," said Anna. "Mr. McNab, is it no? Or I should say Sergeant McNab. What happened to the *Encyclopædia Britannica?*"

"They called me back tae duty to let a younger man gang tae war," said the ex-private detective. "Now I sit behind the counter aw day. Soft for the feet and softer on the brain. Could I hae a word wi' you in private, Mrs. Dougal?"

"I should be in bed anyway," said Elspeth, rising. "Good night, everybody. Come on, Hughie."

For Hugh to be excluded from drama was unthinkable. Said the temporary head of the house, "I am sure, Sergeant, that Mrs. Dougal would want me to stay. We have no secrets from one another."

"Is that a fact?" said Anna. "What about the packet of

Prize Crop cigarettes I found in your blazer pocket? And you a rugger player."

"You pinched them? And there were seventeen left."

"I'll give them back and you can smoke them in front of me instead of dashing off, if you'll take yoursel out of here the now. You'll no be missing anything. Sergeant McNab just wants to give me the gossip of our old kirk at Botanic Gardens. Is that no right, Sergeant?"

Damn! "In that case, good night, Sergeant. Good night, Mother." He left without kissing her.

"I was just about to ring for a wee cup of tea," said Anna. "Will you join me? I'd offer you whisky, but I remember the trouble with your abdomen."

"Nae mair, Mrs. Dougal. I havena had a pain since I rejoined the force."

"The detecting must have been an awfu strain on the nerves."

"That and no drinking proper. We hae a new police doctor, and he says nae harm can come to an ulcer frae a weak whisky and plain water. No soda water, though. Yon gas fair eats you. No wine or beer either, but who wants that when he's allowed the real stuff?"

"Help yoursel, then." She didn't offer to pour. A man should measure his own. "The water in the carafe's fresh." Quickly she added, "Just in case a gentleman like yoursel ducks in. You'll be here about Daisy Grant's death?"

"Aye."

"In that case, would you mind giving me a taet to keep me from the vapors?" He barely wet the bottom of a glass. "You needna be so sparing with it," she adjured him. "I ken it's nasty-tasting stuff, but aw med'cin has to be or it doesna do any good."

"Your health." He drank, pursed his lips, smacked them. "My, that's whusky. Now, Mrs. Dougal, ever since I did yon wee job for you, I've thocht you and James Grant would marry. I handed you aw the evidence he needed for divorce."

"Whatever gave you that idea?"

"Mibbie I wantit tae feel I'd helped make two fine folk happy."

"You're a mite auld for Cupid, Sergeant. Anyway, Mr. Grant wouldna use your evidence lest Daisy take after me and mine."

"Well, well. He's a grand man, yon. And you're no sae bad yoursel. That's why I kept an e'e on Daisy every now and then, and why I asked my pals in Paisley what happened yesterday."

"I dinna doubt it was her brother-in-law."

"Aye. I shouldna tell you, but I'm off duty and I ken you'll keep it tae yoursel." He looked into the glass cupped in both big hands. "I came here the nicht wi' a piece of advice. If it was me, I wouldna see owermuch o' Sergeant Grant till the trial's done. In fact, I wouldna be alone wi' him at aw. You see, Mrs. Dougal, there's nae doubt that Tom Black choked the life out o' Daisy Grant. He's guilty, and the only question now is the extent o' his punishment. If the prosecution can show that Daisy was a defenseless wife driven from her home by the unfaithfulness of her husband, Tom Black'll hang." He sipped his drink thoughtfully. "You're sure there never was aught between you and Grant before she left him?"

"No! I told you that before." She pushed aside a gold-framed picture, dialed a combination, and took out Daisy's letter, in the safe since Jamie had left for war. "Read this. It's what I did with your report, Sergeant. I snookered Daisy into signing a declaration of desertion. After four years Mr. Grant could use that to shed her easy as a collie sheds sheep."

"Indeed he could, Mrs. Dougal."

"Now tell the truth. You're no off duty, are you?"

"No all the way." He was unperturbed. "My Paisley colleagues ken I once did a wee bit checking on the victim. They want aw the background they can get on the murder. You see, wi' no weapon but bare hands, it doesna look premeditated. The more bad the law can learn about Daisy's character, the less chance there is that Tom Black'll hae to take the six-foot drop. Can you prove what you told me the first time? That James Grant showed his wife the gate because she had, so to speak, consorted wi' your late husband?"

"Would it save his neck?" Daisy, who had ruined lives, should not be allowed to take one *post-mortem*.

"I could awmost guarantee it."

"My oldest daughter saw them and kept it to hersel till she couldna hold it any longer."

"Och, the wee lass." He replenished his glass, and she held up her own to be refilled. "I wouldna ask her tae testify against her ain father tae save the King himsel."

"She wouldna have to." From the safe she now took Dorcas's disguised scrawl and the envelope in which it had come. "You'll note the postmark is dated the day before Daisy left Mr. Grant of her own free will."

"May I take these wi' me?" He saw her hesitate. "Dinna fret, Mrs. Dougal. Aw I need is tae prove Daisy Grant was no good before she took up wi' Black. A wee squint at these before the trial, and the prosecutor'll no try tae make her out a weak woman victimized by a wicked man. These prove Daisy was evil and Tom naught but a damn fool."

"And he'll no hang?"

"Scots law's no vindictive."

"Will the word get out?"

"No a chance o' that either."

"McNab, you're a gentleman and a friend."

"Is it handing me ma hat you are? Do you no want tae ken how Daisy met her end?"

"I thought you'd never ask."

"Would you mind ma pipe?" He held up a curly-stemmed brier.

"Go right ahead." Anna sat back: like Dr. Watson.

"Aw the ladies"—*puff*—"in Tom Black's flats"—*puff*—"kent Daisy for what she was." *Puff, puff, puff.* "You're sure you dinna mind? It's no a fit story for a lady's ears."

" 'Judy O'Grady and the Colonel's lady . . .' "

"You and Daisy never were sisters under the skin. That I'll no have."

"On with it, man."

"The war speeded up the deceased's—uh—traffic," he continued, wreathed now in camouflaging smoke. "Daisy was owergreedy, and soon aw the decent folk wantit an end put to the neighborhood scandal. What they didna ken was that the landlord was also a—customer, for where Daisy grew careless, Tom continued careful as a Jerry spy. The woman in the fish-and-chips shop—a good sort yon—tellt me she tried tae talk her husband intae blowing the gaff, but he said he didna have sufficient proof to tak tae Black."

"Men are aw daft, Sergeant, present company excepted."

McNab nodded. "Anyway, Mrs. Fish and Chips decided that if the mister wouldna tattle, she would. After kirk last Sunday—they sit under the same minister—she pulled Tom Black aside and tolt him Daisy Grant was running a—a one-woman—brothel. I shouldna use such a word in front o' you, Mrs. Dougal."

"I ken it doesna mean 'soup kitchen,' Sergeant. What did Black say to that?"

"Nothing. But his informant said she was glad she wasna a man. He turned purple and drew back his fist. Imagine! Tae a woman! Outside the kirk where he was a deacon. Then he got ahold o' himsel and went home wi' his wife to the Sunday joint. Strange. He made a great point to the duty officer about the sirloin being owerdone. He seemed to think that was important."

Of course it was. Nothing would be right. Anna could imagine him trying to rest while the mind churned. The sofa would have prodding lumps, the parlor excess heat, the wing collar daggers to prick the neck, and his wife's "You'll no be feeling poorly?" would surely be repaid with a snarl.

McNab consulted a black-bound notebook. "At two-forty P.M. the suspect donned his frock coat again and proceeded to deceased's home, to which he had a key. He entered wi'out chapping and caught her"—the sergeant struggled with the niceties—"*in flagrante delicto* with a naval rating off *H.M.S. Repulse,* and him but a lad." He snapped his book shut. "On the Sabbath moreover." That seemed to shock him more than the situation or the disparity in ages.

"Apart from his fling wi' Daisy, Black was aye a law-abiding citizen. When the mist cleared, he went to the station and gave himself up. That'll help, o' course." McNab sighed. "In aw ma days, I've never been able tae understand the ordinary man's predilection for working sae hard tae get intae trouble."

Although it meant the last train, a creeping slow local, he wouldn't stay the night. "Yon laddie of yours wasna put off by your wee prevarication, Mrs. Dougal. He'd throw the questions at me the morn's morn, and when he found out I didna even ken the number of the pews in your auld kirk, he'd be on tae me like a young police after a street bookie. I'm good at the dissembling, but I'll no take the chance of lowering a halflin's belief in the honesty of the man in blue. Our reputation is the law's strongest weapon."

"He seemed a decent enough sort," Hugh told his mother next morning over the breakfast herring. He was always down before the girls. "What did Sergeant McNab really want?"

Tell the half truth, and you won't have to tell the whole. "You'll have heard about Mr. Grant's poor wife?"

"Come on, Mother. Just because she's dead. She was the complete rotter. Everyone knew that. Why should the police come to see you about her?"

"They wanted a sketch of her character when she lived here. It seems that if they can show she was aye the bad hat, the man that did her in will no have to hang."

"Mairi says he should get a medal. What did you tell Sergeant McNab?"

"I didna go quite as far as Mairi, but I said that from what I'd heard, she'd been asking to have her neck wrung for a gey long time. You and Mairi must be right good friends to chat about such like."

"Mairi's fun. She's jolly good-looking, as well."

And you're coming up to the age where I'll have to worry about you, too. "Only three herring, Hughie? You'll fade away to a gasworks."

"I'd rather have Cookie's herring fried in oatmeal than pheasant under glass." He pondered the overstatement. "For breakfast anyway."

This, too, proved a busy day for the wires. Dolly Nolan rang up. "Will you ask Sergeant Grant tae save Pat an' me a night of his leave?"

"Why me?"

"Och, Mrs. Dougal . . ." Dolly giggled and hung up.

Harriet Boyd dared the telephone all the way from Brodick. "I think you had better come down here for a visit. The weather's fine—not at all what it was last time you were here. I've been bathing every noon when the gentlemen leave the beach. If I'm not careful, my complexion will turn all nasty and brown. Can you catch the boat tomorrow? Are you listening?"

" 'Course I'm listening." Between the lines, too, Harriet Hepburn. You want me out of here.

"Oh, Anna, what a dreadful way to become a widower! You shouldn't take the slightest chance of getting mixed up in the affair. Think of the children. Shall I meet the pinnace in the morning?"

"If you have nothing better to do. You can aye have a word with yon skeely skipper. Give him my regards, for I'll no be there to do it mysel."

"Three minutes, please."

"Drat," said Harriet. "I don't have any more pennies."

"Ta-ta the now, my auld china."

Anna was touched and amused by Harriet's solicitude, but not at all upset. That condition was reserved for the next call.

"Margot Dougal here. How are you, Anna? Philip and I were talking about you last night and saying how long it has been since we were together. You've never even seen the little estate we've acquired in Perthshire. I do so want to show it to you. Why don't you pack a valise right now and visit us for a few days. Philip could send the Rolls for you from town, and you could come back with him in the evening. He'd love that . . ."

"He'd no such damn thing. If your husband had to be shut up in a motorcar with wee Anna Dougal for two hours, he'd go out the window. If I didn't go first. I'll no be so unkind as to say he means well, but I'd no leave Glen Gryffe the now. I have four doddies about to calve."

The Honorable Margot laughed. "I win my bet. I told Philip you wouldn't come. Not with your—partner coming home. But he insisted I try. Do visit us some other time. I would love to have you for your sake and not for the firm's."

Cook entered. "What wines will we serve the night, Mrs. Dougal? Have you any idea of the gentleman's taste?"

"Lordsakes, Son of McFadden. I'd forgotten aw about him. He's partial to an *apéritif*. Medium dry sherry."

"I thought as Master Hugh would be at the carving, salmon slices and lamb chops. It wouldna do for him tae land a bird in your lawyer's lap."

"With the fish, any dry white then, as long as it's no from Hunland, damn them. And a Châteauneuf-du-pape with the chops. If the French could fight as brawly as they make wine, this bloody war would be ower. What's for afters?"

"We still hae a jar o' raspberry jam left, Mrs. Dougal. I thought a trifle . . ."

"Fine, but we'll pass up dessert wine. I canna stand the sticky sweet stuff. And with the cheese board, serve the port. Mr. McFadden'll no be wanting to sit over it by his lone."

"Wineglasses for Master Hugh?"

"Aye. It's time his education started. He can have a taet of the white and red. He'll need a wee lift to help him ower this dinner."

He did. The guest was constrained. Young people were foreign country to him, and hard as the Dougals tried, the ball of small talk lacked bounce, frequently rolling under the table with a deflationary sigh. With the port, Elspeth and Hugh gratefully excused themselves, she to walk over to see Bella Cockburn, he to take old Chief for an eight-mile stroll on the moors before bedtime.

Then Archibald McFadden began to talk. About himself. From his birth in 1857 to his present position as heir to the most solid legal firm in the West of Scotland. The saga of sixty years lacked interest, for nothing had ever happened to him, and Anna found her eyes watering with suppressed yawns until he said, "This is not the way I imagined it, Mrs. Dougal—Anna. I should be calling on Sir George, the good man. I pondered approaching your brother-in-law, for Philip Dougal is the head of the clan, but then he is not blood kin, is he now?"

It might have been the preamble to a brief, and suddenly she did not want him to present his case, one that he could only lose. He must have been hurt before, and who was she to throw another one to his bread basket? The gypsy prophecy was coming true in part; it was up to her to see that the whole did not materialize. That dart about using him without thought for his feelings . . . Look at the way he was talking now.

"I'm a shy chap, Anna. I always have been. It's hard for me to say . . ."

"Would you no like a spot of brandy, Mr. A.?" Play for time to think.

"Thank you kindly." He seemed glad of the interruption. His back, as he poured, reminded her of her father's, broad-fleshed, stiff, old. Had he ever been young enough for the grand passion? He turned to her again, whiskery face red with embarrassment. "I wrestled with my conscience and yesterday decided it would not be taking unfair advantage of you to approach you directly. I can offer you a strong arm to lean on."

One arm? For the tottering down? When she wanted two around her?

"Hoho!" She slapped her knee. "Now I twig. You're a fine one to caw me Machiavellian, Mr. A."

"I beg your pardon?"

"The legal profession doesna approve of its members soliciting business, that's it, is it no? You're after the Biggart Trust to add to the Dougal affairs, and I dinna blame you. It makes damn good sense. Sit there and enjoy your brandy whiles I go for the papers, and we'll look them ower for a loophole that'll let me drop my papà's lawyers. I'd be glad to be rid of the old fogies, for I canna abide them. They aye make me feel like a gumptionless bairn."

Quickly she left the morning room, although the legal documents were in the safe above her head. That part of her ploy would give him time to change from suitor to lawyer if he was smart enough to sense her motive. Was he, she wondered? She sat in her bedroom for ten minutes, and when she rejoined him saw that the metamorphosis had taken place. No gentleman would light a Corona-Corona before popping the question.

"Gowk that I am," she said. "I thought the papers were in my upstairs safe. They must be down here."

"Anna—Mrs. Dougal, may I say that I have never admired your tact more than I do at this moment?"

So he had seen through her and accepted the unspoken refusal like the gentleman he was. With the document in his hands, he was again poised, sure of himself . . . Relieved? Aye, that too, damn it, but it would have been a proposal if she'd let him stumble on, which was no sae bad and t' hell with gypsy criticism. Anna Dougal didna hurt folk with thought or without. One niggle remained. Had it only been her money?

"Tell me, Mr. A., why would you want a closer association with wee Anna Dougal?" she asked, and he, honest man, knowing she wasn't referring to business ties, gave her the straight of it.

"You make me laugh," he said.

It was enough to make a body cry.

"What did Mr. McFadden want?" asked Hugh the next morning.

"Supposing I told you he was after marrying your wee mamá?"

Hugh dropped his porridge spoon. "Why, he's old enough to be your father."

"For that you can drive the Argyll aw day."

"Mother—you wouldn't—I mean it would hardly be decent. You've been married . . ."

"And I'm old enough to be your mother?"

"Well, after all . . ."

"Hughie, put your porridge back where it belongs. Then you'll no be able to say the wrong thing, for your mouth will be full. My, laddie, what a fine surprise life holds for you."

Chapter Ten

SHE PRESSED HER KNEES against the terrace's stone wall, clung to it to keep from running down the brae like a servant lass with her heart open in her hands for all to see. He marched along the Gryffe, kit bag on his right shoulder, red Cameron kilt swinging, sergeant's yellow stripes on his arm aglint in the morning sun. Gone was the effortless lope of the moor walker. His pace was quicker, in it a determination that spoke of forced slogging and bagpipes stretching the stride of bone-weary troops. Left, right, left, right, left . . . He did not open the garden gate but slung his kit bag over it, his back toward her, and looked across the Gryffe to the village. She saw his shoulders go up slowly as he inhaled deep. Slowly he turned toward the old Maclehose property, then slowly around to the south, and at last up the brae to the big house. She couldn't see if he smiled; the light was that eye-watering bright. She raised a hand shoulder-high and waved a tiny greeting. Up flashed his right to his Glengarry in salute, then he whipped around through the gate and into his empty house.

Anna went into hers and pulled the bell rope gently.

"Nora, please tell Cook that Mr. Grant is home."

"Yess, Mistress Dougal!"

"I baked a cake," said Cookie, "but it doesna seem fitting tae rush it down, and him back for such a reason."

"Take it to him the morn's morn," said Anna. "Once he's over the shock of return."

"Would it be aw right for me tae gang down and see him?"

"Be wrong if you didna. Tell him I'll be home aw day, if he could spare a wee minute." A wee minute? It's the rest of your life I want, Jamie Grant.

She rang up the orphanage and told Johnny Blackadder. From the morning room she watched the bairns he had trained hurry over. Elspeth and Mairi Maclean, in land-girl clothes, trying not to run; Hugh and Morag, not caring, going at a dogtrot, wee Sandy bringing up the rear, the cow's tail; the Super himself, jabbing the turf with his hawthorn stick; Pat Nolan, who knelt on the bank and pulled a quart bottle of ale from the Gryffe, where he must have put it to cool days ago. He wouldn't pull the long face at the reason for the soldier's return. There was no hypocrisy in Pat.

It was noon before her soldier started up the brae, hand in hand with Sandy and Morag, Hugh and Chief behind. She nibbled her lips to redden them, pinched her cheeks, and went out on the terrace.

"Well, Sergeant Grant, come in the house." What's happened to your eyes? "You'll take a bite with us?"

"I'll go round the back. These tackety boots dinna belong on parquet."

"You'll come by the front." And I'll fill the scratches with gold leaf. Jamie Grant walked here. "Morag, run and tell Cookie we'll lunch in thirty minutes. Hughie, drive into the village and pick up my shoes. They should be done by now. The cobbler's had them a fortnight, the lazy rascal. Take

Sandy with you. Mr. Grant, will you walk ower the fields with me first and see what your partner's been up to while you were gone?"

She waited until they were hidden by a thick hedge of fuchsia before she turned, ready to melt into his arms, but they stayed loose at his sides.

More to himself than to her he said, "I'm no the man I was, Anna."

"You are too, Jamie." A lie. His face was aw lines. And strained, like his eyes.

"I've killed folk."

"They would have killed you."

He might not have heard her. "It does something to you. No at first. The first time you dinna feel anything. The Boche was two hundred yard off. I could have been shooting an auld stag for the good of the herd, for aw I cared. But when it goes on and on, becomes two, then ten—closer and closer till you're right on top of them—bayonet fixed . . ." His arms jabbed. "In! Round! Out!" Fingers open like a rake, he reaped a half-dozen blossoms from the hedge, crushed them in his hand, and let their dark blood-red fall on his boots. "'Chlanna nan con thigibh so's gheibh sibh feòil.' Do you ken what that means?" He did not wait for her answer. "Yon's the cry of the Camerons. 'Sons of the hounds, come here and get flesh.'"

"But you're a Grant! 'Stand Fast' is your slogan. You're no a Cameron."

"I am for the duration. One of Lochiel's Own."

"Och, Jamie, leave the regiment for now. A week of Strathgryffe, and you'll be yoursel again."

"I'll no be here that long. I wouldna have come at aw if it werena for Tom Black. Only by a fluke is he behind bars and no me. I ken now I can kill, and I might have then. It's on my conscience to tell him that. Then it's back to the regiment, bearing him no ill will."

What do you bear me? she wanted to cry.

"You understand, Anna?" No jokes of "Mrs. Dougal." "I'd give my hope of heaven—it would be my heaven—to be with you on Seil again. But no the now when I'm needed elsewhere."

"Mibbie it's just as well, Jamie." Giving in for his sake, she told him of McNab's advice to stay apart, and he nodded agreement.

He was not allowed to see the prisoner. He gave his message verbally to an elderly lawyer, out of sympathy with a client who would not defend himself. The police took a statement from him, but did not probe. That would be McNab's doing. They informed him where Daisy was buried, that she had left no will, and that her possessions belonged legally to him.

"Give the sticks and clothes to the Salvation Army," he said.

"And the money, Sergeant?" The policeman opened up a pass book from the British Linen Bank. "Nine hundred and three pound, six shillings and thruppence. After the expenses of the funeral."

The significance of the huge sum sent him to the police lavatory. Then he left to call on the woman trebly bereaved; husband, sister, pride, all gone in two minutes of red rage.

"The money's yours, Maggie Black."

"I'll no touch it. It's bad money."

"Only because it's been in bad hands. Is it no time to return it to good?"

He put the passbook in her lap and left her staring at her felt-slippered feet. She had not looked at him once.

He swung off the local at Dambridge into a soft mist, the still air a saturation of microscopic waterdrops. Instinctively he looked for duck boards and gave a short bark of laughter. Here was no mud, but proper drained and cambered macadam.

"Whisky, Dolly."

At closing time she and Pat helped him to bed in the back

room, and Anna, going to her own, guessed where he was and why his house stayed dark. And no blame to you, Jamie. Would to God I were stoven-drunk mysel. She came no nearer to prayer that night.

Next morning he pulled himself out of his ten-hour stupor and set off for home between sentinel ranks of purple foxgloves, tunic collar unbuttoned, Glengarry half in his pocket, the sun and the westerly breeze welcome hands on his close-cropped hair. The clang of his steel-shod heels on the hard surface of the winding road was a homey tattoo after the endless months of clumping on sodden wood or hauling through deep sucking mud. A train whistle at his back was reassuringly male after the womanly screech of French engines. He stopped to watch the steamer pulling six red-brown carriages up the brae beside him; the driver waved a hand in salute, and he waved back. In the third carriage a soldier leaned far out the window, letting the sights and scents of home wash over him. "Hoo-ooch!" yelled the Jock, then flung open the compartment door, swung onto the step, and dropped off running to trip, roll, and end up at Grant's feet, the cattle fence between them.

"A braw morning to you, Sergeant," said Lance-Corporal Lachlan Dougal, flat on his back.

"You daft wee bugger. Are you trying for a self-inflicted Blighty? Break a leg doing that, and you'd be crimed. I ought to take your number . . ." The lad's smile said he kenned naught of the murder. Good.

"Unpremeditated, Mr. Grant." Lachie rose, dusted off his breeches, vaulted the fence with ease, and stuck forward a hand as big as a shovel. "All the school years, I wanted to try that. Seeing you standing there, I was out before I knew it. How are you, Mr. Grant?"

"Daft wee bugger," repeated Jamie. "Cut back and get your pack, and we'll march thegether, though I dinna ken— one of Lochiel's Own with the H.L.I.?"

"We're both Poor Bloody Infantry, and the P.B.I. has to

join ranks. Can we stretch our legs across the moor? Since we lost our horses, I'm fair sick of marching to the step of the shortest man."

At the bridge over the Gryffe he stopped the older man to look down into the trout pool, limpid clear, running white water above and below.

"There, Mr. Grant," said Lachie softly, pointing into the shade of the overhanging bank where a shadow lay, tail barely moving from side to side to maintain head upstream. "What a beauty. I bet he'd go a pound. Maybe more. I wonder if wee Sandy's learned to guddle yet? I took my first trout by hand when I was nine."

"I should have put the water bailie onto you for a poacher." His smile disappeared. "You'll be on embarkation leave, Lachie."

"Aye. And high bloody time. I've waited almost a year."

"Does your mother ken?"

"Och, there's no point in bothering her." Embarrassed, he flicked a tiny piece of shale from the stone, it dropped, and the brown trout shot upstream into the concealing white water. "What's it like over there, Mr. Grant?"

"The food's bloody awfu, and your palliasse'll no be stuffed with goose feathers. Och, it's no sae bad, though the ving-ky blang-ky and the ving-ky rouge are a proper affront to a man's soul when he's looking for a glass of whisky. And watch out for the mam'selles, Lachie. They're no owerclean, if you ken what I mean."

"So you'll not tell me either. Is that all you old soldiers talk about? Grub, grog, and girls?"

"Do you ken better, Lachie?" You'll learn about the other for yoursel soon enough. "What about Willie Boyd? Is he for off, too?"

"No. The wee menace isn't seventeen yet. They'll not let him go. He screamed so loud they gave him two stripes to quiet him. I'm going to miss Willie. He's damn funny."

"You'll find lots of Willies ower there, Lachie. You'll

hardly meet a man you wouldna be willing to share your last bawbee with. Or your last fag end."

"I've found that out already." Lachie cocked his head. "Listen, Mr. Grant." Faintly, a high thin whistle came downwind.

"A widgeon," said Jamie. "The feeding must be poor on Moss Pond to bring him to grazing land."

"I've never seen one. I'll have to take the glasses up to the Moss when I get back. I don't have enough time now. Only five days for Mother and the family."

"Go now and take your mother with you. She's good at the birding."

"Is she? I didn't know that." He glanced incuriously at the sergeant. "But then a chap never knows anything about his mother. Maybe you could come with us, Mr. Grant, and show us where to look?"

" 'When this bloody war is ower,' Lachie. Right the now I'm awa to my unit." He estimated the height of the sun. "In fact, I better swing my kilt or I'll no catch the next train."

"If there's any petrol in the Argyll, I'll drive you to the station."

"No!" barked Sergeant Grant. Then he put his hand on the boy's shoulder. "You're kind to offer," he said, "but I wouldna take you from your mother. Tell her ta-ta for me and to keep the home fires burning. So long, Lachie. I'm glad you hirpled off the train when you did. You're aw right, lad."

Kit bag on his shoulder, he closed his front door and crossed the burn by the steppingstones to keep out of sight of the big house. From up the brae he heard the hoochs and shouts of a soldier's homecoming, saw the flag flying for the head of the house, and was glad for Anna's sake. Lachie's arrival covered his leaving. Through a clearing in the trees that concealed him, he looked back at Glen Gryffe, slammed his heels together, and saluted the Union Jack. " 'Stand Fast,' " he muttered, about-faced, and marched on.

"What would you like to do most in all the world?" said Morag, perched on one white flannel knee.

"That I can do too, Lachie, please," said Sandy, perched on the other. "I can play tennis, if you don't serve to my backhand the way Hughie always does."

"Have to teach you somehow," said Hugh on the floor, Chief at his side, his back to the inglenook between Elspeth and his mother.

"Come on, Lachie. Let's play tennis," said Morag. "You're dressed for it."

"These shrunken trousers are the only ones that don't go twice around my waist," said Lachie. "You are looking at the new Dougal—all muscle and no middle."

"You do look awfully fit," said Elspeth.

"I won't be if I eat like that all the time. Cookie outdid herself. I'm fair stuffed." He slapped his middle, and a belch surprised him.

" 'Ken him?' " chorused his brothers and sisters. " 'I ken him that well, I dinna need to rift ahint ma haun.' "

"Wherever did you learn such vulgarity?" said Anna.

"From you, Mother dear." Again a chorus.

"I suppose I could play tennis to oblige you," said Lachie. "I'll umpire for Morag and Sandy while my dinner goes down. Then the rest of us can play a set."

"A threesome?" said Elspeth.

"If we had a fourth, we could play mixed doubles." The blush up his neck reassured Anna. He was still only a laddie for all the man's uniform upstairs.

"I'll ring up Bella," said Elspeth, running.

They played till ten-fifteen, when the balls grew blurry as the long Scots light grayed. Then the mistress of the house joined the older young on the terrace for tea, tomato sandwiches and scones, cake and biscuits, until the midges chased them inside.

"Take you home if you like, Bella," said Lachie, stiff as granite.

"Don't bother if it's a trouble," she replied disinterestedly.

"Me for bed," said Elspeth. "Come on, Hughie."

When the Argyll did not roar, Anna went to the bay window of the dining room. Down the brae toward Jamie's home the dim figures walked through the gloaming two feet apart, Lachie swinging Bella's racquet in shadow play, she holding up her skirt from the dew. She was too old for him; long-limbed, well-bred, bonny, and too old for him. Anna felt envy for the girl who walked with her son into the awakening. Jealousy, too. No even a kiss goodbye, Jamie. Up and awa like a moonlight flit as if you couldna pay the rent. If you think Lachie's homecoming makes up for your leaving, you dinna ken a damn about women. And Lachie, you have more understanding of Bella's feelings or wee Anna Dougal will take a tennis racquet to your sturdy backside. Now there's a thought for a mother. Get you to the sideboard and pour a mite of decency back into your daft and glaikit self.

"Thanks for the convoy, Lachie. No need to come all the way to the door."

"I must mind my manners, Bella."

The long driveway, black dark under the oaks before they reached the lights of the house . . . Then it would be too late. Would she slap his face? Willie the Bold said that girls liked to be kissed. *Fat, skinny, short, tall, bonny, ugly— they're aye ready, Lachie. Especially the ugly ones. Try one of them first. They're properly grateful.* Bella wasn't ugly. And he wasn't Willie. How did you do it? You couldn't just grab her. Nor beg permission. *Never ask, Lachie.* Hurry up. The house was just around the bend. Ten more yards of concealment . . .

What's he waiting for? thought Bella. Six feet from the mellow curtain of light, she stumbled. Instinctively his arms encircled her to prevent a fall. "Ow! My ankle!" With care she put foot to the ground. "Ow!" Obediently his grip on her waist tightened. "You're awful strong, Lachie."

She turned up her head, hoping there was light enough for him to see her eyelids drooping.

"Do you feel faint?" he asked anxiously.

"That's not the only reason a girl closes her eyes, Lachie."

It wasn't well done, but with no previous kiss for comparison, that didn't matter at all.

"You have the smoothest face for a man."

"I shaved before dinner," he fibbed, his downy cheek requiring the razor only every other day.

"I must go, Lachie."

"Stay a minute. Please."

"Papá locks up at midnight."

"In Strathgryffe? We never turn the key. Let me carry you, Bella. You shouldn't risk that ankle."

Her smile was as mischievous as wee Morag's. "I didn't turn it at all. I only pretended, so you would have to hold me."

Two more minutes, three . . .

"I really have to go in, Lachie," pushing halfheartedly against his chest.

"Must you?" holding tight.

"I told you, silly. Unless . . ."

"Unless what?"

"I could say good night to Papá and nip out the back door instead of going up to bed."

"How would you get back in?"

"By the trellis. I've climbed it many a time for fun."

Two hours later, while Lachie held his breath, she ran up the trellis and through her window with the ease of an able-bodied seaman mounting to the crow's-nest. Then she leaned out, and in the moonlight he saw her lips frame "I love you."

Lachlan Dougal went home in a daze that persisted until, at the head of the stairs, he saw a light under his mother's door.

Softly he rapped. "Are you all right, Mother?"

"Come in, Lachie."

She was sitting in bed, a magazine in her lap, her fair hair loose above a woolly blue bed jacket. He had never seen her like that before. She looked so *young*.

"You're gey late home, son." To give him time to think up an excuse she said, "Open my windows and draw the curtains, there's a good lad." To help him protect the lady: "Where did you go after you dropped Bella?"

Amused, he caught on. Older people didn't understand. He would no more lay a finger on Bella—she *loved* him. "Over the Pad," he humored his mother. "It was a night for a daunder. Much too grand for bed."

He bent to kiss her brow, but she slipped a hand behind his head and pulled him to her lips, light, quick, kind. "I'm proud to have you for a son, Lachie."

Now what was behind that? He pondered the praise for a good twelve seconds before smiling his way into sleep.

Because of the extenuating circumstances—the murdered woman's way of life, the ultimate provocation, the absence of premeditation, the guilty man's immediate surrender—Tom Black was not condemned to the hangman but sentenced to life imprisonment. In these enlightened times, this meant a maximum of twenty years in jail with time off for good behavior.

On June 7, 1917, in a brilliant limited action the British IInd Army straightened out the Ypres salient, taking Messines Ridge in a matter of hours. Involved were A.N.Z.A.C.s, the 47th London, and—war bringing stranger bedfellows than politics—the combined divisions of the 36th (Ulster) and 16th (Irish) who, fighting side by side, took the village of Wytschaete. Heartened by success, Haig thereupon named July 31 as the date for the Third Battle of Ypres. On July 22, using 2300 guns, he set out to soften up the enemy with the traditional artillery bombardment, a grave error in this low-lying terrain with its intricate drainage system. After nine days and nights of ceaseless roaring, when the cannon finally fell quiet the British were faced with a near-impassable swamp across which to advance on foot.

Unlike Haig, the German High Commander, Erich Ludendorff, had learned from the years of battle in Flanders. Realizing that marshes made ill land for the deep dugouts needed against heavy shelling, he had saved his front-line troops from Haig's barrage, withdrawing them to the rear to be held in reserve behind concrete pillboxes manned by machine guns.

On July 31 the British Empire infantry advanced on a fifteen-mile front in torrential rain that seemed a worse enemy to Sergeant James Grant than the pillboxes hidden in the downpour. The strategically unimportant left of the line made some progress, but the vital right was beaten off at the Menin Road, and forward motion ceased.

On August 16 the British again thrust through the mud and around the water-filled shell holes.

"A body could drown in yin o' they," said one of the few surviving Bantams of the 18th H.L.I.

"You could, Shorty," replied Lance Corporal Lachlan Dougal.

"Eff you, you big string bean. Keep your heid doon an' come on."

"After you, you wee nyaff."

The old soldier heard the thud, then the crack, and whipped around to see his mate falling backwards into the shell hole. Throwing himself on the mud, the Bantam hooked his bayonet into the tunic with the single stripe, floated the six-footer to the bank, and slid him onto half-solid ground. One look said that nothing more need be done. "Aye, a body could drown in there," he muttered. "But no you, Lachie." He turned and shook his fist at the enemy. "You effing bastards!" he shouted. "He was only a effing laddie!"

The memorial service was short, the Strathgryffe church packed, the Dougals in a front pew, the Glen Gryffe staff behind them. Johnny Blackadder was there, and Pat Nolan; "Whisky" Cockburn, Bella's father; Smith the Shipbuilder, the owner of the Paisley Rope Works, Morton the Joiner, Speirs the Garage, Alfredo the Tally. Robert Boyd. Philip Dougal, the mourning band on his left arm doing double duty for his nephew and for his older son killed earlier at Vimy Ridge.

The Reverend Arthur Auchinleck was finding it increasingly difficult to give the bereaved the original solace they deserved. Each loss was personal and merited a consolation equally personal. In this case he stepped back into history and quoted the last words of Mary, Queen of Scots. "*In my end is my beginning.*" Anna closed her mind, years later to find each word carved deep in her womb. She sat head up even through prayer, for lack of control would shame the dead they had come to honor. When a muffled sob broke from Mairi, Anna turned and shook her head "no" to give the girl strength.

"She's a bloody marvel," Pat Nolan told his Dolly. "Sure an' yon Mairi could have set the whole kirk to keening, but the Widow Dougal picked her up with one stern wave of her wee head."

"You must eat," said Bella's mother. "What would Lachie think of a girl who took to her bed?"—and burst into tears.

A telegram arrived at Glen Gryffe. It came from Brodick and consisted of the one word, "Come."

"I couldna leave my bairns," Anna told them.

"Elspeth and I think you should," said Hugh, the black tie making him look older than seventeen. "We talked about it last night."

"And while I'm gone you'll rid the house of your brother's possessions?"

"Morton the Joiner's son could do with his clothes," said Elspeth. "They wouldn't need much altering."

"No his kilt!"

"We'll put that away in mothballs for wee Sandy." The

new head of the house ruffled the youngster's hair. "Though he'll have to grow some to fill it."

Every corner of her home, every tuft of heather reminded her of Lachie. Lachie had never been on Arran . . .

"We could talk about him if you went away," said Morag. "We don't like to in front of you. Your face gets all hard."

"Morag!" cautioned Elspeth.

"It does so. I don't like it one bit. Mamá's too bonny."

Because scores of thousands of mothers who should be in mourning could not afford it, she did not wear black. Shona Dawson met her at the pier, Duncan by the hand. "He's going to school in September, aren't you, my wee man?"

"Gilmorehill," said the child. "Trusty Boyds go to Gilmorehill."

Uncle John, friend of the family and village carter, took her portmanteaus. "I'll drop them at the cottage, Mistress Dougal. No charge at all."

"Aunt Harriet's waiting on the beach," said Shona. "She bought some scrumptious toffee for our chittering bite. It's worth bathing just to get it."

"I can row," said Duncan.

"Only one oar, boastie," said Shona.

"Heavens, Anna Biggart, whoever sold you that hat?" said Harriet, rummaging through a tin box that once had held shortbread but now housed pins, needles, thread, and bits and pieces of silk and velvet. "Let me have the bonnet and I'll retrim it to our taste while you help the bairns with their sand castle. My, it's close today. You brought lovely weather with you."

When the children were in bed, she produced two gills of whisky wheedled from the renter of the thruppence-an-hour dinghies. "Tom the Boat's Aggie drinks too much anyway. Down with it and your defenses. And oh, Anna, you'll have to weep for the both of us, for I can't any more. I'm all cried out."

Every morning she left the end cottage of the Gothic terrace, stout shoes on her feet, a sandwich in the capacious pocket of her tweeds. Alone, she walked the sheep tracks and deer paths of moor and glen, and Lachie went with her every mile. Occasionally he would break away, and she would watch him scale a granite precipice where she did not dare to go; Lachie never could refuse a challenge. Each night she slept eight hours, drugged by the Scots panacea of the body-exhausting walk.

She went up Glen Rosa, its water winding down through the mountains on each hand; scrambled over the Saddle, slid into steep straight Glen Sannox to come out at Corrie and foot the seven miles of shore road back to Brodick. She walked the ten miles of the String from one side of the isle to the other, by Glen Shurig, by Machrie Water to Blackwaterfoot. Then she turned and climbed back up over the spine of Arran. On the ridge of An Tunna she saw a herd of red deer silhouetted against the sky, two stags with soaring antlers and a dozen hinds grazing that minded her of Scarba. None o' that! She took Kitty Boyd's favorite saunter through the Faery Glen and across the Hotel Burn to Lamlash; to King's Cross, departure for Robert the Bruce on his way to defeat the English. "Scotland forever!" she heard Lachie cry. To Whiting Bay and back again. She climbed the road to Corrygills, then up over Dun Fionn onto the Clauchland Hills where the heather, food of the grouse, was abundant and so were they, whirring up at her feet, crying *go-ba-ack! go-ba-ack!* Lachie said they were the trickiest shooting of all, faster than the wind and jeuking all the time.

Telling no one, on the Friday she tackled Goat Fell, following the stiff path through the rhododendrons of the castle grounds, then up green Glenshant Hill, over the burn, and on to granite above the tree line, where cairns guided her to the eastern shoulder. Mist billowed in as she scrambled for the top, hiding it and the drop into the corrie below. She climbed out of the white shroud twenty feet from the summit, and Lachie showed her how to scale the granite boulder big as the tomb of Mausoleus. Her head almost three thousand feet higher than the beach where Harriet sat with other wives and bairns, she stood above a tossing sea of white washing soundlessly against the rocks. No other peak broke the infinity of cloud that looked solid enough to bear her weight all the one-way road to Tir-nan-Og, the Isle of the Ever Young. In the brilliant sun blazing from the blue, she half closed her eyes and on the lids saw Lachie, kilt and shoulders swinging as he "went West" from her forever. Then at last she wept.

"You had no business being alone on the Hill of the Wind," scolded Harriet when her guest reached home. "You were just lucky that the breeze changed with the tide, or you'd be there yet."

"Well, as I'm no, how about a wee taet for the intrepid mountaineer?"

Harriet looked up from the peas she was shelling. "You are quite incredible, Anna Biggart," she said slowly, lovingly. "Already you seem almost back to normal."

"That's the idea, my auld china." I never will be, but no one's to ken, no even you.

Despite ceaseless rain on the morass that was Flanders, the Royal Flying Corps did an excellent job of spotting for the Royal Artillery. After three months and 400,000 additional British Empire casualties, the 1st Division and the 2nd Canadians recaptured a site on the military map where once had stood the village of Passchendaele. Eleven hundred days of fighting brought victory on November 4, 1917, and ended the Battles of Ypres begun by the Germans on October 19, 1914.

The Allied cause prospered elsewhere in 1917. Allenby captured Jerusalem for a moral victory. The loyal South Africans, under General Smuts, finally forced the wily von Lettow-Vorbeck to withdraw, and East Africa ceased to be German.

When the United States declared war in April 1917, that month had seen the British lose 600,000 tons of shipping, dropping the food for her population to a six-weeks' supply. Quickly the United States threw in a fleet of light antisubmarine craft and rapidly built merchant ships to outwit the U-boats. She also loaned money to Britain, whose resources were strained to the limit by her war expenditures of £7,000,000 a day and the financing of her original allies.

Early in '18 the importance of psychology in war was realized for the first time. Alfred Charles William Harmsworth, Viscount Northcliffe, Dublin-born publisher of the *Daily Mail,* was appointed Director of Propaganda designed to break the morale of enemy civilians.

Collaboration now ended the U-boat menace. The United States laid a mine field from Scotland to Norway and blocked the submarine cruisers from the Atlantic; the Dover Patrol of the Royal Navy raided Zeebrugge and Ostend on April 23, 1918, rendering these Belgian bases useless for the smaller submarines that had plagued home waters.

The politicians at last answered Haig's appeals and appointed a supreme commander in chief, the sixty-seven-year-old Field Marshal Ferdinand Foch. In April, well-equipped confident American troops began to arrive at the rate of 300,000 a month, and General Pershing placed his men at the Frenchman's disposal wherever required.

Despite the previous failure of tanks, Winston Churchill, now Minister of Munitions, forced their full production. On August 8 four hundred and fifty of the monsters, deployed as armored cavalry, scored a major strategic gain east of Amiens, which completed the demoralization of the enemy.

The killing, however, continued for almost two more months before Germany could bring herself to request peace with honor from the leader who had argued longest for it, President Wilson of the United States. Foch, with all Allied forces under his hand, wouldn't wait for an answer. Wanting not peace but vengeance, he sent two giant pincers into action against the salient bulging between Ypres and Verdun, the ground that had been blood-soaked, now, for more than fifteen hundred days.

America took two weeks to reply to the peace offer and then demanded unconditional surrender with no honor at all, and this slap to Prussian pride prolonged the fighting. Austria, the ultimatum giver, her army cut in two, her people demoralized by Northcliffe's propaganda, cried "Kamerad" and signed an armistice on November 3. Next day revolution broke out on the German home front, spread rapidly, and opened the door to Socialist leadership. Foch now massed French and Americans—twenty-eight divisions and six hundred tanks—for revenge on the enemy. Faced with annihilation, deserted by its home front, the German High Command evaded Foch's blood lust by surrendering unconditionally to him in his railway carriage in the Forêt de Compiègne at 5 A.M. November 11, 1918.

Six hours later the war ended; the Great War; of sixteen nations; troops involved, 65,000,000; casualties, from all causes, 37,000,000. The greatest war of all time had been won by the Allies.

Haste ye back, Jamie Grant!

But the politicians had other notions. Having sampled dictatorship, they were in no mind to return prewar freedom to the individual. With their certain knowledge of what was best for the greatest number, His Majesty's Government granted priority of demobilization to the skilled workers, those properly fitted to restore the shattered economy. "Foremen first" was the cry, and as most of these had been drafted into service, last in became first out. The volunteer with the proud 1914 star on his tunic found himself sewn into khaki while the conscripts of '17 and '18 joyously redonned "civvies" and sped home to fire up the jobs and the girls they had all left behind.

"It is not fair, Mistress Dougal," said Mairi.

Anna agreed. "Your politician has as much fairness in him as a hen has face," said she.

Miss Dougal came home. No foreman Dorcas, but a new woman painted fit to scandalize the parish, locks cut sleek in a bob, hemline almost calf-high, short hair, short dress both tributes to the emancipation recently granted her sex by Lloyd George. His vote-catching Representation of the People Act gave the franchise to certain British women, and the more daring seized on this inch of political freedom to grab an ell of fashion.

"You return after five years made up like a *fille de joie*," said her mother, unable to rejoice over the return of a shirker. "What happened to the wholesome lass who left here?"

"I used to look like a plate of cold porridge," said the prodigal, aloof, unyielding.

"Are you a good girl, Dorcas?"

"Qu'est-ce que c'est bon?"

She entered into none of her family's activities, took long walks over the moor, kept to her room, spoke little, read much—mainly French novels. Anna, whose linguistics stopped at *Il y avait un fois il demeuraient dans un grand forêt trois ours*, was sure that Dorcas's reading was racier than *Goldilocks and the Three Bears*.

"I understand her no one bit and mysel less," Anna told Harriet in the tearoom of Pettigrew's, the ladies' outfitters. "My oldest bairn is wiser now in the ways of the world than you or I will ever be."

"Subconsciously you don't wish to understand her, Anna. You stopped trying the day you packed her off to St. Thenew's. She minds you of what you would forget."

"Hoho, it's a disciple of Freud I'm breaking scones with the day."

"I never heard of the person. He sounds foreign. I don't need him to tell me what is plain Scottish common sense."

"Is that a fact now?" Anna inspected the three-tiered cake

stand. "Me for a Napoleon, one tasty thing to come out of the Auld Alliance."

"Honestly, Anna, the way you eat. And it doesn't do you any good."

" 'Rab Haw, the Glasgow glutton, ate three loaves and a leg of mutton.' I'm no skinnier than Dorcas. If yon's the coming trend, my figure'll soon be aw the rage." She stuck a limb out from the table, pulled up her silk frock, and eyed her trim ankle and calf with satisfaction.

"Really, Anna!" Blushing, Harriet looked around. "Supposing a gentleman walked in?"

"Get an eyeful, wouldn't he? I've a mind to have my dressmaker put the shears to aw I own."

"You wouldn't."

"Why for no?" She examined her leg again. "With a couple of jewels like that, it's a shame to grudge the lads a wee keek."

"You always were a hussy."

"But you're the only one that kens."

"I wouldn't be surprised if Mr. Grant suspects."

"You took your time getting around to him." Anna consulted the watch attached to her discreet bosom. "One hour and five minute. That's going on for a record."

"Have you heard from him?"

"No later than the day."

"Tell me, Anna"—Harriet leaned forward—"was it—a—love letter?"

"Dinna be daft, Harriet Hepburn."

It had been a letter of love, the kind a man bears for another man, a heartbreaker that came close to spilling her half-full bottle. For he had written a eulogy of her son, and to Jamie, Lachie was all the brave fallen, all the comrades in arms whose handclasps conveyed a closeness withheld from women. She'd have to caw canny with him in the beginning. He had come through three and a half years in the trenches without a physical scratch, but the mental wounds must be gey deep and yet to heal. Well, wee Anna Dougal would supply the balm—if the Army would ever let her, damn them.

Spring came, a lovely spring as if the Strath, too, had decided the time of mourning was over. When daffodil and narcissus had carpeted the lush grass under the oaks, a trunk call came for Dorcas. In minutes she filled two suit-cases. Dorcas! Who could never decide what or how to pack.

"Would you drive me to the station, *Maman?*"

"You're off again? Where are you for?"

"London. To Fiona's. She wants me to pop up there for a few days."

"You dinna go up to London," said Anna, irritated. No even a by-your-leave. "You go down."

"Pure provincialism, pet. London is the greatest city in the world."

"I'll take Glasgow."

"*Chacune.* I really must dash."

"How do you propose to finance this wee jaunt, Dorcas?"

"I transferred what was left of my last letter of credit to Cox's Bank. Son of McFadden was jolly good about money. All through the war it was never late."

"Aye, he's right reliable with the siller." No thanks given to the mother who had ensured it. "Where will you stay?"

"Fiona is redoing a stable in a mews off Regent Street."

"I dinna like the sound of that."

"*Maman,* I'm twenty-three. I left home, to all intents, seven years ago . . ."

"But you were aye chaperoned. Least I thought you were."

"Oh, I was. By Fiona. And she by me. A perfect arrange-ment . . ."

"That I dinna fancy one bit. But as you say, you are ower twenty-one, and if you dinna ken how to behave now . . . Hughie'll run you to the station."

"Afraid to be seen in the village with the black sheep, pet?"

"Damn the fears. And stop calling me 'pet.' I'm no a pekingese."

Then Dorcas was gone, and it was as if she had never returned. To think wee Anna Dougal could have a daughter old enough to gang her ain gait. Without meaning to, the others also nudged her with the years.

"Mother, it's time you had a man to handle the Argyll," said Elspeth.

"That relic?" Hugh hooted. "What chauffeur would take on the care and feeding of a prewar tourer?"

"I canna abide shovers," said Anna. "Anyway, you two do most of the motoring nowadays."

"Well, you never seem to want to drive anymore," said Elspeth.

"Wee Anna Dougal sets fashions. She doesna follow them." It had been different when she was a lone feminist tootling over the roads to the wonder of His Majesty's lieges. She hadn't turned a head in a year; women drivers were that common now, thanks to the War.

"Mother's too unselfish for her own good," said Hugh. "We should leave the Argyll for her whether she wants it or not. The impulse might take her at any time."

"So it's a go-devil of your own that you're after," said Anna. "Did you and Elspeth arrange this wee ploy between you?"

"We do need a new machine," said Hugh, red-faced. "It's almost impossible to get spare parts for an Argyll any more. The firm's been out of business for five years."

Superannuate the chariot that had carried her to Oban? She'd as soon sell Hughie's collie. "I'll keep the Argyll."

"Of course, Mamá," said Elspeth. "But a second motor-car . . ."

"The Arrol-Johnston is a fine piece of machinery," said Hugh. "Scottish-built, too. In Dumfries. Twin cylinders horizontally opposed, two connecting rods to each piston, and a rocking lever between the con rods. It has a bore and stroke

of a hundred and twenty by a hundred and sixty-five milli-
meters . . ."

"Spare a body the innards," said Anna. Lachie had aye
harped on them, too. "Just as long as you dinna ask for a
Rolls Royce. We'll leave that conceit to your Uncle Philip.
Despite your sister Dorcas, this branch of the family's no
that Anglicized."

The few days that Fiona Murray had asked Dorcas to
spend in London expanded into a few weeks. She rarely
wrote. When she did, her letters were offhand and spattered
with nicknames giving no clue to the identity of her fellow
partyers at the Savoy or Claridge's or the Café Royal.

"Lucky dog," said Bella Cockburn. "In London you're in
the swing. Honestly, Elspeth, if we don't meet some men
soon . . ."

The casualties among the Strathgryffe eligibles, the sub-
alterns with swagger sticks, had been heavier than one in
three, the Empire average for all ranks, and the fortunate
handful demobilized were disinterested in children-turned-
ladies in their absence. They tended to stick together in
tipsy pursuit of Glasgow's shopgirls, fair lasses and free for
hedonistic affairs without future. The few slackers who had
evaded the Great Adventure were scorned—permanently—
by the Bellas for their lack of grit or pitied for the physical
unfitness that had kept them out of uniform, either flaw
rendering them ineligible as bridegrooms and potential
fathers.

"Even a flat in Glasgow would be better than this," said
Bella, glancing over the front page of the *Herald* with its
Hatches, Matches, and Dispatches, the paid announcements
of births, marriages, and deaths. They took less time to read,
now that the Dispatches were once again of peacetime
length.

Ensconced in camp chairs, she and Elspeth glowed gently
in the April sun trapped in the sunken garden of Glen
Gryffe. Over the wall came the plunk of a tennis ball as

Morag and the ageless Miss Cuthbert played singles on the grass court. There wasn't a male in sight, not even Hugh—a nice lad, but a child—off for a run in the new motorcar with his mother and the bairn Sandy. Bella picked up a handful of the red gravel that paved the walks and let it dribble through her fingers. "Dear Diary," she said. "Saturday afternoon I spent at the girls' colony. As usual."

"Want to play tennis?" asked Elspeth.

"Uch."

"You used to love the game."

The memory of Lachie dropping between them, Bella angrily opened the paper to the Court news.

"Game and set," sang out Miss Cuthbert. "Jolly good, young 'un. You're playing much better. Now where's the tea you promised me?"

They came swinging down the brick steps, the gym instructress cool and unruffled; Morag's pretty face was red from the extra effort put out by the loser.

"Tea will be here in a minute," said Elspeth. "It's almost four o'clock."

"Good," said Miss Cuthbert. "I'm parched."

"WOW!" yelled Bella.

"Good heavens. Did a bee sting the girl?"

"WOW!" yelled Bella again. "Listen to this. 'Among those attending were Miss Murray of Perthshire and Miss Dougal of Renfrewshire.'"

"Attending what?" demanded Miss Cuthbert, a great one for the society news.

Reverently Bella lowered the *Herald*. "A reception at Buckingham Palace."

Tea was ignored as they clustered around the paper to read the guest list. Her Majesty, the Prince of Wales—*the Prince of Wales!*—Viscount Northcliffe, Mr. and Mrs. Winston Churchill . . . The list was a roster of nobility and leaders.

"And I envied Dorcas before," said Bella numbly.

"Here comes Mamá!" Morag ran to the driveway and

jumped onto the running board of the new Arrol-Johnston. "Dorcas has been to the Palace!"

"Which one?" asked Anna. "Crystal or Picture?"

"Buckingham!"

"In the name of . . . Where did you pick up sic a rumor?"

"No rumor. It's in the *Herald*."

"Stop jouncing. You'll coup the car."

"It has to be Dorcas. She was with Miss Murray of Perthshire. That must have been Fiona. And oh, Mummy, the Prince of Wales was there himself."

"You're so quiet, Mrs. Dougal," said Bella at dinner's end.

"I'm thinking. Nora, I'll take my demitasse in the morning room. By my lone."

Trunks put her through to London, the operators all women now.

"Miss Dougal here." The voice crackled over music and babble.

"What's aw the cacophony? Is it a pub you're living in?"

"*Maman!* This is a surprise. Fiona and I are having a small bash for a few chums. Porky, turn down that gramophone. I'm talking to Scotland."

"I say"—a man laughed—"not in Gaelic, old thing?"

"I heard that," said Anna. "Tell yon Sassenach I'd take my claymore to him if I could reach. Dorcas?"

"Yes, *Maman?*"

"What were you doing at Buckingham Palace?"

"Drinking champagne, my pet, and flirting like mad."

"I didna mean that. Why were you invited?"

"Oh, they needed some youthful femininity. I wore mauve lace, and Murray was adequate in flowered chiffon. It was a bore, really."

"Blasé, aren't you? Dorcas, you werena commanded to the Palace just to even the numbers. Why pick you?"

"For my ravishing beauty, I suppose."

"London's full of stunners. With titles."

"Oh, but H.R.H. is awfully democratic. He likes the lower orders."

"Dinna fence with me, girl, or I'll lunge at you with a stroke you'll no be able to parry."

"How unmaternal."

"Here it comes then. Those cushy years in Switzerland—they didna merit Royal honor unless—Dorcas, could you look your brother Lachie in the eye?"

Ragtime, high voices, braying laughter filled Anna's earpiece for seconds before the answer came.

"Touché," whispered Dorcas.

"Speak up, lass. I canna hear."

"Yes, Mamá, I could."

"That's all I wanted to ken. For misjudging you, I apologize. For mysel, for your brothers and sisters, for the whole damn ignorant village of Strathgryffe."

"Don't be angry with yourself. You were supposed to think the school was a haven for slackers. I can't say more. I shouldn't have said even that." Her voice turned brittle again. "By the way, I have super news. Fiona's engaged to a younger son of a baronet. A major. No money, just his pension for a peg leg, but awfully good bloodline. They'll be married in June."

"Then you'll be home?"

"Sorry, pet. Lord Northcliffe has offered me a job on one of his newspapers."

"He was in the propaganda business, was he no? Were you?"

"Heavens, no. More the horticultural." A pause. "It was jolly difficult to keep gardeners. They'd no sooner learn our ways than they'd pop off. Terribly frustrating. Awfully good-looking chaps, most of them, especially the Italians."

"Hoo-ooooch!"

"*Maman!* My eardrum."

"Sorry, lass. That was the bats leaving my belfry."

Receiver back on its hook, Anna hugged herself. The

Royal honoring, the position from Viscount Northcliffe, the wee hints dropped by Dorcas—Anna Dougal's oldest had helped escaped P. O. W.'s! Just like Nurse Cavell! Wait till Strathgryffe gets an earful of that! Damn. To protect Swiss neutrality, I'm no supposed to let on. That's the reason Dorcas held her wheest. To heck with it. But to her children she disclosed only that Dorcas must have aided the War somehow to be recognized at the Palace and by the Minister of Propaganda.

"I could die for shame at my disloyal thoughts," mumbled Elspeth. "About my own sister . . ."

"Jolly good show, whatever it was," said Hugh.

"Up the Dougals!" shouted Sandy, while Morag smiled and reddened with pleasure.

It wasn't enough for the bursting mother. If Jamie were here he could drop a wee word in Dolly Nolan's lug to spread the news. Och, I'll have a crack with Pat the morn's morn. He'll do fine, and I'll no spill aw the beans, though why fash about a bunch of damn yodelers, now wars are ended for good . . .

"The oldest Dougal girl has taken a job," murmured the gardener sleepily, then gasped "Ooof!" as Mrs. Nolan rolled back on him in surprise.

"I dinna believe it."

"Truth." Pat struggled to free himself from the weight of his wife. "Bejasus, do you need the middle half of the bed?"

"Sorry, lovey. I'll move." Dolly heaved herself over, the mattress convulsed, Pat bounced. "What could yon lass do that's worth a bawbee?"

"Work for a newspaper. In London."

"Dorcas? According to Cookie, she canna even write. Aw these years and barely a scribble."

"Viscount Northcliffe's betting she can. He's the one gave her the post."

"Where did she meet a toff like him?"

"Sure, at Buckingham Palace, no less."

Dolly was better than any town crier, and by week's end

wild conjecture about Dorcas's derring-do had filtered up from kitchen, garage, and stable to parlor and drawing room. Had she come home at that moment, she would have been awarded the keys to Strathgryffe, no further questions asked.

Open combatants could be rewarded openly. On May 19, 1919, the Scots commander of the British Empire forces in France received the Freedom of Glasgow, which had contributed so gallantly. Having put 200,000 of her men in arms, medals abounded in her douce flats and reeking tenements. So did black-draped photographs, empty sleeves, pinned-up trouser legs, silver plates in damaged skulls, shell shock, and lungs permanently scarred by chlorine or mustard gas. A proud city turned out to honor the general who had led the Empire to victory. A grateful Government had raised him to the peerage and awarded him £100,000, tax free. Ordinary citizens had donated their shillings and pence to buy back his ancestral home for him, reaffirming Thomas the Rhymer's medieval prophecy, "Tyde what may betyde, Haig shall be Haig of Bemersyde." Behind arm-linked smiling bobbies, the jam-packed thousands stood in George Square and roared their tribute to Earl Haig as pipes skirled, brass blared, fifes squealed, drums rolled until even the statues of Rabbie Burns and Sir Walter Scott seemed to cheer. Indeed, the whole world applauded the gallant gentleman who had refused to accept money for himself until the Government made provision for the wounded. For the millions killed under his command he could do nothing, but that day in Glasgow he announced the creation of the Earl Haig Benevolent Fund, a Scottish organization whose revenue for the ex-serviceman would come every succeeding Armistice Day from the sale of paper poppies.

May your charity help you sleep, Douglas Haig, thought Anna as she and Harriet made their way down from the huge reviewing stand, wee Duncan between them.

"How many Germans did Earl Haig kill, Mother?" asked the boy. "I mean by himself."

"That's not a nice thing to say, Duncan. Generals don't kill. What do you think, Anna? Jimmy Craig's for tea?"

"We're as likely no to find a pew there as any place."

"My, that's a good cup, and I needed it," said Harriet when they had found seats in the tearooms on Gordon Street. "All that standing—I'm properly exhausted."

"You're no a chicken for aw your cheeping," said Anna.

"Neither are you, Anna Biggart, so don't give yourself airs. Have a parkin." Harriet passed the gingery biscuits of oatmeal and treacle.

"Lose some weight and you'd no tire so easy. I tellt you the wiry ones are coming in fashion. Dorcas sent me a wee article she had in the *Daily Mail*. It's definite. The shape of the future is flat."

"How unladylike. And you don't have to use devious ways to introduce her name. I'm just as proud of her now as you are, so boast away. Does she write about any particular young man?"

"Aye. A different one every week."

"It's time she settled down."

"A spoilsport you are."

"And you're an unnatural mother. I would be worried sick if it were Kitty gallivanting around London's West End, that fast place."

"You wouldna worry a bit if it were yoursel though, and you twenty-three again."

"Oh, Anna, wasn't it a sin the way we were kept down?" said Harriet. "Didn't Lord Weir look handsome? There's something about him . . ."

"If you're no going to bite, Harriet Hepburn, dinna bare your teeth. You've never had sighs for anyone but Robert . . ."

"Lord Weir is Minister for Air," said Duncan. "The gentleman next to me said so. I'm going to be a flier when I grow up."

"Little pitchers, big ears," murmured Harriet. "Change the subject."

"It's dull work sitting here with the auld folk, isn't it, laddie?" Anna smiled down at the bairn, good-looking but more delicate-featured than Lachie at the same age. "Would you fancy a cream horn to liven things up?"

"You've dribbled butter from your scone all over your chin, Duncan," said Harriet. "You may be excused to wash it, first." When he was dutifully gone . . . "Have you heard when Mr. Grant will be demobbed?"

"Only Lloyd George kens that." Anna scowled into her cup. "If I could get my claws into yon Taffy, I'd Welsh-wizard him for keeping my partner from his herd."

When the Armistice was one year old, Willie Boyd came home. Before seeing his own mother he went to see Lachie's, knowing that only after this duty call would he be able to relax in front of the family grate. He was not so stupid as to blame himself for his chum's death, but they had run away together, joined up together. He rode the train to Strath-gryffe, the confidence born of his new head-to-toe "civvies" melting from him, nervousness mounting as he neared the dread meeting. He need not have worried.

"You look grand enough for an officer," said Anna, walking around him to get the full effect of his Shetland tweed suit of Lovat green, Queen's Own tie, Irish linen handkerchief peeping from his left sleeve. "Are you sure it's no Captain Boyd? Wait till Elspeth and Morag get a squint at you. Come ben the house and I'll show you off to the girls in the kitchen. They deserve a treat." He's grown, but he's still no Lachie's height. Lachie would be twenty-one. "May I bring an old friend in to see you, Cookie?"

She mentioned her son's name aloud only once; before a toast in whisky to his memory. Lachie had never tasted his country's barley brew—no to her knowledge.

"Where's your uniform, Willie?" said Sandy. "I thought you were a sergeant."

"Not any more, laddie. William Boyd, Esquire, from now till the cows come toddling home."

"Like to see the new Arrol-Johnston, Willie?" said Hugh.

"Let's put on the gramophone and dance," said Elspeth. "Can you fox-trot, Willie?"

"Can a fish swim?"

"He's awful conceited," Morag whispered to her mother as record and couple spun. "Why Elspeth would want to dance with him . . . I can't stand stuck-up people."

"May I have the pleasure, Morag?" asked Willie, smiling down at the lady in bud.

"Please excuse me," she replied, nose toward the ceiling. "I find the fox-trot nauseating."

"Hoity-toity. Come on, Aunt Anna."

"Lead me to it, laddie." So Morag still had a crush on Willie . . . My, he was light on his feet. Hard lines, Morag. I doubt Willie's the marrying sort. What sort would Lachie have been? Would he and Bella . . . ?

"Aunt Anna, the gentleman is supposed to lead."

"Sorry, Willie. It's been that long since a body birled me around the floor."

"Oh, you beautiful doll"—sang His Master's Voice—"you great big beautiful doll—" The words of the fox-trot didn't fit her, but the sentiment did for sure: "Let me put my arms around you—" A year since the Armistice, and he was still over there. Why couldn't the damn Frogs wind up the Watch on the Rhine? It's their ticker, no Scotland's.

"You're leading again, Aunt Anna."

"It's a hussy I am." Harriet said she was. "You're no to let on to your mother that you came here first," she told Willie. "She'd have my scalp."

He went swinging down the brae into the dark that should have been lighted by Jamie's windows. It is not fair, Mairi had said, and Mairi was right. There was something gey wrong with a system that let out a lad who'd never seen the trenches and hung onto a man who'd done more than his bit. Damn Lloyd George. No reward for the lads who had beaten the Hun. In 1920, one by one they came drifting home to Strathgryffe, no community cheers, no bravos to greet them at the finale as there had been when the curtain went up.

"Maybe England's a land fit for heroes to live in, Mrs. Dougal," Malcolm Loudon, ex-Royal Corps of Signals, said bitterly. "But not poor old Scotland. It's Lloyd George's dole for me."

No jobs for the like of Malcolm. The boomlet enlivening the rest of the country had bypassed the Clyde, where the bellwether shipyards that had saved the nation lay silent and unneeded. From war boom to peace bust went the Glasgow area at the speed of a lift with a broken cable, and the unemployed who had marched to "When this blinking war is over, oh how happy we will be" now snarled "In a sow's arse."

The folk in the big houses, the owners of businesses, could live off their fat. The wine merchants' lorries still backed up to the tradesmen's entrances to unload the cases of wine and spirits, but the Malcolm Loudons rarely had the price of a pint in their pockets to send them off on a daunder to the Dambridge Larder, now more firmly established than ever. The Temperance (Scotland) Act had been passed in London "to promote temperance in Scotland by conferring on the electors in prescribed areas control over the grant and renewal of certificates." On June 1, 1920, "Whisky" Cockburn and his neighbors solemnly repaired to the school and with a handful of reformed drunks did their duty. Under local option they voted Strathgryffe dry for the lower classes, who couldn't handle their liquor. Or afford it by the case.

That James Grant was not there to cast a contrary ballot could be laid at the door of his own barracks. A poor soldier would have been let out, but Jamie was proving as strong in peace as in battle, and to keep him in, his superiors promoted him to regimental sergeant major and added a bar to his D.C.M.

"Damn and hell and bloody," said Anna when she read his letter, full of regret, but shyly proud for all that. Angry feet spurning the turf, she stalked over the Pad to sit above the Clyde and plot. Men were daft. Couldn't they see that the worst aftermath of the war—worse than unemployment— was this new interference with the freedom of the individual? What were medals and rank when they cost a body the right to do and go as he pleased? This is what happened when politics became a salaried occupation instead of an unpaid service to the country. Look at yon Welsh weasel Lloyd George, H.M.'s Prime Minister, selling kingly favors to put cash in his creaky Liberal Party's poke. Openly and blatantly. £10,000 down, and a war profiteer became a knight. Philip Dougal was a heavy contributor to the Conservatives, but surely they'd no play the same dishononorable game when they made their certain return to power. They might. Was Philip out for an accolade? Sir Philip? The thought was enough to give a body the scunners. Her brother-in-law aye had the glad hand for titled folk, one reason he continued so generous to the orphanage. He liked to see his name tucked in behind that of Felicity, Countess of Strathgryffe, chief patroness. Jamie's name should be up at the top, too, after aw he'd done for the bairns. Wouldn't that be a poke in the eye for Philip, S.N.O.B.

Plot jelled.

Next day, dressed in her braws, Anna pushed open the big brass doors of the family firm.

"Mrs. Anna Dougal," she told the alpaca-jacketed receptionist. "I have an appointment with Mr. Dougal." She had telephoned ahead to indicate trouble at the orphanage, sure entry for her to the Managing Director's sanctum.

"I am surprised," he said after a stiff "Good day, Anna. Margot and I had dinner with the Countess only last week. She indicated no crisis."

"Felicity wouldna wish to upset your digestion." Be damned if she'd talk big-house. Let him take her as she liked to be. Anna removed her gloves and blew into the fingers. "Your favorite charity is being negleckit, Philip."

Smiling, he polished pince-nez negligently with silk handkerchief. "I happen to know better. The cash position has never been more sound."

"An orphan's proper upbringing doesna depend entirely on money, brother-in-law. Johnny Blackadder's no as young as he used to be." That didna say he was old; no a man who could play thirty-six holes on a Saturday afternoon, then glean the course for lost balls in the evening. "It's their spiritual welfare that's getting the go-by."

"I beg to differ. Auchinleck, the padre—your own minister —was also present at table. He assured me that the inmates are coming forward to join the Church in gratifying numbers, and no backsliding thereafter."

"There's more to the spiritual than the Kirk. There's the self-confidence that comes from learning a trade. You'll have heard tell of the agricultural school?"

"Vaguely. A peripheral activity, I understand."

"To you, mibbie, but no to the bairns. To them it's the passport to the big world outside. They leave Strathgryffe with a skill and a wee-bit chance to keep off the dole, which comes from your income taxes."

"That is laudable." Philip replaced his glasses. "What is the matter with the—er—school? If Blackadder is too decrepit to run it, he should be replaced."

"He never ran it." Forgive me, Johnny. "The man who did—the power behind it—joined up in fourteen—and they havena let him out yet. He's stuck in Germany guarding Boches when he should be home looking after bairns."

"And you wish him out? Laudable again, Anna." Philip Dougal nodded agreement. "You have come to the right place. I wield considerable influence in Conservative and military circles, and to me this is clearly a case of hardship for the orphans. Anything we can do to keep them from being a charge on the overburdened taxpayer . . . Let me have this fellow's name, rank, and regiment, and I can assure you he will be demobilized."

"It's that easy?"

"When you know the right people. And I do. You can trust me in that."

"I wouldna doubt it for a second." She placed a slip of paper on the mahogany. "Grant, J., Regimental Sergeant Major, 5th Cameron Highlanders."

"Splendid regiment. No man I admire more than Lochiel, Chief of the Clan." Self-satisfied smile faded. "Who did you say?"

"Whom."

He grabbed for the paper. "Why, this is . . ."

" . . . the instructor of the Aggie School at Strathgryffe, your favorite charity, Philip."

The effort to avoid sputtering reddened his face. "I have always thought you unprincipled, but that you would have the effrontery to come to me—appealing to my good nature . . . Did you think me so stupid that I would not see through your maudlin story? You are asking me, Philip Dougal, to revive the association of one of my name with a common farmer, whose marital scandal ended in a degrading killing . . ."

"I never heard of an upgrading murder, Philip, so save your breath to cool your porritch. You promised, and that's that."

"A promise without witnesses is no commitment."

"You'd welsh on it?"

"How dare you imply such a dishonorable action to me?"

Anna sighed. "It's no going to sit well with Felicity to ken you're a welsher. She was that relieved when I told her I would ask you to arrange for Sergeant Major Grant's discharge. 'Philip will manage,' she said. 'Then I won't have to give the M.P. from Paisley—he's that horror Asquith now—a contribution for the Liberal Party.' Ten thousand pound for a knighthood, Philip. What's the going rate for a sergeant major? One thousand pound?"

"I would not give a penny. I wouldn't have to. Gentlemen don't buy favors . . ."

"Nor break promises." Nostrils twitching, he glared at her, and she smiled sweetly back. "The Countess of Strathgryffe has one big fault. She canna keep her mouth shut. Och, I can hear her now. 'Because Philip Dougal was too mean to help the children, I had to donate a thousand pounds to the Liberals. I, a true-blue Tory!' I wouldna be surprised if you were asked to resign from the Conservative Club."

Having swung the sledge hammer, she left. Now all she had to do was wait.

And wait, while the heather bloomed and faded, the nights drew in, and the white fogs of the back end signaled the approach of a second Armistice Day with its two minutes' silence. *Lest we forget*—as if a body could.

"There's a light on in the farmhouse," said Sandy one dreich drenching evening as black as the coat of an Aberdeen Angus. "Do you suppose it's a burglar?"

Elspeth, Hugh, and Morag joined him at the window to peer down the brae at the yellow glow, jagged-edged through the streaming pane.

"No burglar, daftie," said Elspeth softly. "Mr. Grant is home from the wars." She turned to her mother just in time to catch a glimpse of Anna's feet disappearing at the top of the staircase. "Did you hear, Mamá?" she called. "Mr. Grant is back."

"Ask him to come by," floated down before her mother's door closed.

"Scoot, young 'un." Hugh gave Morag a pat on the bottom, and she ran for her oilskin.

"Wait for me," shouted Sandy.

"Mairi!" Elspeth called into the speaking tube. "Mairi! Come down. Mr. Grant's home."

"I'll change my frock!"

They were waiting in the hall—Cook, Nora, Sheila, Mairi a knockout in green shantung, Elspeth, Hugh—when Anna reappeared in her Oban kilt, toes of her black pumps peeping out from the Royal tartan.

"What a stunning outfit, Mamá," said Elspeth. "I've never seen it before."

"Och, I keep it for the Highlands . . ." Where my heart is. "I thought tonight, for one of Lochiel's Own . . . You dinna think I'm owerdressed?"

"Devil a bit," said Hugh. "In that braw regalia you don't look old enough to be my mother."

"For that I'll no begrudge you champagne the night, Hughie. Would you like to ask Mr. Grant to stay for dinner?"

"Throw another pea in the pot, Cookie," said Elspeth, then pulled her mother aside. "Ask Mairi to dine with us, too," she whispered.

Where was the girl's intuition? "Mairi, you'll take dinner with us the night?"

"Thank you, yess."

Let battle commence.

The steel-lined outer door opened and closed; through frosted glass they could see dim shapes wrestling out of foul-weather gear, hear the stumping and scraping of muddied feet. Then the inner door burst wide, Sandy and Morag marched in, and behind them came Jamie—in the dress kilt and ruffles that shouted Oban loud as her own.

The head of the house stuck out his hand. "It's grand to have you back, Mr. Grant," said Hugh.

"Ditto with dots," said Elspeth. The copycat.

"*Ceud mile failte!*" Shyly Mairi wished him a thousand welcomes.

"Och, and here's a Lowland welcome, Jamie Grant." Cookie kissed him soundly on the cheek, and the starched caps of Sheila and Nora came together in a twinly giggle.

"You're home for good then, Mr. Grant," said Anna. "You'll take a sherry with me? Decanter and glasses please, Nora."

"Nae whusky?"

His first words, said with a smile, gave hope that the

agony wait of the past two years had buried the dead.

"We'll have champagne later, Mr. Grant. You wouldna be for mixing the barley and the grape, would you now? You'll dine with us?"

"Off with you, Sheila," commanded Cook. "Afore the fatted calf is a burnt offering, forbye it's saddle of mutton the night."

Course after couse; she in her usual place at the end of the table, Jamie at the other on Hughie's right, between them an expanse of napery broad as the Sound of Mull. The white wine, the red, the champagne—wine of love in Oban, here naught but damn aerated water. He should have written— let her ken he was out. They should be by their lone. On the moor. *Seil would be my heaven,* he'd said. Even in Glasgow, sooty and commercial and anonymous.

Sandy went to bed, then Morag; at ten o'clock Hugh, mind on his morning train. But Elspeth and Mairi, bairns no more, were wide-eyed as a brace of night owls. Elspeth was twenty-two and Mairi was what? Twenty-seven and a beauty who now gave Jamie an account of the farm and did it quietly well, damn it, without boasting.

"Don't belittle yourself, Mairi," said Elspeth. "She's done a grand job, Mr. Grant."

"You all have." He rose to his feet.

"Like every man in the P.B.I. I've dreamed of how it would be to come back. It could have been gey empty, but you made it a chief's reception. Now I better awa down the brae before I say more, sentimental gowk that I am. I'll see you the morn's morn, Mrs. Dougal, for no doubt you'll be pushing my nose into the account books first thing." With the eye away from the others, he gave her a quick wink and was gone.

A wink. A wee bloody wink quick as a flash when a body's looking for a kiss that could take half an hour. An hour, dammit! I've waited six year, but the thought of another round of the clock is awmost more than this wee body can bear.

"Would you believe aw my senses are sharper? The grass is greener, the Gryffe is sparklier, the doddies are blacker, the throstles sing sweeter . . ."

"How about wee Anna Biggart?"

"I have to work up to you, for I canna find the words. They havena been written."

"No even by Rabbie Burns?"

"He hadna the luck to ken you. His love was only 'like a red red rose.' You're the mist of the heather, the moon on Moss Pond, the scent of bog myrtle and lilac, the first bud on the apple tree, the May in full bloom . . ."

"Rabbie, you're outclassed."

"I havena begun yet, Anna."

"That'll do to start." A pause. "You worried me when you were back the—other time."

"I was sorry for mysel. I didna realize how lucky I was. No until Lachie . . ."

She put her fingers over his lips. "None of that, now. Lachie's locked awa where only I can get at him."

"And that's the way with aw the war, Anna. It's inside me. Och, it'll come out when they hold the regimental reunions, but only the laughs. That's what we'll call to mind. The other is private."

"Like us."

"The same. If your bairns could see you now, Mrs. Dougal."

"Jamie, I'm too old for you."

"You dinna have to say things like that to wheedle protestations of burning affection from this old sojer. I love you from my battered feet to my thick heid, and well you ken it."

"That's the trouble. You should have something to show for it, but I'm ower the age of bearing you bairns."

"I look on yours as mine. And there's the orphans. I dinna need weans of my own."

"A lazy man you are. Mairi Maclean would be glad to give you a baker's dozen."

"Godsakes! Where did you get a daft notion like that? We dinna even kick with the same foot."

"Even so, a blind man could tell last night that she's after marrying you. Well, mibbie no a man, but a blind woman. You're a catch, Jamie Grant, a free man now, and a prosperous."

"The last, thanks to you. In aw Scotland there's no a smarter lady."

"You were doing better, Jamie, when you called me the heather mist and the May in bloom. After yon bonny compliments, I'm no envious of Mairi's looks. But I could be of her age."

"Dafter and dafter. Would you want to go back to twenty-six?"

"Twenty-seven and a half."

"Just as bad. Would you tackle the uncertainties of being young again?"

"Kenning what I do now? You bet."

"No this auld fox. 'A woman's as auld as she looks, a man's as auld as he feels' fits us, and I wouldna change it by a day."

"That gets you a kiss." And puts the kibosh on Mairi. "Are you after marrying me then, Jamie?"

He placed his hands behind his head, looked up at the mackerel sky of the halcyon day, took his time before he spoke, and did not answer her question. "I took a wee keek at the books last night before I went to bed," he said. "The farm showed a profit of six hundred pound in 1919—aw yours, for I wasna here to help. If we continue to do as well, I can count on an income for mysel of three hundred pound. That's prosperity to me right enough." He whistled soundlessly for a second. "I'll bet the Dougal Trust puts near that much into the bank for you every damn week."

"No quite, Jamie."

"And on top of that, there's the Biggart money. It must make your cup of tea sweet as lick."

"It's no my fault, Jamie."

"It would be mine if I drank from it, Anna. I wouldna have a friend left in Strathgryffe, including mysel."

"Would you have me give it up then? I would, you ken. Six hundred a year's a sight more than most folk have. I could move into the farmhouse . . ."

"Your bairns would have you committed, and I wouldna blame them. They like me well enough as the farmer down the brae. But as a stepfather? It wouldna work a damn bit."

"So what are we to do? If I canna move in with you, and your pride'll no let you share the wealth I didna earn . . . Och, it's a terrible dilemma. There just isna any way to make an honest woman of wee me."

At her cackle he sighed and closed his eyes.

"So," he said finally. "H.M.S. *Indomitable* has been firing blanks from her popgun to get me to strike my colors. Here they come down then. Will you marry me, Mrs. Dougal?"

"Och, t' hell, Mr. Grant, but it's good of you to ask."